Sunbeam

SUNBEAM

Mark Eklid

To Tom and Jack,

who reminded me how important it is to never give up on your dreams

1

It was the sixth week of Christmas – less than three more to go until the big day – and all through the Royal Alfred Hotel was the noise of parties. Friday night was less than half an hour away from handing over to Saturday morning and while the guests seemed to have embraced the Season To Be Jolly concept, the principle of Good Will To All was in danger of collapse.

In the wood-panelled reception, which had once warmed Victorian high society on winter nights such as this, a screeching row between two drunken young women had suddenly escalated from expletive-laden insults and accusations to swinging fists and handfuls of hair. At the reception desk, a middle-aged couple just back from a nice meal out were staring in wide-eyed realisation that their quiet weekend away might not be all they hoped it would be, while the duty manager, suspended in the act of handing over their key, was plotting with horror the potential path of the squabbling females and the small baying crowd around them towards the large, glittering Christmas tree.

Along one of the corridors leading from the reception, the door to the gents' toilet was pulled halfway open and then slid shut again, not because the person on the other side of it had changed his mind about leaving but because he had lost his grip on the handle. After taking a more calculated hold this time, he steadily pulled the door fully open and emerged unsteadily back on to the corridor, his distinct sway not helped by the chastising tap to the back of the shoulder the door gave him as it closed behind him.

In his creased dark blue suit with a crumpled white shirt open at the neck and stained grey tie, he would have looked less out of place in a skip than in a city centre four-star hotel which still, at most times of the year, clung on to pretensions of being reasonably posh. Though he had thankfully retained enough self-awareness to check his flies were done up, his shirt remained untucked on one side at the front and the bottom button of it was undone, allowing a small, unappealing roll of paunchy flesh to protrude, exposed, where it bulged above the belt line. His uncombed hair was retreating at the temples and was long overdue both a wash and a cut, while his sagging jowl and dark, careworn eyes made him look older than his thirty-seven years, confirming that here was a man whose neglected appearance could not be written off as the excesses of only one night.

Composing himself following the unanticipated contact with the door of the gents, he suppressed a belch and stopped in the middle of the corridor to make sure he was pointing in the right direction. A man in a dinner suit stepped past him with an 'excuse me', and opened the door to the Thornbridge Room on the opposite side of the corridor. His eyes followed the dinner-suited man through to the far end of the room, where entertainer Ronnie de Martino, all the way from Doncaster, was wrapping up his set for the annual golf club dinner dance. Dabbing the perspiration from his brow, the veteran crooner resurrected the last of his well-worn jokes of dubious taste while he cued up the backing track to his grand finale ("Here's a little favourite of mine that was a big hit around the time of the World Cup Italia 90 for the one and only, the iconic Mr Luciano Pavarrrrrotti").

With deliberate and reasonably assured steps, the dishevelled man walked on to the reception area, where the aftermath of the row was still being dealt with. The manager of the Teleshef call centre company had already delegated the task of keeping his two junior colleagues well apart and was now doing his best to placate the duty manager of the hotel, who was protesting about the damage caused to the reputation of the establishment by such outrageous behaviour and was threatening the ultimate sanction – pulling the plug on the disco in the Hopefield Suite and shutting the bar.

Five yards away, one of the chastened combatants, her make-up ruined beyond salvation and her new dress torn, was being consoled on the leather-effect Chesterfield sofa by two friends but was still defiantly vowing, between snivels, that she would get the bitch.

The Birley Suite was across the other side of reception and, largely oblivious to the drama he was leaving behind him, the dishevelled man pushed open the door to it. Inside, he paused again, adjusting his ears to the pounding beat and his eyes to the gloom which was being penetrated in time to the music by the flashing lights of the dance floor. The Ridings Building Society Christmas do was still going strong.

The paper decorations which had not been dragged from their sticky tape fixings to be wrapped around necks like feather boas were sagging in the stale heat. The remains of burst 'Happy Xmas' balloons, trodden into a mess of debris with party poppers and discarded paper hats, stuck to his shoes as he walked deeper into the room, past abandoned tables cluttered by empty glasses.

Young men in their best going-out shirts, their drinks cupped close to their chests for comfort and safety, gazed with predatory eyes from the edge of the dance floor at the girls in party frocks. Bolder work-mates were putting on their well-practiced moves in an attempt to lure a girl or two from a group that had, at its centre, in her sparkly black mid-thigh dress, Stella the savings accounts manager. Even when she was in her normal day-to-day work wear, all her male colleagues unanimously agreed she was really fit for her age and, emboldened by booze, their admiration was reaching deeper and more carnal levels. Only one middle-aged manager, however, his tie dragged loose and his pulling potential no longer regarded seriously by anyone other than himself, dared approach the lovely Stella for a brief hand-on-the-hip boogie and a swift twirl, unaware of jealous younger stares.

In the furthest corner of the room was the bar and the dishevelled man veered deliberately towards it. The stool he had vacated ten minutes earlier had not been taken by anyone else and so he sat back down, scooped a ten-pound note from his trouser pocket and gestured to the barman, who no longer needed confirmation of the order and poured another double rum and coke. As he settled to wait for the drink, he swivelled the stool so that he had his back to the centre of everyone else's attention, rested his elbows on the bar and sighed.

The early part of his night has been spent picking over an unpalatable Christmas meal, in awkward isolation at the end seat of a table he shared with people he had no time for on any other day of the year, content to allow the conversations to swirl around him. That duty done, he decided he had earned the right to sit alone and drink for the rest of the night, his steady progress towards the familiar blurry numbness of intoxication interrupted only by the regular acid eruptions brought on by the food.

In the solitude of his quiet corner, he could drink unnoticed. Having a good time at these functions was practically compulsory but overstepping the mark was still tacitly discouraged and drinking to oblivion was definitely not the right example expected of a senior member of staff. He knew how to be discreet about it. Put your order in when no-one else is at the bar, or occasionally use one of the other bars in the building, if the option is there. Go for doubles, triples even, and always with a mixer so they don't know how much is rum and how much is coke. Knock them back as quickly as you like. Nobody watches you closely enough to count how many you've had. Nobody really cares. As long as you stay upright, you can get away with anything.

Mornings were harder. It was difficult to hide a heavy night before from every other member of staff he would have to pass on his way to the sanctuary of his own small office but, once inside, it was possible to give the impression of being busy by taking the phone off the hook until the head cleared a bit. A livener from the bottle in the briefcase sometimes helped. Always handy to have a few cans of coke and a packet of mints in the drawers as well. Sometimes, he invented appointments at branch offices to give him extra recovery time at home.

Everybody knew anyway. The junior office staff had even invented a grading system for those hungover morning appearances; a scale of one to five ranging from 'slightly' to 'completely'. Most of the more senior staff had been really good about it since he had returned to work there and were still prepared to make allowances. They knew what he had been through. Someone might occasionally chance a quiet 'are you OK?' but none of them really knew what to say and so thought it best to leave him alone.

Frankly, no one was paying the slightest attention to him tonight, especially those who had felt compelled to attempt small talk earlier by the unfortunate luck of the draw in the table plan. They were happy and probably quite relieved to attempt their shouted conversations elsewhere.

They would most likely have preferred it if he had not come at all. He knew it was a mistake too but he had succumbed to the immoderate pleading of Julie, whose job it was to be a helpful first point of contact for visitors to the High Street branch and whose self-appointed mission it was to achieve one hundred per cent attendance at another interminable annual works Christmas do. He had been Julie's toughest challenge but she was one of those at the office whose sympathy had not yet been exhausted and she wasn't about to take no for an answer. She probably thought she was being kind.

Much as he hated to admit it, he quite enjoyed the fact that someone actually went through the motions of making him feel like his presence at the do would be brilliant, even though the truth was nobody could care less whether he was there or not. So he had bought a ticket. That was in October. Only later did it strike him about the date.

Of all the days. One year on.

It would have been easier to just not turn up and then deal with the excuses on Monday, if anyone even noticed he wasn't there. He would have lied. He wouldn't have said anything about why this day, of all days, made him even less inclined to pretend to be sociable. That would have just made him sound as if he was milking it. Lies are easier.

In the end, he decided he would more than likely spend the night pouring the contents of a bottle of rum down his throat and so he might as well have it dispensed by the barman at the Royal Alfred as anywhere else. Perhaps there still was, deep within him, a part of his soul which craved an end to the self-exile he had imposed. Maybe. Anyway, he decided to go. Right now, though, he wished he had decided to pour his own rum at the flat.

One year. So much had gone wrong in that time that he could barely recall what his life had been like before then.

One year. His marriage, home, friends, future – all lost to him now and all because of one stupid decision on one night. Why the hell didn't I...? Ah! Here we go again.

He drained his glass and, practically in a single motion, turned to order another from the barman. Half a minute later, another double rum and coke with two fresh cubes of ice was in his hand and his pocket was lighter by another £7.50.

On the dance floor, Robbie Williams fought to be heard above the tuneless accompaniment of personal banking analysts, mortgage consultants, financial planners and clerical staff who were linked, arms around shoulders and waists, to form a large swaying circle.

Before the noisy huddle could disperse, the next song was already playing. The first few notes were unmistakable and were greeted with whoops of joy from the dance floor. Others were soon on their way to join them. It was the song which has tortured the deepest consciousness of every bar worker, greetings card shop assistant and supermarket checkout person for long weeks of countless years around the same time of year.

The royalties pay-out every Christmas must be enormous. So here it is; another few pennies in Noddy Holder's Pension Plan.

It was time to escape. He drained his glass again, gave an unacknowledged nod of thanks to the barman, who looked as if the end of his shift could not come quickly enough, and after peering around to remember where the exit was, he headed for it.

His lungs appreciated the cool, fresh air even if the rest of him didn't. He shivered with only his flimsy suit jacket for warmth as he emerged into the city centre street, where people walked briskly on their way home or wandered, yawping ostentatiously, immune to the temperature and seemingly in no hurry to call time on their night out.

Christ, three more weeks of this. Bloody Christmas.

There were usually long queues at the taxi ranks at this time, so he turned against the flow and headed towards the back-street taxi company office that had been his last call on many a night spent alone trailing around the quieter pubs, away from the busy bars at the heart of the city centre.

A few minutes later, he walked through the door of the squat, dirty office of Zingy Cabs and was greeted with a world-weary glance from the hard-bitten woman in her fifties who seemed to sit permanently there behind the protective screen of the radio desk. She never offered more than a disdainful flicker of acknowledgement whenever anyone walked through the door. No doubt that is what too much exposure to too many people who have had too much to drink and are either irrationally aggressive or believe they are hilariously funny does to a person. Perhaps she was once as bright and pleasant as Julie the High Street customer representative. Perhaps not. With or without the protection of the screen, she did not look a woman to mess with. With the briefest exchange of eye contact and a discontented sigh, she picked up the radio mike.

'Anybody on their way back to the office?'

'Four-three, just dropped off and on my way back in, five minutes.'

'Be with you in a few minutes, sir, if you would just take a seat,' she said flatly and returned to pawing over a tatty trashy magazine.

He sat on one of a row of grimy plastic chairs and looked at the same old posters on the pin board opposite. Most of them were flyers for nearby takeaways but the largest, handwritten in marker pen on fluorescent yellow card, was an attempt to deter potential fare dodgers and included an unnecessary apostrophe in the word 'cameras'.

Fixed to the wall above the pin board was a battered portable TV with the volume turned up too high. A square-jawed cop in plain clothes was in the process of taking on the whole of gangland armed only with a pistol that apparently never ran out of bullets. He was a very good shot. Just as the cop took out another three of the bad guys, the woman behind the protective screen, without looking up at the TV, reached up a flabby arm and changed channel with the remote control. She then put the remote back down on the counter and flicked over the page of her magazine.

On the TV now, two women, one with bottle-blonde hair and a huge surgically enhanced cleavage and the other darker, with a tattoo of three red roses down the length of one arm from the shoulder to the elbow, were sitting at a table. They were the type who became famous for appearing on reality TV shows and talking vacuous nonsense and were, at this very moment, talking vacuous nonsense on a reality TV show.

He watched them gesturing and preening, not really able and not especially attempting to pick up the thread of what they were talking about, until a car pulled up outside.

'This one mine?' he said. The response came with a single nod, no eye contact.

Out in the cold again, he dodged a rowdy group who were on their way to the pizza and kebab takeaway next door and climbed into the back of an ageing Toyota.

'Bottom of School Lane, right?' said the driver, who was plainly more familiar with the face in his rear-view mirror than his passenger was with the back of the head now in front of him. The driver also knew it was pointless trying to start conversation with this customer. It was a silent fifteen-minute drive.

As the car pulled away again, he took a few steps down the steep side road to the entrance to the flats where he lived, fumbling in his pocket for the key to the main door, when he froze, hearing a whispered voice from up ahead.

'John! John!'

Looking up sharply, he squinted to see the figure of a man cloaked by darkness fifteen yards away on the other side of the street, though there was not enough light to distinguish a face.

'Who is it?'

'John, I need to talk to you.'

His heart was pounding. His brain attempted to work out whether, if he tried to make a run for it now, he could reach the secure main door of the flats and get through it before this man could cut him off. It would be close. Too close. Maybe that would only make him aggressive. Jesus, who is it? How does he know my name?

'Come out into the open, where I can see you.'

'Best not. Look, come over here. It's all right, mate. I'm not a nutter or anything. Trust me.'

Trust me? Mate?

'Look, who the hell are you? I'm not stupid. I'm not falling for this. There's no way I'm going over there. How many of you are there? Leave me alone or I'll shout for help.'

In the few moments of silence that followed, he felt as if he was going to be sick. Make a run for it. Now! Now, while you've got the chance! Then the figure spoke again.

'It's OK. I'm alone. It's me, Stef.'

With that, the figure stepped out of the shadows into where the street light caught his face. He was in his mid-thirties, not especially tall and didn't look especially threatening, with his thinning dark hair and dark-framed glasses. In fact, he looked more apprehensive than dangerous.

John's blood ran cold. He knew that face but he hadn't seen it for a while.

Not for a year. A year to the day, to be precise.

2

You were always a real bugger for that. We'd been for a few beers at the Phoenix and we couldn't have been walking for a minute down White Lane when you told me to hold on a sec.

Christ, Stef, why didn't you just go for one in the pub? But you had already gone through the gap in the hedge where you could get on the path to the golf course. *Hurry up, will you? It's bloody freezing out here.*

I waited for a bit, shuffling my feet and pulling my coat a little tighter for warmth with my hands in the pockets before ambling slow steps further along the roadside path. The air was still, hardly a breath of wind, and the night was crisp; considerably colder than it had been in the pub but quite a mild night really for early December.

I strolled far enough down the path to make you have to catch up and make my point about not wanting to hang around but not so far that it looked as if I was having a strop. Then I peered up at the night sky. The clouds were barely moving. The moon was nearly full and shone through a clear gap between the grey blobs that blotted out vast galaxies. I stumbled slightly as I squinted up and swivelled my head to find any familiar shape of dots in the sky.

It was really quiet. There were closer pubs than the Phoenix but that had been the drinking spot of preference ever since we had been in the sixth form. You could always get served under-age at the Old Harrow as well, but it could be a bit rough there and so a habit grew and a lot of good memories – birthdays, Christmas, New Year, the glorious feeling of acceptance at our first lock-in – were all at the Phoenix. Even though it changed a lot when they did it up and started putting food on, that quarter of an hour walk down White Lane, just across the county border, was never too far. Except when it was raining, of course. On nights like this, though, when the road was quiet and you were between the edge of the city and the tiny rural community that looked as if it had nestled there unnoticed for hundreds of years, with nothing but open field on either side of you, it was blissful.

But pretty chilly. *Come on, Stef, what are you doing?*

I turned to look and there you were; half out from the clearing but not walking my way. You reached down to your pocket and took something out – your wallet? Your phone? That's when I saw him, mostly hidden by your smaller frame and in the darkness but definitely more than a shadow. *Not good. Jesus.*

'Hey!' I shouted and ran towards you. The other one glanced quickly up towards me and, in that instant, I saw your arm reach out to grab his but he jerked it towards you and I saw you bend sharply at the hip and then sink, without straightening, to your knees. There wasn't much light on that part of the road apart from that offered by the moon but I saw a definite glint then in the other one's hand as he pulled it away and turned to run back through the gap in the hedge where you could get on the path to the golf course. *Jesus, Jesus, Jesus.*

I was there in seconds. He had gone but I didn't care. You were perfectly still, kneeling, bowed and crouched as if deep in prayer, though with both hands clutching the left side of your midriff. 'Oh Jesus. Stef! Stef! You OK?'

My hands on your shoulders made you start to fall forward, but I eased you to your left and on to your back. As your jacket fell open, I could see the glistening dark liquid between your fingers. I looked at your face. I will never erase the image of that face, your eyes bulging, desperate, your mouth agape and speechless as if it was taking every effort you could muster to draw every gasping breath into your body, which was now quivering uncontrollably.

'Oh no! Please no! Hold on, Stef, hold on.'

I ripped the scarf from around my neck and eased your shaking fingers from the wound in your side. I pressed the crumpled scarf against it and, with my other hand, reached for my phone in the inside pocket of my coat, fumbling to press in the security code and dial 999.

'Ambulance. White Lane, White Lane near Ridgeway. My mate's been stabbed, he's losing a lot of blood. Yeah, I'm with him. He is breathing. Yeah, I'll stay on, but hurry up.'

A car pulled up alongside us. The window buzzed down. 'You all right, pal?'

'My mate's been stabbed.'

'Oh shhhi—!' He leapt out of the car and I thrust the phone towards him.

'I've called the ambulance. Take it.'

'Hello, hello? Yeah, I'm with him. No, I've just stopped to help. On its way – good. Yeah, I think so – hang on. Is he still breathing, mate?'

Still the eyes wide, wide, pleading, shocked, despairing. Each breath more laboured than the last. 'Hold on, Stef.'

But by the time the ambulance arrived, it was too late.

I've played that scene through my head like a film clip a million times. Why did I have to walk away? If I'd stayed closer he would never have dared take two of us on. Where did he come from? Why didn't you just let him get away when I started running towards you? What were you thinking, trying to grab hold of his arm when he'd got a bloody great knife? Jesus! It was a few quid and a phone. Let him take it. It wasn't... It wasn't... Why didn't I just stay close?

They never got the bastard. Never found the knife, never traced the phone, never traced the cards. Nothing. The trail went cold very quickly. I've played that scene through my head like a film clip a million times and every time I come to the bit where he glanced up, I try to freeze frame and zoom in, but it's useless. He was taller than you – about six foot. Dark clothes, couldn't even say for sure if he was white, black or whatever. That's all I could give them – about six foot tall, dark clothes, not sure if he was white, black or whatever. Some use.

The police did say there had been a report of somebody trying to break into the secretary's office at the golf club that night when there were still about twenty people in the bar. Not the brightest, let's assume. Somebody saw him and scared him off. Said he was six footish, dark clothes, probably white. Six footish, dark clothes, probably white. Some use. CCTV wasn't much help either. They thought maybe he ran across the golf course and was making his way down the path when he saw you having a piss against a tree and thought he might at least cover his bus fare. Easy pickings for a bastard with a bloody great knife. The timings were about right to connect him with the golf club thing, but that was about it. The trail went cold very quickly after that.

That was it. That was how my best friend died on the side of a road at the age of thirty-six from a stab wound inflicted by some bastard with a bloody great knife who had probably just botched a break-in. What a stupid waste. If you'd gone for a piss before we left the pub, if I'd just stayed close instead of wandering off, if you'd just let him get away. Why did you grab at him? Why didn't I stay where I was? I could have stopped it happening, then I wouldn't see that face, those eyes, every day, every night, over and over again.

Now here's your face again. Not the same one as that time, more like it used to be. The expression is a bit like a small boy who's been caught pinching small change from his mum's purse, but it was more like the way I wish I could remember you all the time. You're even wearing the same clothes as that night, before all the blood. It's definitely you, only it can't be. It can't be.

John suddenly felt weak. He staggered backwards towards the wall of the flats until his back pressed against the solid brick, but he could not find the strength in his legs to support him and he slid down the length of the wall until he was sitting on the paving stone. His head fell forward onto his bended knees and his hands cupped around the back of his head so that he was curled almost into a ball.

What's going on with me? What is going on? Twelve months of trying to suppress the anguish – deny it, drown it, whatever – and now this. The last year washed back and overwhelmed him.

Tentatively, Stef moved closer until he could reach out and touch John's arm. John started and drew in a sharp breath, looking up at the form of his dead friend with frightened eyes. Jesus! I actually felt that.

Stef instantly pulled his hand away. 'It's OK, mate, it's OK. Look, I know this is a bit weird but we need to talk. I haven't got long.'

John buried his head again and pressed it even more firmly into his knees with his cupped hands. 'No, no! This can't be happening. I'm losing it. This isn't real.'

Stef sighed and sat beside the sobbing ball of John. 'Look, I've got some stuff to tell you now, John, and I need you to trust me. I am dead, you aren't going mental. I'm not trying to scare you or anything. There is a reason I'm here. I couldn't let you carry on doing what you've been doing to yourself. I want to help. I want you to help yourself.'

John stayed firmly locked in his protective coil but, as much as he wanted to block them out, the words penetrated his defences.

'Please listen to me, mate. I know we always said that when you're dead, you're dead and they either burn you or bury you and that's it but that's not the way it is. Death is actually no big deal. There is an after-life and, I have to tell you, it is way, way better than this one. Listen to me, John, this is important. It's like you are simultaneously everything and everywhere and yet at the same time you're neither anything nor anywhere in particular. You're every grain of sand in the desert, every drop of water in the ocean, every leaf on a tree. It's really cool.'

He paused.

'That probably doesn't make any sense to you, but it is awesome. Because nobody is defined by a physical form there's no inequality, no greed, no judgement, no pain, no suffering. It's really beautiful.'

'Sounds bloody dull.'

A reaction! Not the one he was hoping for, but a reaction all the same.

'It's not! It's wonderful!' Stef paused again. John stayed curled up, but he was

11

not sobbing any more.

'Look, everybody has their time and mine was up a year ago. Nobody can do anything to change it when it's your time to die but your time isn't up. You can still do good here. That's what I'm here to tell you. You have a new destiny now.'

John broke out from his defensive shell and looked straight at the form of his friend with watery, defeated eyes.

'What do you expect me to do? I can't even take care of myself. I couldn't stop you from getting killed that night. I've been killing myself ever since and I've got rid of all the people around me that I cared for until there's nothing left. The only good I could do is to finish what I've started, and, if I did, nobody could care less. They'd burn me and put the ashes in a pot in a room somewhere and nobody would bother coming to pick them up and that would be it. I'd be gone. What am I even saying this for? You're not really Stef. He died a year ago. You're a bad trick of the booze. Why should I even believe this is happening?'

Stef took hold of John's arm.

'This is really real, mate. There was nothing you or anybody else could have done to change what happened to me that night because it was meant to be. Nobody was to blame. You've got to stop raking over what happened and start realising that you can change what happens from now on. This is a big chance for you to save yourself and save others. Everybody gets only a short time on earth and there's so much about it that is beautiful, but we all lose sight of how fantastic it all is and so very few of us realise how much of a positive difference we can all make. It is a wonderful world if we just open our eyes.'

John snorted. 'Great. Now he's turning into Louis Armstrong.'

'Actually, Louis has become a really good friend.'

There was a moment of silence. John stared.

'Nah, I'm having you on. Your face!'

Stef grinned. John rested his head on his knees again.

'Bastard.'

Stef felt they were beginning to reconnect. Like they used to.

'Look, I can understand this is all a bit much but, if you want proof, I'll give it to you. Go and see Jas. Go and see Jas and ask her if you can go and have a look in my study. I still watch over her and I know she left my stuff just as it was. Tell her you want a bit of time alone and then look in the dark blue document wallet marked 'old tax returns' to the left of my desk. Open it at 2015–16 and in there you'll find a red case with a ring in it.'

Stef shrugged. 'I was going to propose on Christmas Day. Had it all planned. Surprise her by taking her to this nice hotel in Scarborough on Christmas Eve, pop the question Christmas Day. I loved her very much.'

'You never said.'

'You'd only have taken the piss.'

John cracked a smile. True.

'Look, you've just said you knew nothing about what I'd planned, so go and find the ring and then you'll know. You'll know this is really happening, John. This isn't a bizarre dream; it's an opportunity you have to embrace. Save yourself, John. Do some good.'

The sound of footsteps from further down the hill and then a woman's laugh made John turn his head. Suddenly aware that he was about to be caught sitting on a pavement beside his dead friend, he turned quickly back to Stef but he was gone.

The couple were up level with him and stopped at the sight of the pathetic slumped figure propped up against the wall.

'Are you OK, pal?' asked the man.

'Fine, fine. Just had one too many. Getting some air. I'm getting up now. I live just here. Thanks.'

The couple moved on and, at the turn onto the main road, glanced back again. John heard the man mutter something and the woman giggle as they moved out of sight. Then he was alone again.

3

He had no choice. That was the only thing close to a conclusion John came to at the end of a tortured night filled with fitful snatches of exhausted sleep mixed with spells in which he lay starkly awake with the same questions running over and over and over in his thoughts.

There had been plenty of other bad nights over the last year but this was different. Not only had old wounds been exposed, again, now his tormented mind echoed with confusing new information that mocked the beliefs he had held to be true.

True? What *was* true?

Even in the stretches of sweaty consciousness in which the minutes passed so slowly, John was no longer sure how much of that night was real and how much was blurred into the screaming images of the dreams that made him crave the power to stay awake.

Had the long descent of the last year taken him close to madness? It seemed so. Sane people do not get visits from their dead friends.

When morning came, John felt more acutely sober than he had for a long, long time and there was still nothing but questions, questions, questions. He realised there was only one option open to him if he was to start finding the answers.

'Hi, Jas. Been a long time.'

John had often told Stef he was punching way above his weight with Jas. It was a charge he was happy to admit to. Even with no make-up and in ludicrously fluffy carpet slippers, she was still a natural beauty, with pale brown skin, gloriously high cheekbones and shining shoulder-length black hair, though those large dark eyes no longer had the sparkle of before. As soon as she opened the door, John realised how shockingly bedraggled he must appear in comparison.

But that was only part of the reason why Jas looked so surprised. John was about the last person she expected to see on her doorstep at 10 o'clock on a Saturday morning.

Of course she had heard the stories about how John had gone off the rails since Stef was killed. Almost exclusively, it was Amy's version of events she heard and, told in the weeks leading up to the split, they did not show John in a good light. By then, Jas had already had to give John up as lost.

In those dreadful first months, when all she wanted was to cease to exist as Jas; to become wholly absorbed by the people closest to her whose words could never console but whose presence was the only thing saving her from a hell of despair, she had tried to reach out to John.

He had been there that night. He had tried to give Stef the final comfort she could not. He still had Stef's blood on his clothing when she saw him in the hospital and she knew then, without a word being spoken, that all was lost. He was the only one who felt the deep, twisting pain as acutely as her and she wanted to reach for him, take him close and not let go until, somehow, their pain eased and the healing began. He was the last connection she had with living Stef and she needed that but when she tried to reach for him he pulled away, when she held him it was like embracing a statue, when she tried to talk to him he could not even look her in the eye.

Not so long after the funeral, when it was as much as Jas could do to find the strength to hold on to the lifebelt herself, she stopped stretching out a hand and had to watch as John drifted slowly out on his own before disappearing below the surface. All she heard after that were the stories. Bad stories.

'Wow, John! What are...? Will you come in?'

John sat, bent forward, at the end of the curved sofa and looked around the room as Jas made coffee and regained her composure. It was much as he remembered it. They had spent ages and a small fortune turning a crumbling and fusty large detached house, barely brought up to date since the 1970s by the old lady who died alone in the main front bedroom, into their modern home; all cashew oak solid wood flooring and tasteful soft furnishings. Jas was the visionary there. Stef was content being led and accepted without complaint the new house rules about footwear etiquette and tidiness. He was just so happy.

'Forgive the clutter, won't you? I was catching up on a bit of work.'

Clutter? John assumed she was referring to the small pile of papers and a pen on the table where she now carefully placed two matching mugs of coffee on coasters.

'You ought to see my place,' he muttered.

'It's been ages, John. How are you?'

How am I? Confused, wracked, exhausted, on the brink of being tossed into chaos by a tormented mind and fearing I might have lost my marbles because I had an encounter with the ghost of your dead former boyfriend.

'Fine. Fine really. How are you?'

'You know, good and bad days but getting there. It was a year yesterday, you know.'

'I know.' He looked down and nodded his head slowly. 'Tough times.'

'Hmm.'

Jas picked up her coffee cup, raised it to her lips without taking a sip because it was plainly too hot and put the cup down again.

'It's good to see you again, John.'

She was still not sure it really was. What was he doing here?

'Have you heard from Amy at all?'

Oh, Amy! Poor Amy. She tried, she really tried, to be the understanding partner. *We'll get through this together*, she promised, and she gave me all the leeway anyone could possibly be entitled to but she really could not cope with the deep, dark moods or understand the destructive drinking binges. In the end, the horrified concern turned to hopeless anguish and she yelled, yelled, yelled at me, trying to get through to the person she desperately wished was still locked inside the calcified shell of her husband.

'Why won't you talk to me? Will you please just go and get help? Can't you see that you are killing yourself? You're killing yourself and you're killing me!'

In the end, when the only way I would deign to close the distance between us for a few moments was through anger and aggression, she left me. She never came back. She got the message. It was over. So much for getting through it together.

John shook his head. 'You?'

'Not so much recently. Not since she started seeing that new bloke.'

New bloke?

'All right for some.'

'She went through a lot as well, John. She deserves to move on.'

'Not as much as some of us.'

'You threatened to kill her with a cricket bat.'

John could not remember the incident, as such, but recalled the accusation being raised when the lawyers were sifting through the details of the divorce, as the remnants of eight years of marriage, plus two more of living together, were shared out.

'She obviously never saw me play. The worst that could have happened is that I

16

would have clipped her with the edge.'

Ah! Inappropriate comment.

'Sorry. Bad joke.'

Jas managed a weak smile.

'Have you been seeing anyone?'

'Noooooo!' John wished he had not made the suggestion sound so absurd but, really, it was. There was no room for even the most casual of acquaintance in his life these days. Who on earth would want to spend serious time with this?

'Me neither. Well, I've been asked out a couple of times and went for a drink with this one guy once but, you know, it just didn't... I'm just not ready yet.'

John nodded sympathetically.

'What about the business?'

John sighed. 'I had to pack it in. There's not much call for an independent financial advisor who's in no fit state to offer independent financial advice and all my clients sort of found IFAs who could.'

'What a pity. You worked so hard to build it up.'

'Yeah.' John shrugged. 'I'm back at the Ridings in their head office. The bloke who interviewed me worked there when I was there before and I think he knew what happened and took pity on me. I get to keep my head down and the work's easy enough. Pays the bills.' He looked around the front room. 'Glad you kept the house.'

Jas took a sip of coffee and put the mug back down. 'Mmm. The mortgage wasn't an issue thanks to that life insurance policy you sorted out for us. It took me weeks until I could bear to set foot in the place alone, but I'm glad I didn't sell up. We put a lot into getting the place how we wanted it and I see Stef everywhere in it. I feel like he's still here with me and I like that feeling, you know? I can look around this house and see happy memories. There were so many.'

'We had some good times, the four of us, didn't we?' prompted John. 'Remember that weekend at the Belfry?'

'Oh god!'

'When Frank Sinatra came on and Stef got up and started singing?'

'I was *sooo* embarrassed!'

'Jumped up on the table at one point, as I remember.'

'I was sure we were going to be thrown out of the hotel.'

'And you could see everybody in the bar turning around and looking at Stef as if to say, "what a dickhead!"'

They were laughing. Together. John couldn't remember the last time he laughed with someone. After a few seconds, the laughter petered out in an air of self-consciousness but, just for a moment, things were different for both of them. It felt good for a moment but now it felt a bit awkward again.

'We never did get around to all going out to New York together like we planned that night, did we?' he added.

'I'm glad you came around, John,' said Jas, finally. 'What made you decide to call, after all this time?'

'I suppose it was with it being a year and I thought about Stef a lot yesterday. I just had a feeling I wanted to come here, see you and, you know, get in touch again.'

'I'm glad you did.'

'I don't suppose I could just have a bit of a look around the house, could I?'

'Of course.' Jas rose to her feet and gestured towards the large dining room, bathed in light from the patio doors that ran almost the full length of the outside wall. The garden had been stripped bare by winter but stretched to where a few birds still fluttered down to feed at the tables and had clearly been maintained with plenty of loving care.

Jas allowed John to lead the way, into the room, hemmed in by the heavy dark red walls, and then out again to the stairs, up towards the guest bedroom where he and Amy had stayed so many times after boozy dinner parties which broke up far too late to contemplate heading home. Past the master bedroom and there it was. Stef's study.

'I don't suppose...' He hesitated. 'I don't suppose I could just spend a few moments in here alone, could I? If that's not too intrusive?'

'No problem. Feel free.' Jas was a little taken aback by the request. 'I'll be downstairs.' She turned to head back down the stairs.

The room was immaculately clean and tidy but was otherwise as Stef had left it.

John sat in the large leather chair and swivelled around to look at the shelves of sports books and novels, with souvenirs of various foreign trips set in every available space. And photos, some of family but mostly of Stef and Jas, some in frames, some not, leaning against the spines of the books. The walls were practically covered with more photos, postcards and prints. It was a busy room. Stef's den, Jas always called it.

One side of the room was more business-like and orderly, with accountancy and business management reference books filling the shelves and no frivolous adornments. Under the L-shaped desk, to the left of the PC set in front of the chair he now sat in, were half a dozen or so hard box files and quite a few more document wallets.

A dark blue wallet, Stef had said, with 'tax returns' written on it. John leaned under the desk to make out the handwritten sticker on the nearest of the document wallets. Not that, not that – ah! Third one, dark blue, 'old tax returns'.

That'll be the one.

He picked it out and opened the catch on the flip top. Which year was it? Can't take much working out. John went through each dividing folder, from the front, taking out the papers within it and peering in until he got to the section marked 2015–16.

There, in the corner at the bottom of the file, was a small red box. John didn't know whether to feel elated or scared. He reached in and took out the box, easing open the stiff top to reveal a gold ring studded with sparkling stones.

'You soft bastard,' he said quietly.

John stared at the ring but was looking way beyond the object in his fingers. So it wasn't just some sort of mad delusion brought on by alcohol. That was something. Quite what the repercussions were beyond there, John could not even attempt to grasp right now. For the moment, it was enough to know that he was not losing it. Not completely, anyway.

'Well bugger me,' he said, closing the lid of the box and replacing everything just the way he had found it.

As he reached the bottom of the stairs, Jas was standing beside the sofa, waiting. She walked towards him and, to his surprise, threw her arms around his neck. John tentatively responded by wrapping his arms around her back. So unexpected, so long since the last time, so... nice. They held the embrace silently for only a few seconds but John felt as self-conscious as a young kid back in the playground, stealing a first kiss in front of all his mates.

Jas broke the hold first and, without moving more than a few inches away, looked straight into John's eyes with purpose.

'We're all finding our own way to move on, John, but it's so much easier if you have people around you who can help. Promise me you'll stay in touch this time.'

John, not entirely sure he could speak anyway, nodded.

'What happened that night was not your fault. I know that and Stef knows that. You can't carry on blaming yourself. You have to start being good to yourself.'

Out on the street again, John heard the front door close behind him and, as he turned to walk back to the car, he took two deep, deep breaths.

He was happy to have seen Jas again. Really. He was. She hadn't slammed the door in his face, hadn't burst into tears and said how she wished it was him who had died and not Stef. She had even offered him a bit of absolution, which was nice of her. Maybe some time he would find the courage and the words to explain to Jas why he had turned up unannounced on her doorstep on a Saturday morning after all these months but, for now, he was just glad to have checked out the ring story and that it had worked out the way he had been told it would.

His dead friend had apparently visited him and offered fairly convincing proof that he wasn't just a figment of an alcohol-addled imagination. That was sort of good.

The easy bit was over with. All he had to do now was get his head around it and work out what it meant.

4

Whatever the next step was and however momentously life-changing it was going to be, John decided the first thing he should do when he stepped back into his flat was to take a shower. This, in itself, was a slight departure from his habit of recent times.

Then he decided to put on fresh clothes for the first time in two days – or was it three? – but this proved to be more of a challenge. In the end, John settled for sorting out the least creased and grubby to wear now and pushed as much as he could from the piles of clothing that littered his bedroom floor into the previously neglected washing machine. In the absence of any washing powder, he reckoned a dishwasher tablet, a free sample he'd decided to hold on to even though he didn't have a dishwasher, would do.

If he had owned a dishwasher, perhaps the pile of plates, pans and mugs heaped in and around the tiny sink in the small kitchen would have been a less daunting sight.

Sizing them up was like reading the layers of rock in a cliff face. The plates peeped out from the bottom of the heap and between them could just be seen a couple of small pans, caked with dried tomato sauce and residual baked beans. On top of them were cereal dishes and fruit bowls, used, presumably, when there were no more clean plates available.

John realised that when the stocks of plates and dishes were exhausted, he must have decided ready meals and takeaways were the way forward. Foil containers and black plastic trays, some of them warped from too long in the microwave, were piled high on top of and among the crockery, with forks, knives and spoons encrusted with everything from lasagne to chicken tikka masala to egg fried rice and, most likely, all three, stuck out of the pile like prongs on a wartime sea mine.

21

On the draining board was a heaped row of used tea bags, from which seeped a trail of brown stain leading to the sink.

Something had to be done, so John delved into the pile in the sink, risking the loss of fingers and upsetting the remains of a tuna pasta bake onto the floor, to manoeuvre the plug into the plughole before filling the sink with clean cold water. Unable to find any washing-up liquid, John tossed the second of his free sample dishwasher tablets into the mix.

That job done, John moved through to the living room.

Could one man really have been solely responsible for emptying so many bottles and cans? In fairness, this was the accumulation of several months of serious drinking and a less-than-dedicated approach to disposing of the empties, but it was a formidable haul.

Rum figured prominently and, judging by the supermarket own brand labels, the choice of which specific rum was less down to taste than finding whichever was the cheapest in whichever supermarket he happened to be in that day. He was careful to vary his supermarket trips so that he wouldn't give away how much he was drinking. Other bottles – gin, vodka, whisky – suggested he had occasionally come across promotions on other spirits too.

Wine bottles, two of them pushed neck first down the side of the sofa, were scattered liberally everywhere except for a neat triangular arrangement of ten at the far end of the room that had been set up for a game of skittles using crushed beer cans, which must have been great fun until he ran out of beer cans close to hand to crush and couldn't be bothered collecting the ones he had tossed at the bottles with unerring inaccuracy.

The few plates, dishes and items of cutlery that were not cluttering the kitchen were at one end of the sofa alongside a mug with a blue culture growing in the bottom, which had been utilised as a safekeeping place for the TV remote control. Beside the front door was a pile, largely of junk mail and takeaway menus, which had, at best, been briefly inspected before being tossed on top of the rest and then completely ignored.

The only way to tell how long any of this scattered detritus had been there was by the depth of dust on or around it and it was evidently quite a long time in many cases. However you looked at it, this was a mess.

John looked at it long and hard, not quite sure how he had allowed it to get so bad. He hadn't realised the flat had become this much of a pigsty. Plainly, he had not been quite aware of many things recently. In a few short hours, he had started to see everything more clearly.

His brain was functioning again. This was good.

But there were more important matters to address right now than cleaning up the flat.

This was not an everyday set of circumstances to try to make sense of and he didn't feel he had come close to grabbing the magnitude of it as yet, so he decided to approach it as methodically as he would have assessed the financial position of one of his former clients. John ripped open an envelope offering a new broadband package from the top of the pile of mail near the door so that he could use it to make notes on and rummaged in the bottom of his briefcase for a pen. He sat down on the sofa and began to write.

John first wrote a number one, followed by the words 'Current Status'. While he was thinking what to put next, he drew a circle around the figure one and then wrote underneath it.

Fucked.

Looking up, John stared at the screwed-up balls of paper, plastic wrappings, empty cans, more bottles and a single trainer that spilled around the waste bin next to the TV – enough to have filled three waste bins. Then he noticed, on the other side of the TV, a half-eaten slice of pizza which had become stuck to the wall after sliding down several inches. Maybe he had disagreed with something on the telly. His aim had let him down but then it can't be easy to throw a half-eaten slice of pizza from what may well have been a prone position on a sofa.

John looked at the trail of tomato puree down the wall and the mouldering remains of the pizza base and crossed out his previous assessment before adding an amendment.

Completely fucked.

That was part one done. John now wrote down a number two followed by the words 'Key Points'. What had Stef said? John scribbled down what he could remember of the previous night's conversation.

2.1 After-life – sand, trees etc.
2.2 Death was meant to be. *(He underlined this.)*
2.3 Change the future.
2.4 I have a new destiny – what the hell does this mean?
2.5 Save yourself, save others.
2.6 Do some good. *(Also underlined).*

He read the six points through again. There was also something about opportunities and the bit about the ring in the folder under the desk but John thought that was a fair summary. He was starting to get a feel for this.

Number three. Circle. 'Course of Action'.

This was the tricky one. He went back to circle the number two while he thought about it a little more, then stared long and hard at the blank space underneath. Then he put a second circle around the number three.

Getting his own life back on track felt like an imposing enough task, let alone finding a way to become some sort of positive influence on other people. How the hell are you supposed to do that?

Change what?

Save who?

Do what?

There must have been something else in what Stef said. Think. Where is the right path? Think. The path that leads to...

Hang on. The important bit here is not *what* Stef said, but the fact that he said it. Stef is dead. If dead Stef was there in front of me, touching my arm so that I could feel his hand pressing against it, telling me stuff, talking about there being an after-life and about the ring in the file in the study – which I couldn't have known about otherwise – that means there really could be an after-life and if there is an after-life, that means there probably must be a... Oh god!

John sat back on the sofa. This was getting a bit serious.

'Well bugger me!' he said to the trail of sprayed beer on the wall just above the TV.

Is this what Stef is telling me? Is he saying my starting point should be that I find religion?

There was only one way to sort this out. Get on the internet.

John began to sift through the mess of his living room in search of his laptop. After ten minutes of overturning and swearing, he found it in a takeaway pizza box. He tried to turn it on. Nothing. Power cable. Where's the bloody power cable?

The bloody power cable was wrapped around the bloody mug tree which was, in turn, in the bloody laundry basket. The bloody laundry basket which was otherwise stuffed with empty cereal boxes in the bloody kitchen. Naturally. What else would a reasonable person put in a laundry basket apart from a mug tree with a power cable wrapped around it and bloody empty cereal boxes? If only he had made this logical step sooner, he could have saved himself another bloody half hour of looking.

John put the power cable into the laptop and then plugged it in. He pressed the power button. After a few seconds, the laptop came to life with a merry little welcome tune and showed a screen that said 'enter password'.

Password? How am I supposed to remember what the bloody password is?

Defeated, he slammed the laptop lid shut.

Phone. Where's my phone?

John tapped the pockets of the jeans he was wearing. Not there. Did I have it when I went to see Jas? He checked the inside pockets of the coat he had tossed over the back of the sofa. Not there.

Yesterday at the do. John went to the bedroom to look for the suit he had worn. The jacket was hung up in the single wardrobe but not the trousers. Trousers. Trousers. Where are the trousers? Normally, he would find them on the end of the bed or among one of the other piles of... Oh shit!

John hurried back to the kitchen, where the washing machine was still labouring through its wash cycle. As the drum turned, he could hear a regular clunk, clunk, clunk sound against the clear glass of the door and, sure enough, he could see, through the thin suds offered by the dishwasher tablet, the black outline of a smart phone.

Dammit! John stood, hands on hips, and considered his options.

There was nothing else for it.

If he wanted answers, he was going to have to do it the hard way.

He was going to have to go to church.

5

For the first time in months, John went to bed sober. Stranger still, he did not even want to have a drink. Part of the reason for that was that it had taken him all afternoon and most of the evening to get the flat into some sort of reasonable order and, unaccustomed to physical exertion recently, he had felt a bit weary. Also, after clearing up so many bottles and cans, the smell of stale booze lingered in his nostrils and not only did the thought of having a drink feel increasingly unappealing, John had felt pricked by shame. How *could* he have let it come to this?

About to open the door to his flat following his second trip to the shop, having under-estimated the number of black bin bags he would need on the first trip, John met his elderly neighbour as she was closing the door of her flat on her way out. He smiled and said hello but the courtesy was not returned. All he got back was a wary frown and a contemptuous curl of the lip.

'Miserable sod,' John said as he closed the door behind him but the encounter later bothered him. He began to imagine what she must have had to put up with over the last few months to have given her such a bad impression of the man on the other side of the adjoining wall.

It began to dawn on him that there must be plenty of people, strangers as well as those who had at one time been so close, who he had alienated recently. There were many bridges to repair.

But when he woke the next morning, clear-headed and refreshed in the restored order of his autumnal cherry and peony-scented bedroom, John felt ready to take on everything he needed to. This was good. The unexpected reunion with Stef had hit him with the subtlety of a cold bucket of water in the face but his senses now felt sharp after months of wandering around in a foggy haze. What did it all mean and how was he meant to utilise this new-found clarity? He did not have a clue but hope surged through his veins again and his eyes had been lifted up and out towards the rest of the world instead of gazing destructively within. For now, that was enough.

He was less sure about the whole church thing, the more he thought about it. His had not been a religious upbringing. Weddings, christenings. That was about the extent of it.

When he was about eight, John remembered going out to call for his pal Neil Finnegan on what must have been a Sunday morning. Finny met him at the door and told John that he couldn't go out yet because his parents were taking him to church.

'Church?' He might as well have said he was about to be immersed in a vat of custard.

'Yeah, it's Palm Sunday. They give you a free Easter egg and everything.'

Finny turned and yelled towards the living room.

'Muuuum! Can John come to church with us?'

Mrs Finny bustled to the door and looked John up and down.

'You can't go like that. Take him to your room, Neil, and he can change into your grey trousers and spare shoes.'

Finny rushed up the stairs. John followed less enthusiastically. He had only come around to play football but Finny was his best mate then and at least this might be better than going home and being bored. The promise of an Easter egg was the deal clincher.

The trousers fitted OK. The shoes were a bit tight. Off they went, Finny bubbly and chatty, his parents silently leading the way, John tagging along. Only as they walked the last fifty yards down the gennal towards the red-brick entrance to St Cyprian's Church did he think about backing out, but Finny was even more effusive than usual and Finny was his pal and so he went in.

Actually, it was all right. The service was a bit rubbish, but a lot of the hymns he knew from school assemblies and he was able to occupy his mind through the dull bits by looking at the pictures on the cream-washed walls and by tracing with his eyes the green painted lines of the wooden supports across the curved roof. He liked that everybody seemed to know each other and were happy and that they said hello and smiled when Mrs Finny introduced them to Neil's friend John.

He did get an Easter egg as well. And a cross made out of a palm leaf. After they went back to Finny's at the end of the service and he got changed back into his jeans and trainers, it was time for John to go back home for Sunday dinner and he ate the egg on the way. It was only a little one but it was nice chocolate and he reckoned if he took it home his mum would tell him he couldn't eat it until after Easter Monday. He showed the cross to his mum and dad when he got home, though.

'Where on earth did you get that from?' said his mum.

'Church. I went with Finny.'

'Church? I thought you were going to play football.'

John's dad thought it was hilarious. For weeks afterwards, whenever there was someone new to say it to and only if John was close by so that his words could cause maximum embarrassment, he would announce: 'Our John's decided he's going to be a priest!'

'Really?'

'Yes. Started taking himself off to church on a Sunday.'

He could be a real pain like that. He showed practically no interest in spending time alone with his son. He never really talked to him about things that mattered in his world. He never showed any affection. He just tried to humiliate him at every opportunity.

So John didn't go to church again. Finny asked once but he said no. It wasn't worth the hassle.

The memory drifted back as he got ready to go to church this Sunday morning. St Cyprian's was over on the other side of the city, so he had decided to go to St Felix, which was closer to the flat and had caught his eye from time to time when he walked past on the way to the bus stop. It was a fine old stone building, slightly obscured by tall fir trees from the path but inviting closer inspection of its grandness in glimpses between the trunks. John thought he had read it was Norman, or part of it was Norman, or it was built by somebody called Norman. Anyway, it was old and imposing – a proper church – and John reasoned that if he was going to be inspired to any sort of religious awakening, it would happen in a setting such as this. So he went to church, to find out if his feelings on the subject had changed in the light of Stef's revelations.

John closed the door to the flat and smiled to himself as he imagined Stef being confronted by St Peter at the Pearly Gates. Knowing Stef, he would have brazened it out but he would have had to do a bit of back-tracking from his usual stance on the subject, that's for sure. Good old Stef, the last of the great pub philosophers.

'Y'see, the thing is.' Stef took a sip of beer and leaned forward – a sure sign that he was about to go off on one.

'The thing is, I've nothing against people having religious beliefs. If they feel a sense of purpose or find strength in their faith, then that's great.'

'That's very good of you.'

'The problem has always been religion itself. The leaders set themselves up as speaking the word of God or being God's representative on earth and it's always just been a way of controlling the masses and protecting their own influence. They

28

accumulate this huge wealth and claim the power of life or death over millions and tell everybody "Follow my commands or it's eternal damnation for you, son" and that's been going on for centuries. It's still happening. Have you any idea how rich the major religions are? They could wipe out all the suffering in the developing world at a stroke but they do nothing. It's obscene. Am I right or what?'

'You're spot on, pal.'

'And, I'll tell you what, how many times through history have ordinary people been dragged off to war because somebody wants to prove 'my god is better than your god' and they always say 'God is on our side' but then so does the other lot and he can't be on every bugger's side, can he? You only have to watch the news to see that religion's the root cause of just about every terrorist atrocity going today. If there really was a god, he would put an end to all that.'

'We'd all be better off without religion.'

'Too right, John. Are you ready for another?'

John lifted the latch of the sturdy gate on the third attempt, betraying the fact that he was about to set foot on an unfamiliar path. As he trod carefully on the worn steps that led up to the church of St Felix, he felt the judgement of the ancient headstones in their irregular rows on either side of the path as they turned their gaze on this unworthy newcomer.

What are you doing here? We are the pious and the devoted. We have earned our place here. You don't deserve to be among us.

John hunched his shoulders against the cold breeze that whipped into his face around the solid stone walls of the church, keeping his eyes on the path ahead. The heavy wooden door, studded with metal as if prepared for a siege, was open and, through it, John could hear background music and the low murmur of voices catching up with each other's family news before the service began. He hesitated before taking the final steps and then turned away, unsure. Slowly shuffling up the path was an old couple. He would at least have to wait until they had cleared the way if he was to back out and go home, so John stepped away from the door and took an exaggerated glance at his watch, hoping to give the impression that he was waiting for someone.

As the old couple tottered past him and though the door, John watched as they headed towards a trestle table set a few yards back from the entrance. A man and a woman rose from their chairs behind the table to greet the couple.

'Morning, Derek, morning, Alice. Cold today, isn't it?'

'Perishing. How are you, Frank? I heard you haven't been very well.'

'Oh, just a bit of a sniffle. Nothing much, thanks anyway.'

John saw a chance to sneak in unnoticed. Go on. Go for it.

Head down, he quickened his step as he moved towards the lines of pews. Almost there...

'Good morning.'

Spotted.

The man and woman behind the table and the old couple had all turned their heads towards him and were smiling. John mumbled 'good morning' back to them and quickly carried on.

He sat at the end of a vacant row towards the back of the church and hunched his shoulders in an involuntary shiver. It wasn't much warmer in here than outside. John pulled his coat a little closer with his hands still in the pockets and looked around.

It was an excellent building. Large girthed pillars built from carved blocks of old stone supported arches which craftsmen, however many hundreds of years ago, had fashioned with precision and elaborately decorated with depictions of strange beasts, some vaguely familiar as belonging to this world and many of imagined creatures from another. Above them were arched windows with, between every other one of them, the origins of huge oak beams bearing the burden of a heavy ceiling which looked like the inside of an upturned hull of a large ship.

Beyond the stone flags of the aisle and through the arch in the stone wall at the centre of the church was a simple altar, watched over by two stained-glass figures set into the window behind it, their hands raised in blessing as the thin light of a December morning attempted to break through.

How many hours – years – had artisans and labourers toiled to create a building such as this – a gloriously elaborate statement of their dedication to a divinity? The naked skill, the imagination, the danger involved was almost inconceivable without the benefit of modern machinery, and yet they created something that future generations somehow lacked the talent to reproduce. What did they have to sacrifice? Was it worth it? If they could possibly have known that, centuries later, their devotion could inspire marvel in even the most ungodly soul, it surely was.

John craned his neck to look at the names carved into the World War One memorial on the wall to his right. He read down the list. Their initials, their rank, their regiment – it somehow never seemed like enough. Who were they? What did they do? What did they dream of doing before the war tore their dreams from them? John read down the names and tried to imagine how their families must have felt when the memorial was first unveiled. Was it pride or anger which pierced their sadness? He thought about how he felt in the weeks and months after Stef was killed and absorbed the bleak lesson of history. Their lives went on. They had to go on. And so those who remained raised another generation to die in another world war. More pain, more anger, more sacrifice.

Turning back to face the front, John saw another, smaller memorial. It was older and was dedicated to a single family, mourning the loss of two sons and a daughter, all aged between twenty-one and twenty-five, their deaths within a few months of each other. The year read 1848. It must have been some sort of epidemic. Jesus! Three of them wiped out like that and not young infants – mature adults. Through the agony of their crushing grief, the parents had decided to commission this marble plaque and dedicate it not only to the memory of their lost ones but also to the glory of their god. How could they do that? How could they see their children taken away from them like that and not feel their faith shaken to the foundations? It was God's will. How can that be right? What did these poor people do wrong to deserve such wretched misfortune? John could not even begin to understand their faith, but he admired it. Perhaps if he understood it, he would have dealt with his own brush with cruel death much better. Maybe he would start to feel it now.

The hum of conversation quietened and the music faded to silence. To the left of the arch at the centre of the church, in the pulpit and waiting patiently for the full attention of the couple of dozen folks in the pews, stood the vicar. A female vicar. John had not anticipated that. She cannot have been any older than him – possibly a little younger. Collar-length blonde hair just touched the fringe of her surplice and John decided she was quite good-looking. Is it a sin to fancy the vicar?

'Good morning, everybody. Cold today, isn't it?'

'Yes,' agreed several voices from the pews.

'Welcome to St Felix. We shall soon get you all warmed up with a spot of singing, so I hope you are all in good voice this morning, but first I wanted to remind you all that there are only nineteen more praising days until Christmas...

(pause for slight murmur of amusement in the congregation)

... and point out to you, in case you haven't already had the chance to look, the beautiful nativity pictures to my left on the board over there which have been sent to us by the children of St Felix Primary School.'

A couple of dozen heads turned to look towards a blue felt pin board, almost entirely covered with A4 sheets of drawings in bold strokes of crayon.

'They really are wonderful, so I hope you will all take the time to have a closer look at the end of the service.'

Seriously doubt it, love, thought John. His feeling of isolation was growing, like an interloper peeking through the curtains at a strange family's gathering. He was impatient for a message that he could connect to. Anything. A verse in a hymn. A line in the sermon. This has to start to mean something.

'So to start our service today, I thought it would be appropriate to sing a hymn that was certainly my favourite when I was a small child and I'm sure it was one of yours too. It's hymn number 60.'

Everyone reached mechanically forward to pick out the crimson-backed books in the racks of the pews in front and rose to their feet. John stood, looked around to check he had picked up the same book as everyone else and turned the pages to find hymn number 60. Here we go. Could this be the message he had been looking for?

The first note sounded from the organ in the balcony behind them.

John turned the pages. 53, 58, 64 – back. 62, 60. Jesus Wants Me For A Sunbeam.

As he walked down the path towards the gate, back past the rows of Dearly Beloveds, Cherished Memories and In Remembrances, John was glad he had not laughed out loud. It would not have been dignified. Though the hymn was not quite the meaningful sign he was hoping for, he sang along and felt much more at ease by the time he retook his seat. Perhaps it was naive to speculate that the message he was looking for could come in one blinding, inspirational flash.

And so he stayed for the rest of the service and he listened to what was said and he joined in the reverent murmur of prayers but they were only words. They did not speak to him. He felt nothing.

If Jesus really did want him for a sunbeam, he was going to have to accept that John was going to do it his own way. That was fair enough, surely. He had not simply dismissed the option. He came to see for himself and now he knew.

It's not for me.

John lifted the latch and heard it fall back into place as the gate closed behind him. He smiled to himself and fastened the top button of his coat.

''kin' sunbeam!'

6

'Good morning, Mr Baldwin, bright and early today.'

Julie was making sure all the leaflets in the racks of the banking hall were correctly sorted and neatly stacked as she prepared to greet the branch's first customers of the day.

'Morning, Julie.' John stopped and turned back to her.

'I thought the do went down very well on Friday.'

'Yes, I think so. Not too many casualties.' She let out a small, uncertain giggle.

'Thanks again for inviting me. I know I haven't exactly been the life and soul recently, but it is appreciated.'

'Oh, you're welcome.' Her hand lingered on the pile of telephone banking user guides as John walked through the door to the offices. What was that all about?

The reaction was similar in the kitchen as the office staff helped themselves to the boxes of biscuits that appeared after lunchtime and were told where they had come from.

'John Baldwin? Really?'

Over the course of the week, they got more and more used to the newcomer, with his smart appearance, casual conversation and cheerful demeanour. By Wednesday, they hardly missed the old John at all. By Thursday, even the barbed whispers over their screens of the juniors in the mortgage team were losing their capacity to draw a reaction.

John was oblivious to the chatter as he set about sorting through months of neglected and misplaced work. It was going to take ages to get straight. He was often the last to leave at night but his conscientious progress was occasionally interrupted by thoughts of what his next step should be beyond the tasks of his role at the Ridings Building Society.

He thought of groups he could get involved with – charities, maybe? Google threw up plenty of options but nothing that really grabbed him.

Late on Thursday afternoon, his new phone – bought to replace the one that he had not been able to revive following its thirty-degree economy wash – rang. It was an unidentified mobile number and John thought about letting it ring out and then, if they didn't leave a message, adding it to the blocked callers list. The last thing he wanted was another bloody PPI cold call. Yes, thank you. I'm a fully qualified independent financial advisor. I would know if I was mis-sold PPI in the past and, no, I wasn't. Go away.

But he didn't let it ring out. He pressed the green answer button.

'Hello, John Baldwin.'

'Hello, Mr Baldwin. My name's Mike Wilshaw. We haven't met but I was given your number by a former colleague of mine.'

'OK, how can I help you?'

'Well I need a bit of guidance from a good IFA and you did some work about a couple of years ago for the bloke I just mentioned – Matt Lemon? He recommended you.'

John sighed.

'I'm sorry but I had to suspend my practice. I'm afraid I don't take on that sort of work anymore.'

'Oh!' Short silence. 'That's a pity.' Another short silence. John decided he would have to make the first move to wrap up the conversation.

'Anyway, I'm sorry I can't...'

'You see, the thing is,' the voice cut across him. 'I'm setting up a charitable trust. I wanted to do something to help out kids from underprivileged backgrounds by giving them access to sport and all sorts of activities, send them on outward bound courses, give them the chance of a few days by the seaside – that sort of thing. Some of these kids have never been on holiday and there's a centre in Skegness which will take them. You should see how much it means to them. It's great for the parents as well to get involved in it, takes a bit of pressure off them all. I've got lots of plans and ideas but I'm afraid I'm not very good on the financial side of things and so I need to find somebody who is. Can you point me towards someone? I'm not expecting them to do it for nothing. I can pay.'

Even before the man finished what he had to say, John had already thought of someone who would have loved to have got involved. Right up his street.

That night in the pub.

'Honestly? You're really going to give up your evenings and weekends to teach some spotty teenagers how to put up a tent and warm up Cup-a-Soup over a paraffin stove and then go with them while they get lost in the Pennines?'

Stef responded to this incredulity with a defiant gulp of beer. 'Yep.'

'Why on earth would you want to do that?'

He laughed. 'It's absolutely brilliant, mate. Some of the kids are genuinely clueless when they start out on their bronze award and by the time they move on to gold, they've learned so much about themselves and how to operate as a responsible young adult within a team. They grow up. I really enjoyed it when I did mine and I want to get involved again as a leader. Didn't you ever want to do the Duke of Edinburgh?'

'Spend my spare time knee-deep in sheep shit? No thanks, pal.'

Stef took another sip. 'It's not for everybody, I'll grant you, but I love all that. I took a lot from it when I did mine and this is my way of giving a bit back, you know?'

John eased back in his chair. 'Mike, isn't it?'

'Yes, that's right.'

'Look, Mike, I don't operate as an IFA anymore but I think I can help you. I think we can help each other, actually. Can we get together to talk about it? I'm free tomorrow evening if you are.'

'So this bloke just called out of the blue?'

Jas leaned forward as John began to tell her about his meeting the previous night.

'I have no idea who the fella is who he says gave him my number – somebody I did a bit for while I was still getting the business established – but yeah. We had a really good chat and he seems like a nice bloke. He used to be a professional cricketer who played at, you know, county level for a few years and he still turns out for one of the big clubs in Sheffield as well as doing the coaching for all their junior sides. He says they've had a few break-ins over the years which were always blamed on the kids from the estate next to the club and he suggested one day that instead of spending more on security to keep these kids out, they make an effort to bring them into the club – give them free coaching and organise matches. He reckoned these kids were too poor to afford their own equipment and so they never got involved in the past and probably thought the club was only for the posh kids. But anyway, since they've been running the free sessions they've been getting dozens of boys and girls turning up – so many that they've had to expand it to two nights. He says they love it and that there are some good little players among them. Some of the parents have been coming down to see them play and – guess what – they haven't had any more break-ins.'

'That's amazing!'

'Anyhow, Mike said that made him think how he could expand the concept to draw in other sports. He says he has loads of contacts in football, cricket – obviously – rugby, athletics and everybody he has talked to has been keen to get involved. That led to him wanting to set up the charity. And it's not only sports, Mike says he wants to bring in people who can teach art and practical skills. He's already identified a residential adventure centre in Derbyshire he'd like to take over eventually and he's approached the people at the holiday centre in Skeggy to see how they could work together. He's got big ideas. It's just a matter of establishing a financial plan to make it work properly and I think I can do that.'

Jas had hardly moved, transfixed by John's re-awakened enthusiasm.

'I think this could be just what I need, Jas – and do you know why it feels right? It's the kind of thing Stef would have got involved in.'

He paused. There. He'd said it.

Tears welled in Jas's big dark eyes. She drew up her hands to dab at them with the inside of her forefingers but one escaped and rolled down her right cheek. She wiped it away but the tears would not stop.

John hesitated but then rose and sat closer, putting a comforting arm around her shoulder. Jas sank her head into his chest and was sobbing now. John embraced her and he too began to cry. He could not remember the last time he had allowed himself to cry. Even on the night Stef was murdered, he hadn't. Not at the funeral either. He was too numb to feel. Not long after that, guilt and self-hatred had been his only friends and they had taken him to fury, desolation and destruction but not tears.

Jas broke the embrace and quickly pulled two tissues from the box on the coffee table in front of them. She gently blew her nose and looked up.

'Sorry, John.'

He shook his head, unable to speak. There was no need to apologise.

She pulled another tissue from the box and used it to wipe a small wet patch on his shoulder. 'Don't worry – tears not snot,' she said.

He managed a smile. 'That's all right then.' He wiped his eyes with the outside of his hands.

She took another tissue and blew her nose again. 'What are we like?'

'I'm sorry if I upset you, Jas. I didn't mean to.'

Jas shook her head and put down the tissues, picking up John's hand and cupping it between hers.

'I'm not upset, John. I think it's really touching that you could look to get involved in something like this and to think of Stef as well. You're right – Stef loved working with kids in the Duke of Edinburgh and this is just the kind of cause he would have got involved in. I think it's lovely that you should do this for both of you and I think it could be really positive to do something in Stef's memory and create a kind of legacy for him. If there's anything I could do as well...'

'I was going to talk to you about that, actually. They will need a website, sooner rather than later, really, to get word out there about the Trust and its aims and with your knowledge of PR and such...'

'Absolutely! I know plenty of people who can set up the site, then I can run it and see to the social media presence as well. Leave that to me.' She picked up a pen and pulled a pad of paper closer to herself.

'What did you say he's calling it?'

'GameOn. Capital G and capital O with no gap between the two words and, thankfully, no exclamation mark.'

Jas wrote it down and underscored it twice, then she put down the pen and took hold of John's hand again. She too felt a surge of restored hope. How good it felt to talk about the future again instead of being content to get through the day-to-day.

'And you never know,' she added. 'You do read about people who have been saved from going off the rails by finding a talent in sport and if this project can stop just one of them from being drawn into crime and maybe going out in a gang with a knife...'

John nodded. Nothing more needed to be said.

There were a few moments of silence between them. It was Jas who broke it.

'I still talk to him, you know. Stef, I mean.' She looked John straight in the eyes, looking for his reaction.

He was startled but tried not to be obvious about it. He had not considered the possibility that Stef might have manifested to anyone else but, of course, if he was going to pop back to earth he was going to want to see Jas. Even more so. Over the last week, John had thought about when or if he would tell Jas about the encounter outside the flat – and the ring – but he hadn't anticipated the right time to do that would come so soon. Or that he would be prompted into the conversation by Jas raising it first.

'You know, when I get home from work I'll talk to Stef as if he was still here and tell him about the usual little boring things that have happened. Just talk out loud. Then sometimes, when the news is on and there's something that I know would have had Stef shouting at the telly, I'll say it for him. Am I going a bit mad?'

John smiled. It was a smile of relief. 'No madder than the rest of us.'

'I suppose it's when he starts answering back that I'll know I've really lost it.'

They shared a slightly self-conscious laugh. Quite. How mad would that be?

'Anyway, I think it's marvellous news about the charity and we'll both have to get together with Mike to swap ideas and talk about how we can get everything up and running,' blurted Jas, keen to change the subject but glad to have made her little confession.

'I said we'd get together in a few days once I've been able to put all the information together that I need and I know he'll be happy to have you on board. I'll let you know when. There was something else I was going to ask you, Jas.'

'OK.'

He hesitated. 'Have you got an address for Amy? I think I should attempt to make my peace with her.'

Jas released his hand and stood, turning to go the well-organised drawer where she kept her organiser. 'Of course.'

'I called to speak to my mum and dad this morning,' he added.

She took out the leather-bound book and closed the drawer. 'How did that go?' She knew the history.

John wrinkled his nose.

'Not well.'

His parents had John when they were both quite young. They married four months before he was born. That was not the way they had planned it. They didn't make the same mistake again. John was an only child.

Despite being landed with the responsibility of parenthood when mum was nineteen and dad was twenty, they did the decent thing and stayed together. Fair play to them for that. But they never entirely embraced the whole parenthood thing. They didn't exactly find their outlook on life transformed by their new bundle of joy. They raised him, provided and cared for him, maybe even loved him, in their way. But John, as adolescent hormones kicked in through his early teens, became aware that he had never really *felt* loved. Maybe that was just their way. He never asked them about it, afraid of what the answer might be. He only knew that his other friends appeared to have closer relationships with their parents.

Occasionally, he could break through his mum's usual air of distracted indifference for long enough to extract a few words of vague advice that might, from time to time, be construed as encouragement, but that was about it. As John grew into his mid-teens, even Dad's barbed put-downs became less and less frequent, to the point where the two of them hardly ever exchanged a word. He came to realise that dad had never properly got over the resentment he must have felt when it dawned on him, not much more than a child himself, that his days as a carefree young adult had been snatched away. That was John's fault.

It was the teachers who saw the potential in the shy kid and slowly coaxed him into expressing his obvious talents. They helped him get the grades he was capable of in his GCSEs and persuaded him to stay on for sixth form. That was when John found all the motivation he needed from within. He realised that if he worked hard and got good grades in his A Levels, he could go to university. University meant independence.

It was easy to put up with going home between terms because he felt resilient now. He neither expected to receive nor sought his parents' interest in his progress.

'How's the course, John?'

'Fine.'

'Oh good.'

That was enough.

Most evenings when he was back home he was working behind the bar at the Birley, earning the extra money he needed to get him through the four years at Nottingham, so he hardly had to spend much time with his parents. That seemed to suit everybody.

It was not so easy to ask if they would mind if he moved back in after he graduated. That was not ideal but, of all the jobs he applied for across the length and breadth of the country, it was the Ridings Building Society who offered to take him on, based at their head office in Sheffield. He could hardly turn that down, so he asked to move back in, just for a short while, with a view to finding a room in a shared house in a couple of months, once he had settled into working life. That was the plan. That would not be so hard.

However, John had not been back for more than a few weeks when his mum casually announced one evening that they were putting the house up for sale because dad had got a new job in Lincoln. It was almost mentioned in passing. She did say that John was welcome to come with them if he wanted to but they both knew that was not going to happen. No chance.

So John moved out, they moved on and that was that. Neither really felt much need to stay in touch very often after then, though there was the occasional phone call.

He only really called when he wanted to let them know how well he was doing. The first promotion. The second promotion. When he passed his diploma to make it possible to quit the building society and set up his own business by the time he was thirty-one. It was never an attempt to earn their approval or admiration or whatever. Though he never truly admitted it to himself, he knew that what he was saying was:

'Look what I have achieved – in spite of you.'

It became his motivation through the tough days after setting up alone, when they had to rely more heavily than he wanted on Amy's salary, when he had to take on every client he could find, no matter how much of a pain in the arse they were. No matter how often he had to explain patiently to them why they were not yet millionaires just because they had put a few quid into an ISA a year ago. They were difficult times but he had to succeed – for him and for Amy so they could start the family of their own that they had put off because John wanted to establish the business first but also so he could show his parents. You should have believed in me.

The phone rang half a dozen or so times before it was picked up.

'Hello.' Sharp rather than friendly. It was him.

'Hello, dad. It's me, John.'

There was a moment as the information registered before a joyless voice answered.

'I thought you were dead or something. Hang on, I'll get your mother.'

Always the arrow. Always aimed to wound. Couldn't he just be civil for once?

'Pauline!' His father's call was muffled to John's ear, as if there was a hand over the mouthpiece at the other end. Muffled but not muted.

'It's John. No, our John. I don't know, you'll have to ask him yourself.'

'Hello, John? What's the matter?'

He sighed. Shouldn't be surprised by the reaction. It had been a long time.

'Nothing. I'm just phoning to see how you are. How both of you are.'

'Oh!' Pause. 'We're fine.' Pause. 'How are you?'

'Fine thanks.'

Pause.

'How's Annie?'

'Amy.'

'Amy – sorry. How's Amy?'

'I haven't seen her for a while. We got divorced.'

'Oh!' Pause. 'These things happen, I suppose.' Pause. 'Did she find somebody else?'

Typical. Why should she want to be with me?

'It wasn't anything like that. We were under a lot of strain after Stef died.'

'Stef – oh, yes. Your friend. I saw a bit about that on the TV news. Terrible business.'

'Yes.'

'Murdered, wasn't he?'

'Yes.'

'Terrible business.'

Pause.

'Did they get who did it?'

'No.'

'Pity.'

Pause. In the background, John heard his father shout out from another room.

'Look, John, it's nice to have heard from you but we're just on our way out. We always go to the shop on a Saturday morning.'

'Oh, OK. Don't let me keep you.'

'It's just that we always pick up Warren and Beverley and we said that we'd be there for 10.30.'

'That's fine. You get off.'

'Bye, then.'

'Bye.'

She hung up. John's chin sunk into his chest. Why should he have expected anything else? That one laboured conversation reached across the years and recalled the thirteen-year-old who was cast adrift every time he reached out for the emotional support he needed to deal with the confusion he felt as he emerged from childhood.

There was a time when their coldness would have crushed him. Not anymore.

'Sod 'em,' he said and snatched up his car keys on his way to tell Jas about his first meeting with Mike Wilshaw.

7

He knew the road. It wasn't that far from where he grew up. He slowed down to look out for the right house number and then pulled in. John drew a deep breath. He was nervous. This was going to be difficult.

There was a short, steep drive separating the two semi-detached houses. Number 20 was on the right. John kept his grip on the steering wheel as he looked towards it through the passenger window, as if holding onto the option of driving away. But he had to do this. He turned the key in the ignition to kill the engine. With another deep breath, he unbuckled the seat belt and opened the car door.

John had been thinking about this for quite a few days, off and on, but he had thought of little else since Jas gave him the address. He had gone over and over what he wanted to say and how Amy might react. Rehearsing time and again, scenario after scenario. Angry, accepting; forgiving, furious. Different scenario after different scenario and yet he still did not want to guess how this was going to go. He knew what he wanted to say – the tone, the words, the sentiment – but that was all he knew.

Though Jas had also been able to give him a phone number, John wanted to do this face to face. It felt like the bravest way, but he now wondered whether he should have taken the softer option. No going back now, though.

There was fairy lights and silver tinsel around the inside of the downstairs bay window but the lights were not turned on. It was only mid-morning. John trod carefully up the drive, the overnight frost still glinting in the pale sunlight, towards the back of a white van which was pulled up in front of a garage. As he walked through the gap between the corner of the house and the back of the van, he read the lettering on the side of the vehicle.

Robert Delaney Joinery
Specialists in Residential & Commercial

John hoped this was the right house. He didn't want to have to go through this for nothing. There was only one way to find out. He rang the doorbell.

'I'll get it,' said a male voice, followed by heavy footsteps, getting louder as they neared the door. The handle turned down and the door opened.

A tall, lean man in his early thirties, looking imposingly strong, sized John up through wary eyes. John had arrived feeling vulnerable and now felt even more so. This must be the new bloke.

'Hello,' the man said.

He had short-cut dark hair and a tight-cropped beard which showed strands of grey on his chin. From around the back of his left leg, the head of a small child peeked out. A girl with long, dark hair, wearing a pink sweatshirt. She watched John closely with the guarded suspicion of a youngster who had hoped to see someone more interesting, more familiar.

'Is Amy around please?'

The man bristled. 'Who wants to know?'

At least he was at the right house.

'I'm John.'

'Are you now?' He clearly recognised the name but offered no opinion. They stood looking each other in the eye. John wanted to say something else but all he could think of was 'don't hit me'.

'I only wanted to...' he offered finally before another voice came from behind the bulk.

'It's OK, Robbie.'

He turned to his right, swivelling on the leg that the small child still held. From behind him and out of the shadow, Amy took a step forward. She'd let her hair grow longer. It suited her. Her face betrayed no emotion. She stared straight into the eyes of her former husband, out of her life but now only a couple of feet away. John knew he had to hold the eye contact. It wasn't a challenge or some sort of contest, but Amy was subjecting him to the deepest of scrutiny – the type that only a person who has known another completely, intimately, at their best and at their worst, can summon to see into a part of the soul where deception cannot hide. The gaze lasted only a few seconds but John felt it cut through him like a razor-sharp blade through soft clay.

She touched the arm of the new bloke. 'It's OK.'

The new bloke held out a hand. Clearly, if Amy said the situation was OK, that was good enough for him. *Impressive levels of trust,* thought John.

'Hi,' he said. 'I'm Rob.'

John took the offering and gave back an uncomfortable smile. It was a very firm grip. Though the words were friendly enough, John knew he was meant to read another message in the handshake. It said: 'Don't mess her about.'

The exchange completed, Amy said, 'Could you take Lizzie into the living room? We'll be in the kitchen.'

'Sure,' Rob replied and turned to sweep up the little girl who had, all the while, been taking in everything with curious eyes. 'Come on, trouble,' he said and she giggled happily.

'Who is that man, Daddy?' Ah, the casual indiscretion of a small child.

'Just a friend of Amy's.'

Amy stayed still for a few seconds more, holding John just beyond the threshold, still not completely sure it was a good idea to allow him to come in further, but then she relented.

'Come on in.'

'Thanks.'

He wiped his feet with exaggerated thoroughness, playing the part of the deferent outsider as well as he could, and then took off his shoes as well, just in case. Amy watched him do it without comment before leading him into the kitchen. There was no invitation for him to take off his coat.

He looked around the kitchen. All stainless steel, oak units and tiling – a far cry from the self-assembly cupboards they had fixed to the papered walls only a couple of months after they moved in together, a lifetime ago.

'Very nice.'

Amy still wasn't prepared to meet the compliment with a concession of the high ground. Her stare was cold and sharp.

'Robbie's a joiner.'

'That's very handy. Seems a nice bloke.'

She flashed him another look. Untrusting, picking over the words for any trace of sarcasm.

'He is. Coffee?'

Without waiting for a reply, she clicked on the kettle and took two mugs from the cupboard.

John felt awkward. He knew that he was meant to.

'Thanks. Lovely little girl. How old is she?'

'Nearly four. She's Robbie's. Her mother left them for another man a couple of weeks before her third birthday. Just ran off.'

'Wow! How can anyone do that to their child? Must have been so tough for him.' John hoped he had got the sympathy levels right.

'Mmm,' said Amy, stirring the boiling water into the mugs. 'You don't have much of a choice when you're left with a small child to care for. He did the right thing. He reached out for help. We were in the same support group.'

John felt the sting in her words. He winced inside.

Amy set the mugs down on two carefully matched coasters on the oak table and sat down.

'Why did you come here, John?'

He took the cue to sit at the opposite end of the table. She fixed her stare on him, waiting for his move. If he thinks he's come here after something, he's got another think coming.

'I can understand what you're probably thinking.' He felt he had to acknowledge and try to defuse the spikiness of her tone. 'I suppose I could have phoned but I thought it best to talk face to face.'

Amy sat back and crossed her arms.

'I know I was an absolute bastard to you when all you were trying to do was help me deal with what happened to Stef and I'm so deeply sorry for that, honestly I am. There's nothing I can say that can make up for what I put you through, I know.'

He paused to allow the words space to breathe.

'I've been a self-absorbed, blind, worthless piece of shit. I've wasted a year of my life and I've thrown away everything we built up together for ten years. I heaped my self-pitying misery on everybody around me – especially you – and that was completely unacceptable, but something happened a week ago that brought me to my senses again. I can see what I became and I no longer want to be that man. I've not had a drink since then and I've started to get my life back together. I know I can never go back and put right everything I got wrong, but I can do better from now on. I feel like I'm at a crossroads and I'm ready to start again on a new path.'

Amy offered nothing back. Much of what he had said she already knew too well.

'I can't change the past but it was important to me to see you and to say that I am really, really, really sorry for what I did to you. I'm not so stupid that I thought I might breeze back into your life and try to win you back or anything like that but I do hope I might one day earn your forgiveness. I'm happy you've moved on and found a new bloke, I truly am. I couldn't just look to move on myself without at least offering my deep regret in the hope that you can accept it for what it is – honest and heartfelt. Nobody has ever known me better than you, Amy, and I hope you believe what I'm saying.'

John looked up, having delivered his contrition with his eyes fixed on the table. Amy's look was still impassive, though John thought he saw the traces of a tear in the corner of her eye.

He held out his hands. 'That's it. That's what I wanted to say.'

She drew a deep breath.

'I appreciate what you're saying, John, and I do believe you mean it.'

He broke a faint smile in relief.

'I don't feel any malice towards you anymore. It took me a long time to reach that stage but I have no more anger. In fact, I don't feel anything for you anymore. I'm glad you're sorting yourself out and I wish you all the best but the part of my life that included you in it is over, John. You killed it.'

'I know, I know…'

'No, I don't think you do, John. You were so pissed, so far beyond the reach of anyone, that you can't possibly know. How could you understand what it's like to see the person you love turn into this unrecognisable monster. It was like living with a dangerous stranger, John. I honestly believed that if I hadn't had you forcibly removed from the house that you might have killed me. I lived your pain with you when Stef was killed but it got so that I became the enemy. You turned all your hate and blame on me – can you imagine what that feels like? You have no idea what it was like to go through that. You weren't there really. I bet you can't even remember it. I bet you can't even remember the police coming to take you away when I had the locks changed and you tried to break down the door and then smashed the kitchen window to try to get in. Can you remember that? Can you imagine how frightening that was? You'd have been thrown in jail if I hadn't dropped the charges. You know, I should have had you locked up because then I wouldn't have had to put up with the phone calls in the middle of the night, all the scary messages pushed through the door, the knowing that you were outside watching the house – I saw you – and wondering if the next time I stepped out of the door I might get attacked. I should have gone straight back to the police because then I wouldn't have had to give up my own home and let you move back in while I lived in a rented bedsit until I could push the divorce through to get what was mine so that I could move on and start living again. But do you know why I decided to deal with it that way? It was because I still loved you and I felt sorry for you but I've moved on now. I don't feel anything for you anymore. So if you're telling me that you've got it together again – great, good for you. I hope you stay on the wagon and have a great life but let me get this clear, I can never forgive you for what you put me through and this is the last time I ever want to see you or even hear from you again. It's completely over between us, John, and I hope you still have sufficient decency within you to respect that.'

Jesus. I can't remember that at all. This is shocking. How could I…

John felt wretched. He struggled to think of a response. Nothing he could say could possibly be adequate. He floundered, shaken and exposed like a beached fish, gasping to express how utterly ashamed he felt.

'I'm…so…sorry,' he mumbled. *What else is there to say?*

'Look, you'll have to go now, John. We were just getting ready to take Lizzie to see Santa when you called.'

'Of course. I'll be off.' He felt completely miserable. Amy had turned the mirror on him and he had caught a glimpse of what he became. He deserved to feel this bad. He put on his shoes and opened the back door to leave. Neither of them said anything more.

Back in the car, John glanced back at the house. The little girl was looking through the bay window at him but then turned her head, hearing her name from within the house, and jumped down in response to the call.

A further thought jabbed at him and twisted in the wound – the self-inflicted wound – reopened by Amy. A glimpse of a future that could have been his. That could have been my little girl – our little girl – waiting at the window for me to get home at night, jumping down to fling her arms around my neck before I had barely been able to get through the door. The child I had persuaded Amy to wait a few years longer for so that I could put everything I had into the business and show my stupid parents how wonderful I was. What a prick! What an opportunity for happiness I had and I threw it all away. What a waste! What a selfish bastard!

Poor Amy. He had created a delusion to suit his own purposes which said that she had left him and did not live up to her promise that they would get through dealing with Stef's death together but he had made it an impossible promise to keep. In the clarity of the last week, he had suspected as much but only now did he comprehend the level of hell he had put her through. She had been the only woman he had ever truly loved. He felt abject. He was the lowest of the low. How could he really believe she was going to offer her forgiveness? He didn't deserve it.

8

Over the course of the rest of that day, John's thoughts grew darker. Amy's truths burnt through his skull and pushed against the thin membrane, not yet mature enough to withstand great pressure, which had newly formed to protect his rational mind from the more destructive forces still within him. That night, alone in his flat, he contemplated oblivion again. He thought about going out to buy a bottle of something to suppress the voices in his head and, for a few moments, considered a more drastic solution. Why not? What have I done to feel I deserve to be alive – when I did that to the woman I loved, when I didn't do enough to prevent the murder of my best friend? Amy was a good woman. Stef was a good man. What am I? I destroy lives.

He paced around the flat, unable to settle, unable to arrest the spiral, and all the while the walls closed in, suffocating him.

It's happening again. Don't let it happen again. Fight it! Fight it!

John grabbed his coat and headed out into the cold, cleansing December night.

Wisps of snow fluttered softly down around him with no wind to hurry them and his breath formed freezing clouds as he drew the frigid air deep into his lungs and exhaled up towards the grey sky. He felt in his coat pocket for his car keys but then changed his mind and put them back. He needed to walk.

It was almost 10 o'clock as John stepped quickly up the steep side road from the entrance to the flats, past the spot, without breaking his stride, where he had crouched as Stef spoke to him. At the top of the road, he turned left towards the city centre.

The main road was quite busy for so late on a Sunday night and John kept his head down to avoid the glare of the headlights coming towards him. He walked briskly to counter the effects of the cold and to exorcise the crushing turmoil of his thoughts, all the while breathing deeply in and out, feeling the pressure ease with every step, every breath.

Past the park, past the hospital, across the ring road and on towards the city centre, its bars and restaurants busy with pre-Christmas revellers. He walked for over an hour and the darkness began to lift. Slowly, slowly he regained control of his thoughts.

Clearly, his behaviour had been worse in those early weeks after the murder than he was aware and being exposed to the true extent of what he had become – what he had become capable of – had shamed him to the core but the perspective he had regained over the last week spoke to him again. None of us can do anything to change the past but that does not mean the past has to be allowed to dictate the future, it told him. He had something to look forward to now, a chance to make amends through deed – a chance to make a difference. The task would be made more difficult if he constantly felt the distraction of a hair shirt. He had to move beyond the past.

It was time to turn back home.

Crossing a road, John flicked a glance left to make sure no car was coming towards him and, a step from the kerb, he stopped. Something further down the dimly lit road he was crossing registered in his consciousness, even though he saw it for barely a fraction of a second. Something was going on down there. All he wanted to do was to walk on and get back to the flat. Walk on! It's nothing. Go home.

But he had to look again.

Three figures. Two tall, dark and ominous. One, in the middle, shorter and hands up at his chest, palms flat, trying to placate. In trouble. Oh no!

The blood drained from John's face. He no longer felt the cold. He was no longer in the middle of the city. It wasn't now any more. It was a year ago. It was a crisp, still early December night on White Lane, just over the county border. John could not move, dare not move, could not breathe. He felt the fear in the back of his throat again – the fear that had scarred so many nights over the last twelve months. He wanted to scream 'Stef!' but the fear would not let the words escape, would not let him scream, would not let him move, would not let him breathe. There was Stef again and someone was in front of him holding a bloody great knife. Not again! Not again!

A movement. A push or a punch. The shorter one in the middle was on the ground and the one in front swung a kick at him. So too did the one behind him. The man was on the ground, knees curled high and arms in front of his face for whatever protection he could get but he was not moving. Helpless. The one in front growled words that John could not make out and kicked again.

John was jerked back to the present. This wasn't his nightmare, it was somebody else's. Whoever it was, he was in trouble. Real trouble.

John was released from his paralysis. A charge of energy shot through him and he screamed! No words but a yell of fury released by a man who no longer felt powerless. He no longer felt the crushing weight on his shoulders of being too late to save his best friend. This wasn't Stef but this was the moment he had turned over in his head time and time and time again ever since and this time he had the chance to change the outcome.

The two attackers were stilled by the sudden noise from the end of the road and turned, attempting to make out who or what it was that was now hurtling towards them at full pelt, roaring at them.

'BASTAAAAARDS!'

In what seemed only a second, the furious shape was suddenly there, thumping into the body of the one who had pushed or punched his victim to the ground and then landed the first kick. The attacker felt the impact under his ribs and the air being knocked out of him before he had the chance to brace against the blow and he was driven back five yards before his spine cracked against the solid brick of the building behind them. His head lashed backwards and hit with a crunch against the wall. He collapsed onto the pavement, stunned.

John picked himself up and turned towards the second attacker, who had watched mesmerised as the raging shadow came from nowhere and took out his accomplice. Now, as he saw a man, older than he was, not especially big, didn't look particularly tough either, his street instinct returned. Whoever this guy was, he was about to be taught not to get involved with something that didn't concern him.

John was back on his feet as the first punch swung towards him. It should have landed somewhere between his left ear and eye socket and would probably have been enough to end this brief, uneven contest there and then. Should have landed.

Not this time. John had never felt like this before. He felt super-human. He saw the punch coming and swerved out of its trajectory. It wasn't an instinctive, defensive movement. This was controlled, calculated. He had time to assess what he needed to do to avoid the flailing fist and took the necessary course of action. Now he had his opponent off-balance. What would be the best way to exploit that? Counter right-hand punch to the nose? Difficult to get full weight behind that punch off the back foot but what about that exposed middle area with a sharp left? Swing and bingo! Landed cleanly around the right kidney area.

The mugger staggered and groaned as the punch sank in but he too had fighting instincts. Wary and hurt, he regained his balance and turned back towards John. This had to end. Now!

He sprang forward but John anticipated the move. No more than a couple of yards were between them but in the time it took his attacker to cover that short distance, John clasped his hands together and brought them sharply up to connect with the jaw of the man pounding towards him, snapping his head back. He went stumbling backwards again, his senses scrambled. John had him.

He took a three-step run-up at the mugger and aimed a kick like he was stroking a conversion attempt at Twickenham but this one made contact with not one ball but two. The mugger sank to the ground with a loud moan. He was bent double, head forward, but John pushed him onto his back with two hands to the head and jumped onto his beaten opponent's chest, pinning his arms to the ground with his knees.

Blow after blow rained down. Right, left, right, delivered with venom. John screamed at the face in front of him as it was torn into a bloodied mess by every punch that landed. The skin on John's knuckles ripped open too as they cracked down onto bone but he felt no pain. He felt exalted, supreme, exonerated. With every lacerating thud of his fists, he felt the agony of the past year releasing like the steam from a pressure valve. This is what retribution feels like.

Then he felt the boot into his ribs and he flew off the prone body of his victim, winded.

John was on his back and, as he regained his awareness, he saw the contorted face of the first mugger snarling at him and saw the glint of the knife which was held only inches from the end of his nose.

'Now I'm gonna fuckin' slice you up!'

The fury had gone. He was normal, human John now and he was about to find out how mortal he was.

So this is how it ends. After a year of living death brought on by a single thrust of one knife, he was going to experience actual death at the point of another. A man not in danger of such an impending painful demise might have appreciated the irony of it.

The flash of blue light startled both of them. Their heads turned sharply towards it at the same time, their eyes squinted in synchrony as they peered and saw the vaguely identifiable figure emerge from the centre of it.

'Police officers! Put down the weapon!' it shouted.

The mugger jumped up, scrambling for the speed in his legs to take him quickly away in the opposite direction from the light before the figure could reach him.

He's going to get away!

No you don't!

John swung his leg at his attacker and just clipped his ankle. It was not much of a contact but it was enough. The mugger was not into his stride anyway and John's trip took away whatever balance he had. He careered sideways, completely unable to control his limbs, and fell. His head hit the kerb with a sickening thud. The mugger twitched once, twice and then was still.

The police officer reached John moments later.

'Sir! Can you hear me? Are you hurt?'

John could hear him but he did not give an answer. He saw the face of the officer and passed out.

9

John sat on the open tailgate of the rapid response ambulance car while the paramedic, in his dark green uniform, carefully put dressings on his bloodied hands. The icy night was doing only a little to numb the throbbing pain. Around his shoulders and over his own coat, John wore a heavy yellow hi-viz police jacket but he was still shivering uncontrollably.

The street was awash with the flashing blues of police car and ambulance lights, the silence of the night broken by the sound of running engines and the indecipherable buzz of emergency service radios. The main road had been cordoned off and beyond the blue tape line curious onlookers were taking pictures on their mobile phones. As he lifted his head, John watched as one of the ambulances pulled away.

'Nearly got you patched up now, John. How are you feeling, mate?' The paramedic looked up into John's eyes from his crouched position, his gaze probing for tell-tale signs of whatever it was he was trained to look for tell-tale signs of.

'Can't stop shivering.'

'That will be the shock, mate. We'll soon have you away from here and up to the Northern General as soon as one of the ambulances comes back. How are the hands?'

John looked at his bandaged hands as they shook with a life of their own. They looked like they belonged to someone else. His fingers, red raw with the cold, were held crooked, numb and useless.

'They hurt.'

'We'll get you something for the pain, mate, when we can have a proper look at you. Oh, look – here we are.'

An ambulance announced its return with a short burst of its siren. A policeman gestured extravagantly to one old man with his dog, who was starting to move out of the way anyway, and drew back the blue tape to let the ambulance through.

'Your taxi awaits, mate,' said the paramedic, rising to his feet. He held out an arm. 'Let me help you up. Gently now. Mind your head.'

John shuffled closer to the edge and tentatively tried to pull himself forward by taking hold of the arm with both hands but he could not grip it and a sharp pain in his right side, where one of the muggers' boots had connected, quickly made him abandon the effort.

'Easy, easy, easy,' offered the paramedic, comfortingly. He dropped into a crouch again and manoeuvred his right shoulder under John's left armpit, stretching to grip his right hip.

'Put your arm around my shoulder. We'll soon have you out of there.'

This time, John made it to his feet, though not painlessly. He stood still, breathing shallowly but as deeply as he dare until the sharp sensation abated.

'Do you want me to get them to bring a wheelchair for you?' said the paramedic.

John looked at the onlookers and shook his head. If he was going to be the star of someone's Facebook page tomorrow, he was going to do all he could to preserve his dignity. He took measured, short steps, supported by the words and sturdy shoulder of the paramedic until they covered the twenty yards to the ambulance.

The ambulance back doors were being opened in readiness as they took the final steps.

'This is John,' said the paramedic to his colleague from the ambulance.

'Hi, John. My name's Alison.'

John smiled back.

'John here fought off two perpetrators to help out a man who was being attacked. He's sustained quite a bit of superficial damage to his hands and I suspect there are several broken bones in there as well. He's also suffering significant discomfort to his right side with query broken ribs but I don't think there's anything more sinister going on in there that we need to be concerned about. I haven't given him any analgesic as yet. I'll leave him in your capables. All the best, mate.'

The paramedic softly patted John on the back after he unhooked himself from the arm around his shoulder.

'Thanks very much,' John said as the man walked away.

'Wow, a real-life superhero, eh?' said the paramedic, without a hint of irony but a little too much as if she was talking to a ten year old. 'I don't think this is your cape, though.'

She eased the police jacket off John's shoulders.

'Excuse me, love, I think this belongs to one of yours,' she called to the police officer on blue tape duty.

'Oh, right. Thanks, love,' he replied and left his post to retrieve the jacket.

'Right, let's get you in then, John. It's warmer in there – you look perished.' She helped him towards the ramp at the back of the ambulance and he glanced up. The sight made his blood run cold. The inside of an ambulance. John could see Stef's body, his face covered, being lifted into the back on a trolley while he, too overwhelmed to comprehend what was happening, too stunned to hear the words of the police officer who was standing right next to him, just stared. Stared at the lifeless form on the stretcher as it was strapped and secured. Stared until the rear doors were slammed shut and the ambulance set off, blue lights flashing but no sirens. No need for sirens.

'Are you all right, love?' The paramedic felt the hesitation as John took his first step onto the ramp.

'Yeah, I just... Yeah, I'm OK.' And he moved forward again.

As she fastened him in, she chatted and asked questions which John responded to with a nod or a shake of the head. His thoughts were racing in other directions.

It could have been me.

What if the police had not arrived at just that moment? Another ten seconds and they could have been loading my dead body onto an ambulance, taking their photos to record exactly where I fell, washing my blood off the freezing road surface after everyone else had left the scene. Oh, Christ! I could have got myself killed. What the hell was I thinking?

He saw again the face, distorted by rage, of the attacker above him, so close that he could smell the booze on his breath and see the spittle as it glistened on his lower lip. He could feel the weight, pinning him, helpless, to the floor as the knife lingered above him, as foreboding as an executioner's axe, poised to strike its final fatal blow – but, in this case, maybe only after being used to trace lines of punishment across his skin for daring to make his intervention. He shuddered at the thought of what might have been.

A further thought occurred. That face. He only saw it for a few seconds but could it be the same face? Was it really possible that he had stumbled on Stef's killer? The odds must be outrageous but what if fate had decided to take such an extraordinary twist and hand him the ultimate opportunity for redemption?

'And is it tender when I press here?'

John, perched with his bare legs over the edge of the trolley in the cubicle at the accident and emergency department, stiffened and pressed down with his palms into the padded plastic.

'Yes,' he confirmed, summoning what little breath he felt he could muster.

'Sorry,' said the doctor. 'What about here?'

'Shit almighty!' His toes curled so forcefully that, had he been wearing shoes, he thought they would have burst through the soles. 'Yes,' he added, quite unnecessarily.

'Sorry,' said the doctor again. Mercifully, this time she stood up and began to take off her Latex gloves.

'You must have taken quite a nasty blow there but I'm happy there is no further damage inside the chest cavity. I'm going to send you down to X-ray to make sure and to see what the extent of the damage to your ribs is. We'll get them to see if there are any broken bones in those hands, too. In the meantime, I'll ask the nurse to bring you something for the pain and, hopefully, after the x-rays come back, we'll be able to send you home. Are you taking any medication?'

'No. No, I'm not taking anything.'

'Do you have any allergies?'

'Not that I know of.'

'Is there anything you would like to ask me?'

John shook his head. 'No, that's good, thank you very much. Sorry for swearing.'

The doctor smiled. 'I've heard worse.'

She pulled back the cubicle curtain, swishing it closed again behind her.

John slid off the trolley to his feet and stretched gingerly to try to ease the stiffness in his side. Over the course of his half-hour wait in the cubicle at A&E, his shivering had stopped, the throbbing pain in his hands had become a dull ache as the warmth of the hospital had tingled his fingers back to life and, up to the point where the doctor had stepped up the thoroughness of her examination, he had begun to draw half-breaths without feeling as if someone was twisting a spike into his right side. He had stopped feeling quite so spooked by the whole experience as well.

The nurse who had earlier helped him out of his clothes and into the blue gown pulled open the curtain holding a small paper cup of tablets and a plastic cup of water. He stood as John washed down the pills.

'They should get on top of the pain for you and give you a more comfortable night. Don't take anything else before you go to bed but you can start taking paracetamol in the morning and take them regularly for a few days. It should all settle down soon,' said the nurse.

'Fine.' John perched on the side of the trolley again.

'If the pain does get too much, you should go to see your GP and they can give you something stronger.'

'OK.'

'Someone will come to fetch you to go to X-ray soon because I don't think they're very busy tonight but there's a policeman waiting to see you if you're ready to talk to him now.'

'Sure, show him in.' The nurse left and, a few seconds later, the curtain opened again.

'Now then, Rocky, how's it going?'

It was the officer who appeared out of the blue light just as John was contemplating a painful demise. His was also the first face John saw when he came around after passing out and his was the jacket John had worn over his shoulders as he was discreetly led away, while three other policemen and then the paramedics dealt with the bloody aftermath of the fight.

John stood to greet him. 'A lot better than I might have been if you hadn't got there when you did. I can't thank you enough.'

'You know what they say, good timing is the essence of good police work – or is that good comedy? Either way, you're the one who deserves the praise in this little episode. I've just been in to see the fella you went to help and he reckons you saved his life. Said those two scrotes told him they were going to teach him a lesson for being the wrong colour in the wrong part of town, basically. Said you tore into them like Bruce Lee with a grudge. He's a very relieved and grateful man.'

John felt the colour rise in his cheeks. 'How badly hurt was he?'

'He'll be fine, thankfully. It could have been much nastier.'

'What about the others?'

The officer took a deep breath.

'One was declared dead at the scene. He hit his head pretty flush on the kerb as he tried to run away. The other is under arrest and is being treated for various facial injuries plus two very sore testicles.'

John felt his legs weaken and he leaned back against the trolley. *Dead? Jesus, I killed a man!*

'Christ, that's terrible.'

The officer moved closer and sat beside John.

'It's not a pleasant thing to contemplate, I know, but between you and me, completely unofficially, I'd think of it like this. If you hadn't been so brave as to take action as you did I reckon we might still have been dealing with a dead body at the scene tonight and in that case it would have been an innocent man who had done nothing more than wander down the wrong road at the wrong time and met up with a couple of bad 'uns. The way it is, we've got one dead scumbag and another scumbag in custody who, hopefully, is now incapable of producing any more scumbag kids in the future. You've got to ask yourself, which is the better outcome here?'

John nodded. 'I suppose so.' It still did not feel like a good outcome, though.

He turned and looked the policeman in the eyes, panicked. 'I tripped him up. I stuck my foot out and that's why he fell. I killed him.'

'You attempted to prevent a suspect from getting away. I was there, remember. He got up to run and you did what anybody would have done in the circumstances. It was an instinctive reaction. He didn't die because you tripped him, he died because he committed a crime and then tried to evade arrest. As far as I'm concerned, there's no question of you being treated as a suspect here. As far as I'm concerned, they ought to be giving you a bloody medal. Don't forget, he was holding a knife in your face and, for all intents and purposes, was about to use it. Don't waste any sympathy on him. He was definitely not worth it.'

The officer allowed John a few seconds to process his thoughts and then added: 'I'm going to need to take a few details from you tonight and ask you to provide us with a brief summary of the incident as you recall it. Over the next couple of days, we'd like to send an officer to see you at home to take a full statement but it's up to you whether you agree to do so or not. You have to understand that if you do provide a full statement, you will in all likelihood be called to court as a witness in the event of a prosecution. Do you understand that, John?'

He nodded.

'And would you be willing to provide a full statement?'

'Definitely. If it helps put that bastard in jail, absolutely.'

The officer smiled and took out his notebook.

'Another thing,' said John. 'Just over a year ago, a friend of mine was killed in a knife attack. A robbery that went wrong. They never got the man who did it. I know it's a bit of a long shot but do you think there's a chance either of those two tonight could have been the one who stabbed my best mate?'

There was a discernible, still-raw edge of desperation in the words as John forced them past the lump which formed in his throat as he began to speak. The policeman heard it and his expression became serious.

'I can certainly look into that. What was your friend's name?'

'Stefan Werner. Single F in Stefan and then W, E, R, N, E, R. It was December the eighth last year when it happened.'

The policeman wrote down the details. 'I'll have a word with the officers who worked on the case. Leave it with me.'

The curtains opened again and a young man with a name badge pinned to his white shirt and a lanyard around his neck pushed in a wheelchair. 'Excuse me, I've come to take Mr Baldwin to X-ray.'

'I'll come with you,' said the officer. 'We can sort out the rest while you're waiting to have your picture taken but, if you've a minute, there's a man two cubicles down who is very keen to see you.'

'Sure,' said John and he looked at the porter for approval. He shrugged his shoulders in a 'why not?' kind of way.

The officer peered round the curtain in the next-but-one cubicle and then gestured for John to be pushed through.

On the bed, a man who looked in his early fifties was shuffling back to raise himself from his recline to sitting up. He winced with every small movement. The clean white of a fresh dressing on the top of his shaven head stood out against the darkness of his skin. He wore a neatly shaped beard which started from a narrow point in line with the top of his ears and in his right earlobe sparkled a gold earring with a stone set in it. As he positioned his backside against the fold of the bed, he looked up at John.

'Here he is – my guardian angel!' There was a light but distinct Caribbean inflection in his accent.

John got out of the wheelchair and walked towards the bed. The man was holding out both hands, ready to greet him. John held out his left hand and the man gently grasped his forearm, well away from the dressings. John noticed that the man's bottom lip was quite badly split.

'Thank you, thank you, thank you. You saved my life. What is your name?'

'John Baldwin.'

'Well, John Baldwin, you are a hero. My name is Gregory Fredericks and I am forever in your debt. You are an extraordinary man, my brother. Jermaine.' Gregory turned to look at the huge well-dressed man who stood like a sentinel in the corner of the cubicle.

'You had better watch out, Jermaine, because John Baldwin here will be taking your job.'

The man in the corner shuffled his feet and allowed the faintest of smiles to crack his stern expression, though only for a moment. He didn't look the type that anyone with an ounce of sense would challenge in order to take his job, or anything else for that matter.

'Jermaine here is pissed off because I gave him the slip and wandered off by myself tonight but I won't be doing that again for a good while,' confided Gregory. 'How are you? Not too badly hurt, I hope,' he added, looking down at the dressings.

'I'll be fine, thanks. They're just taking me down to X-ray to make sure. How are you?'

'A bit banged up. They're going to keep me in tonight to keep an eye on me but

I'll survive, thanks to you. If you hadn't shown up they would have been laying me out instead of patching me up. Those two ignorant fuckers called me a black-this and a black-that and said they were going to stamp on my head! They gave me no reason to feel they weren't telling the truth. Robbing bastards! If they came calling around my old neighbourhood they would not have been so sure of themselves. Thank the good Lord for sending you to stop them, brother.'

He turned again to his surly protector. 'Jermaine, give him one of my personal cards.' Jermaine reached into his inside jacket pocket and took out a wallet.

Gregory took a firmer grip of John's forearm and looked into his eyes to show his sincerity.

'Keep hold of this card. If there is ever anything I can do for you, you only need to call this number and I will do everything I can to help, I promise.'

John flushed. 'There really is no need, Gregory. I was only doing what anyone would have in that situation.'

'Take the card. I owe you my life, John Baldwin.'

Jermaine handed John the business card. Gregory squeezed his forearm once more and then released his grip.

John sat back in the wheelchair and held up the card to say thank you and goodbye.

'God bless you, brother,' called Gregory as he was reversed out of the cubicle.

The porter spun the wheelchair around one hundred and eighty degrees to face down the hospital corridor, through the door pointing the way to the x-ray department.

'That's you sorted for gig tickets for the rest of your life,' he said.

John looked bemused and craned his neck to look back at the porter. 'What do you mean?'

'Don't you know him? That's Gregory Fredericks. He's one of the biggest figures in the music industry in Europe.'

10

'Have-a-go hero saves top pop promoter.' Jas was reading from the front page of the Tuesday edition of *The Star*, which she had waved over-excitedly at John as soon as she walked into the flat.

'Then, under that it says: "Sheffield man fought off two" – that's "two" in capital letters and in red type, if you don't mind – "fought off two attackers to rescue man who was being attacked". I wish I could meet this wonderful person so that I could shake him by the hand.'

John held up both his heavily bandaged hands and, tilting his head sideways, gave Jas a sardonic look, though he was fully aware she did not need the reminder.

'Aww, sorry! That was cruel. How are they?'

'One cracked knuckle, no breaks, no broken ribs either, so I must be made of tougher stuff than I realised. Still hurts like buggery, though.'

Jas stood up from the sofa and threw her arms around John's neck. 'I'm so proud of you.' She released him and sat down again. 'You must be really proud of yourself.'

He screwed up his face. 'I am...but. You know why I'm not getting carried away about all of this.'

Her shoulders sagged. 'I do, John. I understand but surely this proves to you that if everything had worked out differently that night – if you'd been able to get there in time – things could have been different. You couldn't change what happened that night because it was not meant to be.'

'Somebody else told me that as well.'

'They were right. I know – everybody knew – that you and Stef were closer than brothers and that you would have given your own life to save him that night, just the same as he would have given his to save you. The point is that you were able to make that difference this time and, when the opportunity was there, you rose to the occasion, just like you would have done if you could've that night. That's undeniable now.'

Her words warmed him. He'd needed to hear them. 'Thanks, Jas. That means a lot.'

She picked up the newspaper again. 'You're front page news, for god's sake, Baldwin. And I heard you on Radio Sheffield as well.'

'Keep a look out,' he interjected. 'BBC and ITV local news have been in touch as well and are sending somebody around tomorrow.'

'That's brilliant! Look at this here.' She scanned down the front page for the passage she wanted to find. 'It says:

Mr Baldwin, 37, has recently helped launch a new charity, GameOn, in memory of a friend who was murdered a year ago in a street attack.

'You don't mind me saying that, I hope?'

Jas shook her head, emphatically. 'Not at all. Apart from anything, you can't buy publicity like this, you know. This is great exposure for the charity.'

She leaned forward in the seat. 'Do the police think either of the attackers could have been involved in Stef's death?'

'No,' John replied, firmly. 'The policeman I saw at the hospital told me he would check it out and he phoned me yesterday. He said both of them were inside on the night Stef was attacked. They were doing three counts each for robbery and racially aggravated assault. Nice people.'

Jas looked disappointed. 'Pity,' she said. 'I was hoping it was them. I was hoping it was the one who is dead. I want the man who attacked Stef to be dead.'

John understood the sentiment, but he was a little taken aback by the venom in her voice. He had never heard Jas say a single spiteful word in all the years he had known her.

'Really?'

'Totally. I want him dead and, if he's got a family, I want them to suffer like we've suffered. If they gave me a gun, I would kill him myself. Wouldn't you?'

John was disconcerted. 'I guess so. I don't know. I've never really been an eye for an eye kind of person. I want him found and brought to justice, certainly—'

'And spend the rest of his life warmed and fed at the taxpayer's expense? No. He doesn't deserve to be alive. He doesn't deserve to be allowed to walk on the face of this earth. I want him dead.'

There was silence between them. It was hard for John to know what to say next.

Jas spoke first.

'Anyway, I've got a bone to pick with you. Why didn't you phone me to pick you up from the hospital?' She was normal Jas again.

'It was very late,' he answered. 'It was after two before they said I could go home and I knew you had to work the next day, so it was easier to jump in a taxi. I just wanted to get home and try to get a bit of kip. I didn't get a great deal, as it turned out, because of the ribs.'

'You could have called me in the morning. I'd have been able to leave what I was doing to come around and take care of you.'

He shook his head. 'Thanks but I spent most of the day dozing on the sofa – in between answering the door to talk to reporters. I felt a bit knackered, to be honest. I figured I might as well leave it until the evening to let you know because there wasn't a great deal you could do, except act as my media manager.'

She smiled. 'You know I would have come round if you'd asked. Anyway, what were you doing out in that part of town at that time of night?'

'That's another story,' he said with a sigh and told her about his visit to Amy. He spared none of the grisly details.

'Oh my god! I didn't know half of that! Amy told me a little bit about what had gone on but nothing like as much as—'

'I had no idea either. Not really. As you can imagine, it wasn't easy to hear.'

'I can bet.'

'And when I saw the little girl at the window and thought about the life I could have had, with Amy and a family, well. It knocked me sideways. I felt like I was back to square one, to be honest. I felt totally wrecked. I just decided I had to get out of the flat and get some air, to clear my head, you know? I had to try to stop myself from sinking into the blackness again.'

Jas moved closer and placed her hand on his arm.

'It's frightening to know that you have such cruelty inside you,' he added.

'That wasn't the real John. It was an extreme situation which provoked an extreme reaction, but it wasn't the real you. You know what made it worse, though, don't you? If you had just let people in instead of bottling it all up until you couldn't keep it from exploding and destroying everything around you, you could have dealt with it all much better. You would have coped, like the rest of us did.'

'I know, I know.'

'The good thing is that you feel able to talk about it now. That's better. And it's a good thing that you faced up to Amy. I know she said a lot of hurtful things but, don't forget, Amy has been carrying that hurt around with her for months, even though she did go to counselling, and she would have rehearsed that conversation with you hundreds and hundreds of times. Now it's all out in the open and that will be good for Amy, too. She doesn't hate you, John. You can't love someone as much as she loved you and then go so far in the opposite direction. She needed to lash out this once and make that part of her moving-on process. She will find it in her heart to forgive you one day, I'm sure.'

'Thanks. I hope so.'

He really wanted that to be true but feared the process could be a long one.

Jas was back at the flat the following evening. The two of them were waiting for Mike Wilshaw to arrive. He buzzed at the front door to be let into the building and John, moving more freely now, waited at his door to greet him.

'Hi, John. Sorry I'm a few minutes late. I was watching you on *Look North*. Bloody brilliant that, mate. Well done!'

He was tall, around six foot three, and his physique was still lean like a sportsman, though he didn't look the type who had ever been especially athletic. Mike was unbuttoning his heavy black overcoat as he stepped into the room to reveal a navy blue v-necked sweater with an embroidered club crest on it and well-pressed dark grey trousers. His hair was dark, greying at the temples, and he was in good shape for a man of his age. He was forty-two. John knew that because he had Googled him.

Michael Patrick Edward Wilshaw, RHB OB, Yorkshire (1993–1995), Derbyshire (1996–2002), Worcestershire (2003-2006).

He had liked Mike from the moment they first shook hands. He had a comfortable manner and was easy company, with not a hint of the former professional sportsman arrogance John had been wary of before they got together. They had made each other laugh right from the start – not forced laughter but natural, like they had known each other for years. Importantly, John was impressed by how clearly Mike was able to articulate his thoughts in setting out his plans for the charity, how passionately he spoke about why he wanted to help kids from deprived backgrounds and what a difference he felt GameOn could make. *Here is a man who knows his mind,* thought John, *and has the drive to see his ambitions through.* Though his sporting career had not been a sparkling one, John could imagine how hard Mike must have worked to get as far as he did and how tough an opponent he must have made himself.

'Can't get away from me at the moment, I'm afraid. Mike, this is Jas.'

Mike's hand reached out. 'Hi, Jas. John told me about you on the phone. Great news that you want to help out. I'm really grateful. Lovely to meet you.'

Jas was instantly charmed. 'Nice to meet you too, Mike.'

'And you're in PR and Marketing, I believe,' he added. 'That will be very useful. We can't rely on this fella to generate all the publicity for us all the time.'

'I hope you didn't mind my connecting my past with what we have in mind for the charity, by the way,' interrupted John. 'I feel like I kind of hijacked the cause a bit.'

'Of course not,' Mike replied. 'What's most important at this stage is getting the word out there. We're going into this with our own motivations but the purpose is the same, that's all that matters. I think it's great that you mentioned GameOn in your interviews. We're not even properly up and running yet and already a wide range of people will have heard of us. That can only be good, can't it, Jas?'

'Absolutely. I told him the same myself.'

'That's all right then,' said John. 'I'll get the kettle on and then we can talk about what we're going to do next.'

Mike did most of the talking. He told them about the coast-to-coast walk, the Sheffield to Amsterdam cycle ride, the Three Peaks Challenge, the 24-hour cricket net session and the other fundraising ideas that people had already offered to arrange. There was positively a buzz of excitement between the three of them.

'We also need to look into building up a portfolio of corporate partners as another revenue stream,' added Jas. 'I deal with clients who might be interested in a partnership with us because it would be great PR for them, especially as we are aiming to benefit young people primarily. I can send out proposals to them.'

'That's great, Jas. Get the word out as widely as you can and I'll always be more than happy to meet with them myself if you think that would be useful. I had another thought about something we need to look into as well.' Mike leaned forward and turned to look straight at John.

'I think it would be a good idea for you to get involved in something else pretty soon. People will identify your face and your name with the charity now and so I'd like us to find a way to keep your face and name out there.'

'What have you got in mind?'

'Something eye-catching, for sure. Some sort of fundraiser that would make the newspapers and the radio and the TV take notice again and would really engage the public.'

'Hmm, I think you're right,' agreed Jas. 'We shouldn't lose this momentum.'

'Fair enough,' said John, 'but I'm not very good at sports, I haven't ridden a bike since I was about twelve and the only publicity you would get if I tried to climb three mountains in one day would involve me dying of a heart attack about halfway up the second.'

'How about a boxing challenge?' suggested Jas. 'Take on the man who beat up two muggers. Obviously, you'd only be taking them on one at a time, so that would be no problem for you.'

They all laughed.

'I think it should be something separate to the events which have already been organised. Something a bit different,' added Mike.

Quiet fell between them for a few moments.

'Skydive?' asked Jas.

'No way! I'm bad enough getting on a plane when I haven't got to jump out of it as well.'

'How about an abseil? Down the side of the town hall or something?' added Mike.

'I'm really not very good with heights. This is the point I'm making. There must be something a little closer to ground level.'

Jas had picked up her tablet to search for ideas.

'Marathon running, no. Bungee jumping, hardly. Car wash, no. Swimming, no. Firewalking.' She looked up from the tablet. 'Firewalking.'

The idea was not shot down.

'It's possible,' said Mike. 'We could set up somewhere prominent in the middle of town, on a pedestrianised area maybe. A couple of the people at the club are well in with the council and I could ask them to look into it. This could work.'

'Take a look at this then,' said Jas. She turned the tablet to show the two men a video. A line of people of both sexes and all ages trod purposefully along a path of smouldering cinders while spectators whooped and cheered each one of them and a fat man with a microphone yelled out encouragement.

John eased back into his chair. They didn't look especially brave and they didn't seem to be in pain. How hard could it be?

'Obviously, you wouldn't be doing it on your own. We could get other people involved and get them to pick up sponsorship. And, just think,' added Jas. 'For someone who could reasonably say he's been through hell this last year, there's a neat symbolism in this.'

Been through hell. That might be a bit of an over-dramatisation and symbolising the past year by treading over hot coals might be a little over-simplistic, but it kind of works. It might even go some way to drawing a line through everything that did happen.

'OK, then,' said John, with resolve. 'Firewalking it is.'

11

Though he had been advised to stay off for the full week, John decided to go into work on Friday. The police had taken their statement, the media interest had died down and he felt at a loose end, so he went in – earlier than usual to avoid drawing any attention to himself.

So much for that. A mid-morning internal phone call told him he was wanted in the boss's office and, as he stepped through his door, it seemed the entire staff was waiting in ambush. Someone had even bought a cake with the Superman logo on it. Initially embarrassed as he was and though he had to urge everyone to not be quite so enthusiastic in their hugs and handshakes, John had to admit to himself he was quite touched by it all.

It was the last weekday before the Christmas break and no-one appeared to be much in the mood for work. By late afternoon, those who were not on the Saturday shift began to do the rounds of sharing their last Christmas wishes and gradually the main floor of the office fell quiet. John looked at his watch. Almost half past six. Time to go. He thought about what he could prepare for his evening meal and then what? A bit of telly? That was the thing about giving up drinking – it leaves plenty of spare evenings for a single man to fill.

He looked around the office and wondered if there was any cake left, then he sauntered over to the water cooler and half-filled a plastic cup.

'Cheers,' he said to the empty office and raised the cup to his lips.

As he did so, the door opened. It was Stella, the savings accounts manager.

'Oh, hi, John. Working late?'

Stella had started at the building society a few weeks before John joined – when he left university and, presumably, she had just finished her A Levels. She was certainly a few years younger. Back then, she was rarely short of offers from more experienced – male – staff members offering to spend time with her, generously willing to pass on the benefit of their knowledge. John observed from a distance. Stella was out of his league and he could accept that. He took his comfort in the odd stolen admiring glance, when he was sure awkward eye contact could be avoided, and from watching the way she met the unwanted approaches with cool indifference until each would-be suitor was forced to drag his simmering, unrequited hormones back to his own desk.

Even in those early days, he could tell that she was smarter than most and that she was not the type to rely on her looks as a way to get herself noticed. He respected her all the more for that. In time, both of them were marked down for moving on to bigger things within their departments and that gave them a sort of bond. Professional common ground. Being handed more responsibility at such a relatively early stage in her career made Stella a target for petty jealousies more than amorous intent, especially among those whose approaches had been rebuffed in those early days, but that did not seem to bother her, nor did it impact on the way she interacted with her colleagues. She bore the added burden of leadership easily. She was a natural.

'Just finishing off a few things before the break. What are you doing back here?'

She was still in her work clothes but her auburn hair, invariably worn up or in a ponytail during business hours, had been allowed to fall naturally over her shoulders. She was always undeniably very attractive, but the full effect of her hair unleashed made her almost intimidatingly so.

'I had to pop back to pick up some things I forgot. You're not staying much longer, are you? You're putting the rest of us to shame.'

John dropped the plastic cup in a bin. 'No, I'm done now. Just about to log off and bugger off, so to speak.'

Stella smiled and walked over to the staff lockers, searching for her keys in her bag. John turned to go back to his office. As he sat at his chair to shut down his computer, Stella followed him in.

'I'll just wait for you and then we can lock up together,' she said.

'Sure. I'll only be a minute.'

Stella moved from the doorway to the Yucca plant in the corner of the office and delicately touched its leaves. John watched her all the way.

'I thought you were very brave to help out that man who was being assaulted.'

John gave what had become a well-practiced, self-effacing shrug. 'It was one of those things you do on instinct. It's only later that you think about it and realise that it could have backfired on you.'

'It was very brave. You're being modest. You risked your life to help a stranger and you were actually injured. Not many people would have done that. You deserve all the recognition you get.' She spoke the words with such authority that John thought it was not his place to argue the point further.

'Thanks.'

Stella glided across the office to a chair in the opposite corner. She sat down, crossed her legs and smiled at him. John felt like he was about to be interviewed.

Say something. 'Did you get what you came in for?' Why did you say that? Of course she got what she came back for. That's why she came back.

'Yes. My own fault. I was in a hurry because I needed to drop the boys off with their dad for the weekend. They're going to the Christmas funfair in the morning and then he's taking them to see United in the afternoon. A real dad and lads' day. It's strange that he finds it easier to make the time to do that sort of thing with them now than he did before we split up. I don't know why it takes going through a divorce for some men to realise what they had all the time. Have you got any kids, John?'

'No. No kids. I got divorced as well – a few months ago.'

'That's a shame. You seemed well matched.' John remembered Stella had been invited to his and Amy's wedding evening do.

'It happens to the best of us, I suppose,' he replied.

'True.'

The computer screen told John it was in the process of shutting down, but it seemed to be taking longer than usual. He bundled a few loose sheets of paper together and put them in his top drawer, attempting to divert himself from a growing sense of being scrutinised.

'And I heard about the charity you are setting up. That sounds fascinating, a really good cause. Isn't it odd how you can work alongside someone for so many years and still know so little about them?'

'I guess so. We're waiting for the final paperwork to go through with the charity people but we should be properly up and running soon. People are already organising fundraising events for us.'

Stella lifted her left hand and ran it through her hair, tucking it behind her ear.

'I think I might like to get involved in your charity. You'll have to tell me more about it.' She stood up and walked to the edge of John's desk, opposite him.

'It would be good to have you on board. I'll be happy to tell you all about it.' *Is it getting warm in here?*

'Perhaps we could go for a coffee sometime.'

She walked round the side of the desk and sat on the corner of it. 'How about now?'

The alarm buzzed, waking John from his dream. He flicked out his hand and dabbed at the buttons on top of the alarm until the noise stopped, then he prised open an eye to check the time. Seven a.m. Saturday. It's Saturday. He had forgotten to turn off the alarm.

Then he remembered why it had slipped his mind.

He turned to make sure it was real. She was lying on her side facing away from him and he watched as her shoulder rose slightly with every slow, rhythmic breath. Her bare shoulder and arm was outside the duvet and John noticed for the first time the tattoo on her right shoulder blade – a black outline of a star with a comet trail of decreasingly smaller stars, coloured red and blue, falling from it in an S shape and others dotted between which had been drawn to create the impression that they were twinkling. Stella's stars. The tail of it disappeared beneath the duvet and John's eyes followed the line of her body down to the dip of her waist and to where it rose in the curve of her hip. It was real all right.

They hadn't talked very much about the charity. Neither had they retreated all that often to the shared safety of work talk. A coffee was followed by a meal and then, when John had convinced himself that even he could not be misinterpreting the signs, he had suggested they go back to his flat. He held his breath slightly as he did, just in case he was making a horrible misjudgement, but he hadn't read it wrong.

He leaned closer and kissed her delicately on the shoulder, then gently stroked back her hair to kiss her again on the neck behind her ear. She stirred and turned onto her back.

'Mmmm. What time is it?'

'Seven o'clock. I forgot to turn the alarm off.'

She smiled and her eyes drew him close so that he could kiss her again, on the lips this time.

'You were lovely,' she said, softly.

He thought she was being generous. It had been a long time. At the very least, he was content that he had not lacked anything in terms of enthusiasm.

'You were wonderful,' he replied – and meant it. They kissed again.

She wriggled and then arched her back in a stifled yawn. She stilled and her eyes stayed closed, as if she was about to fall asleep again. He watched her for a few snatched moments more. Christ, she's gorgeous!

'I'll go and make us a cup of tea.'

She drew a deep breath. Her eyes stayed closed.

'Yes please,' she said, drowsily. Then her blue eyes flashed into life again. 'And bring it back to bed.'

They had lunch at the flat and both said that they would like to carry on seeing each other, though they agreed they would keep the relationship quiet at work.

Neither wanted to be the subject of office gossip.

After lunch, Stella went home to change and tackle all her household jobs before the kids were returned to her the next morning, which was Christmas Eve. Far from feeling sad to see her go as they said their goodbyes, John was overwhelmingly elated. He leaned against the door after seeing Stella on her way and a huge smile spread across his face, like a naughty child who had got away with stealing and secretly eating a whole tray of cakes.

'You fucking beauty,' he said out loud, possibly a little too loud. He hoped the woman in the next flat had not heard the outburst and then crouched into a series of silent fist pumps. Though he had not had a huge amount of sleep the night before and had exerted himself in another fairly long session of lovemaking in the morning, John felt like he had the boundless energy of a teenager. He had not felt this way since the early days with Amy.

There was no way he could just lounge about in the flat that afternoon. He felt he would burst if he did not keep moving, so he decided to walk to the shop to stock up for Christmas Day and pushed his trolley with the swagger of a rock star. Make way for the undisputable King of Testosterone, chosen lover of the exquisite Stella. He felt as if his new prowess could not be more obvious to everyone he encountered if he had worn the words across his swollen chest on a t-shirt.

The euphoria could not be sustained and John fell asleep on the sofa watching the nine o'clock news that evening, waking up with a crick in his neck just as Gary Lineker and Alan Shearer were discussing a dubious penalty for Everton on *Match of the Day*. He felt a bit washed-out the next morning, too, but Stella and their hours of glorious carnal pleasure filled his every thought. He could not wait to see her again and told her so in texts, hoping his words struck the right balance between keen and obsessive.

But Stella had her children to occupy her attention on Christmas Day and John had a date to keep with the other woman in his life.

He and Jas had made a pact. They had promised to go together, on Christmas morning, to visit the spot where Stef's life ended. John hadn't been there since that night, just over a year earlier, and Jas had been unable to bear to make the journey herself. But they'd decided the time was right. It was another step forward that they had to take and they wanted to take it together.

John pulled up in the car park of the Old Harrow, which was now a Bangladeshi restaurant, and they made the half-mile walk towards the county border, on the road that led to the Phoenix, in silence. There was nothing to say. The morning was mild and drizzly and they huddled close, arm in arm, as John tried to manoeuvre Jas' inadequately flimsy umbrella so that it kept off the rain and did not blow inside out in the breeze.

Cars drove by almost constantly, packed with people on their way to deliver presents to friends and family, sending spray over the two figures on the narrow path and creating rushes of air to further test the integrity of the umbrella, but as they neared the spot, there were suddenly no more cars. There, on the road out towards the Phoenix and at the place close to the gap in the hedge where you could get on the path to the golf course, there was no one and nothing, not even a sound. There was just the two of them.

John slowed as they approached the spot and Jas looked at him. Their eyes met. He told her this was the place and she understood without the need for words to be exchanged. They stopped. There was no mark, no memorial, to distinguish what had happened there only a year or so earlier, nothing to let passers-by know how a life had been cruelly ripped from the body of a man who had so much more to give, but the two people who cherished his memory most dearly knew.

They stood and they remembered. Then Jas raised the single red rose she had carried with her to her lips, kissed its tight bud and gently placed the flower on the place on the path where Stef had drawn his last desperate breath. Each of them said their silent farewells and they turned to walk, arm in arm, back to the car.

'I'm glad we did that,' said Jas, finally, as they drove out of the car park.

'Me too,' John replied. 'And I'm glad we did it together.'

'I couldn't have done it on my own,' added Jas, after a moment, staring straight forward.

'Me neither.'

When they reached Jas' house, she turned to him. 'Are you sure you won't come with me to have Christmas dinner at my parents'? They would be really happy to have you there and they always prepare far too much food for the five of us.'

He shook his head. 'It's a very kind offer, Jas, but I'm OK on my own, honestly. I've bought myself a little chicken roast, pigs in blankets, the lot. You have a lovely day with your family.'

She smiled. 'Call me if you change your mind. Happy Christmas, John.' She leaned over and kissed him on the cheek. 'And thanks for today.'

'Pleasure.'

Jas unclipped the seatbelt and opened the car door. 'Happy Christmas to you, too, and thanks for everything.'

He watched as she walked to the home she and Stef had made for each other, waved and closed the door.

Alone later that afternoon, John felt tremendously content. He enjoyed the meal he cooked for himself, *Toy Story 3* was on the TV and life was good again.

He put the wooden tray, with its now-empty plate, down on the floor and eased back on the sofa. A contented smile spread across his face before he released a short, satisfying fart.

All the while he had been cooking his meal he had thought about what the future might hold. Maybe he would be able to pick up the threads of his IFA business again, leave the building society job and combine the business with running the charity. Then one day, perhaps he might move in with Stella and he could become a step-dad to her two boys – take them ten pin bowling, maybe take them to watch a Test match or a Twenty20 international. Kids seemed a lot keener on the one-day cricket these days. He knew he was getting well ahead of himself but how good it felt to be looking forward again, with optimism. His dark days seemed so long ago and yet how long ago was it? A couple of weeks?

What a couple of weeks it had been. Really, just over two weeks. He did a quick mental calculation of the days, just to make sure. Seventeen days. Wow! Seventeen days since Stef's unexpected intervention changed the course of his life – and now look. The irrationally large burden of guilt he had carried for a year was gone, he had made his peace, as best he could, with the people he had hurt through his darkest days and his life had a purpose again. What's more, he had copped off with the best-looking woman in the whole of the Ridings Building Society. Yes, life was good again.

There was no doubt in his mind that his change of fortune was not down to chance. Sceptical though he was at first, John was now convinced that the hand of Stef was all over everything that had happened to him in these last seventeen days. The call out of the blue from Mike who just happened, of all the potential financial advisors out there, to be given John's number to offer him the chance to become involved in a cause he could believe in and use as a means to do good. Walking through a part of town he wouldn't normally be in at an hour when he wouldn't normally be out just in time to save Gregory from a severe and possibly fatal beating and proving to himself that he had the courage inside him to not let that happen. Returning to work earlier than he planned and still being in the office when Stella, who just happened to have forgotten to take everything with her when she initially left for the day and had left her children with their father for the night, popped back in. These were not coincidences. These were examples of Stef manoeuvring his destiny. Didn't he say, that night seventeen days ago, that he wanted to help? Wanted to help John to help himself? That's what Stef was doing. Somehow he was manipulating fate to provide opportunities that John could pick up and run with – as a way to improve his life and the lives of others. He did not feel buffeted by forces out of his control, because it was still in his power to take the opportunities he was being offered or decline them.

This is my life – and it is blessed.

John raised his glass of orange squash and looked to the ceiling.

'Stef, old mate, I know you said you could be everywhere and anywhere at the same time, so if you just happen to be in the vicinity right now, I wanted to say thanks very much. I don't know where I would have been now if you hadn't decided to use up one of your manifestation cards in paying me a visit – probably lying in a pool of my own vomit or something – but, anyway, I'm very grateful to you for giving me the kick up the arse I needed and setting me back on the right road.

'Mike's a great bloke. I was trying to work out the other day whether or not he might have been playing one of those times we went down for the day to Chesterfield, but I think that might have been a bit before his time. Anyway, he's still a good fella and I love the charity we are getting going together. You probably know that I've agreed to do a firewalk to raise some money for it, which might not be such a great idea, the more I think about it, but I'll do it all the same. It's better than tramping for hour after hour through fields full of cowpats, which I know you would probably have preferred. Sod that. But I'm really excited about helping to make this thing work and it's terrific that Jas is getting involved as well. She's doing really well, by the way, but then you probably knew that as well.

'It was a very nice touch with the mugging. Thanks for making it possible for me to do the Bruce Willis bit there, especially because it made me feel better about not being able to save your sorry arse. But, seriously, mate, I needed that and I understand now that sometimes situations are beyond our control and that all we can do is take control of situations we are able to influence. I understand that now but I still wish I'd been able to save you that night. I know, I know – it wasn't meant to be, your time was up and there was nothing anybody could have done about it but I wish it wasn't that way because I still miss you loads, mate. I'm glad I've sort of got you back, at least.

'Most importantly, thanks for sending Stella my way. I have no idea how you managed to get a beautiful woman like that to go for an ugly bastard like me but whatever it was you did, you know, absolutely brilliant. Keep up the good work.

'If you see the big boss man, please pass on my regards and say sorry I didn't pick up the religion thing but I hope he understands. Sorry as well for having unwholesome thoughts about one of his lady vicars. I promise to keep trying to do the right thing and if that's not enough for him when the time comes for me to stand in front of St Peter and justify my life, then there's not a great deal I can do about that. Still, if you can get in, I reckon I must have a good chance. Anyway, put in a word for me if you see him. Oh, and happy birthday to him and all that.

'That's about all I've got to say for now. I hope you're still keeping an eye out for me, I'll look after Jas all I can and I look forward to seeing what you've got lined up next. If there's anything I can do for you in return, you know where I am. Cheers, Stef – and thanks for giving me my life back. You're a good 'un.'

John raised his glass again and settled down to watch the rest of the film.

12

The Boxing Day bank holiday was over and it was back to work for the staff at the Ridings Building Society, though the quieter roads on the drive in was a reminder that not everyone was facing the same jolting realisation that their Christmas break was over.

John did not appear to regard himself as one of the unfortunate ones as he walked, with a spring in his step, through the main doors of the city centre branch. Neither did Julie appear to be wishing she was still tucked up in her warm bed as she greeted him with her usual cheerful smile.

'Morning, Mr Baldwin. Did you have a nice Christmas?'

'Great, thank you, Julie. How was yours?'

'Very nice, thanks. Hope you have a lovely day.'

Nice girl, thought John, as he keyed the code into the security panel and walked on to the main office floor.

'Morning, everyone.'

Most people were already at their desks and some were clearly not entirely happy about that as John scanned the room. Stella was not at her desk but then he saw her, talking to one of the juniors about something on a screen, and his heart seemed to stop for a moment. She glanced up at him but looked straight back down at the screen and continued talking, her expression unchanged. He knew what that meant and carried on walking to his office, before he gave anything away.

The morning passed smoothly enough and, early in the afternoon, the phone on his desk pinged to let him know that he had a text message. It was from Jas.

I'm in the lobby at your branch. Can you pop out to see me for a second? VERY exciting news!!!

The words were followed by three excited-face emojis. Three exclamation marks and three excited-face emojis. It must be good. He went to meet her.

They hugged as they met halfway across the banking hall floor.

There was a pretty long queue of customers waiting to be served at the desks and Julie was helping a middle-aged couple find the right leaflet for their needs, with another older couple watching her closely, clearly keen that there should be no doubt they were waiting to be assisted next. John looked towards the corner of the room, where three people sat at the small cluster of tables, two of them leafing through the free newspapers and none of them seemingly wanting anything other than a sit down and a bit of warmth. One of the tables, with two chairs at it, was free, though.

'Shall we have a sit down?'

'What is it that's so exciting it demands three exclamation marks?' he asked.

'Well.' Jas leaned forward. She obviously had news she was bursting to share. John tried to look cool, but he was intrigued.

'You know Dean Stone?'

'The crap actor?'

She ignored the response. 'You know he's from Sheffield?'

'I believe he's mentioned it once or twice. Wasn't he in that dreadful film years ago, set in Sheffield, about the pub footballer who went from obscurity to scoring the winning goal in the FA Cup final in the space of about a week? Possibly one of the cheesiest films of all time, as I remember.'

'He's one of the biggest movie stars in the world and he's been in some top TV series as well.'

John sensed he might be ruining her moment. 'Yeah, you're right. Sorry. I don't think I've ever stopped hating him for that film where he ended up in bed with Scarlett Johansson. Carry on.'

'Well, did you know that he's got a new film out called *Into the Fires of Hell* where he plays a scientist who has to lead a team into the crater of a volcano and set off some explosives to stop it erupting and covering a major city in America in molten lava?'

'I haven't heard of it. Sounds like a typical Dean Stone film though.'

'It's just about to open at the cinemas.'

'OK.' What is this leading up to? Is she suggesting a night out at the pictures?

'I saw a trailer for it on TV while I was putting out a tweet on the charity account, you know, trying to raise some publicity about the firewalk. Anyway, I thought it would be an idea to follow Dean Stone on the account, tag him into one of the tweets and see if that would get us a few more followers. Look, this is what I put.'

She opened her bag, took out her phone and opened the app.

'Here it is. "@therealdeanstone Think you can take the heat? Let's see you walk over red-hot coals in our @gameontrust firewalk on January 26", then I put hashtag realtoughguys.'

'Great idea, Jas. Did it get us any followers?'

'Did it?' Her eyes opened really wide, like a child with a new toy. 'He only bloody replied himself, didn't he?'

Suddenly, John understood why Jas was excited. 'Bloody hell!'

'Look, look.' She turned the screen so that John could read it. She did not need to read the words to recite them. 'He says: "always up for a challenge @gameontrust – count me in".'

'Are you sure that's really him?' This was beginning to sound a bit too good to be true.

'It's him! He's got, like, millions of followers and he retweeted the conversation out to all of them. We've had so many likes and follows because of this my phone has been going mental. I've had to turn the sound off and, this is the best bit, he followed us so that he could send a direct message. Look!'

Jas tapped at her phone again. 'We had quite a long conversation, actually,' she added. 'He said he's in the country doing a promotional tour for the film – chat shows and press interviews, that sort of thing – but that he's in Sheffield to visit family on the day of the firewalk – how freakish is that? – and that he wants to do the walk to help us out. It turns out he grew up on the estate at the back of Mike's cricket club and, when he read up about us, he liked what we were trying to do. He says he'll have to clear it with the insurance people and all that but he says he thinks the studio will love the publicity angle for the film and will go along with it. He even gave me the contact details for his PA and told me to sort out the rest with them. Isn't that brilliant?'

John's head was reeling. 'Fantastic, Jas.'

She was still in full excited flow. 'Just think of all the exposure this could get us. We're talking national media here, not just the local papers, radio and telly. It'll mean a lot more outlay on stewards and police and all that but it could make us a packet if we get this right. Oh my god, if Dean Stone really turns up and does the firewalk – even if he just turns up and doesn't do the walk – I might actually have to shag him.'

The extent of the possibilities was also beginning to dawn on John. 'I might shag him as well,' he said.

Jas jumped to her feet and John rose too. She flung her arms around his neck and gave him a kiss on the lips with an exaggerated mmmmmuhh. As she broke the contact, John looked over her shoulder and saw Stella, just returning from lunch, staring at him, wide-eyed. Jas noticed his sudden distraction and turned to look, just as Stella hurried on her way towards the security door to the office.

'What is it, John? Oh, are you two....?'

He nodded.

'Wow, John, she's really pretty. When did that happen?'

'Just before Christmas. I was going to tell you about it. We're keeping it hush-hush at work to avoid, you know.'

Jas had a big, mischievous grin on her face. John was blushing slightly.

'You old dog, Baldwin. I hope I've not....'

'Nah, it'll be fine. I'll explain.'

'I wouldn't want to....'

'It's fine, Jas. Look, I'd better get back to work. Fantastic news about Dean Stone. Can I leave you to get in touch with Mike this afternoon because he'll have to call his contacts at the council? He'll have to push them to give us a prime city centre spot for this – one of the pedestrianised areas, preferably – but we'll have to move fast to get all the details secured and make all the extra arrangements, then we can start putting the word out there that Dean Stone is going to be doing it with us. This is going to be huge, Jas, brilliant work. I'll call you tonight to catch up.'

They hugged again and John headed back to his office.

He walked back without looking towards Stella's desk and sat down. What's the best way to handle this? He didn't know Stella anything like well enough to judge. There was nothing to hide but allowing the situation to pass without explanation for very long would not be good. Just then, his phone pinged with another text. It was her.

Can I come to see you now?

OK, now. That works.

Of course. Pop over.

A minute later, Stella walked in carrying a bunch of files, no doubt to give the impression she was on a work-related mission. She closed the door behind her and stood in front of him.

'I want you to know that I'm not the naturally jealous type and I'm not about to claim possession of you just because we spent one night together but my ex was seeing other women and that's why we divorced, which has left me with trust issues regarding men, so I have to ask. Was that a situation I need to know about?'

He loved her candour. Amy used to be so hard to read sometimes.

'That was Jas,' he replied, attempting to strike the same forthright tone. 'You know the friend of mine who was killed a year ago?'

She nodded.

'Well Jas was his partner. They lived together. I've known Jas for years and she's a good friend, more like a sister really. We're working together to get the charity going. We certainly don't have that sort of a relationship, so no, there are no issues there.'

Stella nodded again. 'OK,' she said finally.

'I'm sorry you had those sorts of problems with your ex, I can't imagine how disturbing that must be, but not all men are like that. I was never even tempted to play around in eleven years together when I was with my ex and I couldn't do that to you either.'

'Fine,' she said, placated. 'I needed to ask.'

'I understand that. We've both been through difficulties and that makes it especially important we're straight up with each other all the time.'

'Agreed.' She was no longer clutching the files to her chest with such purpose and her expression softened again. She sat down.

'Jas had some awesome news, actually,' John added, hoping to further defuse the mood.

'You know Dean Stone?'

'The actor?'

'That's the one. Jas somehow established a rapport with him on social media and he says he's going to do the firewalk with us next month. At the very least, hopefully, he'll turn up and give us his support. Isn't that incredible?'

'Dean Stone. Really? That's really good. He's from Sheffield, isn't he?'

John smiled. 'I believe so.'

'I might have to sign up for this firewalk myself. I've always had a bit of a thing for him, actually.'

John eased back in his chair. 'You know, I'm by no means an expert in these matters but I can't for the life of me understand what women see in him.'

'He's a bit rough around the edges, earthy, quite sexy really. I think he reminds women of the bad lad that they were always warned about but secretly wanted to go with. Yes, that's it. He's a man of action and lots of women like that.'

'I see.' John folded his hands across his chest. 'If or when he turns up at the firewalk I'll have to make sure you get the chance to meet your action man, if you'd like – as long as you don't end up running off with him.'

She smiled. 'I can make no promises.'

He sat forward again. 'In the meantime, can we see each other this week?'

'I'd like that. I can't ask you to come to mine yet because it would be too confusing for the boys. It took them a long time to get used to their mother and father living separately and I don't want to upset that just now.'

'I can understand that.'

'But I can ask my mum to babysit for the night and come over to yours. I'll have to let you know which night she can do.'

'Perfect. Any night will be good for me.' He hesitated and then added: 'I was thinking as well, maybe one of the weekends when the boys go to their dad's we could go away somewhere for a night or two.'

'Hmm. It would have to be somewhere not too far away, in case I need to get back for the boys, and somewhere we could go without being seen together by anyone from here but that would be nice. David is due to have them again not next weekend but the weekend after, so maybe then.'

'Excellent. I'll come up with a few ideas.'

Stella gathered up the files from her knee and stood. She walked to John and planted a soft kiss on his lips, then wiped his lips with her forefinger to remove any trace of lipstick. She smiled and her blue eyes flashed vividly at him again before she turned to leave the office.

John watched her bottom as she sashayed towards the main floor and then disappeared from view.

'Baldwin,' he said in a low voice, 'you are a lucky bastard.'

13

The night with Stella was arranged for Friday. John made them a meal and then they cuddled together on the sofa while she drank wine and he sipped water. They decided York was a good choice for an overnight trip away and talked about it while a Dean Stone film played to itself on the TV. They paid no attention to the plot, preferring to spend the time getting to know each other a little better.

Saturday night had been set aside for a GameOn meeting. They had plenty to discuss.

'The council people have been very helpful, especially since we told them about Dean.' Mike was taking control of the meeting again. 'They're very excited about the return of one of the city's most famous sons and want as much of a share of the kudos as they can get their hands on, so they've been quick to approve the company we nominated for taking care of organising the firewalk and they've confirmed that we can go ahead with Friday, January 26, on a site on the Moor, which, as we know, is fully pedestrianised. That's perfect, really, and we're lucky that they've been prepared to pull out all the stops with this because they can drag their feet at times. They've told us we can have Saturday the 27th as a reserve day if the weather's too bad on the Friday but let's hope we don't need it. That's a complication we could really do without.'

John nodded his approval. Jas was scribbling notes on a pad.

'As we know, they are health and safety mad these days, so they're insisting all sorts of measures are put in place to accommodate a big crowd showing up to see Dean, but none of them are insurmountable in our time frame and the firewalk company is very experienced when it comes to these events and have been able to reassure the council to a large degree, so it's all looking good from that point of view.

What they have said is that it will be a maximum of twenty-five people actually doing the walk. Obviously, you, John, and Dean will take two of those slots and we will have to be very selective about who fills the others. I thought we could set a minimum sponsorship target for anyone who puts themselves forward – and I believe, Jas, there's already plenty of them.'

'Quite a few,' she replied.

'If we set a minimum target, it should really sharpen the focus and make our potential firewalkers push for sponsors, like runners have to if they want to do the major marathons. Obviously we would have to set a deadline, say about week and a half to two weeks before the event, for them to meet the target before we can settle on the final list. However, I thought it might also be an idea to make maybe one or two of the slots available for someone in the local media to do the walk. It would be a good way of keeping them on our side, looking to the long term, and we could easily encourage them to make a contribution in return for, say, getting a bit of exclusive time with Dean as well. What do you think?'

'I think that would be a good idea,' confirmed Jas.

'Me too,' added John.

'So what's the latest with the Charity Commission, John?'

'Still in the process but the feedback I've had is that there's an excellent chance we will be fully registered before the 26th. It doesn't stop us promoting events like this to raise funds before they give the go-ahead but we just have to be careful not to put anything out that suggests we are a registered charity until we actually are.'

'Already OK with that,' said Jas. 'The web page has been up and running for a few days now.'

'Very nice it is, too,' interrupted Mike.

'Thanks. A colleague of mine did it for us. There's nothing on there yet to say we are registered but it is spelled out in the aims and ambitions section that we're moving towards it. Obviously, I'll update that when the confirmation comes through. I've placed the link to the fundraising page prominently on the home page and I've included the link on all our social media posts as well. We've already had well over £12,000 pledged without really trying yet and that's only going to grow massively. Our reach on social media because of Dean is just phenomenal. I've never known anything like it.'

'Excellent. What about the mainstream media?' asked Mike.

'I've emailed out a press release to just about everybody I could think of and I've had plenty of positive responses. I've recruited one of the girls I used to work with to help me manage that side of it and make sure everybody gets what they want. The BBC was straight onto it and talking in terms of live links on the night – possibly even going out nationally, which would be wonderful. We're never going to get this sort of opportunity for national exposure again, so I'll make sure we make the most of it.'

'Great work, Jas,' said John.

'I was in the process of putting something together for potential corporate partners before it broke that Dean was with us, so I've put that on hold,' she added. 'They are starting to come to us! What I thought is we could offer three levels of corporate sponsorship and get them to commit annually and, as part of that, we can encourage them with a VIP package for the firewalk night, where they get to spend a little time in a VIP room with Dean and have a drink or two, have their photos taken by an official photographer, get autographs, that sort of thing. Also, I thought we could advertise a limited number of chances for the public to get a signed photo with Dean for, say, £50 a time. I've already put that to his PA as a proposal and she reckons he'll be fine with that.'

'This is all very encouraging, people. What about doing the walk, John? I presume you'll have to have some sort of training.'

'Yeah, they say they get everybody together for a preparation day, some sort of three-hour seminar, which sounds fine. I'm looking forward to finding out what it's all about,' said John.

'I appreciate these are going to be a busy four weeks – just less than four weeks, actually – for us, especially trying to balance this alongside the day jobs, but I think it's important we also keep an eye on what we do after the firewalk,' added Mike.

'This is going to create a lot of momentum for us and I don't want to lose that because we are all taking a breath after this event is out of the way, so keep coming up with the ideas. I was thinking maybe we could organise a football match with well-known former players from United and Wednesday. I could rope in some of my old cricket team-mates as well because a lot of them used to fancy themselves as footballers and then, when the weather improves, we could get them all involved in a cricket match – make it a sort of two-sport challenge.'

Jas and John nodded their approval.

'What about a concert?' suggested John.

Mike considered the idea. 'Yeah, that would work, put us in front of a different kind of crowd, but personally I know nobody who's involved in a group or whatever. Do either of you two?'

'Well, no,' said John, reaching into his inside jacket pocket for his wallet. 'But thankfully...' He pulled out a business card. 'I do have the personal telephone number of one of the most important figures in the European music industry.'

'Ahh! That might do it!'

'The man who was attacked,' recalled Jas. 'Gregory…'

'Fredericks. He said I should call him if there was anything I needed and he seemed a top bloke, so I don't think he was just saying it. With his contacts, I'm sure he'll be able to pull a few strings and point us in the direction of someone who could organise a bit of a concert and maybe even set us up with somebody people have actually heard of as a headliner. He might even be able to sort us out some memorabilia that we could use as a raffle prize at some stage. I'll give him a call.'

Back at his flat after the meeting, John looked at his watch. Ten past nine. Is it too late to call Gregory now? What are you thinking? It's Saturday night and he's in the music industry – he's hardly likely to be getting into his pyjamas, is he?

He took out the card again and keyed the number into his phone. It started to ring – a long, single buzz which meant the number he was calling was abroad. The timing might be even worse than he first feared. He considered hanging up but the call was answered within seconds.

'Hello, this is Gregory. Who's that?'

'Gregory, hi. It's John Baldwin from Sheffield.'

There was a moment of silence before Gregory responded. Could he have forgotten me already?

'John! Good to hear from you, brother!'

John was relieved. 'You too, Gregory. I hope I'm not disturbing you in the middle of the night.'

'Not at all, not at all. It's just after five in the evening here. I'm at my place in Jamaica for a little bit of rest and recuperation, you know, to get over our little exchange of opinions with those two guys in the back alley. It's a cool twenty-eight degrees and I'm sipping a cold beer while I dip my toes in the pool. How are things in England?'

'Well, I just had to scrape the frost off my car windscreen before I drove home but pretty good apart from that. Are you feeling better now?'

'Almost one hundred per cent, thank you, brother, but I might just stretch out my recovery for another couple of weeks. I don't like the thought of all that cold weather. Are you good?'

'Very good thanks.'

'And what can I do for you?'

It hadn't taken him long to realise this was not a social call. He must be so used to dealing with people who wanted him to do them favours. John felt awkward. He hoped Gregory was not already regretting handing over his card.

'I'm not calling for myself, Gregory, I'm calling on behalf of a charity I'm helping to establish. We're planning to work with children and their families from deprived areas in the city to help them to improve their lives, basically. We'll be working with them through sport, crafts and music and one of the fundraising ideas we've had is to organise a concert. That's where we were hoping you might be able to help out.'

'I see.' Gregory paused. 'I'm sure there will be something I can do. Come and see me in London when I return. I'll be back by the end of the month. Do you see the office number on the card I gave you?'

John picked up the card from the arm of the sofa. 'Yes, I've got it.'

'Call them and make an appointment. Come down to see me, I'll take you and your people out for lunch and I'll do everything I can to help because I want to show you what it means to me that you put yourself in danger to save my life. Give my people a call.'

'That's really good of you, Gregory. I will look forward to seeing you again.'

'You too, brother.'

14

Monday was New Year's Day – a date for renewal, an opportunity for everyone to declare an intention to start afresh on a better path. Having taken that step several weeks ahead of all the determined dieters and would-be non-smokers, John felt no need to make a pledge he might have no better than a fifty per cent chance of seeing through, but he did decide to make good use of the extra day off by beginning the process of reviving his independent financial advisory business.

Doing so left him with a slight feeling of betrayal. The building society had been good to him and had taken him back at a time when his life had been in enough of a mess without throwing in the added complication of being broke. He might have been hopeless but he had mercifully retained enough good sense to make sure he didn't also end up homeless. However, he did not want to be a compliance officer all his life.

No matter how frustrating it might have been at times to deal with the unrealistic expectations of unreasonable clients, he did not want to see the many hours of study to earn his qualifications go to waste. The desire for independence burnt within him again – the dream of establishing a business to the level where he could be selective about whose money he chose to invest with. Those were the times he had thought about a lot in the early months, while he was compiling his mental hit list of clients he would refuse to work with again once the business became well enough established. Making plenty of money and having choices. That was the goal.

It was back to the building society on Tuesday and that meant the considerable bonus of being able to see Stella again, even if their relationship remained a clandestine one.

There was no doubt that the secrecy gave John a buzz. The feeling that they were pulling off a deception in plain sight was intoxicating and exciting, but he found the camouflage increasingly difficult to maintain. He could not look at Stella without wanting to hold her, and not even being able to talk to her for fear of arousing suspicion demanded all the restraint he could muster.

He found himself paying far more frequent visits to the water cooler than usual, just so that he could pilfer a look in her direction over the edge of his plastic cup, or making personal visits to garner information from colleagues instead of firing off an email, just so that he could pass close by her and breathe in her scent. And so he spent his days, perpetually drawn into the gravitational pull of Stella, knowing that he would again be repelled by the force of their secret. It was not easy but their overnight stay in York was closer by the day. The thought sustained him as he picked at the scraps of their covert accord.

By Friday, the trip was almost in touching distance but the heightened anticipation was punctured by a morning phone call.

'Mr Baldwin? Hello there, it's Detective Constable Harrison from Sheffield CID.'

It was the officer who had visited him to take his statement after the attack on Gregory.

'Oh, hi. What can I do for you?'

The tone of the policeman's voice changed.

'I wanted to give you a call regarding our investigation. I should say this is just me giving you a word to the wise, it's not an official call, as such.'

'OK.'

'It's just that the solicitor acting for Kyle Jarvis and Craig Thomas, the two who carried out the assault on Mr Fredericks, has been told that in your statement you admitted to having tripped Jarvis as he tried to get away. He's trying to push for a charge of unlawful killing against you.'

John felt the colour drain from his face. 'Really?'

'He's also prompted Thomas to make an official complaint in his statement alleging that you used unreasonable force against him. Look, I wouldn't get too worried about this...'

Good as it was of the policeman to offer that comforting opinion, it had come too late. John felt sick. 'OK,' he just about managed to reply, unconvincingly.

'This solicitor is a slippery piece of work and he's trying it on, that's all. He's not got a leg to stand on, as far as we're concerned, and he's probably just trying to earn a bit of leniency for Thomas. They've already indicated, when he was up in front of the magistrates, that he's going to plead guilty, so he'll go to Crown Court for sentencing in a couple of weeks and he'll get sent down for a long time, especially with his record. This whole counter-allegation thing is a smokescreen. The courts won't fall for that.'

'Will I have to go to court?'

'Not unless he changes his plea. He's admitted guilt, so the sentencing hearing won't take that long and the procedure is that once we've got him safely put away, we are obliged to launch a new case to follow up Thomas' allegation. We'll then ask you to come to the station to walk through your statement again, this time under caution.'

'Does that mean I'll be arrested?'

'Certainly not at this stage and possibly not at all. What we'll do is look at all the evidence, including your statement, and pass everything on to the Crown Prosecution Service for them to decide if there's a case to answer but they have to be satisfied that prosecuting you would be in the public interest as well and I can't see them deciding to bring charges for that reason alone, never mind the fact that you've done nothing wrong here. Most likely they'll make the decision not to proceed and you'll get a letter through the post and that will be the end of it.'

'What about the other one – the unlawful killing?'

'There'll be an inquest into the Jarvis death but that won't be for months and I doubt you'll be called to give evidence at that. I also very much doubt the coroner will come up with a verdict of unlawful killing. Look, as I said, you've done nothing wrong and I wouldn't worry about it but I thought I should make you aware of what is happening and, if you've got a solicitor, I would alert them to this so they can get on top of it quickly. You'll probably hear nothing more about it but I wanted to give you a friendly warning.'

'I appreciate that. Can I give you a call if there's anything else I want to ask?'

'Of course. You've got my card, haven't you?'

'I have.'

'Call whenever you need me. I hope you have a good weekend, Mr Baldwin.'

The revelation shook John, but he resolved to put it behind him. It was not going to affect his trip with Stella, though he decided he would tell her about it as they strolled through York the following day.

'And what did your solicitor say?' she asked, anxiously.

'He said the same as the policeman. They're bluffing. They've no grounds. That sort of thing.'

'Good.'

They walked in silence for a while. The day was bright, cold and fresh and there were plenty of day-trippers around. You could pick them out by the way they moved at their own pace, as if they were ambling through an art gallery, not caring if they interrupted the flow of people around them by stopping to gaze at the upper levels of the wood-panelled buildings which loomed over the narrow street, pointing to ancient dates which confirmed the authenticity of the chocolate box scene they had travelled to see. They paid no heed to the locals who ducked and swerved through the crowd to get about their everyday lives at their everyday pace and the locals, in turn, paid no heed to them, like animals in a zoo compound who had long since grown oblivious to the presence of squawking children and curious adults.

'How can these people live with themselves?' said Stella at last.

'Who?'

'The solicitors for the two who attacked that poor man. How can they even think of turning it back around on you when you were the one who acted like a hero? They ought to be locked up with the lowlife they make their living out of. They're bastards, the lot of them.'

'They're just trying it on.' John was less concerned with defending those attempting to damage him than he was with trying to protect the romantic mood of the weekend. 'It won't come to anything, I'm sure. Forget about them. Fancy a coffee?'

'Yes.' Stella snapped out of her anger. 'That would be lovely.'

John steered them across the street to a tea room, despite its ludicrously quaint name which was no doubt intended to lure in beguiled tourists who wanted to stay on-theme. Better that than one of the ubiquitous international chains which had infected the uniqueness of the scene like an aggressive alien species, as they seemed to have done everywhere. John always avoided them when he travelled away from his home city, feeling that to use them would make him as unadventurous as the people who visited strange, exotic parts of the world and then went out to eat at a McDonald's.

The inside of the tea room was cramped and busy, but there were spare tables. At the side of the counter was a large display of cakes behind a sign which advertised their home-baked credentials, each of them looking like a single slice would provide enough calories for a family of adults for a month. John eyed them greedily but resisted and they waited their turn to order coffees from a young man who appeared to be still getting to grips with the Saturday job and constantly sought affirmation from the middle-aged woman who was busy preparing lattes and cappuccinos at the steaming, hissing coffee machine.

They found a table for two towards the back of the shop and sat down. Stella scooped a spoonful of chocolate-dusted froth off the top of her cappuccino, but paused before she brought the spoon to her mouth.

'Why did you and your wife – Amy, was it?'

John nodded.

'Why did you and Amy split up?'

He was prepared. He had already come to realise that Stella was not a woman to dodge an issue where there was an option to confront it head on and he had thought through what he would say in reply when this subject was raised.

'It was my fault. When Stef was killed, I went to pieces. I felt like I was to blame and I wouldn't listen to anybody who tried to tell me anything different. I didn't want to talk to anyone about it because I didn't think that anybody could possibly understand how I felt and so I tried to deal with it on my own in my own way. And my own way was that I tried to drink the feelings away. It was the worst thing I could have done – I know that now – but I've never been one to rely on other people because I grew up never being able to rely on other people. Amy couldn't understand that, of course, and she tried to bring me to my senses but the more she tried to pull me back from the brink, the more I pulled in the opposite direction until I started to treat her attempts to help as a conflict. It wasn't my finest hour.'

Stella listened silently and intently. John took a sip from his coffee.

'There was a period of several weeks – I honestly have no idea exactly how long it went on – where I was so wrapped up in the booze and the anger that I had no control over my actions any more. I behaved absolutely appallingly towards Amy. I was aggressive, confrontational, irrational, impossible to live with until, quite rightly, she decided she had had enough and left me to it. She did the right thing. I hate to think what might have happened if she hadn't. Anyway, I kind of emerged from the worst of it after Amy left and wallowed in self-hatred for a time while she started the divorce proceedings. I was still drinking far too much but I did have a few lucid periods and realised I had to do something about finding a new place to live, finding a job to pay for it, that sort of thing, and that's how I ended up back at the Ridings but I was still a mess.'

'You didn't hide it very well, I have to say,' interrupted Stella. 'What changed?'

'I suppose you could say I had an epiphany,' he replied, taking another sip. 'I suddenly saw myself for what I'd become and decided to change. I haven't touched a drop since and I've got my life back.'

It wasn't a lie, so he didn't feel bad about the version of the truth he had decided to present. It just wasn't the full story. He didn't feel it was appropriate yet to tell her exactly what happened to draw him out of his worst state. Not yet. The time would come.

'I'm thankful I was able to get back on track but, as I said, I'm deeply ashamed of what I put Amy through. I did go to see her a couple of weeks ago to at least start the process of trying to put things right but she was still pretty unforgiving about it, as you can imagine – and I can't blame her. I can't make up for what I did but I can make sure I'm a better person in the future and that's what I've decided to do.'

'That's quite a story. I appreciate your honesty.'

Stella's expression was giving nothing away. John hoped he had not said too much. He knew he was taking a chance by exposing his past in its full hideous detail but he did not want to hide it from her. It was important that she knew. He thought she would understand.

'You were plainly under a lot of emotional strain and made mistakes, but I think it takes a brave man to recognise that and not shy away from it. That's good. I'm glad you told me.'

'Does it change the way you see me? Do you feel any differently about us?' John held his breath.

She considered her response. 'No. I know you better now than I did ten minutes ago and that's a good thing. I think what you put your wife through must have been appalling, but there were clearly deep psychological issues at play which made you behave in a way that was completely out of character and the important thing now is that you recognised them and have faced them. Nobody should condemn a person for the sins of their past when they show true remorse and move to set the record straight. Everybody deserves a second chance when they've shown they've earned it. I don't see you in a worse light, I see you in a clearer light and it doesn't make me feel differently about our relationship. Besides,' her face softened and she smiled, 'the hotel's already paid for.'

John's head dropped in relief. The woman was truly remarkable.

'Would you like to know about me and David?' she added.

He didn't expect that. 'If you're happy to tell me, yes.'

'There's nothing to hide,' she said as she idly stirred what remained of her cup of coffee. 'We started going out when we were fifteen. He was the coolest boy in the year who all the girls wanted to go out with, so I was very happy about that. David was always smart but he wasn't very academically gifted and he left school at sixteen to get a job while I stopped on for A Levels, which was good for me because he was earning money and could afford to take me out. When I finished sixth form I decided not to go to university so that I could stay close to David, which upset my parents and was a huge mistake – I can see that now. Big mistake. Anyhow, that's when I started work at the Ridings.

'We got married when I was twenty-three and that was fine but David decided he wanted us to start a family sooner rather than later. I was just beginning to make real progress in my career at that time and I was ambitious. I'd been in the job long enough to know that I could take on one of the senior positions at the branch and almost certainly do it a lot better than some of the people in post, then I thought I could use that as a stepping stone to a bigger job somewhere else but David kept on about wanting kids and I gave in. We had Jamie a week before my twenty-sixth and Liam two years later and, don't get me wrong, my kids are the most important people in my life and I wouldn't be without them for the world but I knew there were people in the company who were probably thinking "there's no point giving her a job higher up because she's only going to leave to have babies soon" and I hated that I'd proved them right. It's very hard to break those attitudes down even when you come back off maternity leave.'

John nodded, sympathetically. It was about all he could offer.

'It's tough when you've got a baby and a toddler and David wasn't much help. All I got from him was a lot of self-pitying whining about how I wasn't paying any attention to him anymore and how he felt like it just wasn't the same between us now that I had – *I had* – the boys. Honestly, it was like having three children in the house. It created a lot of tension between us and eventually I found out that he had been seeking comfort elsewhere. That was that. I kicked him out.'

'What a shame. He must want his head examining.'

Stella let out a short laugh. 'Thanks for the vote of confidence. I think what it boiled down to was that we got together too young and we were very different people when we were twenty-five than we were when we were fifteen, but that's the way of the world, I suppose. Anyway, I... oh, for crying out loud!'

She had glanced over John's shoulder but suddenly bowed her head. He moved to see what had caught her eye. 'What is it?'

'Don't turn around!' she hissed. He looked back at her. 'It's Becky from my savings team. I don't think she's seen us.'

Stella kept her head bowed, peeping across the shop. 'She's looking for a table. Go away! It's too busy in here. Go somewhere else. She's still looking around. Oh god, she's waving.'

Her expression was forced into a smile as she mouthed the word 'hi' over John's shoulder. She dipped her head again and resumed her surreptitious commentary.

'Oh no, don't come over! Just get a drink and sit down. She's coming over!'

Stella sat up and drew her shoulders back, ready to face the music with dignity. The game was up.

'Hi, Becky,' she said, without enthusiasm.

'Oh hi, Stella! I said to my mum I thought it was you but you're never sure when you see somebody some place you don't expect to see them, are you?'

John tried, without making it too obvious, to hide his face from the young woman who was now at his side, but there was no escape.

'Oh hello, Mr Baldwin,' she said, surprised.

He looked up. Becky's round face lit up with delight as the realisation of her discovery dawned.

'Hello, Becky. Fancy seeing you here.'

She was the cat who had not only got the cream but had stumbled on a full dairy herd's worth. Oh, this is good! This is really good!

'Fancy,' she replied, barely able to contain her joy.

A few seconds of silence passed. Only two of the three people around the table found them awkward. Finally, Becky delivered the merciful final blow.

'Well, I'll leave you two alone. Enjoy.'

Stella waited until Becky had turned away before her fixed expression dropped and she muttered 'fuck' sharply under her breath.

'Of all the people we could have bumped into. This will be all over Facebook in five minutes. It's a wonder she didn't ask us to pose for a selfie with her. Fuck!'

John allowed her initial irritation to subside. 'Do you know what, who cares? People were bound to find out sometime and it's going to be sooner than we expected, but what the hell! Our relationship doesn't compromise what we do professionally in the slightest and, what's most important, I'm so happy to be with you that I want everybody to know about it. We might give the gossips ammunition for a day or two but they'll soon get bored of that and move on to talking about something else. It won't affect us. You're the best thing to happen to me for a long time, Stella, and I don't want us to slink around in secrecy all the time.'

She looked straight back at him, not angry anymore.

'That's very sweet of you, John, and I'm so happy to be with you too. You are just the sort of man I need in my life right now, but you don't understand. You don't know what it's like to be a woman in an environment which is still dominated by older men in many ways. Especially when you're young, it's very difficult to get people to take you seriously and when you do begin to move up the ladder on merit, people still say you've only got there because you flashed your breasts at the bosses. I've heard them say it. That's why I decided very early on in my time of working at the Ridings that I would keep my private life and my professional life completely separate. I broke my rule for you and I don't regret that, but... Oh, I don't know! I knew we couldn't hide away for ever, but I just didn't want it to get out this way. If we were going to let everyone know, I wanted it to be on our terms.'

He could see her frustration. Having matters out of her control was clearly not Stella's thing.

'I can understand that but let's not allow this to spoil our weekend.'

She sighed. 'No. No, it won't.'

'In that case, I wish to propose a toast.' John raised his coffee cup. Stella half-smiled back, amused but bemused.

'Bollocks to Becky,' he said.

She laughed and raised her cup to clink against his. 'Bollocks to Becky and bollocks to the lot of them,' she added. They both drained the rest of their coffee.

'Now let's go to see the Minster.'

They drove back the following afternoon. The trip had been all John hoped it would be, despite the unexpected encounter in the tea room. He was sure now that he was in love but didn't yet feel confident enough to say so, just in case Stella was not growing into the relationship at the same pace. He knew they were completely at ease with each other and that was enough for now.

He had suggested the news about their affair might not have been brought to the attention of a wider audience after all, but Stella was adamant discretion was not one of Becky's natural qualities and so he expected to attract a few knowing glances when he arrived at work on Monday morning.

'Morning, Julie.'

She was busying herself as usual in the banking hall. 'Morning, Mr Baldwin. Did you have a nice weekend?'

It was nothing more than she would say any other Monday morning, but the words seemed to carry a different resonance this time. You're just being over-sensitive, John.

'Lovely, thanks. How about you?'

He passed through the security door to the main office with a smile on his face. Just a normal morning. Nobody hiding away here. 'Morning all.'

Those who normally returned the greeting did so. Maybe they were seeing him in a different way. He was trying not to show that he was looking for signs.

'John, could you come here please?'

It was Stella. That definitely provoked added interest around the office. They were waiting to see what was about to happen. He walked over to her desk.

'Could I have your attention for a second?' she announced. She didn't need to ask twice. The room was quiet apart from one telephone, which rang unanswered.

'No doubt many of you will be aware that John and I are in a relationship and have been for a few weeks. Quite why this should be of interest to anyone else, I do not know but there you have it. Now, if we could all just get on with our jobs please instead of wasting time on gossiping, that would be appreciated.'

Stella sat down and started typing on her keyboard. A few faces looked towards John for a reaction, but he shrugged as if to confirm 'like she said' and they turned away. John went to his office but before he could take off his coat, one of the assistant managers tapped on the door.

He offered his clenched hand for a fist-pump, which John half-heartedly accepted.

'Nice one, John. I didn't know you had it in you,' he beamed. John stared blankly back. *What do you want me to say?*

'But seriously, after everything you've been through lately, I'm really happy for you, both of you. I hope it works out.'

'Thanks, Gordon. I appreciate that,' He did. The man left. John took off his coat, hung it up on the hook behind his door and sat at his desk. If he had ever felt happier, he could not recall when that time was.

15

The firewalk was only a few days away. The time had passed quickly and there had been no shortage of fine detail to sift through but they had hit no snags and, much to their relief, the Charity Commission had approved GameOn's charitable status with days to spare. A get-together had been called for two nights before the event with all the volunteers they had recruited to help make sure the evening ran smoothly but John, Mike and Jas also decided they should meet for one last time a day earlier than that.

'So what was the training seminar like then, John?' Mike was handing out copies of the event schedule and the notes he had prepared for the volunteers.

'It was pretty good, actually.' His expectations had been lower than that. Too many training days with a team-building element had dulled his enthusiasm for group activities served up to promote self-discovery.

'There was lots of positive affirmation sloganeering and talk about finding a better you, that sort of thing, but actually a lot of what they said about preparing your mind for the challenge, focusing on conquering the fear rather than the fear itself and the practical bits about the best way to walk on hot embers without getting burnt were all very useful. I feel completely prepared for it now.'

'That's a relief. We'd look a bit daft if you pulled out at this stage.' Mike sat down. 'All still OK with our Hollywood superstar as well, I hope, Jas.'

She put up two thumbs. 'All good. I called his PA again today and she says he's looking forward to it.'

'Marvellous. What's the latest on sponsorship?'

'Well.' Jas flicked through her notes. 'The other twenty-three walkers are confirmed and have all been busy raising money, by the looks of things. We have eight corporate partners and we've sold thirty-six VIP packages. I'll be disappointed if we can't turn at least a few of them into corporate partners by the time we're finished. We've also sold out all the fifty-pound packages. I'm beginning to wish we had gone in a bit higher with them but that's fine. In all, I'd estimate we'll be well on our way to six figures in the bank by the time all the bucket collections and such are counted, which is brilliant.'

'That's great. We just have to hope it doesn't piddle down and that all the media turns up now.' Mike sat back in his chair until it creaked. 'Anybody aware of anything else we need to look at?'

The other two shook their heads.

'In that case, I suggest we go to the pub for a well-earned pint.' He checked himself. 'Sorry, John. Well-earned orange and lemonade.'

John grinned. 'You're buying.'

'Agreed!'

As they stood to gather their notes and put on their coats, Jas turned to John.

'Heard anything yet?' she asked, discreetly. He had told her that Craig Thomas was due to appear in Crown Court two days earlier on a charge of racially aggravated assault causing grievous bodily harm.

'Yes. He pleaded guilty and got four and a half years, which I'm told is just about the maximum they could have gone for, seeing as he admitted it. With his previous, I'm not surprised. It's just a matter of waiting for the police to get in touch now and, when they do, I'll go in and go through my statement again but this time I'll need to have my solicitor with me.'

'It's not right!'

He shrugged. 'It's what they've got to do. An official complaint was made and they have to look into it, then it's up to the CPS to decide if there's a case to answer. The police tell me they don't think it will go any further, so I'm pretty relaxed about it. There's nothing I can do about it either way.'

Jas reached over and squeezed his hand in support.

'It'll be all right,' he added, reassuringly.

Mike was at the door waiting. 'Are we going to the pub, or what?'

It was a crisp, cold but, happily, dry winter evening and already a couple of hundred people, wrapped up in preparation for a long and chilly vigil, had gathered on the pedestrianised walkway. Many were in place at the metal barriers on either side of the fifteen-foot-long mound of glowing coals, no longer flaming as the time for the firewalk drew close but still radiating welcome heat to warm the noses and cheeks of those who stood as close as they were allowed. The big department stores on either side were closed, but the dimmed-down light from the buildings helped the dotted street lamps illuminate the growing crowd, whose number was being swelled by the minute by curious passers-by on their way home from work. The steam rose from three fast food vans and the sizzle of the cooking added to the crackle in the atmosphere. There was just under thirty-five minutes to go.

John had barely stopped all day as meticulous attention was given to the smooth running of the event, but he stood still now and took the chance to look around. It all felt unreal. It was only a few weeks since the germ of an idea took root and, for all their planning, it had somehow felt like it was all still a theoretical exercise. But now that he'd allowed himself a moment to stop and take it all in, the realisation sank in for the first time. Jesus, this is actually going to happen!

Stranger still, he was standing in the glare of a small but powerful spotlight waiting to give his first live TV interview.

'They're coming over to us in just over a minute,' said the female interviewer. 'Are you feeling OK?'

'Yeah, fine.' It wasn't the time to make any sort of confession about how odd the whole experience was.

'As I said, I'll do a piece to camera first and then pull you into the conversation. You don't need to move any closer to me when I start the interview because Wilko,' she glanced over towards the cameraman in position behind his tripod, 'will have the shot. Then I'll ask you a little bit about the event, a bit about the charity and we'll talk about Dean. OK?'

John nodded.

She touched her earpiece and talked towards the microphone which was mounted on the camera. 'Ready when you are.'

It was almost time, clearly. John felt a flutter of nerves. The interviewer looked towards the cameraman again. 'OK, Wilko?' He responded with a thumbs-up. She drew a couple of deep breaths and her mouth moved slightly as she mentally rehearsed what she was about to say. Then the signal was given and the expression on her face changed as quickly as if a switch had been flicked.

'Yes, Harry. It is quite a chilly night here in the centre of Sheffield but, as you can see, that hasn't put off the hundreds of people who have come down here tonight to see film star Dean Stone literally walking through fire.' She did a quarter turn to her right to point out the jostling crowd that had amassed behind her in hope of appearing on the telly. They cheered, as prompted.

'The final preparations are being made to get ready for the firewalk and although the flames have died down now, I can tell you that there is still a lot of heat coming off those coals. The temperature, I'm told, is over 1,200 degrees Fahrenheit and that is hot enough to melt aluminium. We have just about half an hour now until the start of the firewalk and I have with me one of the organisers for the event.' She glanced down at her notes. 'John Baldwin of the GameOn Trust.'

She turned to her left. 'John, you must be delighted to have such great support for your event tonight.'

'Yes, absolutely, Michelle. A lot of planning goes into organising an event such as this, as you can imagine, with lots of people involved, but it looks as if all that effort is going to be worthwhile.'

Michelle was nodding earnestly. 'So tell us a bit about the GameOn Trust. The charity hasn't been going for very long, I gather.'

'That's right. In fact, we only received approval of our charitable status a few days ago. This is our first major fundraising event and, really, we started out only a month or so ago with the aim of giving young people from some of the more underprivileged areas of the city the opportunity to express themselves through sport and the arts because so many of them just don't have the money to access the facilities in our city. Our ambitions have already been raised because of the fantastic support we've had for tonight's event and now we're hoping to be able to branch out by perhaps offering funding for education and apprenticeship packages among the communities we have targeted as needing help. As we grow, we'd like to expand our operation to other areas around South Yorkshire and, maybe one day, become a national body. These are exciting times.'

'Indeed, and it must help when you can draw on support from one of the world's biggest film stars. How did it come about that Dean Stone became involved in GameOn and what has it been like working alongside a Hollywood icon? He is from Sheffield originally, of course.'

'Yes, that's right. The contact with Dean came about completely by chance, really. One of my colleagues, Jas, sent out a bit of a challenge to him in a message on Twitter and he replied to her, which came completely out of the blue. He said he wanted to get involved because he grew up in one of the communities we wanted to work with and he's been good to his word.'

'Have you had the chance to talk to him yet?'

'Not yet. We're incredibly grateful to him for agreeing to come down and support our cause – and, of course, he is going to do the firewalk with us.'

'And you are going to be walking on fire as well, I hear. Are you looking forward to that?'

'Well, Michelle, you could say it's quite an extreme way to warm up your toes on a cold night such as this but, yes, I am looking forward to it. It will be an experience.'

'We will look forward to watching you.' She turned back to the camera. 'I might just join in myself to get warm! Back to you in the studio, Harry.'

She waited in pose for a couple of seconds longer until the signal came through her ear that the live link was over. 'OK, OK thanks,' she said and then turned back to John.

'That was great, John. You said there was a chance we could have a few words with Dean after the firewalk?'

'As far as I understand, yes. Jas is handling that side of things, but I believe Dean is happy to.'

She smiled in relief. 'Wonderful. We'd better let you get ready, then. Thanks again, John.'

John walked through the gathering crowd to the marquee set aside as a VIP area and showed his credentials to the two security men in their heavy orange coats. Inside, the fan heaters were doing an excellent job and John gave an exaggerated shiver as if to shake off the cold of the outside. There was around fifty or sixty people inside, standing around in clusters with many of them congregated around the bar area, drinks in hand. He looked around and saw Stella chatting to Jas. They seemed to be getting along very well. He stood and watched them for a moment. They were the two people he cared for most in the world. He loved them both, in different ways, and it gave him a happy glow within to see them, separate strands of his life brought together and no longer strangers because he was now their common ground. He walked towards them.

Stella saw him first and she smiled hello as he came closer. Jas turned and said: 'Here he is. You must have known we were talking about you.'

Standing close to Stella were two small boys. She had said she planned to bring them along, which John was happy about. It felt like a first step towards allowing him into their lives. He said 'hi' to her, thinking it best not to kiss her, as he wanted to, while he was being surveyed by their young eyes for the first time.

'It's a good job I got here before you got to all the juicy bits.'

He looked down at the two boys and tried to look kindly. They were snug in matching black coats and both wore red and white football scarves and hats. The seven year old stood tall and bold and had his mother's handsome features, including her blue eyes. He stared at John fearlessly. The five year old had a paler complexion and brown eyes. Stella had said he looked more like his father. He held his mother's hand but had already become weary of looking at this newcomer and was staring around the room. He appeared keen to set off and explore on his own, had he not been restrained by his mother.

'This is Jamie and this is Liam,' Stella made the introductions. John dropped to his haunches to be closer to the boys' level and said hello. The oldest watched as he did, the youngest acknowledged him with a momentary peek and then carried on perusing the crowd.

'This is John, one of mummy's friends from work. He's going to be walking on the hot coals soon.'

The oldest took in the information and considered. 'Won't you get burnt?'

'Ah!' said John. 'These are special hot coals that only grown-ups can walk over without getting burnt. Ordinary hot coals would burn you and you should always stay well away from them because fire is dangerous, but these ones will be fine.'

For someone with no previous experience of responsible parenting he thought that was not half bad. He looked up at Stella and got an approving smile. First hurdle safely negotiated. He rose back to his feet.

'How did the interview go?' asked Jas.

'Fine, good. I feel like I'm getting to be a bit of a veteran at this now. There's a decent crowd building up out there.'

Jas glanced at her watch. 'I ought to start to get all the walkers ready to go very soon. Have you had the chance to say hello to Dean yet?'

'No, I haven't actually.'

'I'll introduce you. Excuse us a sec, Stella.'

They wandered towards the other side of the marquee. Jas touched John's arm and said quietly: 'I think she's lovely.'

He smiled back. 'Good. So do I.'

In the corner was a large banner promoting the film *Into the Fires of Hell* in vivid reds and oranges, with a picture of Dean Stone, being fearless, in a silver and presumably fire-resistant suit, dominating the right side of it. His supporting stars, similarly attired and equally intrepid, followed close behind in the picture, though the perspective of the shot made them appear smaller and proportionately less fearless than the main man. In front of the banner and with his back to them as they walked across the tent, the real Dean Stone was performing for another supporting cast of six or seven. They laughed simultaneously as he delivered the punch line to his story. A man in his mid-forties, a large belly hanging over his jeans and with the red shirt beneath his dark suit jacket opened one button too many to expose his excessive chest hair, was laughing loudest. He held up the hand that was not cradling a large gin and tonic for Dean to grasp in a manly, arm-wrestling handshake and pulled the star to him in a chest-bump hug.

'Absolutely brilliant, Dean. Absolutely brilliant,' he said. 'Look, it's been great to meet you and thanks a lot for the photo.'

'No problem at all.'

'Brilliant, mate. And good luck with the film.' With that, the man released his grip and left to tell the others in his party what a great bloke Dean Stone is.

Jas saw her chance. 'Dean, can I introduce you to John Baldwin, one of our co-founders. He's the one who is going to be doing the firewalk with you tonight.'

The actor turned to face John and offered his hand in a conventional handshake. His lean face was tanned beneath carefully manicured hair and his chin had a carefully manicured two or three days of stubble on it. His smile was easy and distinctly roguish, exaggerating the crease of dimples on his cheeks and pushing up the lines around his thin green eyes, which retained the rascally quality that had so frequently over the years led to him being cast as the bad guy or the not-so-good good guy.

'Good to meet you, John.'

'Good to meet you, too. I can't thank you enough for giving up your time to support us tonight.'

'No problem, no problem.' He made no attempt at false modesty but accepted the thanks without belittling the sentiment.

'It really does make such a difference to us and to the young people we'll be able to help because of the money we've raised tonight.'

'Happy to be able to help. A Sheffield lad always keeps his word, isn't that right?'

They broke off their handshake and John gave a nod towards the film promotion banner, which had been the backdrop for the evening's VIP photo opportunities. 'How has the tour been going?'

Dean looked towards the banner. 'It's been very good, ta. The reviews have been pretty good so far as well, which is always a bit of a relief. Are you planning to go to see it yourself, John?'

He nodded. 'Oh yes, definitely.' Probably not, actually.

'Do you,' he glanced up at the others in his entourage knowingly, 'do you like watching my films then, John?'

'Yes, of course. Big fan. I was watching one again the other night, actually.' *What's going on here? Does this bloke want me to stroke his ego or what?*

'Good, good.' He glanced at his entourage again. They appeared barely able to contain themselves. *Am I being set up here?* 'It's just that I've been told that you didn't have a very high opinion of me anymore. Something to do with a certain bedroom scene I did some years ago.'

Jas! He gave her a chastening glare. She blushed. The people with Dean giggled. John thought momentarily about revealing what Jas had promised to do if everything worked out as planned but he dismissed the thought as ungallant.

'I see. I've been stitched up here, haven't I?' He felt his own cheeks redden.

'Nothing personal, it's just that I've always had a bit of a thing for Scarlett Johansson.'

Dean smiled and clapped him firmly on the arm. 'I can understand that. She's a nice lass, is Scarlett. I'll tell you what.' He moved close to John, as if to pass on a confidence. 'If you're ever over in LA, give me a call and I'll see if I can put in a word for you.'

He looked at his people to see if they properly appreciated the joke. They did.

'I'll hold you to that.' Thanks, Jas. Thanks a lot.

She provided her own excuse to leave. 'Look at the time! You two had better get your shoes and socks off and get ready. I need to make sure everybody else is prepared. See you in five minutes.' With that, she scurried through the door at the back of the marquee, holding her clipboard.

'I'll see you out there,' said John and he went back to join Stella and her boys.

Back out in the chilly air, a snake of the other walkers had already formed in front of an imitation turf mat, laid out just before the strip of still-smouldering coals, which flickered and glowed brighter orange and yellow as they caught the night breezes. The first walkers, in shorts or with trousers rolled up to the knee, looked nervously excited as they jiggled and fidgeted to dispel the tension and stay warm. The ones behind them craned their necks to get a better look at the task ahead. John was to walk next to last, with Dean providing the grand finale.

Music was playing through the speakers on either side of the marquee behind them and, by the side of the mat, a man wearing a hoodie top and baseball cap, which both bore the logo of the walk's organising company, was yelling into a microphone in an effort to ramp up the atmosphere.

'Are you ready for this, Sheffield?' he called. Beyond the metal barriers on either side, over which hung the GameOn Trust placards that had been made for the occasion, the crowd cheered in response. There was so many of them that they appeared to shrink the narrow avenue between. Those in the first three rows jostled to find gaps to position their smart phones so they could take pictures and videos and, further back, young children had been lifted onto shoulders to get a better view. Beyond them, John could see people standing on the fixed benches and balanced on the metal cages which protected the base of the trees, clinging to the branches for security.

'Give it up for our brave firewalkers!' shouted the man on the mic. The crowd cheered louder.

'I want you to give a huge cheer to all our firewalkers here tonight and celebrate with each and every one of them as they complete what will be, for all of them, a very special journey. Don't forget, these people have gone through professional training to prepare them for what they are about to do so, whatever you do, do not try this at home. If, however, you want to learn how to firewalk yourselves, please pick up one of our flyers before you leave. Now ARE – YOU – READY?'

The roar confirmed that they were and the man gestured for the first walker, a large woman in her fifties who was wearing a GameOn Trust t-shirt, to step forward. She waved her arms above her head and performed a little jig of excitement before settling into a purposeful, upright six steps across the hot coals. By the time she had wiped her feet on the mat at the other end to knock off any bits that might have stuck to her soles and sent a huge whoop of joy into the night sky, the second walker was on his way too.

'Dean! Dean!'

The people close to the starting end of the walkway called to attract his attention and took their photos and held out scraps of paper for him to sign. John looked around and there was the star of the show, emerged from the marquee for his big scene. Dean smiled and waved self-effacingly to both sides, as if to attempt to pacify them without wanting to make himself a distraction. He looked back down the walkway and clapped as, one by one, the volunteers completed their challenge.

John looked at the line of people yet to come. Only eight or nine more now and then it was his turn. He unexpectedly began to feel afraid. With all the distractions of the day, time had sort of crept up on him. He was not sure he was ready. He thought back to what was said in the training seminar – clear your mind, be positive, tell yourself you can do this, focus on the end. Only about half a dozen before him now. Clear your mind, be positive, tell yourself you can do this, focus on the end.

One by one, they strode out across the coals. Only two to go. This is it. Come on, John. Focus. One more. He stepped forward in line behind a man in an orange shirt. The last one in the line.

As the man in orange took his first step, a huge feeling of calm surged through John's body. He saw the orange of the shirt move from him and fade into a blur, even though the figure was only a few feet away. The faces in the crowd, even those on the front row, were indistinguishable and the sound of their cheering became muffled, like he was hearing them from beneath water. The flash of their phones seemed to last for seconds instead of fractions of seconds and he blinked his eyes against the light. He saw the arms of the man on the mic waving him forward, a slow-motion wave, and he saw the man's mouth move in exaggerated expression of unheard words.

A hand patted down on John's shoulder twice, three times, and he turned his head to see Dean smiling, uttering encouragement that could not be made out through the distancing woolliness that had settled between them. It was time to go. John stepped forward on to the mat, each step feeling so slow and heavy that it reverberated up his legs, through his torso and thudded into his brain. He was by the edge of the strip of coals now and he stopped. He looked down at his bare feet and then up again, along the fifteen feet of smoking black and orange which seemed to go on forever. He could see two figures balancing TV cameras on their shoulders and three photographers in their official lime green tabards, waiting no doubt for the man behind him to take his steps across the coals.

The crowd was still cheering and, through the sea of obscured faces, John's eye was drawn. One head stood out clear and sharp in his sight. Only one. It was a man's. A man who could not have been more than twenty-four to twenty-five years old. He wore a dark cap with a hood pulled over it. He was taller than most of those around him but not so much that he stood out from the crowd, other than to John's eye. His head was in profile at first, a thin face with a flattened nose under which was the tuft of a moustache and straggly beard. He was watching the photographers, preparing to take their shots, and then his head turned, slowly, to look down towards where John waited, mesmerised by the sight of this one face, around twenty-five feet away. As the man gazed down, he craned forward slightly to get a better view and their eyes met. As they met, the distance between them seemed to shrink until John felt he could almost reach out and touch that face.

The eyes of the man were cool and curious but, as they met John's, they narrowed. He stared and John could read the processes going on behind them. Recognition. Both of them felt it. They knew it. In the same instant, they both knew where they recognised each other from. It was a still, cool night a couple of weeks before Christmas, on a road that crossed the county border, close to the gap in the hedge where you could get on the path to the golf course.

The man's eyes widened in momentary panic and he turned, pushing his way through the crowd. John watched the back of his frame as he barged through the people in his way. He's getting away! Don't let him get away again!

He yelled, so loud and so unexpectedly that even the man on the mic was silenced.

'Stop that man!'

The world was back to normal speed again, but John could see nothing except the back of the hooded figure edging through the crowd. Energy surged through him as he sprang into a sprint, showering spits of glowing embers and smoke over those in his wake as he gained traction on the loose coals, his feet skidding and scattering debris behind him as he covered the distance of the strip in four strides and headed straight for the gap in the metal barrier where the previous walkers had made their exit. He sprinted past the cameras, driving forward much more smoothly now on the mat and flagstones, until he came to the extended barrier to his right and vaulted it in one leap. He landed, jarring his ankle, but sprinted on, hoping to catch sight of the hooded figure again. He slowed and stopped, looking around. The man was gone.

John bent forward with his hands on his knees and tried to get his breath back, realising the exertion for the first time. He looked down at his bare, sooty feet on the flags of the pedestrianised street.

'Oh shit! What have I done?'

He stood up tall and turned around. Faces and phones, hundreds of them, it seemed, were pointed his way. John bowed his head and limped back towards the VIP marquee.

16

Stella was the first person he saw back at the marquee. She wrapped him in a protective hug which he was in no hurry to break free from. 'You OK, babe?' she said softly in his ear.

John raised his head from her shoulder and looked her in the eye. 'I saw him. I saw Stef's killer.'

Before she could respond, Jas had joined them.

'Oh my god, John. Are you all right?'

Stella released him and took a step back. This was going to be difficult.

'I saw the man who killed Stef, Jas. It was him. He was there in the crowd.'

Jas brought her hands up to her face. Mike had wandered over to them now.

'Are you sure it was him?' asked Stella.

He nodded. 'As sure as I can be. I really think so. I looked straight at him and he looked at me. He knew that I knew and that was why he turned away and scarpered. He'd got away before I could get there.'

'I'm going to be sick,' said Jas through her hands. Stella put her arm around Jas' shoulder and began to lead her towards the door.

'Come and get some air.'

She turned back to glance at John and Mike. 'Could you keep an eye on the boys, please?' Then she looked to her two sons, who had watched the whole scene with wide-eyed fascination. 'Stay with these two gentlemen please, boys, until mummy gets back. I'll only be a minute.'

Mike gave John a firm stare. 'Are you OK?'

John ruffled his hair with both hands, as if waking from a deep sleep. 'I'm fine. I'm just a bit, you know… I'm not sure what I'm feeling like, to be honest. But I'm fine.'

A voice from over his shoulder made him spin round.

'Excuse me, John?'

It was a ruddy-faced man who looked in his early thirties. John vaguely recognised him but was not instantly sure where from.

'I'm Richard Lancaster from *The Star*? We spoke when you were involved in that attack a few weeks ago?' John remembered now. He also recalled that he had an irritating raised inflection habit which meant he made statements sound like questions.

'Oh, hi, Richard. You did the walk with us tonight, didn't you? Did you enjoy it?'

'It was great, thanks. I didn't make quite as spectacular an entrance as you though. I wonder if you could spare me a minute?'

'Er, sure.' He looked to Mike. Mike took his cue and began to lead Stella's two boys away.

'Let's go and wait over here for your mum to get back. I see you're both United fans. Who's your favourite player, then?'

A thought occurred. 'You're not going to write something taking the piss, are you?'

The reporter shook his head. 'No. I saw what you did and I'm sure there had to be a reason for that. I just wondered what it was that made you chase off like you did?' As he spoke, he reached into his coat pocket, brought out his smartphone and began to select the voice recording mode.

It was an opportunity to explain himself. John decided to take a chance and trust him.

'You remember when we spoke last time that I told you that my best friend was murdered a year ago?'

The reporter nodded.

'Well, I saw the man who did it in the crowd tonight. I'm fairly certain it was him.'

'What makes you so sure? I thought you told me you couldn't give the police a very good description of the man on the night.'

'I couldn't but I saw him tonight and, I don't know, I just recognised him. Maybe the information was there all the time, locked away in a corner of my brain, and it just needed an incident like this to bring it all back into focus. Anyway, I knew it was him straightaway and, by the way he looked back at me, he recognised me and he knew I knew it was him. That's why he ran away and that's why I chased after him.'

'That's incredible. How did that make you feel?'

John considered. 'Kind of numb, really. It was a shock, I suppose. I wasn't particularly angry but when I saw him trying to get away I panicked and I wanted to stop him. I want him to pay for what he did. I want them to catch him and send him to prison for killing my best friend. That's what was going through my head.'

'What do you plan to do next?'

'Er, I don't really know. I hadn't planned for this. I'll go to see the police again, I suppose. I'll go to see them, give them a bit more of a description and see if that can kick-start the investigation into Stef's murder. We know he is still out there now, still in Sheffield. The police might have a better chance of catching him if I can give them more of an idea of what he looks like. They might even be able to pick him up on CCTV. There must be hundreds of cameras around this part of town.'

'So you will be calling on the police to re-open the investigation?'

'I don't suppose it ever really closed but they might be able to get some fresh leads from this, give it a bit of momentum. If we can get a better description out there, somebody might recognise him. Somebody will know who he is. If you could put something in your report appealing for people to come forward, that would be a huge help.'

John looked over the reporter's shoulder and saw, across the marquee, that Dean Stone and his entourage were getting ready to leave.

'Richard, I must go and have a word with Dean before he leaves. Have you got everything you want?'

The reporter nodded again. 'That's great thanks, John. I've spoken to Dean myself and I've got some good quotes from Mike and the leader of the council and from a few of the people in the crowd. It should make a nice piece.'

'Great.' John was already breaking away from their conversation to make sure he could intercept Dean. 'And you won't write anything that makes me look like a knob, will you?'

'I don't do that sort of thing,' said the reporter as his subject backed away. He had his story. He quickly dialled through to the office to suggest to the night editor that he might want to rethink his plans for the next day's edition.

Dean was walking towards the door when John caught him up and put his hand on the actor's shoulder. He looked around and smiled broadly.

'Here he is – it's Johnny Storm!' he said and slapped John on the upper arm. 'All right there, pal? If you'd have said it was a race I'd have gone into training.'

His jocularity did not make John feel any less embarrassed.

'I'm really sorry about that, Dean. I hope I didn't flick any bits of coal on you.'

'I should think about half the people here copped for a bit of it! Hey, you want to watch out for that big lad on the microphone. He's looking for you. I think you burnt three holes in his hoodie.' He slapped John on the arm again. 'Seriously, buddy, don't worry about it. Funniest thing I've seen in ages, to be honest.'

John felt relieved. The thought that he might have upset the star guest horrified him.

'That's good of you to say and thanks again for giving up your time to do all this for us tonight.' He reached out to offer a handshake. Dean grabbed it firmly. 'It really is appreciated.'

'No problem. Look, I'm going to do a bit of press while the car is brought around but good luck with everything with the charity. You've got my contacts now and if there's anything I can do for you in the future, get in touch and I'll help out if I can.'

'Much appreciated.'

With that, Dean Stone gave John a wink and was gone.

Jas and Stella had returned. Jas had regained her colour and Stella was holding the hand of her youngest son. As John reached them, Stella gave a reassuring smile and left them, walking towards where Mike and Jamie seemed to be getting along famously.

'Are you feeling better?'

'Mmm, yes,' said Jas. 'I'm glad you managed to see Dean before he left to say thank you again.'

'Yeah, he said we should get in touch if there's anything else we want from him, which was nice. He was very good about the whole running thing.'

'He was actually really good when it happened as well. Everybody was a bit shocked when you set off and there were lots of people making sure they hadn't got bits of coal on their clothes and so on but he stepped up and got their attention again, then did the walk and took his time coming back to the marquee signing autographs and doing selfies. He was really brilliant.'

'He turned out to be a top bloke.'

'Yeah, he did.'

There was a moment of quiet between them before Jas decided they had skirted around the issue for long enough.

'Are you really sure it was him?'

'As sure as I can be. There was this connection between us and that's what makes me feel it really was him. It's hard to explain it but I felt pretty certain at the time.'

'Are you going to tell the police?'

'First thing in the morning. I'll go down there and tell them everything I remember and I'll look through their books of mug shots, if they still do that sort of thing. This could bring them closer to catching him, Jas. At last.'

She dipped her hands into her coat pockets and tensed her shoulders, as if a shiver had gone through her soul.

'I hope so. Catch the bastard and string him up.'

There was no point in his arguing. He understood what she was feeling. He put his arm around her and drew her close in a comforting cuddle.

'Come on, let's get you home.'

He spent much of Saturday morning in the police station, telling them about the previous evening's experience and overseeing as they put together an e-fit picture. They could not quite get it to look as he wanted it to, but he reckoned the final effort was close enough.

He called Jas on his way back to the car.

'Have you seen a paper yet?' she asked, after he had delivered his update.

'Nooo, not yet,' he replied, warily.

'They've done a really nice job. You should pick one up while you're in town. You need to get online when you get home as well because this whole thing last night has gone mad. You wouldn't believe how many people have put footage and pictures on social media and you've already got thousands of views on YouTube. The clip has been in the top five most viewed on the BBC and the ITV websites all day. You've gone viral, John!'

He did not greet the news with the same enthusiasm. He'd have preferred the whole matter to go away quietly.

'I've had loads of calls and emails from press wanting to interview you. What do you want me to do about them?'

He sighed. It wasn't going to go away quietly. 'I'll talk to the people who bothered to respond and help us out when you sent out the original press release but not the rest. They can bugger off. Send me through some numbers and I'll call them when I get home.'

They ended the call. John felt self-conscious and turned up the collar of his coat. On the corner of the street was a heavily wrapped-up older man sitting behind a small red stand who was selling newspapers. A bill poster attached to the front of the stand read: 'Man Chases Friend's Killer.' He walked over to buy a copy and unfolded it to look at the front page.

'I SPOTTED MY MATE'S KILLER' said the headline, underneath a slightly blurry picture of John chasing over the coals, a half-crazed look on his face, sending sparks and black smoke spraying over the people behind him. Many of them were recoiling, the flat palms of their hands up in a reflex reaction to stop themselves from being hit by debris. He could pick out Dean Stone in the background, turned to his side with his leg held up for protection and an expression of utter bemusement on his face.

'Oh my god,' John said to himself. Then he read the sub-head, in smaller type:

'Firerunner John says he was chasing a murderer as sparks fly at Dean Stone charity event.'

Firerunner? Oh, I see. A bit contrived, but OK.

He folded up the newspaper, stuffed it in his pocket and scurried away, before he was recognised.

He tried to be accommodating with all his interviewers, even those who seemed to him to be angling for him to commit to a 'Mr Bean tries his hand at being a vigilante' line, but it was wearying to go over the same story so many times, answering the same questions, and he looked forward to returning to the normal rhythms of the workplace on Monday.

'Morning, Mr Baldwin.'

'Morning, Julie.'

He tapped the code into the security keypad and walked through to the main office floor, ready to greet the usual people the usual way but no one wanted to catch his eye. They busied themselves as if he was not there. OK, perhaps just as well. He carried on walking towards his office.

As he put his hand on the door handle and pushed down, a single voice yelled out from behind him.

'Stop that man!'

If the massed laughter all around the office was not enough to make John aware he had walked into a well-planned set-up, the sight as his office door swung open surely did.

On the back wall facing him, A4-sized sheets of paper, each with a single letter printed on it, spelled out the words: STOP THAT MAN. Other sheets, many of them bearing the same sentence and others filled with blown-up still pictures of John in full flight, the type of which he had seen quite enough of on social media all weekend, were stuck randomly to the walls, his seat, his desk and even his plant.

Great, he thought. Now I've got a catchphrase.

There was only one thing for it. He set down his bag and turned to face his tormentors. They cheered and applauded, so he walked between them, holding out his hands for high-fives. When he reached the smirking Stella, he grabbed her and kissed her, provoking more applause and a single wolf whistle. Then he turned to face the rest of them and they quietened as he prepared to speak.

'I want you to know that I regard this as a wanton misuse of company resources.'

They cheered and applauded again.

'Thank you, everybody. My public humiliation is now complete. Thank you again.'

He walked back to his office, exchanging more high-fives. The noise of cheering was replaced by a buzz of mutual appreciation at a job well done as he disappeared behind his door and looked around again. It must have taken them ages. It didn't seem right to begin dismantling it at once, so he removed the sheet from his chair, peeled off another from his computer screen and sat down. The weekend post had already been put on his desk so, while the computer started up, he began to open his mail.

The fourth one he opened contained a single sheet of paper. He unfolded it and all the happy feeling of the morning's reception disappeared from him like air rushing out of a balloon. He put down the sheet on the desk and then picked it up again to make sure he had read it right.

Three short sentences, in block capitals and clearly printed off a computer, stared back at him.

WE NO YOUR A KILLER
WERE COMING AFTER YOU
JARVO WILL BE REVENGED

17

'It doesn't say much for the education standards in this country, that's for sure.'

DC Harrison put the note, now in a clear plastic police evidence bag, back down on the table of the customer consultation room. John was glad that DC Harrison had been on duty and was able to come down himself to collect the note. Having had to start his story from scratch with an unfamiliar officer on Saturday, it was a relief to see someone who knew the background to this case. It was also a comfort.

Being threatened through the post had shaken him. He was aware that there were plenty of people out there whose attitude to casual violence was much different to his own but he had managed to steer well clear of them for most of his life. Up until the last year or so, anyway. This was a type of danger he had never known before and he needed the reassurance of being able to enlist the protection of someone more familiar with it.

'What should I do?' he asked.

'I'd certainly be a lot more vigilant for a while,' said the policeman. 'These sorts of threats are often just that – threats. If there is somebody out there who really wanted to get you, they will usually just get on with it rather than writing to you to tell you about it. We do treat these matters very seriously because you can never dismiss them as just threats, but my instinct here is that they're just trying to put the wind up you.'

John stood up, still feeling agitated. 'In that case, they've succeeded.'

'I know it's easier said than done, but don't let it stop you going about your normal life. If you do see anything suspicious or spot anyone you don't know hanging around your house or workplace, though, give us a call immediately. I'll give you a card with all the emergency numbers so you can put them in your phone or you can always call my number direct. If you get another one of these through the post, again, give us a call straightaway. If it comes with the same sort of printed address on the envelope and you think it's from the same source, call us before you open it.'

'Yes I will.' John sat down again. 'Do you think you'll be able to get anything off this letter to help you?'

The officer picked up the bag again and pulled a face. 'Doubt it, to be honest. I'll pass it on and see if we can get any prints off it but I'd be surprised if they were thick enough to handle it without gloves. It must have been a lot more interesting in the old days when they used to send notes put together from bits cut out from a newspaper. At least then you would be able to work out if they were a *Sun* reader or *Daily Mail* reader. These days, any idiot can print one off from a computer.' He looked at the note wistfully, as if lamenting a golden age that this modern imitator could not measure up to.

'What we do have is a pretty comprehensive list of known associates of our late and not-so- lamented Mr Jarvis, so that's a decent starting point. We'll look into it all we can but, mostly, as far as you are concerned, it's just a matter of keeping your wits about you for potential danger.'

John shuffled uncomfortably in his seat. 'I will.' He rose again. 'Thanks for coming down, DC Harrison.' He held out his hand.

'Tom.' They shook hands. 'I could also say something about you keeping a low profile but from what I've seen all over the telly and the papers this weekend, I think I might be a bit too late there.'

'Oh yes, that.' John smiled sheepishly. 'It did go a bit mad, didn't it?'

'Seriously, though, it's not a good idea to go chasing after felons like that. You have to leave that sort of thing to us. You could have been putting yourself in a very dangerous situation. What if you had caught him? What then?'

'I know. I wasn't really thinking it through at the time. It was an instinctive thing.'

'The same applies if you see anything suspicious you think might be connected to this letter. Don't confront them, whatever you do. Call us.'

John opened the door for the policeman to leave. 'Rest assured that the only running I'll be doing if I think these people are coming for me is very quickly and in the opposite direction.'

On his way back to the office, his phone rang.

'Hello, John Baldwin.'

'Good morning, Mr Baldwin, this is Detective Sergeant Reece from Sheffield CID.'

'I'm afraid you've just missed him.'

'Sorry?'

'Your DC Harrison. He's just left.'

There was a short silence at the other end of the line.

'I think we must be a little at cross purposes here,' said the slightly perplexed detective.

They wouldn't be calling me to talk to their own officer, would they? That must have sounded like a really thick thing to say.

'I'm sorry but I've just been talking to DC Harrison about an issue and I thought...never mind. How can I help you?'

'Oh, I see. I'm actually calling in regard to a complaint of an alleged assault committed by you against a Craig Christopher Thomas on December the 17th. I believe you have been made fully aware of the circumstances of the complaint.'

John knew this call was coming but with everything else that had been happening over the last couple of weeks, he had put it to the back of his mind. *Jesus, it never rains.*

'Yes, I'm aware.'

'Then you should know that we are in the process of collating evidence regarding the complaint before it is passed to the Crown Prosecution Service for them to make a judgement on whether or not to proceed with a prosecution. As part of that process, we would like to make an appointment for you to come to the station to give us your statement.'

'I already gave my statement after the original incident. I told you everything.'

'I understand that, Mr Baldwin, but this is now being treated as a separate offence and so we would need to go through it with you again. You'll be interviewed under caution this time, so we would recommend you have a solicitor present. If you haven't got a legal representative, we can arrange for one to be present for you.'

'That's OK. I've got a solicitor. When do you need me to come down?'

Bloody hell! I might qualify for my own car parking space soon.

'Sometime in the next couple of days would be appreciated.'

Friday was out because he was going down to London to see Gregory Fredericks with Mike and Jas. It would have to be before then.

'I'll have to talk to my solicitor to make sure he's available. Can we make it Wednesday or Thursday? I'll call you when I know which day.'

'That was about it really.' John took a second bite from the sausage and tomato sandwich he had hastily bought just before the train arrived and chewed warily. It might not have been so bad an idea to skip breakfast altogether. He tried to mask the after-taste with a slurp of cappuccino.

'So you've not been arrested?' Mike asked. He and Jas sat across the table. John found it hard not to feel as if he was being interviewed again.

'No. It was an interview under caution, that's what they called it. The process is they look at the evidence and hand it all over to the CPS. From what I understand, the CPS has to decide if there's enough evidence to prosecute first off but then they have to decide if it's in the public interest as well. It's like if someone breaks into your home and you catch them trying to nick your telly and the burglar gets injured as you try to stop him making off with it. Strictly speaking, you've assaulted him but the law has to decide if you were using reasonable force in the situation or if you were acting to defend yourself or someone else. That's how the law protects people acting in the way I did when you come across nasty little scrotes like Craig Thomas and his mate.'

'And your solicitor says that's why the CPS won't prosecute.' Jas was wearing her concerned look.

'That's what he says. He said he couldn't see how the CPS would want to take somebody to court for basically coming to the aid of a man being attacked, especially seeing as the attack was racially motivated. He doesn't think the CPS would want to be seen to be sending out the wrong message.'

'Hope not. Was he badly hurt, this Thomas bloke?'

Mike's question made John wince. He had, in truth, been shocked at what he had done when the extent of the injuries were read out in the interview. He hadn't thought he was capable of inflicting so much physical harm on anyone.

'Er, fairly badly. Depressed fracture of the cheekbone, hairline fracture around the eye socket, a couple of cuts that needed stitches and a ruptured testicle.'

It was Mike's turn to wince. 'Ouch! Remind me not to get into an argument with you the next time we have a budget meeting.'

'I didn't think I'd hurt him that much.' John shuffled uncomfortably. 'I kind of jumped on his chest after the kick to the balls had put him on the ground and the rest of it was a bit of a blur. It was all a bit frenzied, in truth. So much anger was coming out and he just happened to be in the firing line. I didn't put it like that to the police, of course, but I was out of control. If his mate hadn't sent me flying with a kick to the ribs, Christ knows what I might have done to him. Perhaps I do deserve to be prosecuted for that.'

Jas reached across the table and touched his hand. 'He had it coming to him. You're not the guilty one here. You were so brave to put yourself at risk to save somebody else. I'm proud of what you did.'

'Too right,' added Mike.

'Thanks. Anyway, let's not talk about that anymore.' John screwed up his nose at the prospect of finishing his sausage sandwich and wrapped the last third of it in a paper serviette instead. 'We've got a big day ahead of us.'

They had caught the train to get them to St Pancras at just before 11.30am, allowing plenty of time to negotiate the Tube to London Bridge station. The appointment was at 12.30 and they had been told the walk to the offices of Callaloo Enterprises was only five minutes from the underground stop.

They were heading for the banks of the Thames and, with time to spare, they wandered across the piazza at the centre of a cluster of modern office blocks, having identified the one they were looking for, to take a closer look at the river. To their left was HMS *Belfast*, the old fighting ship, still imposing and dignified in retirement. The always impressive Tower Bridge, instantly recognisable as a symbol of the city's majesty, was to their right, leading to the brooding Tower of London on the opposite bank. Though he had never wished to live there, visiting London had never lost its capacity to thrill, as far as John was concerned. Amid the perpetual bustle and noise of the busy modern city, there was always an opportunity to escape to somewhere wondrous and historically significant. He loved that.

Jas took a picture on her phone of the three of them with Tower Bridge as the backdrop and then Mike suggested they go to make themselves known at Reception.

Up the four shallow steps from the piazza, they passed through one of the two large revolving doors and stepped into the reception area of the building. The heels of Jas' shoes clicked on the dark grey tiled floor. Dominating the wall to their right was a huge TV screen, easily eight feet high and almost twice as wide, which was showing a rolling news programme with sub-titles, though the newsreader's voice could be faintly heard above the noise of the activity on the main floor. On the opposite side of the room were two red sofas and matching chairs set around two low tables which had newspapers and magazines scattered over them. The walls were black with sparkling flecks which looked like a million distant stars and a silver board upon it detailed which companies occupied which floors within the building. Callaloo Enterprises, they already knew from the address on the card, was on the third floor.

The reception desk was towards the right, about two-thirds of the way across the floor. Three members of staff, two women and a man, smartly dressed and wearing ID badges on lanyards around their necks, sat behind the desk. John headed to the one who was not already dealing with other visitors; a young woman with her dark hair scraped back into a tight ponytail beneath her phone headset.

'Excuse me, we've come to see Gregory Fredericks at Callaloo Enterprises,' he said.

'Have you got an appointment?' she replied without looking up from the computer screen and without stopping tapping on her keyboard.

'Yes, 12.30.'

'Name please.'

'Baldwin.'

She stopped typing and speedily pressed four numbers on the phone keypad. As she waited for the call to be answered, she typed a few more commands into the computer.

'I have a Mr Baldwin to see Mr Fredericks. OK, thanks.' She hung up and looked up at John for the first time. 'Someone will be down to collect you in a few minutes. Could I ask you to sign in for me? How many are there of you?'

John glanced around at his two colleagues. 'Three.' Perhaps she was too busy to do the calculation herself.

She slapped a clipboard and a pen onto the upper level of the split-tier desk. 'Could you all fill in your details for me, please?' While John picked up the pen and started writing his name, she opened the drawer to her right and began to untangle three visitors' passes.

John passed the pen to Jas while the receptionist returned to her typing and Mike had also signed in by the time a young man in a blue suit stepped up behind the reception desk.

'Mr Baldwin?' He looked between John and Mike, waiting for enlightenment.

'Yes, that's me.'

'Oh hi!' The young man smiled broadly and shot out his hand. 'I'm Oscar, Mr Fredericks' assistant.' He shook John's hand vigorously and then offered the same to Jas and Mike with a smile and a 'hi'.

'Have you signed in already?' He peered at the list on the clipboard. 'Good. If you could just grab a visitors' pass each, I'll take you up.'

John picked up the passes from where the receptionist had put them down and handed them out. He turned back to her and muttered 'thank you', without acknowledgement.

Oscar had made his way to the three sets of waist-high glass security doors, which opened with a beep as a steady stream of people touched their passes to the card reader, and was waiting for them with a cheerful face. Two tall and sturdy security men, in black suits and red ties, watched the flow of people through the gates, their hands clasped behind their backs. The three touched their visitors' passes against the reader and were beeped through to where Oscar was already waiting eagerly to usher them towards the lifts.

One of the lifts was already at ground level and they stepped inside. Oscar pressed the button for the third floor and the doors closed.

'Have you met Mr Fredericks before?'

'I have. Just the once,' replied John.

'He's an exceptionally nice man,' offered Oscar.

'A very handy employer if you are looking for concert tickets as well, I should imagine.'

'Absolutely. He handles all the big names. Promotes, manages, produces – I don't know how he finds the energy and, do you know, he still always finds the time to make sure everybody who works for him feels special and that they are all playing an important role in the organisation.'

'You must enjoy working here then.'

'I love it. I never want to leave.'

The lift doors opened and they followed Oscar's brisk pace down the corridor to their left. He held open a door to the right for them to walk through into a small but lively open-plan office space and led them towards the corner office. He tapped on the door and poked his head around it.

'Your visitors are here,' he said and then turned back to his three escorts, opening the door wider for them to go through.

Gregory was already out from behind his desk and on his way across his office with arms out wide. A smart grey checked waistcoat, matching his trousers, restrained his generous waistline and beneath it he wore a jade green shirt. He was shorter than John recalled but, then again, this was the first time he had seen Gregory on his feet, apart from at a distance in the gloomy dark of that back street. His broad smile lit up the room as he stepped towards John with purpose. There was no avoiding the hug.

'John, how are you doing, my brother?'

They patted each other on the back and parted, though Gregory kept his hands around John's upper arms. 'It is so good to see you again.'

'You too, Gregory. Thankfully, you look an awful lot better than the last time.'

He laughed. 'That would not have been very hard.' Gregory glanced to where the other two were standing back, not wishing to intrude on the reunion. John stepped out of the embrace.

'Gregory, this is Jas Grewal. She's a freelance marketing and PR specialist and has been handling that side of the operation for the charity.'

Jas held out her hand to shake but Gregory took it, bent slowly and kissed it. Her initial surprise soon turned to demure pleasure.

'May I say how beautiful you look?'

'You may. Thank you very much.'

'You have to be so careful these days in case you cause offence. How can it be offensive to pay someone a compliment?'

Jas was clearly not finding it a problem.

'And this is Mike Wilshaw. Mike's the founder of the GameOn Trust and a former professional cricketer.'

'Really,' said Gregory and shook Mike's hand warmly. 'Have you ever been on tour to the West Indies?'

'Unfortunately not. I was never good enough to play internationally but I did get the chance to play against just about all the international sides when they toured over here. As a matter of fact, Jimmy Adams gave me my maiden first-class wicket in 1995.'

Gregory looked impressed. 'Good player – and a Jamaican, too.'

'Indeed. I should add that he was caught on the boundary but it doesn't say that in the scorebook,' added Mike, self-effacingly.

'It still counts. Did you know I grew up in the same area of Kingston as Courtney Walsh? We are both Half Way Tree boys. We played in the same high school team at Excelsior. I taught him all he knows!' Gregory laughed heartily at his own joke.

He noticed Jas was smiling politely at an exchange she felt she had nothing to contribute to. 'I could talk about cricket all day but you didn't come here to speak about that. Please, have a seat.'

They took up the three chairs set out for them while Gregory turned to go back to the other side of his desk. 'Hey!' he suddenly spun and pointed at John.

'I was told our mutual friend got sent to jail.'

John nodded. 'Four and a half years.'

'I hope he never gets out of there and, as for the other one, I hope he rots in Hell.'

John felt a momentary pang of anxiety as the memory of the letter popped back into his consciousness. He hadn't told the others about it yet. Maybe on the way home.

'So you wanted to ask me about putting on a concert.' Gregory was smiling warmly again. His moods swung a little but his bad moments didn't appear to linger long.

'Well.' John had been nominated to take the lead in putting forward their case. 'As you know, we're looking to establish a new charity called the GameOn Trust with the aim of helping young people and their families from underprivileged backgrounds. We're starting small by giving kids in Sheffield opportunities in sport, adventure weekends, that sort of thing, but, in time, we're aiming to help people from a wider area and expand the scope of what we can offer to education and training but all of this, of course, needs funding. We have a brochure that we've been handing out to potential corporate sponsors.'

Prompted, Mike reached into his case and handed over a brochure to Gregory, who thumbed through it as John continued to talk.

'One of the fundraising ideas we had was to put on a music concert. We've had an early idea for a name – A Gig for GameOn.'

'Gig for GameOn,' nodded Gregory, appreciatively, still looking at the brochure. 'Not bad.'

'That was one of Jas' ideas.' She gave a coy half-smile at Gregory as he looked up at her.

'What we don't have is any experience or knowledge of what it takes to put on a small concert. That's where we were hoping you might be able to help out. We're not talking about anything big here, nothing on the scale of some of the huge events you've put on in the past. We were thinking maybe three or four acts, a venue that can hold a few hundred or so, that sort of thing.'

Gregory was nodding but was not looking at the three expectant faces in front of him. He put down the brochure and stared straight at John.

'I think you can do better than that.' He stood up and peered out through the big picture window as a red and white sightseeing boat chugged slowly along the brown water.

John looked at Mike. Jas looked at John. They had thought a low-key approach to selling their idea would be the best way. Keep it friendly. Maybe they had misjudged Gregory.

He talked with his back to them. They could see the towers of Tower Bridge through the window behind him. 'Do you remember when we last met?'

'Of course,' said John.

'The reason I was in Sheffield was to talk to the council people there. We have been in negotiation about putting on a huge summer festival next year; three days of many of the top acts in the world at a central venue in one of the big parks with four satellite venues around the city, staging a diverse range of music for all tastes. The aim was to make it one of the biggest festivals in Europe and, in time, make it *the* biggest.'

He turned around to face them again. 'The reason I slipped away from my minder, Jermaine, and was out on the streets so late when you met me that first time was because I felt like celebrating. We had signed the deal that day. The festival is going to be announced next week.'

'Wow!' said John.

'So let me tell you what I can do for you.' Gregory wandered back to his seat. 'I will put on your charity concert for you this summer. We can make it an outdoor event and that will give us the chance to make it a bit of a test run. We'll use it to generate publicity for the main event next year and put on maybe six or seven good acts, plus put word out that there will be a mystery special guest performing. All our share of the profit from that event will go to you. Then I will make you a preferred charity partner for the main festival itself, which will allow you privileges you can use to make money from, and I will sign over a small percentage of the overall profits from the festival. How does that sound?'

There was silence. None of them could quite believe what they were hearing.

'Amazing,' said Jas, finally.

'Good. That's done then. I'll go and speak to one of my assistants now and make some arrangements for the rest of the day. What time are you planning to catch the train home?'

'Er, just after eight,' said Mike.

'Perfect. My assistant will give you a tour to show you what we do here, then we will sit you down with the people who are in charge of this festival project so that you can find out all about it and I'll assign someone to work with you to organise your charity concert. They will be able to talk you through what it entails and answer all your questions but you will be leaving all the arrangements with them because they know what they are doing. After that, I'll take you to a place that serves the best West Indian food in London and we will eat before I have someone drive you to catch your train home. Does that sound OK?'

'Sounds, well…wonderful,' said John.

Gregory clapped his hands once and stood to leave the office. As the door closed behind him, the three of them looked at each other, wide-eyed and dumbstruck.

'Well, what do you think?' asked Mike at last. 'Should we accept his terms?'

The others nodded slowly, as if weighing up their options.

'He did say it would only be a *small* percentage of the profits,' said Jas.

'I noticed that,' added John. 'I think we ought to hold out for twenty-five per cent or we withdraw our support.'

They nodded sagely at each other before Jas began to giggle. They were still laughing, like kids on the back row of the bus, when Gregory returned to his office.

18

They instructed the taxi driver to make Jas's house the first stop-off point from the train station. As it pulled up, Jas turned to her two fellow passengers.

'I was thinking, Dean Stone is on the *Noel Walker Show* tonight.' She glanced at her watch. 'It's only just started, how do you fancy coming in to watch it?'

John was in no hurry to get back to his flat. 'Yeah, why not?'

'I'll pass, if you don't mind,' said Mike. 'I'd like to get home. It's been a long day.'

'Sure?' Jas asked.

He nodded.

John reached for his wallet to make a contribution towards the taxi fare but Mike intervened.

'No, this one's on me. Today was incredible. Thanks, both of you, for everything you've done. This is way beyond anything I imagined we could achieve in so short a time. I'll give you a ring to talk about when we can get together next but we've done some tremendous work today.'

They said their goodbyes and the two of them got out of the taxi, then waited as Mike was driven away.

As they stepped up to the gate, John asked, casually: 'Did you get to shag Dean Stone in the end?'

Her face and tone was indignation itself. 'No!'

She opened the gate and stepped onto the short path. 'I might do, though, if you manage to get it on with Scarlett.'

Actually, he hadn't reprimanded her yet about giving up that detail on the night of the firewalk. 'Yeah, what on earth did you want to tell him that for, by the way?'

She shrugged. 'I don't know. I suppose I got excited and it slipped out.'

125

They walked to the front door and Jas opened her bag to find her keys.

John chuckled.

'What?' she asked.

'Nothing. Just a thought. It's my brain. It's nothing.' He lowered his head to try to disguise the wide smirk on his face.

She was not about to let that pass. 'Tell me.'

'Honestly, it's nothing. You wouldn't like it.'

'Baldwin!' She gripped his forearm to add a physical element to the mock threat in her tone. 'Tell me!'

'OK, OK.'

She eased the grip.

'It's just when you said about getting excited and it slipping out. I was going to ask if that's what Dean said as well.'

'John!' She shot him a chastening look and thumped him on the arm.

He rubbed it, smiling mischievously, as she put the key in the lock. 'That really hurt.'

'Good.' The intruder alarm began to beep as she opened the door. 'You deserved it.'

He rubbed his arm again, relishing the rebuke. 'Told you that you wouldn't like it.'

They took off their coats and Jas took them to hang up.

'Do you want something to drink?'

'Just some water please.'

She picked up the remote control and the TV sparked into life. She scrolled to the menu and made her selection.

'I'm going to have a glass of wine, do you mind?'

'Of course not.'

John sat down on the sofa. The first guest was already being introduced. John vaguely recognised him as some sort of celebrity chef.

Jas placed a glass of iced water on a coaster in front of John and put her wine on another before sitting on the sofa beside him. Noel was introducing his next guest – an actress neither of them had heard of – and she jiggled out of the lurid orange background in a perilously low-cut black dress.

'Good god, look at her! I hope that tit tape holds out.'

John was looking but he didn't share Jas' concern for the adhesive qualities of the tape.

Dean Stone was next to be roared onto the stage and he took the seat on the sofa closest to the host. He looked comfortable in his surroundings but not completely at ease. It seemed weird to see him in full celebrity mode so soon after meeting him in much more casual surroundings.

The banter was soon in full swing, with Noel pulling the strings and getting the biggest laughs from an enthusiastic audience. Around ten minutes in, he spoke directly to Dean, who had been a little on the periphery of the conversation so far. He asked about the new film.

'And you've plainly developed a bit of a taste for fiery danger, haven't you, Dean? Tell us about how you were sprayed with red-hot coals this week.'

Jas nudged John and set down her glass. She leaned forward and turned up the volume, listening intently. He began to fear he was about to be exposed to a whole new level of public ridicule.

'It wasn't planned that way but yeah. I did a firewalk for a charity while I was back home for a few days and it was an interesting experience, shall we say.'

'Well,' said Noel. 'I think we should have a look.' The screen filled with the TV footage of the firewalk.

'Oh Christ!' said John.

A woman in a black sweatshirt walked over the coals and the man in an orange shirt waited his turn. John watched himself standing stock still a yard further back, transfixed. He had avoided looking at the footage since the night. From what Jas had told him, that made him just about the only person in the world who had not seen it. Now a few million were about to re-live it with him.

'So we can see you there, Dean. You look really up for it, I must say. I'm not sure I'd be so keen. There must be better ways of treating your verrucas.'

John watched as Dean patted him on the back and he stepped tentatively forward.

'Hold on. This bloke doesn't look like he fancies it. Whoaaaa!'

The audience shrieked as John's arm shot out, his mouth opened in a yell to the near distance and he set off at a furious pace, scattering fragments of glowing coals everywhere and making everyone around him duck and cover up. It looked worse than he thought it would and John held his hands to his face. Jas touched his arm supportively but made no effort to save him from his suffering. She appeared to find it terribly funny.

'What was that all about?' asked Noel, struggling to make his voice heard above the reaction from the audience.

'I was a bit surprised myself,' said Dean.

'I mean, did he not understand what it entailed? It is fire*walking*. The clue's in the name. What was it that made him set off like that? Did you ask?'

Dean shuffled in his seat. 'I did hear about it later. Apparently, he saw somebody who he thought had murdered one of his friends.'

'Oh my gosh!' said the actress.

'Are we sure about this?' Noel wasn't about to let the mood change. 'That sounds like a bit of a dog-ate-my-homework type of excuse to me. He could have just seen a bloke who owed him a fiver.'

'By the looks of him, he could have seen that the burger van was just leaving,' chimed in the chef.

John looked down at his waist. He had lost about a stone since he had stopped drinking, but there was still a bit of a roll above his belt.

'Bit harsh,' he said.

Jas was in hysterics. 'Stop that van!' she managed to splutter out between breaths.

'And did he manage to catch this mysterious man in the crowd?' asked Noel.

'Not so far as I know,' answered Dean. 'I think he might have been hallucinating.'

'What are you saying, Dean?' Noel knitted his brow. 'Are you suggesting they were burning something else on that fire apart from coal?'

Eventually, the conversation moved on and John's colour began to return to normal. Jas wiped the tears from the corners of her eyes with the back of her hands and took another sip of wine. 'Oh, that was so funny,' she said.

John looked at her and smiled. It was good to see her so happy, even if it had been at his expense. His phone beeped with an incoming text message and he reached into his pocket to retrieve it.

'Who's it from?' asked Jas.

'Stella.' He sighed. 'Are you watching Noel Walker, colon, closed bracket, maybe we should have put "stop that van" on the posters.'

'That's what I said! How spooky is that?'

'Great minds.' John began typing his reply, trying to come up with a form of words less acerbic than the tone of his verbal response.

'Poor John!' Jas said and gently touched his face. 'Just think, a few weeks ago you were an unknown ordinary bloke who worked in a building society and now you're having the piss taken out of you on one of the most popular shows on television. What's it like to be so famous?'

He chuckled quietly. 'A bit surreal, to be honest.'

'Seriously, though,' Jas put her glass back on the coaster and sat up straight. 'Do you think about everything that's happened in the last couple of months?'

John pressed send and the message went on its way with a whoosh. 'All the time.'

'I mean, up until that day you came knocking on my door we hadn't seen each other in literally ages, neither of us had met Mike and had no idea about his plan for starting up a charity, we had never heard of Gregory and Dean Stone was just somebody we saw in films and on the telly.'

'It's true.'

'But now look. You're back to the John I knew before Stef died and you've found a lovely new girlfriend and a bizarre combination of fate and circumstances have led us to all these fabulous new people and made it possible for us to become involved in a cause that – well, who knows how big it might become and how many people's lives it could improve? How did all this happen? It surely can't all be coincidence. There's got to be a reason for it.'

'I completely agree.' John was watching Jas intently, but she was not really paying much attention back. He got the impression she was getting something off her chest that she had been thinking through for a while. He started to feel like he knew where the conversation was heading.

'Do you know what I think? I think it's Stef. I think he's looking down on us and taking care of us. I know you don't believe in that sort of thing but I think it's the only explanation. I think we've still got Stef in our lives.'

She looked at him at last, waiting for his reaction. He shrugged and nodded. There was no point trying to put her off the scent. She was a smart woman and had figured it out. He was always going to tell her when he felt brave enough and had told himself he would know when the time was right. It looked as if the time had come.

'I think so too.'

She appeared surprised by his answer. 'Do you really?'

He nodded again. 'I do.'

'I'm really glad you've said that, John, because I wanted to tell you what I'd like to do and I didn't want you to think I'm being stupid.' She took his hand. 'I want to go to see a spiritualist. You know, a clairvoyant. Not one of those people who set themselves up at fairs or on Blackpool seafront, a proper one. I want to see if they can put me in touch with Stef again. What do you think? Am I being stupid?'

He could see in her eyes that she was desperate for his support. Desperate for someone to understand why she needed the answers she was looking for. Desperate to put her mind at ease at last. Desperate to connect with the love of her life again.

He wanted her to find her solace in the same way as he had found his. Her way was not the way.

'You're not being stupid, Jas. I understand what you're going through, honestly I do, but you don't need to go to a spiritualist. You see, I don't only *think* Stef is looking out for us, I *know* he is.'

His certainty silenced her. She had anticipated John would disapprove of the spiritualist plan but not in this way. What did he mean *know*?

'Do you remember when I came around to see you for the first time in all those months? I asked you if I could have some time in Stef's study alone? Do you remember that?'

It wasn't a detail Jas had especially remembered about the day. The fact that John appeared at all, out of the blue, was all she really recalled, but she nodded.

'It was because I was looking for something. Something I didn't know was there until the day before. Let me show you.'

He stood, and led her up the stairs. As they got closer to the study, she hesitated, suddenly wary without understanding why.

He sensed her reluctance. 'It's OK.'

She followed him through the door. Everything was just as it always was, every other time she had stepped into the room to clean, taking comfort as she ran her fingers over the books and photos and files, taking care to leave everything just the way she found it.

John looked around and tried to recall which of the files he was looking for. He got down on his knees and peered at the stacked box files and document wallets under the desk. Which one, which one? The dark blue one. Old tax returns. That's the one. He pulled it out and opened the catch, thumbing through the individually divided folders until he came to the one that had a small red box concealed at the bottom of it.

He stood and, without touching the box, held the file open for Jas to see. She peered in and then looked up, back into John's eyes. She was confused.

'It's fine, Jas. Here, take it out.'

Cautiously, she reached in and took out the box, then looked again at John.

'Open it. It's yours.'

She prised open the lid of the box and the sparkle of the stones under the ceiling light took her breath. She stared at the gold band and gently moved the box so that the diamonds glistened in turn. It was beautiful, but what...? Her hand began to shake and her legs felt weak. She propped herself against the arm of the office chair and then lowered herself into it, still gazing at the ring, unable to take her eyes off it.

John put down the file and crouched down to be at Jas' eye level. She was lost. He wanted to tell her everything.

'Did Stef say anything about going away for Christmas?'

She thought, snapping out of the enchantment the ring had cast on her. 'Yes. Yes, he did. He told me we were going to leave on Christmas Eve and come back the day after Boxing Day but he wouldn't tell me where we were going. He liked surprises.'

'He was going to take you to Scarborough.' She peered hard at John. *How does he know that? Scarborough?* That was where Stef took her on their first weekend away, not long after they started going out together. They had such a fantastic time. The old Victorian hotel, overlooking the long curve of South Shore beach, was beautiful, the weather baking hot and whenever she dreamily recollected it, she was able to say to herself that that was the weekend she truly knew, for the first time, that she had met the man she would love for ever.

'Jas, he was going to ask you to marry him on Christmas Day.'

He placed his hand on her arm and rubbed softly. Above anything else, that was the news he had dreaded having to break to Jas because he knew saying those words would be, at the same time, both gloriously delightful and devastatingly cruel.

She looked back at the box in her hand and burst into tears. Uncontrollable, inconsolable. John went to put his arm around her but the gesture felt hopelessly inadequate. She sobbed, the gold and diamonds glinting through the wash of her tears. There was no point in his doing or saying anything until she had allowed the emotion to flood out, as it had to.

Finally, she was composed enough to be able to speak.

'You knew about all this? Scarborough? The proposal? You knew and you didn't say anything to me for all this time?' There was anger and frustration in her voice.

'Not quite all the time. I only found out about it the day before I came round to see you in December. You see.' He bowed his head and took a deep breath. There was no easy way to say this. 'That's when Stef told me.'

Her anger burnt deeper, fuelled by this new confusion. *What is he saying? He's ripping my world apart and talking in riddles. Who the hell do you think you are, tormenting me like this? What the hell are you talking about?*

'I was on my way back to the flat after a night out – I'd been drinking heavily again – and Stef was waiting for me on the opposite side of the street. He called my name. I didn't know who it was at first, of course, but then he stepped into the light and it was him. He looked just the same as he did when we set off to go to the Phoenix that night a year earlier and he touched my arm, Jas. He touched me and I felt the weight of his hand just as if he was alive, I swear. I was pissed that night but I know I really saw him and I really felt that touch on my arm. He was as close and as real as we are now.'

Jas shrugged off his arm from her shoulder and rose sharply to her feet. She glared down at him, angry and agitated.

'What are you talking about? How can that be true? Why would Stef return from the dead just to tell you about going to Scarborough and this fucking ring?' She hurled it at him. 'You're not making any sense, John. You were out of your mind because of the fucking boozing. You're still out of your fucking mind.'

John picked up the ring, still securely in its box, and set it safely on the desk. 'That wasn't all he told me, of course. He told me he wanted to help me to save myself from what I had become since the night of the murder. He told me I should stop blaming myself for his death and that I should get my life back on track and do some good. That's why he came to me. He wanted to save my life. He *has* saved my life.'

Jas was becalmed. She was listening.

'He told me about the ring so that he could prove to me that I wasn't having some sort of alcohol-induced breakdown. Up until then, I had no idea the ring was here. You have to believe me.'

His words dissipated her fury. She wanted to believe him.

'But why did he only come to you? Why hasn't he appeared to me? Why, John?' It was an anguished appeal.

John stood and put his arms around her.

'I don't know, Jas. I really don't. I've asked myself that same question and that's partly what has stopped me from telling you all of this sooner. He wanted to save me because he said I had a new destiny and I had no idea what that meant at the time but through everything that's happened since, I'm beginning to understand. I don't know why he appeared to me and not you. I've no idea how these things work and I wish he could come to you and you could see and hold him again, but all I know is that he loved you very much and he will always be looking over you.'

She pulled away from their embrace and picked up the jewellery box. She took out the ring and eased it onto the third finger of her left hand. It fitted perfectly.

They hugged again. He held her with one arm and, with his other hand, stroked her soft dark hair as she nestled her head into his shoulder. Jas looked up at him with dark, sad eyes, hesitated and then moved to kiss him.

Their lips were together for just a moment or two too long. Dangerously long. Neither of them recoiled from it, though they both knew they should.

Jas pulled away and they gazed at each other. There they stood, silently and precariously on the edge of a deep ravine from which there would be no climbing back. The steepness of the drop was reflected in each other's eyes and they almost dared each other to step out into the black void of the new uncertain reality at their feet.

It was John who stepped away from the brink.

'Jas, I can't...we can't do this.'

'No, John, you're right. I'm so sorry, I...'

'No, I'm sorry, this is my fault.'

'It's not. I was...'

Jas turned, desperate to get away. She walked quickly down the stairs. John followed, keeping his distance. By the time he reached the bottom of the stairs, Jas was in the kitchen, rinsing out her wine glass.

'Jas, I'm so sorry. I don't know what I was thinking.'

She did not turn around.

'Just go, John. I think you should leave. I need to be on my own to think. Leave me alone.'

He felt awful. 'Can I do anything?'

She dropped the wine glass on the tiled floor and it shattered into a thousand pieces.

'Just go!' she yelled.

He had done enough. He collected his overcoat and left.

19

By around 9.30 the next morning, he reckoned he had waited long enough. It had been the longest of nights and he had barely slept. In one irrational, unguarded moment, he felt as if he had betrayed the two women in his life and was consumed by the fear that it might have cost him his relationships with them both.

How did I let it happen?

John was sure that he would not have got carried away to the point where an already regrettable situation could have escalated into an irretrievably awkward one and he felt confident Jas would not have allowed it to go that far either, but the emotional charge in that one kiss was undeniable.

He would be lying if he said he hadn't always found Jas attractive. Of course he did. She was a very beautiful woman, in every way, but she was Stef's partner and they were friends. Friends should not become lovers, not even once and by mistake. There was a line that should not be crossed because once it was, the dynamic between them would be changed forever.

What really disappointed him was that he allowed himself to stay in the moment for just that second too long. He could have just cut it short at a peck or kissed her on the cheek and then they could have told themselves it would never have been anything more than that. Then he could have stayed to support her until the whirlwind of new information he had given her had blown through and order was restored, but he had left her to deal with it alone – and had thrown in added psychological chaos for good measure. What must she have gone through after he left?

He had to talk to her and find out if she was OK.

The words he wanted to say had ricocheted around his mind all night. He ran through them again as he selected Jas' number in his directory and pressed the button to call it.

It did not even ring.

'Hi, this is Jas. I'm not available right now, please leave a message.'

He hung up. It would not have been right to say what he had to say to an answering service. She must still be angry with him and had blocked him.

I'll try again in a bit.

The next time was the same. And the time after that. And the time after that.

It was not like Jas to stay cross for so long. He began to feel concerned that her emotional state might be closer to despair than anger. He decided he should call round to the house.

The curtains, upstairs and downstairs, were open as John got out of the car and pulled up his collar against the wind and rain. He tried to decide whether that was a good or a bad sign.

He scurried up the path, hesitated long enough to draw a deep breath and then knocked on the door. There was no answer. Against the noise of the weather, it was hard to hear if there was any sound of movement inside the house, so he knocked again and waited. Nothing.

He took out his phone and called her number. Straight to answerphone again.

He stepped off the path and onto the small sodden strip of grass which barely warranted being called a front garden and cupped his hand against the glass of the front window. He saw no sign of her.

He walked round the back of the row of houses to where Jas usually parked her car. It was not there.

So he went back to his car and headed back to the flat.

John kept ringing through the afternoon and called around again. It was getting dark by then but there were no lights on in the house and still no car in the parking space.

This was really worrying. He tried to fight off his worst nagging anxiety. She couldn't have done something desperate, could she? Jas was not like that. But he knew better than most that everyone has their breaking point and maybe she had reached hers. Maybe she had taken the information he'd given her and decided that if she could no longer be with Stef in this world, she'd join him in the next. After all, hadn't John offered confirmation that Stef was there, waiting for her?

His rational mind said she had probably sought comfort from her parents or one of her sisters instead. She probably didn't want to hear from anyone outside that close protective circle right now. He could take that. As long as she was safe.

He thought about calling Jas' mum and dad just to make sure she was there but what if she wasn't? What if they had been trying to call her too? If he phoned and they didn't know where she was and they found out he didn't know where she was, he would be causing them an awful lot of anxiety as well. They might panic. They might call the police and report her missing. Then the police would want to know why she had gone missing. Then it would be a bigger mess.

And all the while he was trying to convince himself there was a perfectly reasonable explanation. She was safe and sound but just didn't want to talk to him. That was understandable. That was the most likely scenario. He just wished he knew.

Stella came to the flat that evening, which, ordinarily, he would have looked forward to immensely. He told her all about the day in London and Gregory's plan and tried to allow the excitement he had felt for so much of the previous day shine through, but she could tell he was not himself.

What could he say? He couldn't tell her what had happened because she might not have believed it had been an innocent mistake. Her marriage had ended because her husband was playing around and that had shaken her trust in men. She had told him as much. She would have dumped him, most likely, and he could not face that possibility. So he told her he was tired. He was, actually. He just didn't tell her why.

They went to bed but neither of them was really in the mood for sex. So they talked for a while longer and he pretended he was falling asleep. Then he lay, wide awake, and watched as Stella slept beside him. He could not stand the thought of losing her. He could not stand the thought of losing Jas either. Where was she?

When Stella left the next morning to pick up her sons from her parents' home, John called Jas again. It was the answering service again, and this time he left a message.

'Hi, Jas, it's me. I'm worried. I need to hear you're OK even if you don't want to talk to me. A text is all I need. Please. Thanks.'

Then he sent her a text with a similar message. He had no reply to that either. He drove around to the house again. Twice. It was just the same.

By the time Monday morning arrived, John's gloomier thoughts had won the battle for supremacy. He tried to call again, shortly after his alarm signalled the end of another night of sleepless turmoil, but without success again.

He decided he would set off for work earlier than usual, park up and try once more. If it was the answering service again, he would call Jas' family to see if they knew where she was and, if they didn't, he would go to the police station and report her missing. Tell them everything. It would be his only option.

He turned off the engine and took out his phone. There was hardly anyone around. He had never been so early that he had managed to park on the first floor at this multi-storey before. His finger hovered over the call button, hardly daring to do what he needed to do for the fear that the response would be the one he expected to hear.

Come on, John.

He pressed the button.

It rang!

It rang three times, four times. Then a voice came on the line.

'Hi, John.' She sounded flat. Not typical Jas. But it was her. Tears of relief filled his eyes.

'Oh, thank Christ, Jas. Where are you? Are you OK?'

There was a pause. 'I'm OK. I'm in Scarborough.'

Scarborough! Of course!

'I'm so glad to hear your voice, Jas. I've been worried sick all weekend. I felt really bad about what happened on Friday night and I thought... Well, you're safe and that's all that matters. Jas, I'm so sorry. Please forgive me.'

'I'm the one who should be saying sorry. You were trying to make me feel better and you've got a gorgeous girlfriend and I started coming on to you like a silly sixteen year old. What must you think of me? I felt so embarrassed with myself. I couldn't bear to let you look at my face, I was so ashamed. It was my fault.'

'It wasn't your fault.'

'But it was. After you calmed me down and you were being really kind and holding me, I just wanted Stef so badly and I guess I just needed to feel wanted back, but it was so wrong of me to put that on you. That was so unfair.'

'I was the one who put an awful lot on you but, look, we were both feeling pretty emotional and our emotions led us somewhere we wouldn't have gone otherwise, but it was just a confused moment. We wouldn't have let it go any further. You're like a sister to me, Jas, and I'm not into that sort of thing.'

She reacted with a short, nervous laugh. It was good to hear.

'You're right, John. We just got carried away but that was it. I'm so glad you don't think badly of me. What do you say we try to forget it ever happened?'

'Agreed. Still mates?'

'Still mates.'

Thank Christ for that!

'So, what have you been doing in Scarborough?'

'Getting blown about and soaked to the skin, mostly, to be honest. I couldn't sleep that night after you left and I was getting more and more upset with myself, so I packed a few things, jumped in my car at around five in the morning and decided I would drive to Scarborough. I was running away, I suppose. Anyway, I went to the hotel on the seafront where Stef and I stayed all those years ago because I thought if he had planned to take me away for Christmas, that would have been the hotel he would have booked us into. He was a sentimental old sod that way. Anyway, there were plenty of rooms to spare.'

'Fancy that, on the East Yorkshire coast in early February!'

'I know! So I booked in for a few days. I decided to leave the phone switched off because I just wanted to be alone to, you know, think it all through. Take it all in. It was a lot to get my head around and I needed space. I'm sorry for the silence. I saw this morning I've got about a million missed calls from you. Sorry to put you through that.'

'That's OK.'

'I spent most of the first day in my room but I decided I should go out for a walk yesterday morning and I'm glad I did. I walked around the harbour and I thought about some of the places I went with Stef. There was this place on the harbour opposite all the amusement arcades which sold the most delicious fudge, but that was still closed for the winter, so I walked into the town, up to the church where one of the Brontës is buried and up to the castle.'

'The castle!'

'Yeah, it was so windy and rainy up there and I felt like what's-her-name out of *Wuthering Heights*. The woman in the kiosk looked at me as if I was mental for wanting to go in but I went out onto the headland and looked out to the north shore and then back at the south shore and watched all the huge waves blowing in off the North Sea and, do you know what? All of a sudden it went really calm and the sun came out. I think it might have been the only spot on the whole east coast to be in the sunshine but it shone on the castle and on me and I knew he was there with me. I felt him there. I couldn't see him but I felt his presence. I just stood there, with no other living soul near me, lifted my face to the sun and I felt so calm, kind of serene. I felt whole again. I had my Stef with me.'

'I'm so happy for you, Jas.'

'It was lovely. I stayed there for ages, just me and Stef. Then an old man started giving me odd looks while he was walking his terrier, so I decided to go back to the hotel. But by the time I got back I didn't feel disturbed any more.

'I felt like I had figured it out. What he did for you, as his best friend, was typical Stef and I can't be jealous of that. I can't feel left out because you and him shared an experience I couldn't be a part of because I had my own special experience with Stef. I can't have him with me, physically, any more and I will miss seeing him and being able to hold him, probably every day for the rest of my life but, in other ways, I never really lost him. To know that he is definitely out there is the next best thing. I can live with that.'

John sat and listened and basked in the warmth of her words, just as she had soaked up the pale sunshine at the castle. For the first time, he felt sure he had done the right thing by telling Jas about his experience that night outside the flat.

'I'll always be here for you as well, Jas, when you need me. When are you thinking about coming home?'

'Maybe tomorrow,' she replied. 'I'm just about to go for breakfast in the hotel and then I might go to Peasholm Park to feed the ducks, unless it's lagging down again.'

'I'll see you then. I'm really glad it worked out for you – and I'm glad we've sorted things out.'

'Me too. See you soon, John.' They hung up.

For at least ten minutes more, he sat in the car, a weekend of anxiety slowly draining from him. He barely moved. He had never felt such a profound sense of relief. Gradually, he no longer felt as if his heart was going to beat out of his chest and he looked at his watch. It was still early but he might as well head into work. Maybe call in somewhere and pick up a coffee on the way. Yes, a coffee would be good. He opened the car door and got out.

Over the concrete barrier, the traffic was building and umbrellas gave whatever shelter they could against the pouring rain for a steady flow of people on their way to work. It was another week and life was back to normal. John took two long, cleansing breaths of air. Thank god for normal.

He opened the back door to retrieve his own umbrella. There was no sign of the rain stopping anytime soon. He peered out again at the cars splashing through the streams of water which ran down the main road outside and noticed one man without an umbrella, head bowed as he battled into the face of the driving rain. Poor bugger. He'll be completely saturated by the time he gets to wherever he's heading. As the man stepped miserably out of view past a shop doorway, John noticed another hunched figure, taking shelter and looking as if he was waiting to decide whether or not to make a run for it. He didn't have an umbrella either. In fact, he didn't even appear to be wearing a proper coat. Just some sort of hooded top, pulled over a cap.

He was lighting a cigarette. A puff of smoke billowed out from the doorway and the man peeked from his shelter to gaze up to the sky. He no longer had the thin beard on his chin but John knew it was him again. Just as he knew at the firewalk.

John locked the car and checked where the nearest stairway was. He had to get down there before the man got away again.

What if he has gone by the time I get there?

John looked out again, taking cover behind a concrete pillar. As he did, the man drew again on his cigarette, cupped it in his hand and dashed out from the doorway, heading down the road.

Go! John ran to the stairway and virtually flung himself down the two flights of stairs, apologising as he did for almost colliding with a couple heading in the opposite direction. He burst into the street and looked around, frantically. The rain was so heavy he could hardly see as it hit his face, so he put up his umbrella.

There he was, walking quickly down the main road. As quickly as John spotted him, he took a right turn and was out of view again. John ran after him, holding his umbrella high as he dodged around the other pedestrians, and reached inside his coat for his phone.

At the junction where he had seen the hooded figure turn, he stopped running. The man was still in sight and the gap between them had been closed. It was enough to keep him in sight and stay discreetly distant. Good. It was time to call for back-up.

'Hello, DC Harrison, Sheffield CID.'

'Tom, hello, it's John Baldwin from the Ridings Building Society.'

'Oh hello, John. What can I do for you this beautiful morning?'

'I've seen him again, the man who killed my friend. I'm following him. He hasn't seen me this time.'

'Right.' The policeman's voice was serious but calm. 'Do not go anywhere near him, John. Keep well back. What I need you to do is to stay on your phone and talk me through where he's heading and then I'll get a couple of cars out to you. Which road are you on now and which direction are you walking?'

'I'm on Mappin Street heading towards Broad Lane. He's about twenty yards in front of me and coming towards the end of the road. I don't know which way he's looking to go at the end yet.'

'That's OK. Just keep an eye on him. I can get somebody out there in five minutes, you just keep telling me where he's going and I'll...'

'Hello? Tom?'

John looked at his phone. The screen was blank. In his distracted state, he must have forgotten to charge it last night.

'Oh, you have just got to be bloody kidding me!'

He pressed the on button a few times, just in case, but the phone was dead. Irritated, he pushed it into his coat pocket and looked up again just as the man turned left at the end of the road, heading out of town. He hurried to catch up, afraid of losing sight of his target again, but the man had not made another diversion. He was walking along the main road, his top turning an ever-darker colour as the rain soaked it through, the occasional puff of smoke rising above his head as he drew another suck on his cigarette.

What to do now? John looked around, in case a policeman just happened to be close by. No luck. Maybe if he stuck to the major roads there was a good chance he would see one on foot or be able to flag down a car. Either way, he had to keep following.

The man came to the roundabout on the ring road and stopped at the pedestrian crossing. John held back and hid his face with his umbrella, occasionally breaking cover to sneak a glance ahead. When the pedestrian crossing lights turned to green, he scurried forward before they changed. For an agonising few seconds, they were together on the central island before the next set of lights turned green and all those on foot were able to complete their crossing. John dropped back to a safer distance.

He was heading past the university building but before he reached the children's hospital, the man turned sharply to look down the road, in John's direction. He pulled down his umbrella again, but the man was watching for a gap in the traffic and dashed across, glancing left before making it to the other side.

John didn't think he had been seen but decided to stay on the opposite side of the road to see what the next move would be. He did not have to wait long. The man walked between the tall carved terracotta pillars of the main entrance and through to Weston Park.

Getting across the left-hand lane of the busy road was easy, but John was made to wait until he could squeeze through a gap in the traffic heading towards town, as cars slowed in the build up towards the roundabout. He passed by the ornate Victorian iron gates and into the park. There was the man, still not too far ahead. Good.

He was on the lower of the two paths, just about beyond the steps on his left leading up to the museum. Then he stepped off the path and walked over the sodden grass towards the pale blue-green Victorian bandstand. John stopped, hoping he was mostly hidden by a small tree without looking as if he was obviously hiding, and watched out of the corner of his eye. The man reached the shelter of the bandstand and brushed the shoulders of his soaking top to remove whatever excess water he could. Then he reached into his pocket and took out his cigarettes. After lighting one, the man looked around. It looked as if he might be waiting for someone.

This is useful, thought John. Hopefully, he will stay there long enough for the police to arrive. He decided it was best to stay where he was and observe. Bide his time.

Minutes passed. The man finished his cigarette and still there was no sign of the police, no sound of a siren. Where are they? There truly is never one around when you need one.

As he waited, John re-thought his tactics. What if the police were not coming?

He had left them a huge scope of possible areas to search because his phone had packed up before they reached the main road and before he could say which direction they were heading. Perhaps he should be more proactive.

John had considered previously what he would do if he came face to face with this man. Would he be angry and try to fight him? Not really his style. Not brave enough. Should he talk to him, as a reasonable man should, and persuade him to give himself up? That would be a huge gamble and would be to assume that the man was reasonable enough to listen, which might be a hell of a leap of faith – but then again. Ever since he saw him at the firewalk, John had considered the possibility that Stef's attacker was not a natural killer. Perhaps it was just a botched mugging, as the police had suggested at the time. Stef had lunged at the man and he panicked. He hadn't meant to kill. Perhaps the man had been haunted by guilt ever since and could be persuaded to give himself up. If he could, wasn't John the man to persuade him? Was that why fate – Stef – had decreed their paths should cross again? It was worth a shot. This could be his only chance.

Steeling himself, John angled his umbrella towards the bandstand and walked on. He carried on beyond where the man had gone onto the grass to approach the bandstand from a different direction. Best not go towards the man head on. He stepped gingerly onto the grass just after a large tree and squelched his way across, attempting to avoid the puddles which would have soaked his shoes even more than they already were. He reached the opposite side of the bandstand without being spotted.

The man was fidgety, appearing impatient at being kept waiting. What would be the best way to approach him? John decided he should walk around the bandstand and stay below the level of the man, to show a little submissiveness maybe. Make himself a less-intimidating presence.

At his feet, he noticed a sturdy length of tree branch, around twelve inches long and quite thick. He thought about picking it up and hiding it behind his back, for possible protection, but decided that could be sending the wrong message. He walked around the bandstand.

The man glanced at John and then stared. He recognised him again.

'Shit! You again!' Alarmed, he looked to break away but John was right in front of him now, only a couple of feet away.

'It's all right. I only want to talk.' He tried to look as unthreatening as he could, which was never really a danger he had to face normally.

The man's eyes flashed – wild, cornered. 'No chance!'

He lunged at John and lashed out, connecting with his fist to the left of John's jaw.

The world swam around him. He was vaguely aware of the man bursting past him and tearing away and broadly conscious that his umbrella was no longer in his hand and the rain was falling on his head but mostly he was mindful that his legs no longer appeared to be connected to the rest of his body and were incapable of supporting his weight. He stumbled and then fell forward, blurry darkness filling his eyes and water filling his mouth and nostrils. Gasping and spluttering, he wanted to lift his head but no longer had the power to do so. Then there was nothing.

20

His head still felt as if it was in a spin as John opened his eyes again but then he realised it wasn't the world that was spinning, it was him.

He was sitting on a children's playground roundabout. Specifically, he was on a children's roundabout on one of the old tennis courts close to the house where he had grown up. As it gently turned, he noticed the pond, where he had spent so many youthful days skimming stones and peeking into the grass on the edge of the water looking for small frogs. The community centre, a large sandy-brown brick building which was never really utilised properly, was beyond the pond, next to the garages where they would play football, using one of the garage doors as a goal. Behind that rose, red brick and charmless, the sturdy outline of St Cyprian's Church.

On the far wall of the converted tennis court he could still see the three lines he had scratched with a stone to make impromptu cricket stumps, a target for practicing his off-spin bowling. He had spent hours alone bowling at that wall, trying to hit the same spot he had marked out on the ground time after time, trying to toughen the skin on the middle finger of his right hand, trying to develop his action until, in his mind's eye at least, it looked just like Carl Hooper's.

It was all so familiar but had been buried in the past for so long that being in the middle of it again made no sense.

'That little plan worked out well, I must say.'

The voice startled John. He turned his head towards the direction it came from, as the roundabout turned to complete its circuit. He already knew who it was. Casually rocking on a swing was Stef.

Now his mind was making sense of it and the conclusion it leapt to hit with the force of a truck, overwhelming him with a wave of helpless despair. So that's it. It's over.

'What! No! Not yet!'

Stef stepped off the swing and stopped the slow rotation of the roundabout with his hand.

'Don't worry, you're not being taken. It's not your time.'

John threw back his head and let out a gasp of relief.

Stef sat on the next segment of the roundabout. 'You know how they say in your last few moments you see your life flashing before your eyes? This is what you might call a bit of a freeze frame and since you gave me the opportunity, I wanted to have a catch-up. Sorry if I scared you a bit there.'

'So I'm OK – is that what you're saying?' John's panic had not completely subsided.

'You're fine. You are, however, drowning in a puddle, you dozy sod. Honestly, of all the daft scrapes you've got yourself into, this has to be the daftest but somebody out jogging has seen it all and is coming to help you. Technically, you're alive the whole time.'

John brought his hands to his face. In that fleeting second of dread, the prospect of seeing his future snatched away terrified him. The situation was still one he could barely comprehend but the one slither of information he had just been given was the only thing that mattered.

I'm not dead. I didn't want to die yet.

'I have to ask, though – what on earth did you think you were doing?'

John ran his fingers through his hair. 'How do you mean?'

There was an edge of irate indignation in the way Stef asked the question, like he had caught a small child trying to push a lollipop stick into a plug socket.

'I mean, why did you just walk straight up to a man who – let me remind you – has a bit of form when it comes to violent attacks and stand right in front of him so the only option he had for making his escape was to batter you out of the way?'

'I thought if I talked to him and...'

'You didn't honestly believe you could appeal to his better nature, did you? This is a desperate, violent beast you're dealing with and when he sees you, he sees somebody who has come to take his freedom away. If he had a conscience, don't you think he would have given himself up at some stage in the last year or so? He doesn't want to answer for his crimes. He's a wild animal and you can't force a wild animal into a corner then be surprised when it bites your hand off.'

'I hear what you're saying, but...'

'No, I don't think you do, John. I don't think you understand how privileged you are to get the second chance I was able to give you and, believe me, you are only scratching the surface of what you can achieve in this new direction you're heading.

I'll protect you but that doesn't make you bulletproof. I can't always take care of you if you make stupid decisions like this.'

He saw it now. He was here because Stef needed to give him the tough love treatment. Beside him he saw a man who had been denied the opportunity to achieve everything he was capable of in life and had taken the only other option available to him – to find fulfilment through his closest friend. Lord knows what he had risked to do that but he had reached out because John was squandering the most precious gift, his life, and needed saving from himself. John realised his recklessness had been the behaviour of an unappreciative child.

'Yeah, I understand. Sorry, mate. I get it. I won't do that again.'

Stef sighed. 'I've helped you and now I need you to help me. This is important to me. You know I want you to get this guy. I can't touch him. I want you to make him pay for what he did to me but you've got to be smarter. I'm not saying that you shouldn't have confronted him in the park but you saw the tree branch – why didn't you pick it up? He comes at you, you whack him and it's job done – or just whack him with it anyway. Say it was self-defence, nobody would know any different.'

'Are you serious?' John scrutinised his friend's face for a sign. Stef had always been a bit of a wind-up artist but he could usually read when he was being set up. He saw nothing this time.

'I couldn't have killed him. I want him to pay for what he did but surely that's not the right way.'

The expression on Stef's face was unchanged. He was serious.

'There's justice and there's justice, my friend. All I'm saying is that we all face the ultimate judgement one day and for people like him, that day might as well come sooner rather than later.'

John stepped up off the roundabout. The suggestion disturbed him. He had heard Jas say several times that she wanted the killer dead, but Stef was making it sound as if he was actually being granted permission – encouraged, even.

'I know what you're thinking. I know the thought of it goes against the grain for you, but I wouldn't ask you to do this unless it was the right course. Think about it. If you had killed this guy it would have been no different to how it worked out with the thug you tripped who smacked his head on the kerb. Say the police had caught him instead, then what? He would have been sent to prison for a few years, then he would have been released, attacked somebody else – more than likely – and ruined more lives. That one got what was coming to him and you know it. The same applies here.'

The words stung John. After being initially troubled by the realisation of what he had done when he had flicked out his foot to trip Jarvis on the night Gregory was attacked, his conscience had been at ease since. He had quickly grown to feel comfortable with the outcome.

But to do the same again – willingly rather than unwittingly – that was a different matter. He didn't feel capable.

'That was different. That was an accident. I didn't want to kill him and I don't want to kill this man. If I can play a part in bringing him to justice then I will because it's important to me as well that he pays for what he's done but it's not for me to set the price. That's not my decision to take. I can't decide what punishment is right for him in this life or the next. I'm only a man.'

Stef held up his hand. 'OK, fine. You do what you think is right, that's your choice to make. You know what my preference is but it's your decision. All I can do is put the opportunities your way. All I'm saying is, whether you change your mind or not, I'll try to make sure no unfortunate repercussions come your way, whatever decision you feel you have to take. I can protect you, John. Just think about that.'

John didn't want to think about it. The conversation had left him unsettled. He was angry with his friend for suggesting he should consider it.

'Look, I can't keep you here for very much longer. I don't want us to part on bad terms,' said Stef.

He stood and the two of them hugged. 'Still mates?' John nodded. Still mates. He could never stay cross at Stef for long.

'Good. There's somebody else who wanted to see you.'

Somebody else? John was puzzled. Stef's eyes directed him towards the swings.

He turned. There was a man of a similar age, maybe a little younger, leaning against the bars of the swing. John was not totally sure who it was at first but then he spoke.

'Allreet there, Smurf?'

Nobody had called him that since uni. The north-east accent was the clincher.

'Good god. Shaggy.'

Shaggy had the room next to John's in the halls of residence in the first year and they hit it off straightaway. He got his nickname in the first couple of weeks because one of the other lads reckoned he looked like the character in *Scooby-Do*. It stuck. It could have been worse. One of the other blokes on their floor in halls, a shy kid on John's course who looked as if he hadn't been more than fifty yards away from his mother for the eighteen years of his life before then, threw up all over his room on the first night after the pub and became known to all as Hughie for the next four years. Poor kid! What was his real name?

Everybody had a nickname. It was like a badge of acceptance. John got his because he used to wear an oversized red woollen hat which somebody said looked as if he had nicked it off Papa Smurf. The rest was nickname evolution.

Shaggy was great company, at first. They lived in shared houses together, with a couple of other friends, for the next two years while Shaggy completed his degree in – what was it? – Sociology, or something like that. They completely embraced the student life together until he met Tracy early in his final year. He changed after that. She was nice enough but was really insecure and very clingy. The rest of them advised him to dump her because she sucked all the life out of him but he wouldn't listen. He was obsessed by her. She practically moved in and they would sit together, always touching, having their private whispered conversations, oblivious to the other three.

Their behaviour was even the basis for a drinking game – the three of them had to take a drink for every use of a pet name, public show of affection, time they laughed at an unshared joke or actually initiated a conversation with someone else in the group, though those were increasingly infrequent occasions. It completely spoiled the dynamic of the house.

It was almost a relief when Shaggy and Tracy finished their courses and moved on. Shaggy completely fluffed his finals because he didn't do enough work. That was a real pity. John never heard from him after then.

'How are you?' John checked himself. In light of their current situation, that might have been a stupid thing to ask. 'Sorry, obviously you can't be... I mean, I guess you must be...what happened?'

'Aww, you know.' Shaggy shrugged and wandered languidly to the roundabout. 'Car accident five years ago. My fault. I was driving like a lunatic. The only good thing was I didn't take anybody with me.'

They embraced. He looked older than the Shaggy of John's memory but the features were as distinct as the accent. The hair was shorter, though, and the dress sense definitely better.

'I'm sorry about that. I had no idea.'

'Well, I should have stayed in touch,' Shaggy said, wistfully. 'I'm not sure you would have wanted me to, really. I was a right prick in that third year.'

John shrugged. 'We all make mistakes. Did you stay with Tracy?'

'Oh, aye!' His mood lifted. 'We got married and had a couple of kids, like. Actually, Tracy is the reason I wanted to see you.'

'Why's that?'

He appeared troubled again. 'Well, after I was taken, all sudden like, Tracy was in a mess and this other guy moved in on her. A builder. A real twat, actually. He started taking decisions for her when she was still really vulnerable and, before you know it, he's got her down to the register office and the house – which was paid for, out of the insurance, by the way – has been transferred over into his name. He tells her it's better that way, with him being in the trade, like, which is complete bullshit but you know what Tracy's like. She's no head for that sort of thing. Anyway, he's a bully and won't let her have a life of her own, he's made her stop seeing her friends and family, checks her phone to see who she's been calling. Total arsehole. He hits the kids as well, which I would never do.'

John sighed. His heart went out to his old friend. 'That's terrible, mate, but what can I do?'

'Thing is,' added Shaggy, desperation in his eyes. 'He's into some pretty nasty porno stuff as well. Downloads it onto a computer he won't let anybody else go near. Really horrible stuff. My little girl's eight now and I'm really scared of what he might do to her. I thought you might be able to go to the coppers and tell them what he's got on his computer so they put him away and don't let him anywhere near Tracy and the kids again. I'm absolutely terrified for them. Can you help me?'

'I'll see what I can do, but I don't—'

Shaggy grabbed hold of John by the arms. 'Anything, pal. You're the only chance I've got. They live not far from you – in Rotherham. It's Harrogate Street, number 86. She's called Williamson now. Thanks, Smurf.'

'Oh, thank god!'

John opened his eyes to see a woman in her early twenties, wearing a luminous yellow beany hat and matching jacket, peering over him with concern. She asked if he was OK but he couldn't reply for coughing. It was as if someone had sneaked up and pushed him into a swimming pool and half the contents of it had shot up his nose before he had the chance to brace himself. He propped himself on one shoulder to try to clear his airway and the woman, not quite knowing what else she could do, patted him firmly on the back. He held up his hand, both to signal that he was OK and that he'd had enough of the patting, and she stopped, pressing her hand comfortingly on his shoulder instead. The coughing would not stop but he was able to draw enough of a breath to croak 'thank you' between hacks.

She looked up and then called out 'over here!' taking her hand off his shoulder to wave. John glanced up to see two policemen running across the grass towards them.

'Are you John Baldwin?' one of them asked as they got close.

He nodded as positively as he could and coughed some more.

The officer spoke into his radio. 'We've found him. He's by the bandstand in Weston Park, looks like he's been attacked. No sign of the suspect.'

'I think he was unconscious when I got here. I saw a man hit him,' said the woman.

'Which way did he go?' asked the officer.

She pointed. 'That way.'

'Suspect last seen heading towards the Crookes Valley Road exit of the park,' he said into the radio. The second officer set off at a fast trot in the direction the woman had pointed. 'PC Danson in pursuit.'

The remaining officer dropped to his haunches, rain dripping off the front of his cap. 'Are you all right, John?'

He nodded again, coughed again and squeaked out in a failing voice: 'Just need to sit up.'

The policeman in front and the woman behind helped John rise from his recline to sitting, leaning forward. He felt the water seeping through the seat of his trousers.

'Thanks.' The new posture helped and he drew croaky breaths as the coughing grew more intermittent.

'You say someone hit him?' the officer was addressing the woman.

'Yes, I was out running and I saw this man with his umbrella up approach another man who was standing just by the bandstand, then he sort of lunged forward and hit this gentleman and ran off.'

'Are you hurt, John?'

The policeman stared intently at him and put his hand on John's arm.

'No, I'm fine. Can you just help me up please?'

With support, he rose to his feet and felt steady on his legs. He looked around. 'My umbrella.'

The other two offered a cursory look in all directions. 'Must have blown away, I'm afraid. Let's get you over to the museum and out of the rain.'

Policeman on one arm and jogger on the other, John made steady progress across the grass, then up the steps and finally under the cover of the columned entrance to the museum. They sat him on a bench.

'Do you need me anymore?' asked the woman.

'I'll just take your details, if I could please, love. We might need you to give a statement, if that's OK.'

'Of course. No problem.'

The two of them wandered a few steps away as the officer retrieved his notebook from the inside pocket of his coat, leaving John to gather his thoughts – again. Extraordinary events were becoming a regular occurrence.

The officer finished writing and the woman looked over towards John. 'I hope you're feeling OK,' she said.

He smiled in an attempt to show that he was. 'Thank you so much,' he said. 'I'm sorry to have delayed you.'

'That's all right,' she replied with a smile of her own and then she stepped out into the rain again to continue her seriously interrupted morning run.

The officer sat on the bench beside John. 'I'd like to take you up to the Hallamshire for them to check you over – just in case.'

'That won't be necessary, honestly. I'm fine now. I just took a bit of water down the wrong way but I've cleared that now. I'll be OK.'

'Are you sure?'

The second officer arrived back, out of breath and very wet. 'No sign of him,' he said.

John stood before the two policemen could come together to insist he went to hospital.

'Look, thanks very much, both of you, for your help but I just want to get home and get out of these wet clothes. My car isn't far away. DC Harrison in CID has my contact details but you might have to wait a bit to call me because my phone went dead. Tell him I'll come in to see him, tomorrow maybe, and tell him everything I can. Oh and please apologise to everyone from me for leading you on a wild goose chase. I'll make sure my phone is fully charged all the time from now on.'

He offered handshakes to the two officers and set off, attempting to give every impression he was completely steady on his feet as they watched him go, towards the park exit where he had walked in what seemed like such a long time ago.

The rain was still hammering down. As he walked through it down the main road towards the city centre, he became aware of the strange looks he was attracting from people walking in the opposite direction. He looked down and realised he was covered in mud all down his front. He wiped his face and looked at his muddy hand. He felt in his pockets for a tissue and wiped as much of the mud off his face as he could. The rain was doing a fine job cleaning away the rest. He could not have felt any wetter.

All he wanted was to get back to the flat but, despite his reassuring words to the policemen, he knew it might not be a good idea to drive. He watched for a taxi but saw none, so he decided to head towards work. It wasn't much further than it was to the car park anyway.

Soaked and bedraggled, he walked through the main doors to the banking hall. Customers turned and stared, as if a homeless man had wandered in. Then Julie spotted him.

'Mr Baldwin!' she shrieked, plainly alarmed, and bustled to him.

'I had a bit of an accident, Julie.'

'Are you all right?' She turned and gestured to another staff member. 'Go and fetch Stella.'

'I'm fine. I might just have a little sit down, though.'

He suddenly felt dizzy again and slumped into a chair. Julie crouched beside him. Moments later, Stella dashed into the hall.

'John! What on earth?' She cupped his face in her hands and wiped a smear of dirt from his cheek, disquieted, as her eyes scanned for signs of a wound. 'What happened? Are you OK?'

'Fine, honestly. A bit wet though.'

'I'd better get you home. Julie, can you call us a taxi, please?'

Julie set off to complete her task. Stella looked him up and down.

'Look at the state of you. How did you get like this?'

He shrugged. 'It's been a strange morning.'

21

The warm water of the shower hit John's face in sharp, tingling jets and he moved his head to allow its invigorating flow to cleanse his mind of the haunting thought that he had never stared into the eyes of his own mortality quite so closely.

Christ, I thought I was dead!

He had not been allowed to dwell on the thought for long but it had been long enough. Long enough to appreciate the value of everything he feared he was about to leave behind. Long enough to unsettle him. Maybe that had been the idea. Maybe Stef thought he needed to appreciate everything he had a little more. Everything he had that Stef had led him to. Maybe that was what this morning had been about.

He let the warm water of the shower wash over him until his thoughts began to settle in among the many others which had redrawn the map of his everyday life lately. It was a long shower but it served its purpose. He dried and put on his towelling dressing gown, feeling warm and renewed. Stella was waiting in the living room with hot drinks for both of them. He sat beside her.

'I've put your dirty things in the washing machine and I've turned the heating on,' she declared. 'Now, are you going to tell me what happened?'

What happened? Now there was a question.

'I saw the man who killed Stef, again,' he said. 'I spotted him just after I'd parked up in the multi-storey and he didn't see me this time, so I followed him. I was going to stay close by and lead the police to him by telling them where he was heading but my phone ran out of charge, so I just had to tail him and hope they turned up in time. Anyhow, I followed him to Weston Park and he was hanging around by the bandstand, like he was waiting for someone. I watched him but then I got it into my head that I could talk him into giving himself up.'

Stella raised her eyebrows.

'I know, I know. Anyway, it didn't work out. He hit me and I fell forward into a puddle. I think I blacked out for a short while until this woman out jogging came to help.'

'Good god, John!'

'It's all right. Technically, I was alive the whole time.'

'Technically? What do you mean, technically?'

She was right to look alarmed. That was the wrong thing to say. It was time to trust her with the truth. It was time to tell her everything.

'I've got something I need to tell you, Stella. There's no way of saying this without it sounding totally weird, so I'm just going to say it.'

He told her about the night of the staff Christmas do, about seeing Stef and what Stef had said to him. He told her about how fate had led him to a series of life-changing opportunities ever since. He told her about breaking the news to Jas and why he had appeared so distracted over the weekend – though he drew a discreet veil over the detail of the kiss, which he thought might have over-complicated the situation a little too much – and then he told her about the playground on the old tennis courts and his reunion with Shaggy.

He told her it all in the same matter-of-fact way he might have told her about a trip to the supermarket. He made no attempt to inject a sense of drama and no attempt to play it down. To do either was unnecessary. He just told it as it was. She listened to every word attentively. She appeared neither frightened nor unbelieving. She absorbed the information without giving anything away.

'So, that's it,' he said, at last, leaning forward to pick up his coffee cup. 'That's my life. That's the bloke you've hooked up with. I see dead people.'

He sipped at the now-cold coffee. She said nothing. He needed her reaction. She took a long, deep breath.

'So that first night, outside the flat, was that the epiphany you told me about when we were in York?'

'That's right.'

She nodded and was quiet again. He hadn't expected Stella to react in the same way as Jas had but he thought she would be more animated than this.

'You're taking this very calmly, I must say. I hope you don't think I'm making all this up. I've not got some sort of psychosis.'

'Oh, I believe you.' Stella grabbed hold of his hand. 'It's just quite a lot to take in. I mean, I was sent to quite a traditional Catholic school, so this is not a new concept to me. We were told stories of apparitions – the Virgin Mary and the saints – until we knew them by heart, but for it to happen to someone close makes it so much more…wow! I've never known anyone this has actually happened to. This is really fascinating. Some might call it miraculous, you know. At the very least it's a blessing. You can say you have seen proof of the after-life, which most people spend their whole lives accepting purely on the strength of their faith. That is so powerful. It must turn your whole world upside down.'

Her rush of enthusiasm made John feel happy but also slightly embarrassed that she appeared to see the whole picture on a much broader scale in two minutes than he had in a couple of months.

'Well, it has, I suppose' he said, contemplatively. 'It's true that it changed the course of my life because I was heading to a very dark place before all this happened but it's not made me feel any more religious, oddly. I'm not sure why that should be but I never felt you have to be a religious man to be a good man previously and I still don't. It has made me realise life is more than a biological accident but I don't think it's intrinsically changed who I am. If anything, it's brought me back to who I was but now I feel like I have added purpose in my life.'

'But for a spirit to come to you, choose you for a special mission, that must make you feel special, surely? No disrespect intended here but you must think "why me?" Of all the people in the world, why have *you* been given this chance?'

John eased back on the sofa. He hadn't attempted to explain his feelings to anyone before and it was not easy to find the words.

'You do think that at first, you're right. I can only think that Stef came to me because he was trying to protect me, as a mate would, and maybe, beyond that, he saw in me an opportunity to achieve things in life that he couldn't. But you do still feel a bit of a fraud at first, to be honest. You feel unworthy and confused, like you're wondering whether you are supposed to suddenly start working towards something hugely significant but, thankfully, I had Mike Wilshaw and his charity sent to me and then you realise that you can only achieve anything by taking one small step at a time. That's what I'm trying to do. I don't think I'm special or superior, that would be wrong, I look at it as a responsibility I've been given where I should make the most of a situation and use it to benefit as many people as I can. Where that'll lead me, I don't know, but for now it's in trying to develop the charity. It's not world peace but it is trying to make the world a better place one small step at a time. I hope that doesn't sound too sanctimonious.'

Stella had been staring intently into his eyes the whole time. She was captivated.

'Not at all. It sounds like you've been able to come to terms with a huge change in your life in a very practical way and I think that's admirable.'

'What I've also come to realise more recently is that Stef needs me to help catch the man responsible for his death. He's led me to him twice now and I feel sure he'll lead me to him again. It's like he cannot rest while the killer is still out there and he needs me to help him find peace. I think that's a big part of the reason why it had to be me because I'm the only connection he has between him and what happened that night. I can understand that and I want to catch the killer, of course I do, but I'm struggling with what he said to me today.'

'How do you mean?'

'Well, the first time I saw him, at the firewalk, I thought it might just be Stef giving a nudge to the investigation but the second time, today at the park, was different. I know it wasn't the smartest move to approach him like that, I can see that now, but I got the impression from what Stef said to me that he wanted me to take this guy out rather than hand him in and I'm just not comfortable with that. At all. I mean, if he wanted me to lead the police to him, why did my phone pack in?'

'It could just be because you forgot to charge it properly. Everyone does that.'

'Yes, but nothing in my life has been that simple lately. I don't believe in coincidences anymore. I was left in a situation where it was me and him and I had to make a choice. Maybe I made the wrong one but Stef was saying I should have picked up the tree branch I saw and hit him with it. He said it would be better if this guy was dead and facing judgement in the next life than facing justice in this and I can't get my head around that.'

'But you can understand why Stef would feel that way, can't you? He's the man who robbed him of his future. That's unforgivable, surely. Don't you hate him as well?'

'No, I don't hate him. I hate what he did but I can't hate him without understanding why he did it. Maybe he was desperate for money and the situation escalated badly. I know that if you go out with a knife and threaten somebody with it you can't claim it wasn't your fault if everything goes wrong, but that doesn't make him a cold-blooded killer. Maybe he just made bad choices. We all make bad choices and, when we do, we have to face the consequences, but it's not for me to decide what his punishment should be. It's not for me to decide whether someone should live or die. I just want him caught and put in jail. You must understand that, don't you?'

'I know what you're saying, John, and I think you're right. Setting out for revenge is wrong, no matter what the other person has done. You're right to do what you believe is the right thing to do. Didn't you say Stef told you that himself?'

'He did. He let me know what his preference would be, but he said it was my choice.'

'Then that's how you should play it. What are you going to do about your other friend?'

'Shaggy? I've not really given it much thought yet, to be honest. I'll take it to the police and see what they suggest.'

'I think you should. He's still a friend who needs your help. Even if he isn't with us any more, that's what it comes down to.' Stella checked herself, as if she had heard the words spoken by another person. 'Am I really talking about you helping out a dead man? I can't believe we're having this conversation!'

'I know. Welcome to my world.'

Their awkward laughter lightened the mood. It had been a strange discussion, but John was glad it had happened. He felt unburdened.

'Thanks for listening, Stell, and thanks for understanding. I don't know what I would do without you.'

He leaned forward and kissed her.

'I'm happy you felt you could talk to me like this. It's a strange position to be in but I hope I can help you all I can.' Stella looked at her watch. 'I should be getting back to work.'

He put his hand on her thigh. 'Can't work wait for another half an hour?'

'No need to ask if you're feeling better.' She gently but discouragingly took his hand off her leg and put it down on his own. 'Sorry, tiger, I've got things to do.'

She stood and smiled, then bent over to kiss John on the forehead. 'And you should get some rest. If you start to feel unwell, call the doctor. Otherwise, just take it easy for the rest of today and I'll see you tomorrow.'

He tried to take the advice, but he couldn't stay still. Too many thoughts were getting in the way. For a start, he needed confirmation that this latest bizarre episode was not a product of his imagination. He decided to see if he could find an old news report about Shaggy's accident and turned on his laptop.

He typed in 'Brendan Forbes car death' and hit return.

There it was. A report in the *Rotherham Advertiser* from five years ago.

'Man named after fatal crash in Wickersley'.

He clicked on the link and read on.

'Police have named the man who was killed in a road accident in the early hours of Friday morning as 32-year-old father of two Brendan Forbes, from Rotherham.

'Mr Forbes was the driver of a car which left the road and hit a tree on a bend in Wickersley. He was pronounced dead at the scene.

'It is not believed any other vehicle was involved in the accident and police investigators say it is possible Mr Forbes lost control of his car in icy conditions.

'An inquest is to be opened to establish the likely cause of the accident.'

Poor Shaggy.

The report saddened John, but it also gave him the reassurance he was looking for. He couldn't have known anything about the crash unless the encounter this morning really had happened. There was some comfort in that.

He decided he had to get out of the flat, so he got dressed and set off to catch a bus to pick up his car from the multi-storey. Then he might tie up the loose ends with the police over the morning's events and put out feelers to see if there was anything he could do to help Shaggy. At the very least, he felt he owed the police the courtesy of a face-to-face apology for messing things up.

The skies were still ominously heavy but the rain had stopped, which made the walk from the bus stop to the car park much more pleasant, in the continued absence of an umbrella on stand-by.

He walked up the steps where he had almost sent the young couple flying earlier in the day and paid for his stay at the ticket machine which, thankfully, accepted the ticket which had been almost in a state of pulp when Stella had retrieved it from his suit trouser pocket.

The hazard lights on his car blinked twice as he pressed the pad on his key to unlock the doors but, as he drew closer, John realised something was wrong.

'Aw, for god's sake.'

There was a stone, the size of a fist, on the bonnet of the car. Then he saw where it had hit the driver's side of the windscreen. The concave shape of glass shards had somehow resisted the impact without shattering but, clearly, the car was not going to be driven anywhere for a while.

'Bollocks.'

He stood, inspecting the damage and fighting the urge to swear longer and louder, before locking the car again and setting off to try to find anyone who looked as if they worked at the car park.

'And did you manage to find anybody?' DC Harrison stretched back in his seat and folded his hands across his rounded middle.

John scoffed. 'Did I hell. The best I could find was a phone number on the board near the payment machine, so I called it while I was waiting for the man to come to repair the windscreen. I wanted to know if they might have access to some CCTV footage showing who threw the stone at my car but the bloke who answered said they only had cameras at key points inside the car park and so that's no good. He kept banging on about how they couldn't accept liability for damage and how it clearly says so on notices and I lost it a bit with him at that stage, to be honest. I shouldn't have, I know, but I was feeling more than a little bit pissed off by then.

'Anyway, the windscreen man came pretty quickly, which was good, and sorted me out. He said I shouldn't drive the car for an hour to let the glue set, or whatever, and that was when I called you. I left it about twenty minutes and I'd had enough by then, so I decided it would be all right if I drove it steady but when I put my ticket into the machine to get out, it was rejected. It kept saying the ticket was invalid, so I parked up and called the number again.'

'I bet he was glad to hear from you again.' There was a barely disguised smirk on the policeman's face. He was enjoying this tale of woe.

'I did start by apologising for calling him a cock earlier but I'm not sure that made a difference. He told me the machine wouldn't accept my ticket because I'd left it too long after paying and that he would have to get somebody out. He said they'd get there as soon as possible. Three-quarters of an hour it took.'

'Oh dear!' said DC Harrison with a chuckle.

'Three-quarters of a bloody hour! Where did they send him from? Bloody Manchester? When he eventually turned up, he wanted to charge me twenty-five quid for a lost ticket and there was no way I was going to pay that, so we had a bit of a stand-off. In the end, I think he let me out just to get rid of me. At least the windscreen had time to set by then. So sorry it's a bit later than I said I'd be here, but that's why.'

The policeman sat forward, still smiling. 'It was worth the wait, quite frankly. I thought I'd had a bad day until you showed up! Who do you think it was who damaged your car? The man you followed?'

John shook his head. 'Couldn't have been. He didn't see me until we were in the park, so he can't have known where I was parked. I'm wondering if it was Jarvis' lot.'

'Could just have been kids. That's not unknown.'

'Possible. I'm just getting a bit paranoid, I suppose.'

'I'll see if we can pull anything off CCTV in the area and we might get lucky there.'

John hesitated. 'There was one more thing.'

The policeman, who had begun to gather his papers in front of him, waited.

'I've had a tip-off about the new partner of a woman I went to uni with. I've been told he's into seriously deranged porn and that there are young kids in the house, so this friend of mine is worried there's a safeguarding issue.'

'I see.' DC Harrison clicked the top of his pen and began to write. 'What's your friend's name?'

'He said he couldn't get directly involved. It's complicated. That's why he came to me.'

'OK then, what about the person he suspects of possessing this porno stuff – what are we talking about here? Images? Film?'

'I don't specifically know what it is but his name's Williamson. I don't have a first name for him. His wife's Tracy – she's the uni friend. I've written their address down.'

He passed over a slip of paper. The policeman transcribed the details onto his own sheet.

'Is there anything you can do?'

DC Harrison surveyed his scribblings and took a deep breath.

'It's not really my field but we have teams who deal with this sort of thing. It's possible he's been downloading from known sites or has been operating on the dark web and they might already be aware of him through traced IP addresses and such, so I'll pass on what you've given me and see if they have enough to go on. The problem is, see, that you can't just go bursting into somebody's house and seizing their computers on suspicion, you have to have a form of proof that you can take to the magistrates to apply for a warrant before you can go in but, as I say, I'll refer what you've told me to them and see what they know. If there's kiddies in the house, that should move it up the priority list. I'll also have a word with Social Services and see if they regard this as an at-risk situation, so we'll see. Leave it with me.'

They shook hands and John left. Back in his car, he was relieved he had set the wheels in motion but felt he should do more. He decided he should drive over to see for himself if Tracy and her kids were safe or not.

22

'I've decided to have a bit of a get-together for my birthday.'

It was great to see the sparkle in Jas' eyes again. There was no trace of hesitancy in her embrace when they greeted each other. No discomfiture. They had put it behind them. She was also wearing the ring.

'Nothing big, just a few family and friends at a restaurant and maybe a few drinks after. I was thinking the Saturday after my birthday – the tenth.'

She was not the only one in a buoyant mood. They had been able to put an up-to-date figure on the amount they had raised so far for the GameOn Trust and it was much more than they had dared hope for at first. Gregory's people had also provided them with a ballpark estimate of what they might stand to make from the summer concert and then the festival weekend and it was an eye-watering amount. For the first time, they had discussed allocating funds and setting projects in motion. It felt like a seminal moment had been reached.

'You will be there, won't you, John? And Stella, too, of course. How is Stella, by the way?'

'Oh, she's great, thanks.'

As a matter of fact, she'd been a bit off for the last few days at work. Distant, actually. She said the boys had gone down with one of those bugs that were doing the rounds and she was tired. He hoped she wasn't going down with something as well.

'Don't forget it's Valentine's Day next Wednesday! Very important day for young lovers!'

He smiled. 'All in hand, thank you very much, Jas.'

'And what about you, Mike? Are you able to come to my birthday bash next month? It's on the tenth. Bring your good lady as well.'

'Would it be all right if I brought the missus instead? She'd start to suspect otherwise. Thanks, Jas, we'd love to be there.'

Mike caught hold of John's arm just as he was beginning to put his coat on.

'You know what I was saying earlier, John, about the meeting with the people in the community and my mate at the council? Could you be there, too? You understand the finances a lot better than I do.'

'Sure.' John carried on putting on the coat. 'Just let me know where and when.'

'It probably won't be until towards next weekend – the 16th or 17th. I'll confirm the details soon.'

'Great. Either day should work for me.'

'Fabulous. It really feels like we're moving forward now, doesn't it?'

John thought about Mike's words while he was driving to Rotherham the following day. It was astonishing how far they had travelled together in so short a time. Little over two months ago, the closest they had come to meeting each other was that John thought he might have seen Mike playing cricket and yet here they were, setting out plans to spend tens of thousands of pounds on charity projects. It would not be long until decisions would have to be made about engaging people to run the charity full time. Mike would be the ideal man for the job to head it, if he was able to make the commitment, this was for sure. He made a mental note to raise the subject when they met later in the week. They would need someone to take it on or very soon the charity would outgrow them.

Harrogate Street was easy to find. The area wasn't great. He could see that it might have been perfectly respectable at one time but, like so many similar communities which had previously leaned heavily on coal mining, it had become rundown when the mine was closed. It was hard to escape the impression that the communities had long since given up because the world had long since given up on them.

After parking his car, John had a good look up and down the street before convincing himself it probably would be safe enough to lock up and leave it for a short while. He had pulled in behind a battered red van. On the side of the van, in chipped white lettering, it said 'VJW Builders'. This must be the place, then. There was no number he could see on the house the van was parked outside but the number eighty was roughly painted on the wall of the house three doors down, so John reasoned he must be at the right one. He was not at all convinced this was a good idea. His instinct told him to get back in the car and drive away but he had promised Shaggy he would do all he could. Seeing for himself that Tracy was safe was part of that. He drew on his reserves of resolve and locked the car, pressing the keypad again a few steps on to make sure it had locked properly.

A narrow pathway separated the blocks of four houses and number eighty-six was one of the end terraces. The back garden was not only badly overgrown and uncared for, it was littered with piles of scaffolding pipe, heaps of rubble, breeze blocks and practically empty cement bags. Definitely a builder. Definitely not a gardener.

Reluctantly, John approached the back door. A movement out of the corner of his eye caught his attention and he turned to see a dog squatting in the next garden.

Jesus! Get on with it and get out of here.

He knocked on the door.

Because he was expecting to see Tracy, he knew it was her but if he had passed her on the street, he would never have recognised her. She looked at least ten years older than he knew she actually was. Her hair was lank and shapeless, her features world-weary and drawn. Even at university, that unreal liberated world between restrained childhood and responsible adulthood, she was hardly carefree and had the capacity to drain the spirit from the most gregarious of souls when left alone with them for only ten minutes, but her appearance now was shocking. She was dead behind the eyes. Crushed. She stared at John without recognising him, looking as if she barely had the will to respond even if she had known who he was. He looked back, stunned into silence himself, before he could force words from his mouth.

'Hi, Tracy. It's John Baldwin. From uni. I used to share a house with Shaggy.'

The faintest of lights glimmered in her eyes for a moment.

'Oh hi, Smurf. What are you doing here?'

'I only found out a couple of days or so ago about the accident. I'm really sorry, Tracy. I wish I'd known at the time so that I could have done something to help you.'

'That's OK.' The small glimmer was gone in an instant. Her gaze wandered from John's face and away to a distant place, five years ago. She had never really left there. 'Can't be helped.'

The door was suddenly wrenched out of her grasp, widening the small gap she had allowed herself and exposing a hulking figure behind her.

The word intimidating was insufficient. He was intimidating in the same way as the north face of the Eiger is a bit steep. Menace seethed from every bristle on his chin and from every smudge of tattoo on his broad neck and thick-veined arms. He wore a white vest which stretched over a torso that looked as if he had won it in a fight with a silverback gorilla. His stare turned John's blood cold and made him feel as if all his bodily fluids were about to trickle out of him through his large intestine but he stood his ground, barely capable, in truth, of doing otherwise.

'Who the fuck are you?' it growled.

John tried to coax words from his suddenly dry throat but, thankfully, Tracy helped him out.

'This is John. He's an old friend of Brendan's from university.'

The words appeared to suppress the creature's urge to make an immediate physical intervention. That was as much as John hoped for right now.

'Can't be much of a friend, he's been dead five years.' Its glare remained fixed on the face of the unwanted intruder. 'Tell him to fuck off.'

With that, it turned and retreated within its lair, satisfied the boundaries were not under threat.

He was a charmer all right.

'Are you safe, Tracy?' John asked in a hushed voice.

She nodded, unconvincingly. 'Vince is just very protective. He's been good to us really.'

A voice boomed out from within the house and made her visibly flinch.

'TRACY!'

'I'd better go now, Smurf.' She moved to close the door.

'Wait a second.' He reached into his inside pocket for his wallet and drew out a business card. 'If you need me for anything, just call.'

She took the card and quickly smuggled it up her sleeve. With a thin, apologetic smile, the door was closed.

John was flustered. He wanted to get away from there as quickly as he could, while he could, but it was obvious Tracy was in a predicament. Leaving her felt like a betrayal, but this was not a situation he could make better here and now. Seeing her so vulnerable and so diminished had shaken him – and what about the kids? He had not seen a sign of the kids. What must their lives be like, sharing a home with The Thing's less kindly half-brother? It was a frightening thought. He felt compelled to do something but powerless to act. It was not a pleasant feeling.

Thankfully, the car was still there and so he drove away, unscathed but nevertheless a lesser man.

'Honestly, Stell, you should have seen the size of him.'

He needed to talk. He needed the distraction and so he had called her from the car as soon as he had navigated his way back to the main road.

'There were bricks in that back yard with teeth marks on them.'

Indulgent smiles do not really transmit very well in a telephone conversation, but John knew he was getting one of Stella's indulgent smiles right then.

'You do talk rubbish sometimes,' she said.

He laughed. 'Fair point, but he was huge and really aggressive with it. I mean, like nasty aggressive. You wouldn't want to pick a fight with him and you definitely wouldn't want to share a house with him. I felt really scared for Tracy because you could see her nerves were frayed from his constant presence and what must he do to her? What does he do to the kids? It's not a safe environment. I felt really bad leaving them there.'

'What else could you have done? Practically, what else could you have done other than what you have done, which is to pass your concerns on to the people who can actually do something about it?'

She was right, of course.

'I know, but it just makes you feel sort of inadequate.'

He was momentarily distracted from his sense of inadequacy by a taxi driver pulling up sharply in front of him and flicking on his hazard lights. John swerved around him and muttered.

'Dickhead.'

'What was that?'

'Nothing. Just a taxi driver being a dickhead.'

'Don't start thinking you have to take it into your own hands with this builder. Your last attempt at going hands-on wasn't exactly a roaring success.'

Stella wasn't the type to let her emotions show, but he had been able to tell that she was concerned about what had happened at the bandstand.

'I won't be doing anything daft, don't worry. I just hope the police can get him before anything bad happens.'

She was quiet. She had seemed distracted all through the conversation.

'Anyway, are you OK? How are the boys?'

'They're getting better, thanks. They're not happy with me that I won't let their dad take them to the football this afternoon, which I think is a good sign. It's been a horrible bug. Half the school have been off with it.'

'And you? You've not got it as well, have you?'

'No, no. I'm fine. Just a bit, you know.'

He decided not to pry further. She was clearly not in the mood to talk about it.

'OK. Call me if you need me to get you anything while you're taking care of the boys.'

'I will. Thanks. See you on Monday.' The traffic lights changed on the roundabout over the motorway and he drove on, back towards home.

It was his turn to be concerned. He had never heard Stella sound so flat. He reckoned that it must be because they were getting to know each other better. People tend to make less of an effort to keep up an outward appearance when they are with someone close. That was probably all it was.

23

Monday was not usually an especially busy day, but this one was. The first job urgently requiring John's attention landed on his desk early in the morning and was swiftly followed by another. Then another. He wasn't aware that anything big was coming up but suddenly everybody above him seemed to be acting as if there was.

At not long after four in the afternoon, his phone rang. It was not a number already in his address book – a mobile number. He was in the middle of a long, detailed document and thought about declining the call, but it had already distracted him by then and so he picked up.

'Hello, John Baldwin.'

Silence. Great. No doubt soon to be followed by the inevitable background noise of a call centre. Not this time. There was a noise. Sobbing.

'Hello, who is this?'

It was an awful sound. Whoever it was sounded so overcome that they could not get their words out.

'It's OK. Just take a deep breath and try to relax.'

He allowed whoever it was time to compose themselves. He hoped his tone had reassured them.

'That's good. Now, how can I help?'

The sobbing became less overwhelming, more controlled. It sounded like a child or a woman.

Finally, they spoke.

'John, it's Tracy.'

Oh, Jesus! He's attacked her!

'Tracy, are you hurt? What's happened?'

'He's going to kill me.'

She started sobbing again and wailing. Proper panicked anguish.

'I'm going to call the police, Tracy. Is he there in the house? Are the kids safe?'

She needed to compose herself again. He needed to hear her answer.

'Tracy, are the kids safe?'

'We're all right but it's Charlie, the eldest. He's done a very bad thing. Oh god! Vince is going to go spare!'

He allowed her a few moments while he tried to think.

'What has he done?'

She was clearly fighting panic again.

'He's broken Vince's computer. He knows he's not allowed to go on it but he found out where Vince keeps his passwords and went on it to play one of those games. You know, Warfare or something. Vince won't let him play them usually because he says they're too violent.'

Christ! That's rich.

'But you know what eleven year olds are like. All his mates play them. He says he's never done it before but he sneaked up when he got back from school and now he's broken it. Oh god! It's my fault. I should have stopped him. Vince is going to blame me.'

This is a problem. I must get them out of the house.

'Tracy, when does Vince get home? I don't want you or the kids there when he gets back. It's not safe. Where can you go until he has the chance to calm down a bit?'

'He won't be back until Friday. He's gone to do a flat conversion job down south somewhere. He's away all week.'

Thank Christ.

'This is good. We can get the computer fixed before he gets back. What exactly has happened to it?'

'Charlie said it was taking ages to load after he put the passwords in and then it came up with an error message. Lots of numbers and something like 'unknown fatal box error' or something. He was terrified when he came to me and we tried to do restarts and forced crashes and whatever, but it still kept coming up with the same message. What can we do?'

What *can* we do?

'I'm no computer expert, Tracy, but I think we ought to let somebody take a look who does know about them. Do you know anybody?'

'No.'

'Neither do I. Look, give me five minutes. I'll find somewhere that fixes them close to where you are and get them to sort it out. I'll call you straight back.'

He tapped the search into his own computer and found a repair shop at a retail park a couple of miles from Tracy's house. He checked the opening times. Open until eight. Perfect. He dialled their number.

'Hello, Tech Shop. Nathan speaking.'

'Oh, hi. A friend of mine has got an urgent problem and needs to bring in their computer to see if you can fix it. The thing is, she needs it back before Friday or she's in big trouble. Do you think you could do it in that time scale?'

'Friday? We normally say it could take longer than that because it depends what has gone wrong, you see. Let me have a look at how much we've got booked in.'

'Thanks. It would really be helping her out of a big hole. It needs to be done pretty urgently.'

John could hear keyboard tapping followed by mildly exasperated blowing sounds.

'Sorry, the system's running really slow today.'

That's not exactly reassuring.

'Here we are. You're in luck. We're not very busy this week. What did she say the problem was?'

'She said it wouldn't load properly and then kept coming up with the same error message when they tried doing force quits.'

'OK. What kind of error message?'

'She was a bit vague. I don't think she's really very technical. At least the computer was still turning on. That's got to be a good sign, hasn't it?'

'Maybe.'

Was it ever possible to get a straight answer out of an IT guy? The ones he occasionally had to deal with at work were the same. It was as if they felt sharing their knowledge might weaken the grip of superiority they held over the less computer-savvy masses.

'I'll get her to bring it to you tonight. Please do your best for her.'

'Well, I can't guarantee we'll be able to fix it until we have a look but we will do our best.'

'Thanks. Nathan, isn't it?'

'That's right.'

'Nathan, you're a top man. Her name is Tracy Williamson. As I say, she'll bring it to you today – maybe half an hour or so. Whatever it costs, I'll take care of that. Put it on my card.'

He passed on his card details and hung up, then called Tracy.

She had stopped crying but still sounded anxious.

'I've just phoned the people at the retail park up the road. I told him you need it back before Friday and he said he'd sort it out.'

'Thank god – but I can't afford an expensive computer repair.'

'Never mind about that. This one's on me.'

'I can't let you—'

'I couldn't be there to help you after the accident but I can do this for you. I insist.'

She fell quiet.

'Bless you, Smurf. Brendan always said you were a good 'un.'

'Yeah, well. He was a good mate. Can you get anybody to run you over to the retail park straight away?'

'Not really.'

'What about a taxi?'

'I haven't got any money for a taxi. I'll catch the bus.'

Jesus! Does that bastard not even give her any money?

'You can't take a computer on the bus. I'll sort you out a taxi and tell them to wait for you to bring you back. I'll get them to come over to you straight away. Get your son to disconnect all the wires to the main box and tell him to take all the passwords with you. I'm sure they'll need them.'

'I'll do that. Thanks, Smurf. You've saved my life.'

After arranging the taxi, John sat back in his chair with a large sigh of relief. That could have worked out a lot worse.

Then he figured out how it could work out a lot better.

'You again? We're going to have to be careful. My wife will start thinking there's something up.'

'Ha, ha! You're not really my type.'

'How can I help you, John?'

He had really come to like DC Harrison. There were no sides to him. A proper copper.

'It's about the bloke I told you about with the dodgy stuff on his computer.'

'Oh, yes. I passed that information up the line to the right people. Not heard anything back yet, mind.'

'I didn't expect so yet but you might like to contact them again because, as we speak, the computer in question is being taken to the repair shop for fixing.'

'Now that's interesting.'

'Am I right in thinking that if a repair shop finds indecent images on a computer they report that to the police and then you don't need a warrant to seize it?'

'They're not obliged to but they usually do if they find anything.'

'Well, if I tell you which repair shop this computer is being taken to and your people make sure they have a look to see what they can find, might that hurry along the process a little?'

He heard the click of a pen down the line.

'Tell me where it's been taken.'

The work had not gone away, but John felt he needed to give Stella an update before he could crack on with it.

She was at her desk, typing. She looked up as he approached her and forced a smile.

'Hey, Stell, I've got a bit of news for you. Have you got ten minutes for a coffee?'

She glanced at the three small piles of papers to her left.

'Not really. I have to get this lot done and I wanted to get off on time tonight to pick up the boys from my mother's because she's off out tonight and I haven't been able to get anything like as much done as I wanted to today. Is it urgent?'

'No, no, it can wait. I'll call you tonight, if that's OK.' Her reluctance bothered him.

'Sure. Leave it until after eight though, will you?' She started typing again.

'Yeah, fine. I'll speak to you then.'

He waited for a further response, but there was none.

'You OK, Stell?'

She looked up and seemed to have to check herself from appearing irritated by the question.

'I'm fine, John, or at least I will be when I can get this done.'

'I understand. I've booked the table for Wednesday, by the way.'

He hoped the mention of their Valentine's Day plans might lift her mood.

She stopped typing.

'I was going to talk to you about that, actually. Can we just have a meal around your place, instead? I don't feel up to going out. Is that all right?'

John felt hurt. Normally, the notion of a romantic night in would suit him better. Generally, he thought of Valentine's Day as a ludicrously over-commercialised excuse to boost the profits of the greetings card industry, but he had been prepared to go along with it, as it was their first together, and was actually looking forward to it.

'If that's what you want. I'll cancel the table, then.'

She was typing again.

He wandered back to his office, crestfallen.

Something was wrong. He shared with many of his gender the common fault of not always being reliably perceptive to the subtle moods of the female, but this was unmistakable.

Something was wrong. The more he tried to work it out, the more his lack of insight fed his fears. The more his fears grew, the worse it looked for him.

She's thinking of calling it off.

He had asked himself many times in their early days why a beautiful woman like Stella had chosen an ordinary bloke like him. She could have her pick of so many men. Why me? He liked to think it was because she was impressed by the changes he had made in his life and, after going through the break-up of her own marriage, she had decided to attach a different set of values to what she wanted in a relationship. Maybe she had decided sturdy and reliable was what she was looking for, like taking comfort from slipping on an old and cosy pullover. That's what he was to her – an old and cosy pullover.

Then he had told her everything. That was a mistake. She thought she was getting into a nice, straightforward relationship with a sturdy and reliable guy and then she had found out he was really more of a cross between Sylvester Stallone and Derek Acorah. He had become too complicated and now she wanted out.

He thought about raising his concerns over the phone that night but lacked courage. He decided it would not be appropriate to raise the issue the following day at work. He resolved to leave it until she came around on Wednesday night.

Happy Valentine's Day. So much for that.

But he also decided not to feel sorry for himself. While there was still a chance he could change her mind, he was going to try to take it. So he did the nice meal, the dozen red roses, the sparkling non-alcoholic wine, the candles – the works. He might not be the man she thought he was but he could still be a man she wanted.

He buzzed her through at the security door downstairs and waited, bouquet in hand, trying not to let his nervousness show.

She looked magnificent. Her auburn hair was immaculately styled and fell over her shoulders onto the lacy neckline of her royal blue dress as she slipped off her coat. Her earrings twinkled in silver and blue and her lips were full and red. There was no doubt she had wanted to look good and even less doubt that she had achieved it.

'You look absolutely gorgeous.'

She smiled, but it was an uncertain smile, like she was setting out on a blind date.

'Thank you. The flat looks nice.'

He was momentarily stunned, but then remembered to step forward to present the roses. She was clearly trying not to, but tears sprung to the corners of her eyes anyway and made them glisten even more.

'I'm sorry, John. This is all so very lovely of you.'

He put the flowers down on the sofa and held her. He could not say anything, even if he had been able to think of the right words. She wrapped her arms around his back and then slid them down to his hips so that she could look into his eyes.

'I love you.'

They were the words he had dreamt of hearing from her. He knew he loved her but he had been reluctant to say so, just in case she felt it was too early in their relationship. There. She had said it. He should be the happiest man in the world but he still felt as if they were the opening words of a gentle let-down. I love you, but...

'I love you too, Stell.'

The tears rose again and she made no attempt to dab at them. This was agony.

'Come on, Stell. I know there's something. You have to tell me.'

She mustered her courage and looked him in the eye again.

'I'm pregnant.'

His first instinct was to laugh. He was glad later that he didn't obey his first instinct.

Unfortunately, he had no idea what his second instinct was. Not for what seemed like an age, anyway. He just stood and looked at her. Not one single, discernible, clear thought came into his head. He was as helpless and detached as someone must feel as they fall from a great height, in the moments before the ground looms to hit them with a thud. He was no more able to process those two words that he was to comprehend the secrets of the universe. He just stood and looked at her, as pitifully shocked as a puppy that had fallen through thin ice into a pond, until the awareness dawned. She was aching for him to say something. Anything.

'That's...wonderful. I mean, really...wonderful.'

He pulled her close again.

Pregnant? Christ! I'm going to be a dad.

'This is great, Stell. Oh god! This is so good.'

He released his grip.

'Are you certain? I mean, we were using...'

'I know. I'm late and I'm never late. I did two tests and then I did a third this afternoon, just to be sure. Same result. I know my body.'

'Wow, fantastic!' He was beginning to get giddy now. 'How pregnant are you? I mean, how many weeks?'

'Only three or four, I would say. It's very early days. The thing is, John, I don't think I can go through this again.'

The puppy, just as it looked as if it had scrambled to the shore, slipped back into the pond.

'What do you mean?'

'I mean we've barely known each other five minutes and I can't help feeling that's not long enough to be having a baby together. My boys have been through a lot, what with the divorce, and they've adjusted really well but add in a new baby and I don't know what that will do to them. Babies are hard work, John. They would be bound to feel excluded. And then I would have to give up work again, just as I was beginning to feel I could start to move forward in my career, and it's like I said to you before, I would be giving them the excuse to keep me down on the shop floor and I don't want them to have that excuse. There's just so much not right about this. The timing is all wrong.'

No wonder she had not been acting herself in recent days. John understood now. In so short a time, however, the thought of fatherhood meant so much to him. He had to reassure her.

'It doesn't have to be that way, Stell.'

He manoeuvred her to the sofa and they sat down.

'You won't be doing it alone. I'll be there with you and I'll do the whole dad thing, I promise. I can do nappies and all that. We can be a proper family. I can give up the lease on this place and we can all live together. I can never be the boys' dad and I wouldn't dream of getting between them and their real dad but I can be there for them and teach them how to play cricket and still do everything I can for the baby as well. It can work, Stell. We can make it work. And by the time you go on maternity leave I will have got my business up and running again and when the baby is a bit bigger, we'll be able to develop the business together. Sod the building society. They don't appreciate you, anyway. We'll be financially independent because we'll make a great team. There's the charity as well. You can help run the charity. We're going to need to employ people to manage it at this rate and you'll be perfect at that.'

She was crying again, but they seemed like happy tears this time.

'I know we've only been together a few weeks but I do love you, Stell, and I know we're right together. You said to me that you thought my seeing Stef was a blessing – well, this is a blessing. The baby is a blessing. It means we are meant for each other.'

They held each other and cried together. In the kitchen, the braised chicken in tomato and basil sauce was overcooking beyond redemption. Neither of them cared in the slightest.

24

The meal was ruined, the sparkling non-alcoholic wine remained uncorked and the roses looked a bit sorry for themselves after being left out of water overnight, but it had been an excellent Valentine's Day.

The woman he loved had told him she loved him too and that they were going to have a baby. For a man who believed he was about to get dumped, that counted as a result.

Fatherhood. Oh my lord!

John had never really considered he was the type. Even in the days when Amy had first tentatively suggested that she would like to start a family, he had not even remotely warmed to the idea. He persuaded her it would be wiser to build the business first. Give them a stable base, he had rationalised it. All he was really doing was trying to put her off so that she might grow out of the idea and realise that what they had together was too good to jeopardise. Just think of the holidays, the impromptu days out, the disposable income, the freedom. Swap that for sleepless nights and screaming brats? No thanks!

He had never got past the stage of looking at fraught parents trying to placate bawling toddlers without feeling a shudder down his spine. Even when he encountered happy fathers sharing a game with joyously giggling children, he never viewed the scene with envy. He always saw what the fathers must have had to give up rather than seeing what they had gained.

No doubt his unhappy relationship with his father had coloured his own view of parenthood.

That was until he saw the little girl in the front window at Amy's house. Then he saw what the appeal was. Then he realised what he was missing.

Stella was right when she said the timing could have been better, certainly from the point of view of their relatively young relationship, but would the timing ever be completely right? He would be thirty-eight by the time the baby was born, forty-three by the time he/she started school, fifty-six by the time he/she went off to university. He didn't want to be waiting much longer.

Besides, this felt right. He was going to be a dad – and that was just awesome!

Stella conquered her reservations. They talked into the night about the life they were going to make together and she had answered all his questions about the practicalities of each stage of the pregnancy. They came to a conclusion about the likely day of conception and had joked about how they might have to name the baby after one of the lead characters in the TV show they had started watching together before they became...distracted. Is Daenerys really such a bad name for a girl?

The following morning, they travelled to work together and she held his hand between gear changes. They were perfectly content.

'Don't say anything to anybody at work, will you?' she said as they pulled into the car park.

Unnecessarily, John thought.

'Of course not.'

'They'll all find out soon enough. It's still very early days. I don't want everybody clucking around. Nobody else needs to know yet.'

'I know, Stell. I'm not daft.' He closed the car door and then opened it again to retrieve the key from the ignition.

'It's just that... '

'I understand, Stell. I'll not say a word.' He opened the car boot to take out their work bags and passed Stella hers. 'Business as usual.'

She smiled. 'Business as usual.'

It felt far from business as usual as he laboured over his normal mundane morning tasks. Life was different. How much more will it change over the coming months, years even? The thought was exciting and terrifying in equal measure.

What if I'm not cut out to be a dad?

My parents had me too young and resented it for more or less every second of my childhood. What if Stell grows to resent me? She was right. We've hardly had time to get to know each other at all. Not properly. What if it's too soon and I'm a useless dad?

His phone rang, breaking the spiral of self-doubt. Tracy.

'Hey, Tracy.'

'Smurf, they've arrested him. Vince. He's been arrested. They just called me this morning, you know, the police. The police down south. Oh my god, Smurf, what have I done?' She blurted out the words. She was panicking again.

'Calm down, Tracy, you haven't done anything wrong. What did the police say?'

'Oh, god!' He could hear her breathing was shallow. 'They said Vince had got himself in a bit of a scrap in a pub and he spent the night in the cells, but they've kept him in because the police in Sheffield want to talk to him about his computer. Something to do with stuff they've found on his computer. Oh god, I've got him in some serious trouble. He's going to kill me!'

John tried to think fast. The last thing he wanted was for this to backfire horribly on Tracy.

'First of all, if they've found something nasty on his computer, you're certainly not to blame for that. That would be down to Vince and Vince alone. Don't forget, he wouldn't let you or the kids anywhere near the computer and it looks like this was the reason why. Whatever type of sick material it is they've found, you are definitely not responsible for it being there. It's a good thing the computer broke when it did because otherwise you wouldn't have needed to take it in to be fixed and then the police wouldn't have been alerted to what was stored on it, then who knows what Vince could have done next? If they've found something like child porn or whatever, your kids could have been in danger, Tracy. Think about that.'

He heard a strangled 'Oh god!' down the line as Tracy contemplated the suggestion.

'Sometimes these things happen for a reason, Tracy. If the computer had broken when Vince was home there was no way he would risk the material on it being discovered and so he would have carried on getting away with it. It was a good thing it broke when it did, don't you see that?'

'I suppose so,' she said after a small pause.

'The most important thing now is that you and the kids are protected. I'm going to give you a number for someone I know in the police at Sheffield. He's a good man. He'll be able to point you towards the right people to make sure Vince can't hurt you or the kids ever again. I want you to trust him and take whatever help the police and Social Services give you. Are you OK with that?'

'Yes.' It was a hesitant response. 'Yes, I will. If that's what you think is for the best.'

'It has to be what *you* think is for the best, Tracy. Do you want to stop Vince from coming back to your home?'

'Yes, I suppose.'

'Would you feel safer if he wasn't there?'

'Yes. Yes, you're right, Smurf. I'll do as you say.'

'Good.' He looked up the number on his phone and read it out to her. Her lack

176

of self-confidence shocked him and her hopeless dependence on this brutal man who had moved in on her life when she was at her most vulnerable both sickened and angered him. He hoped she would take the right course now, but could not be entirely confident that she would. His support and encouragement would be needed for a while yet.

'You are going to call him, aren't you, Tracy?'

'Yes. Yes I am.'

'Call him straightaway, won't you.'

'I will, yes.'

'OK, that's good. Do what's best for your kids, Tracy.'

'You're right. Thanks, Smurf.'

She hung up. He sat back in his chair. The thought of her allowing that man back through the door was too awful. Surely, she will let the police help her.

I'll call them myself later, make sure she did what she said she would.

The phone rang again. John looked to see who it was. It was not the number he usually called Tom Harrison on but it looked similar. Maybe it was about the computer thing. They could be calling to thank him for helping them get their hands on Vince Williamson.

'Hello, John Baldwin.'

'Hello, Mr Baldwin, this is DS Webster from South Yorkshire CID.'

He did not know the name.

'Hello there.'

'Mr Baldwin, I'm calling regarding the complaint of an alleged assault on Sunday, December the 17th last year involving yourself and a Craig Christopher Thomas.'

'Oh yes.' At last. This has been hanging over me for long enough. About time all the loose ends were tidied up.

'As you will recall, the statements we took from all parties and the medical evidence were sent to the Crown Prosecution Service for their consideration to see if charges should be brought in regard to this alleged offence and we have now had their response. The CPS have decided that there is sufficient cause to warrant a prosecution in this case...'

'What!'

'...and I'm going to have to ask you to present yourself to the police station, where you will be formally charged with the offence of Assault Occasioning Actual Bodily Harm, contrary to section 47 of the Offences against the Person Act 1861.'

'Jesus! This is ridiculous!'

'I should warn you that failure to present yourself...'

'I'm not going to run away, am I?' John became aware that his tone was a little too aggressive. Might not be a good idea to come across as someone who actually might be capable of a serious assault in case this was being recorded as evidence.

'I'm sorry but I'm absolutely shocked that the CPS are willing to take it this far. This is ludicrous. I stepped in to prevent a man from being quite likely killed here. Are you sure this is what they've decided?'

'Quite sure, sir.'

John paced around his office, unable to contain his frustration.

'I'll come in to Snig Hill as soon as I can make the right arrangements.'

'Will you arrange for your own legal representation or do you want us to arrange for a solicitor to be present on your behalf?'

John caught sight of the waste bin in the corner of his eye and was sorely tempted to aim a huge kick at it.

'No. I'll bring my own solicitor. This is absolutely ridiculous. I'll be there and I'll have my solicitor with me. I'll let you know when I can arrange a time that suits us both. This is totally outrageous. It's no wonder this country's in such a mess if this is how the CPS wastes everybody's time and money.'

He hung up and slammed the phone down onto the desk.

Outside, on the main office floor, those in nearby desks whose ears had picked up the sound of a raised voice flinched at the roar of anguish from the enclosed office space behind them, followed by the light thud of what seemed to be a cylindrical metal object hitting the wall.

'It won't come to that.'

Max Monaghan of the law firm Toombs, Tonks and Taylor was nothing if not a man eternally confident in his professed judgement, even though his most recent confident judgement – that the CPS would dismiss the complaint of assault as a clear case of reasonable force used in self-defence or the protection of another and therefore it was plainly not in the public interest to pursue a prosecution – had proved slightly wide of the mark. His confident judgement now – that the case would surely be quickly dismissed in court through the weight of evidence in favour of the defendant and that the CPS would be rightly rebuked by the magistrate for bringing the case to court in the first place – was in response to John pointing out, as they left the police station following the formal reading of the charge, that he had read there was a maximum sentence of five years in prison for ABH.

'No point even contemplating the possibility of being found guilty because you are innocent. This prosecution should not have seen the light of day. Scandalously poor judgement by the CPS.'

He was perhaps twenty years older than John and his permanently arched eyebrows gave the impression he was perpetually in a state of agitation, though attention was usually drawn from his expression by his habit of wearing consistently appalling ties. Today's was a pink, blue, yellow and several other clashing colours combination of diamond shapes, made even more hideous by the red with white pinstripes shirt he had selected to set it against.

Toombs, Tonks and Taylor had acted for John all the way through setting up the business and through the divorce and, up until very recently, he had never felt any reason to doubt that Max Monaghan's confident judgement was anything less than completely sound. He still felt that way through the last day and a half, actually. As his state of mind flitted between various degrees of anger, exasperation and indignation, he remained convinced that his current situation was, indeed, the result of scandalously poor judgement on the part of the CPS. That did not stop him from being concerned enough to check what the punishment might be, however.

Stella reacted with calming reassurance when he told her of the development. She was really good about it. Jas tried to hide her usual initial reaction to bad news – to worry that the worst outcome was a practical inevitability – behind a mask of righteous pique but, in the end, it was John who had to do most of the comforting there. He decided it was wise to inform his line manager what was going on too and he was broadly supportive, though not, John thought, convincingly so. Perhaps he was concerned about possible damage to the image of the company.

However, the confident judgement of Max Monaghan was that no one need have any concerns over undesirable conclusions.

'I'll consult with one of the partners, but I'm certain she will say the same as I've already told you. No chance of anything other than a speedy dismissal by the court. Shouldn't have come to this in the first place. We'll speak again soon.'

With that, Max Monaghan shook John's hand vigorously and turned to hurry back to the offices of Toombs, Tonks and Taylor. John watched him go. The process of being charged made him feel like he was a criminal already and had shaken his belief that he was the innocent party in this matter. His solicitor may have been entirely confident that the justice system would come down firmly in his favour, but he was now less so.

25

Nearly a quarter to eleven. The business at the police station had taken less time than he anticipated. John had arranged to meet Mike at midday at the community hall, where they were going to discuss the best use of the money they had raised in the firewalk with community leaders and Mike's mate from the council.

'Bollocks.'

He should have been excited about the meeting. This was what they had been working towards since he first met up with Mike. He was excited about it really. It was just that he felt a little flat right now and wished he hadn't said he would go, or that it was another day, or...

He also wished he didn't have so much time to waste until then. What was it, ten minutes in the car? Could go for a coffee, set off about twenty to? That's a long time to sit nursing a cappuccino and feeling sorry for yourself. Bollocks.

Then he decided. Leave the car in the multi-storey, walk to the meeting. It was a nice enough day. Didn't look like it would rain. The walk would clear his mind. The meeting will be a welcome distraction. Something positive. Forget about the bloody court case. Think about GameOn and the good it will do. Think about Stella. And the baby.

So John set off walking. As he did, he reached into his pocket for his phone.

He had promised to tell Stella how he got on at the police station.

'Hey, Stell.'

'Hi, how was it?'

Alien, intimidating, humiliating, scary.

'It was OK. Just a formality really.'

'How long do they think it will be until you have to go to court?'

'Two weeks, three maybe. Hopefully, it'll all be dealt with at the magistrates in one go. The solicitor still thinks it'll be over with very quickly and that the charges will be dismissed.'

'I'm sure he's right.'

'I hope so.' John wished he had responded more positively.

'You know so. What are you up to before you meet up with Mike?'

'I decided to walk there. I've got plenty of time. I thought the walk would do me good.'

Stella could sense his vulnerability.

'Do you want me to come to meet up with you?'

'No, no, I'm fine. You've got the boys to see to. I'll clear my head with the walk and look forward to the meeting. I'm not going to let myself get wound up about the court case because there's nothing I can do about that. It'll be sorted, like the solicitor said. Are you still OK for tonight?'

'Of course.'

'I'll tell you about the meeting then. Looking forward to seeing you later. Love you.'

'Love you too.'

The call diverted John's attention from having to walk past the Magistrates' Court and soon he was heading over the river, past the takeaways and convenience stores clinging on to life on the long-forgotten periphery of the city centre and heading towards the old Wicker railway arches.

The community hall seemed a long way away but already this felt like a good idea. As the sound of the weir faded behind him, John felt as if he was putting distance between himself and what was to come. There really is nothing to be gained from fretting about it. It's going to happen and that's it. All I can do is have faith in the system and in the strength of my case.

In Max Monaghan we trust.

There really did seem to be a lot of couples with children around. Dads pushing pushchairs, a mum with the youngest child straddled on her hip and an older one holding her hand. Perhaps there were always this many families around and he just didn't notice. He noticed them now and tried to imagine himself in their position. How does that feel? It was still too crazy an idea to envisage. But he was warming to the concept.

John tried to recall times he and his parents went out together as a family, even if it was only on a trip to the shops. There must have been times but he could not recall one. Yes, there were times he went out with mum, to get new shoes for school or just to be with her as she picked up a few things for tea. Dad was never there, though. Even when they had their week by the seaside – Scarborough, Skeggy or

Brid usually – it was always dad doing his own thing and mum who led the occasional trip to the park or who supervised digging in the sand, on the days when the wind off the North Sea made it tolerable for an adult to be on the beach. Mealtimes at the B&B were just about the only times they were all three together. He barely noticed that then, never asked why it should be that way. It was just normal.

At home, he was largely left to entertain himself and spent hours making model aeroplane kits or painting plastic soldiers. It was practically a production line. His bedroom must have permanently reeked of enamel paint and turpentine. Large portions of the summer holidays were spent in front of the TV or playing games with his friends. He could never recall feeling bored. Or neglected, for that matter. It was just normal.

There was one time, he recalled, when he was maybe eight or nine and mum finally consented to take him to the fair which came to the top field every year. Dad didn't come, of course. The crowds, the lights, the sounds – it was immensely thrilling and he could not understand why mum appeared to regard it as so potentially dangerous. They never saw any trouble but mum insisted he stayed within arm's length. If that was the condition of being able to be there, it was worth obeying.

She wouldn't go with him on the Waltzer. Oh no! It's far too fast! Look at the way those men are spinning the cars around! I'd be sick! We'd both be sick! No way!

As a concession, she gave him fifty pence – an advance against next week's pocket money – so that he could have a go at throwing a ping pong ball into a glass goldfish bowl. After it was pointed out that it was his own money he was spending and if he wanted to waste it this way it was his responsibility and that nobody ever won on these things and that it was undoubtedly a big con because the ping pong balls were no bigger than the opening to the bowls, she handed over the coin and he gave it to the fairground man in the scruffy cap, once his attention could be drawn from the three teenage girls further around the brightly painted circular stall.

'Unlucky, ladies, fancy another go?'

Two of the girls had already turned away. The third shook her head and quickly broke eye contact, rushing to join her friends.

He took John's money without a word and handed over three ping pong balls, turning back to gaze towards where the three girls had gone.

The first ball hit the rim of one bowl and bobbled between several others before settling to a rest in a gap. Without even looking, he could see mum rolling her eyes disapprovingly. What a waste of money!

Come on! Take aim. Go for that one right in the middle.

With the ball between his thumb and forefinger, he cocked his wrist once, twice, like a dart player sizing up a treble twenty, and let the ball go. It arced towards the target but bounced off the rim again. This time, however, it took three, four more deviations before falling neatly in the mouth of one of the bowls and rattling to the bottom.

'Yes!' John threw his arms to the air in triumph.

'Have you won?' His mother turned her head belatedly back to the scene of glory, having been distracted by the perils all around her.

The man in the cap also noticed the celebration.

'We have a winner!' he announced to anyone close enough to hear above the noise of the dodgems, hoping they might be tempted to have a go themselves, now that they had been presented with irrefutable evidence of how fair a challenge it was.

'Well done, young man. Here's your prize.' He began to reach down beneath the shelf.

'Hang on, he's got another go yet!' Mum was suddenly fully invested. John held up the third ball as confirmation.

The man stood up again and crossed his arms, waiting.

John took aim, trying to replicate his winning technique. One, two and release. The ball pinged off one bowl, two bowls and then deviated sharply over the edge to rest at the fairground man's feet.

Who cares? I won!

The man bent to pick up the third ball and handed over the prize. It was a plaster frog, crudely painted green with patches of white around its base and a smear of red smudged across its smiling lips. John looked at it in his hands and traced his finger around the air bubble indentation on its back. His fifty pence would probably have paid for one hundred of them but that wasn't the point. He had won it and that made it as precious as the World Cup.

He marched into the front room proudly with his trophy. Mum promised him he could put it on the mantelpiece. He made a space and placed it down, standing back in admiration. In his chair, dad peered over the top of his newspaper.

'What the bloody hell is that?'

'It's a frog ornament. I won it.'

'At the fair,' reminded mum, in case dad had forgotten where they had been.

His parents stared at each other for a moment, her non-committal, him incredulous. He shook his head and turned back to his paper.

'Bloody hideous.'

The following morning, before going in for breakfast, John went to look at his prize again but it was gone. Dad was in the kitchen.

'Have you seen my frog?'

He barely acknowledged the question. 'Your mum knocked it off the mantelpiece accidentally. I had to throw it away.' He carried on stirring his tea.

John was quiet through breakfast. There was no point making a fuss about his loss. It would only have resulted in a telling-off. He decided he would salvage the pieces of the ornament from the bin and glue them back together. Once he had painted it properly, no one would be able to tell it had ever been broken.

Waiting until the kitchen was empty, he delved into the bin and felt around. His hand touched the plaster of the frog. It seemed like quite a large piece. He pulled it out and looked at it. It was intact.

Why would dad say it had been broken when it wasn't? Did mum know she had been given the blame? He thought about putting the question to her but decided not to. She may have been part of the decision to throw it away. So he took the frog to his room and secreted it away to protect it from further risk of disposal.

It stayed there for a week. John thought about painting it properly but he didn't have the right type of green and, besides, when he looked at it, it no longer looked like victory. It looked like disdain. Like lies. Like betrayal.

He hid it in his coat and took it to the pond, throwing it as far as he could and watching as the ripples it made expanded and faded until there was no trace. Then he went home and never asked to go to the fair again.

The car horn startled him. He was pretty sure pedestrians had the right of way crossing over a side street but John was aware that his thoughts had drifted elsewhere and held up his hand to the irate driver to own up to his apparent mistake.

Several people around him had their attention caught by the sudden blast of the horn but, quickly satisfied it was nothing more than the reaction of a dickhead driver to a dozy pedestrian, they paid it little heed. John glanced up to make sure they were no longer looking at him and, on the pavement, he stopped. Up ahead, maybe fifteen or twenty yards, shuffling away, shoulders hunched, head bowed, was a man, a youngish man judging by the way he was moving.

Him again. He knew it.

He was moving quite quickly. A nudge from a passing shoulder made John stumble and jolted him into pursuit.

Hell, what do I do?

He took out his phone. Plenty of charge this time.

'Hello, Sheffield CID, DC Dearden speaking.'

'Is Tom Harrison available please?'

'I'm afraid it's his day off today. How can I help?'

Bugger. Tell the tale again.

'Yes. My name's John Baldwin. I was witness to a murder a year or so ago and

I've spotted the man responsible. I'm walking behind him and following him.'

'I see.' The policeman's tone changed. 'Whereabouts are you, sir?'

'I'm on Burngreave Road. There's a doctor's to the left and a road coming up to the right. It's called...' He waited until he could read the sign. 'Abbeydale. No, Abbeyfield. Abbeyfield Road.'

'I'm with you. I'll get a unit to you as soon as I can but please stay on the line and, whatever you do, do not approach him. Have you got that, Mr Baldwin?'

John recalled that his last attempt at close contact did not work out well.

'I understand. How quickly can you get somebody here? He's walking quite quickly. I can keep him in sight but I don't want to risk losing him again.'

'My colleague is putting a call out now, sir. We should have a car in the area. Have you still got eyes on him?'

'Yes. He's about twenty yards ahead. We're just passing the park on the right.' Jesus, don't let him take off into a park again.

The man skipped across the road towards the park but stayed on the path, heading towards the next junction. The pace of the pursuit was making John pant for air but he did not think his prey had spotted him. He was sure the man could outrun him easily if he had wanted to make it a footrace.

'He's following the road right at the junction up, what is it? Barnsley Road?'

'I've got you. Up Barnsley Road. We've got a car on the way to you now, Mr Baldwin. Are you still OK?'

'Fine, fine.' His heart felt like it was about to burst out of his chest, less through the exertion as with anxiety. He must get this man this time.

A bus pulled into a stop thirty yards ahead of the man. There were plenty of people waiting to get on it. The man could easily get there in time to catch the bus if that was his intention. Thankfully, it wasn't.

'He's crossing the road again. I'm holding back because I don't want him to see me. I think he's heading for the road by the school. He is. He's going up it. I'm setting off again to make sure I don't lose sight of him.'

John broke into a run, dashing between the traffic to cross the busy main road. He saw the man take another turn to the left, just before what looked like a block of flats. He ran again.

'He's turned off the road. I'm just getting to where he went now.' He was getting quite breathless.

'There are some flats and he's gone up what seems to be a driveway leading behind the flats. I can't see him anymore but that's definitely where he went.'

The policeman remained quiet, considering his move. 'I want you to stay where you are now, Mr Baldwin. This could be too dangerous. The car is almost with you and we will take it from there.'

'But he could have disappeared by then.' John, getting his breath back, felt his panic rise. This might be his last chance. 'I'm just going to go a few yards up the driveway to see if he's there. I won't approach him.'

'Just stay where you are please, sir. I cannot guarantee your safety if you go any further.'

'It's OK. It's just a driveway.'

John edged up the driveway, nervously.

'Can't see him yet.'

'Do not go any further, Mr Baldwin.'

'I'm OK.'

Beyond the rough stone driveway behind the flats was a parking area with eight red-painted garages which appeared barely big enough to get a car into. Cars, one red, one white and one silver, were parked outside three of them.

Litter swirled in the breeze and a scrawny ginger and black tabby cat eyed John suspiciously as he craned his neck around the corner to inspect the open space between the flats and the garages. He could not see the man. Maybe he was hiding but John had sensed nothing to make him feel the man knew he was being followed.

At his side of the garages was an opening. Beyond it, John could see piles of dumped debris and a clump of trees and a well-worn muddy path. It looked like it might be a short-cut. Maybe that was why the man came this way.

He looked behind him and listened carefully for the sound of an approaching police car. There was nothing. He dropped the arm holding his phone to his side, not daring to speak into it in case he somehow alerted his prey, wherever he may be. He took a deep breath and stepped forward towards the path.

Bare trees stood either side of a trail, made by the regular tramp of feet, which cut a diagonal line across a patch of neglected ground. Discarded bags of rubbish were propped against a wooden fence to his left which partitioned the area from the back of someone's home. The fence, the garages and the trees gave the area an ominous sense of enclosure. It was not a place to be alone at night. Not really a place to be alone at any time. As John's eyes followed the line of the trail, he thought he could see a gap opening out on to a street. That must be where the man went. He set his gaze on the gap, trying to blank out everything else around him, and walked on.

Can't let him get away.

A hefty blow from behind, two open hands forcefully hitting him around the shoulder blades, knocked the air out of his lungs and sent John tumbling forwards. He landed on his knees, bracing himself against the fall with his hands, and spun around to sit on his backside and see where the hit came from. But he already knew.

Him.

He stood over John, malevolence in his eyes, his hand already reaching inside his jacket. As he pulled out his hand, John could see he was gripping the handle of a long knife. The blade never seemed to stop coming. Shit.

As the man withdrew the blade slowly, deliberately, it snagged on the lining of his jacket. He looked to see where it had caught and pulled sharply, freeing the end of the blade but sending the knife spinning loose from his grasp. It landed, flat on the ground, at John's feet. He quickly seized it and held it towards his assailant, using his other hand to ease himself to his feet again. The man lunged, trying to knock the knife loose, but John reacted to avoid the blow and stood tall, glaring at the man – not in fear anymore, but in conquest. I've got him.

The man looked around him. In withdrawing from his lunge he had backed himself into a corner between the garages and a tree. As John stepped forward, he was penned in. There was only one way for him to escape and, right now, it was not a good option.

John glanced down at the knife. It was maybe eight inches long, the sort of kitchen knife you could buy from a supermarket. As he looked at it, pale February sunshine broke through the clouds and, in a glint off the blade, John thought he could see Stef's shocked face, his eyes beseeching as his breath shortened and the life pumped from him through the gaping wound on the left side of his abdomen.

'Is this the one?' He glowered back towards the man, his heart full of rancour. 'Is this the knife you killed my mate with?'

The man's thin face showed no sign of submission. He stared back in arrogant defiance.

He no longer wore the straggly beard he had when John saw him at the firewalk and, from the wisps left exposed beneath his baseball cap, it looked as if he had changed his hair colour too, in an attempt to keep one step ahead of the photofit maybe.

A cheerless smile exposed his tobacco-stained teeth.

'Do you think I'm fucking stupid? I got rid of that one ages ago.'

Rage surged through John. He wanted to plunge the knife into the cold heart of this worthless murderer in front of him. End it now. But deep within him, the voice of restraint urged him to hold back. It wanted answers, not retribution.

'Why did you do it?'

'It was his own fucking fault.' The dark eyes remained impassive. 'He shouldn't have come at me. I didn't want to stab him, I only wanted to rob him. He only had to hand over his stuff and he'd have still been alive but he came at me. He gave me no choice. Stupid fucker.'

John could not comprehend the callousness. How could he at this moment – any moment – speak so contemptuously about a man whose life he took so needlessly? No remorse at all. He had no words to capture the hatred he felt for this man. All the loathing he had tormented himself with for a year was misdirected. Here was the culpable one. Here. Right in front of him.

'So come on then, let's sort this.' The man's eyes narrowed, challenging his opponent to make his move. 'This is what you wanted, isn't it? This is why you've been following me. Well, here's your chance. Let's see what you've got.'

John shook his head. 'I haven't been following you.'

'Don't give me that. You've been trailing me for weeks.'

'No, I haven't been following you, I've been led to you because you need to realise that you have to give yourself up. I don't want to fight you; I want to take you in. You did a terrible thing and you have to face the consequences. I want proper justice for what you did.'

The man sneered. 'The only justice there is where I come from is revenge and don't pretend you're any better than that because that's all you're interested in an' all. That's why you won't leave me alone.' He pointed his finger at John, accusingly. 'I made one mistake. I had to go out robbing because I didn't have any money and it went wrong but you don't know what that's like, do you? I made one mistake and I haven't done anything wrong since. I haven't broken any laws since then but you won't leave me alone, will you? Well, here's where it ends. When I saw you the last time, in the shop...'

What last time in the shop? I never saw him in a shop.

'... that got me thinking. The coppers haven't got anything on me or they'd have picked me up by now, so it's just you, you're the only thing that connects me to that night. I reckoned my best option was to wait until the next time you followed me, drag you to a place where there's nobody else about and see to it, once and for all. You're out of the way and I'm free of it for good.'

John glanced down at the knife in his hand. 'Except it didn't go to plan, did it?'

'Yeah, but what are you going to do about that? Your kind haven't got the balls.'

The man took a step forward until he was only a couple of feet from the point of the blade. John stepped back.

'See, you're scared shitless. You couldn't do it. That's why I'm going to walk away from here and then you'd better start looking over your shoulder because the next time we see each other it'll be me after you and you'll end up in a hole in the ground just like your mate. What do you think to that, then? You going to do something about it or are you going to pussy out?'

He stepped forward again.

'Come on then, show me what you've got. Come on.'

He was right. John knew he could do nothing. He couldn't stab this man. That would make him no better. His heart pounded and his mouth was so dry that he could not have answered back even if he could have found the words to speak. He was powerless.

'Thought so. Pussy.'

The man looked down at the knife. John's arm trembled so much it could barely hold onto the blade.

He's going to try to take it off me. He's going to try to knock it free and then I'm done for. I can't let him have it. I can't let him go.

He took another step back until he could almost feel the fence against his back. There was nowhere else to go. This was his last move.

Stab him! Stab him! Stab him!

From the depths of his soul, he found the power to speak.

'Get back or I will use this. I will.'

His faltering voice was far from intimidating but the words appeared to make the man reconsider his decision to strike. They stared at each other. The man was no longer trapped but John knew he couldn't just walk away. Not without the knife. It was the evidence that would lead the police to him. Something had to give. There was no other way.

'Stay right where you are!'

The voice startled both men. John looked to see two policemen emerging through the gap beside the garages. His foe moved to start running towards the far end of the muddy trail but two more policemen were coming through the trees.

'Put down the weapon!'

John hurriedly threw down the knife by his side. Two of the policemen already had the man in their grasp. One of them was securing his arms behind his back with handcuffs while the other frisked him vigorously.

'Mr Baldwin?'

The policeman had his hand on John's shoulder.

'Are you all right?'

John felt his heart was about to explode. His ears pulsed with the furious drumbeat, his eyes blackened and bulged and his whole skull seemed as if it was about to pop like an over-inflated balloon. The constricting tightness across his chest made him gasp for air and his legs began to buckle.

He grabbed the policeman's arm with both hands and began to lower himself to the ground for fear that he might collapse.

'Just need a second,' he wheezed as he landed on the soft ground, the small of his back against the wooden fence.

The policeman crouched beside him.

'Try to take deep breaths, sir. Nice and steady. Do you have a history of heart or respiratory problems? Sir, do you have any medication you need me to help you with?'

John raised his knees and rested his arms on them, trying to slow down his breathing and ease the restraining force around his rib cage. He shook his head.

A second policeman came forward.

'Shall I call for the paramedics?'

His colleague was staring intently at John, watching as he began to recover control of his body. Breathing. Slowly, deeply.

'Are you going to be all right, Mr Baldwin?'

'I think so.' Slowly, deeply, the storm moving into the distance. 'It was just...'

'Take your time, sir. That must have been a very traumatic experience for you. Take your time and let me know when you want me to help you.'

The policeman rose to his feet and turned to his colleague. 'I think he's OK.'

The second one nodded and shook out a plastic evidence bag to gather the knife.

John stayed still, concentrating on each breath, grateful not to be the focus of attention while the policemen went about their business. Grateful to still be alive. Jesus, that was horrible!

'Is this your mobile phone, Mr Baldwin?'

The officer had exposed the phone as he poked between the dead leaves and rubbish with his baton.

My phone. John patted the inside pocket where he usually kept it. It wasn't there. Then he remembered. It was in his hand as he stepped into the clearing, held by his side. Then he got whacked from behind and it must have...

'Yeah, I think so. It was knocked out of my hand.'

The officer picked it up and looked at it, then lifted it to his ear.

'Hello?' He paused. 'I think it's still connected. Hello? Who is this please?'

A broad smile spread across his face.

'Harry! How are you? It's Eddie Flynn. Yeah, we're with him now. Yeah, he's OK, just getting his head back together. Yeah, we've got him in custody, they're bringing him in now. Hang on, yeah, I'll pass you over.'

He offered the phone to John.

'It's DC Dearden.'

John took the phone.

'Hi. Have you been on the line the whole time?'

'Yes, sir. I heard every word and we've got it recorded. We've got him.'

26

He stood on the front doorstep and raised his hand to knock on the door but then hesitated. He felt more nervous about calling in on Jas unannounced this time than he had all those weeks ago when they hadn't seen each other for almost a year.

John rang Stella from the back of the police car as he was being taken back to the station to give his statement. She listened quietly as he told her the tale of his latest bout of utter recklessness, listening without rebuking him for his foolishness even once. She simply asked for reassurance that he was unharmed and told him that she would meet him at the police station. There was no point in him attempting to dissuade her this time and nor did he want to. He needed her.

He also rang Mike and apologised for his no-show at the meeting. Mike was more animated in his response to the story of John's unavoidable delay and, after saying that the meeting was productive and that he would brief him on the details at a more suitable time, shook his head as he hung up and silently wondered what sort of lunatic he had gone into business with.

But he could not ring Jas to tell her about it. That had to be done face to face. Stella, of course, agreed. So, after going through what was becoming the familiar routine of giving a statement to the police and picking up his car from the multi-storey, John called home to change out of his muddy clothes and drove around to Jas' house.

It was getting dark by that time and the wind had picked up, blowing icy spots of rain against the back of his head as he stood, a suspended portrait of a man about to knock on a door, until he raised the conviction to rap his knuckles against it.

Jas opened the door, wearing a large loose pullover and jeans. Her hair was pulled back into a ponytail and she smiled warmly when she saw who her unexpected caller was.

'Hi, John. Come on in.'

She peered outside as he wiped his feet on the mat and began to take off his shoes.

'Looks like it's turning a bit nasty out there. It was lovely earlier. I met up with my sister up town – you know Anuja, don't you? – and it was really quite nice to say it's still February. I was just about to make myself a cuppa, do you fancy one?'

John hung up his coat on the hooks beside the door. 'Thanks. Coffee would be great.'

She set off for the kitchen and, without turning back, called out: 'You didn't have to come around to tell me, you know. A phone call would have been fine.'

He was momentarily confused. She couldn't already know.

'What do you mean?'

She reappeared from the kitchen holding two mugs. 'Not that it isn't nice to see you, of course, but I didn't expect you to come straight around to tell me about it.'

She disappeared from sight again and John heard the click of the kettle being switched on.

The meeting. She's talking about the meeting.

He sat down and rehearsed again, as he had several times on the way over, how he would break the real news.

A minute or so later, Jas came back into the room carrying the two steaming mugs, carefully setting them down on coasters.

'So, how did it go?' She sat opposite him and leaned forward in anticipation.

Here we go.

'Actually, I didn't get to the meeting.'

'Oh!' She appeared slightly taken aback.

Just say it.

'Jas, they've got him. The man who killed Stef. He's under arrest.'

He allowed space for the enormity of the words to boil down until they were small enough to be absorbed. Jas was completely still as she processed them and digested their significance until the first tears welled in the corners of her eyes.

'Are you OK?' he asked, gently.

'I think so,' she dabbed at her eyes. 'I mean, like, wow!'

He stood and went to sit beside her, reaching to cup her left hand between his.

'How did they get him? This is the man you saw at the firewalk and in the park, right?'

John nodded. 'His name's Anthony Chaplin, apparently. I saw him again and followed him. Stef led me to him again. Thankfully, the police got there in time to nick him this time.'

'What happened?'

He told her the story. The pursuit, the clearing behind the garages. The knife.

'John, that was such a dangerous thing to do. I mean, like, you were really brave but he might have killed you.'

There was panic in her eyes. They were beyond concern. She could not stand the thought of losing someone else who meant so much to her, especially to the same hand.

He shrugged. 'Do you know what, Jas, I knew it wasn't a good situation but when we were there facing each other, just like that time at the bandstand, I felt Stef was with me and that he wouldn't let me come to any harm. Don't get me wrong, I was absolutely bloody terrified but I also felt kind of safe in a strange way. I know for sure it's been Stef all along who's been steering me into these situations – though Christ knows how – and that he wouldn't have done it if he didn't know I would be OK. Does that make any sense?'

Jas nodded. Faith in Stef was the bond which united them.

'It was strange, you know,' he continued. 'There was a moment there when we were facing each other, not much more than a yard or so apart, and I had the knife in my hand and I could virtually feel Stef's presence on my shoulder telling me to stick it in him. I know that's what he wanted me to do and I'm sure that's why he put me in precisely that position but I just couldn't, Jas. I just couldn't kill him, no matter how much of a bastard he is and no matter what he's done. Was that wrong? Do you think I've let Stef down?'

She withdrew her hand from between his and gripped his arm. 'You shouldn't think that way, John. You did what you thought was right.'

'I did, but it's not what Stef really wanted and it's not what you wanted either. You said you wanted him dead as well.'

That was true. She had told him several times, though without realising that decision could be in John's hands one day.

'That was the anger talking,' she said. 'What you say you'd like to do and what you actually would do in that situation are different things. Stef was the same. You know as well as I do, he couldn't stop himself from picking an argument if he was in one of his moods and somebody said something that irritated him but that was only because he liked showing them he knew more than they did. It was a game to him. He'd always stop short of pushing them too far because he was absolutely hopeless at confrontation.'

'Most of the time he did. Do you remember that time at your cousin's wedding do?'

'Sanjay's?'

'That's the one. When that bloke wanted to take him outside for winding him up in an argument about – what was it? – something to do with politics.'

'Oh yeah! That bloke really took it the wrong way, didn't he?'

'He was a bit of a cock, as I remember.'

'And Stef was like, "are we going now, Jas? Isn't it time we were going home?" and I was like, "I'm not leaving early just because you wound somebody up again. It's your own fault".'

John laughed. 'He could be a real pain in the arse sometimes, couldn't he?'

'He really could.' Jas sighed. 'Bless him.'

John shook his head, ruefully, and drew a deep breath. 'Yeah.'

'But seriously,' said Jas. 'I couldn't have put a knife in that man if it was me in your position, neither could Stef and I'm glad you didn't either. You could have ended up in serious trouble.'

Trouble! *More* trouble.

'Ha! That's another thing. I haven't told you this bit yet.'

John reclined in the chair. Jas remained still.

'I've been charged with ABH for when I stopped the men from attacking Gregory. I was called down to the police station this morning for them to charge me.'

'You're kidding! How could they? That's ridiculous!'

'I know. You should have seen the desk sergeant's face when he saw me, covered in mud, being brought in by two coppers a couple of hours after he'd booked me in to be charged with assault. I think he was wondering if I'd set some kind of record.'

The attempt at levity was lost on Jas. 'I can't believe they're putting you through that. Poor you. You must be horrified.'

He shrugged. 'The solicitor says it won't come to anything. I know he's said that all along and yet here we are, but I do still think there's no way they can find me guilty, so I'm OK with it. I could do without it, all the same.'

'I bet.' Jas' expression brimmed with sympathy and concern.

'I don't regret any of it, though, Jas.' He looked straight at her. He didn't want her to think she needed to feel sorry for him.

'I'm proud of myself for stopping Gregory from taking a beating from those thugs and I'm so happy that I've been able to put the man who killed Stef behind bars. I still think about that night so often and think about how it might have turned out differently – if I'd stayed closer, if I'd got to him quicker. If I'd stayed where I was instead of wandering off because I was a bit irritated at Stef not going for a pee before we left the pub, that bastard Chaplin might have seen there was two of us and might not have attempted to rob Stef. That might have meant some other poor sod would have been attacked, but Stef would still be alive. I can't tell you how much it still hurts that I couldn't save Stef that night but now I feel like I've done my best for him and that he can rest easy. I spent a year or so feeling so helpless about what happened but now I've helped bring his killer to justice and that means so much to me. You understand that, don't you?'

The tears trickled down the side of Jas' face. She understood the pain of loss and the despair of helplessness all too well. She had cursed the circumstances of that night which had brought her to the brink of devastation and wished it could have worked out differently, though she had never sought to attach blame for the futility of her wishes on anyone other than the killer. She wanted John to forgive himself and to be at peace with himself, just as she desired nothing more than to be able to remember Stef for the love they shared, untinged by the horror, the anger, the hurt of the night he was taken away from her. There would be the trial to get through but maybe after then, with this man having been brought to justice, maybe they could both move on.

Never without Stef but without acrimony.

'Of course I do.'

'I know you do.' He gently brushed away her tear with the back of his hand and rose to kiss her on the forehead. 'Are you going to be OK?'

She nodded and smiled.

'I should go. I'm off out with Stella tonight and she won't be happy if I'm not ready in time.'

Jas got up to give him a hug.

'Thanks for coming to see me, John, and thanks for everything you've done for Stef.'

She released him. 'How is Stella?'

That's yet *another* thing! Not yet. He and Stella had promised each other not to tell anyone yet and this was certainly not the right time.

'She's great, thanks.'

John turned the key in the ignition and waved at Jas in the open door. She waved back before retreating to the warmth inside.

He clicked the seatbelt into place and exhaled, relieved that Jas had taken the news as she did. He eased off the handbrake and drove away, the wipers sweeping away the steady dabs of spotting rain.

He hadn't expected her to be angry, in spite of her vehemence the other times when they had discussed the preferred fate of the killer. Not angry, but he half-expected her reaction to be more emotional than it was. Perhaps there would be private tears when she had time to gather her thoughts. He would ring her tomorrow.

She might want to talk about it some more.

Jas will be fine. She's strong. She's had to be strong. This time, he was there to help her. As importantly, he was allowing her to help him stay strong. That's the way it should have been last time.

Stef would understand too.

John smiled to himself at the memory of the near-skirmish at the wedding do. Good old Stef. He could be an irritating sod but he was a good mate.

He really was a good mate. That's the way he should be remembered. For the first time, John felt as if he was ready to move beyond the memories that had for too long cast so dark a shadow over the good times. Order had been restored. Justice served.

It was time to get back to a normal life.

'I hope I did all right by you today, pal,' he said to the sun visor.

'We got him. I hope you can rest easy now, I really do. I'm glad you helped me get him and I hope you're happy with the way it's turned out. I think it's the right solution.

'We make a decent team, don't we, but I think we should put that aside now. I think it's time for me to do it all by myself the rest of the way. You know, let nature run its course.

'I'll never stop being grateful for everything you've done for me, you know that. You saved my life and everything I do from now on will be to make the most of this second chance you've given me, but I need to do it my way now.

'What I'm trying to say, Stef, is that I might make the occasional mistake from here on but that's all part of being human and I've got to be willing to take that chance. Maybe it's time you stop taking a hand in my life now and let me take care of it the rest of the way. As I said, I'm eternally grateful and whatever I achieve from now until I the day I die, I'll be doing it for both of us but I have to do it alone. I hope you can respect that.

'Maybe we'll meet again in the next world, pal. I hope you have a good eternity until then. See you, Stef.'

John felt the silence in his car. He switched on the radio and tried to turn his mind to deciding what he was going to wear to go to the restaurant with Stella.

27

'Morning, Julie.'

She was completing her final checks on a new display in the banking hall ready for the first customers of the week. It was a life-size cut-out of a young woman with a smiling face you could trust who was wearing regulation Ridings Building Society uniform and was plainly very excited to have the chance to tell everyone about the exclusive fabulous new loyalty saver rate for new and existing customers (not all customers may be eligible, see a staff member for full terms and conditions).

'Morning, Mr Baldwin.'

At the door to the main office floor stood Pavel. Pavel was a security man and Pavel was huge. He was at least six foot four and a great Eastern European slab of a man. John would occasionally see him working the door at some of the livelier pubs in the city centre, back in the days when John used to get around the less lively pubs in the city centre on a regular basis. Here was a man who recognised where his natural assets lay and had set out to utilise them fully. You would not mess with Pavel. Pavel was not, however, usually stationed at the door to the main office floor.

'Morning, Pavel.'

John raised his hand to press the code numbers into the security keypad but Pavel put his considerable frame in the way to prevent him.

'You are to see Mr O'Connell straight away, sir,' he said.

'OK.' John waited for Pavel to move. Pavel did not move.

'Can you let me past then, Pavel, and I'll pop up.'

Pavel prodded at the keypad with his thick forefinger and opened the door himself. Instead of holding it open for John, he went through it first and then began to punch the code into a second keypad to his left to open the door to the upstairs management suite. He held the door open for John to go through.

Odd. 'Thank you, Pavel.'

As he began to climb the stairs, John became aware that Pavel was still behind him and heading upstairs too. He turned to speak over his shoulder.

'There's no need for you to come up as well. I know the way.'

Pavel lumbered on, the stairs creaking under the weight as he carefully placed as much of his big black boots as he could against the narrow steps, like a grizzly bear navigating a mountain ledge.

'I have been told to stay with you, sir.'

John was perplexed. What could have happened over the weekend that was so urgent? Oh, Christ! It couldn't be some kind of comeback over the ABH charge, could it?

At the top of the stairs, John turned right and knocked on the first door. The sign read 'TW O'Connell, Manager.'

'Come in.'

Pavel took up sentry duty outside the office and John opened the door.

The man behind the desk looked over the top of his glasses. 'Ah, John. Come in.'

He was a short, rotund man close to retirement age who had a bald head, wore round-rimmed glasses and had a moustache. The staff had nicknamed him Captain Mainwaring. It was meant affectionately and based purely on physical resemblance. Everybody liked Mr O'Connell. John was grateful to him for taking him back onto the staff in the dark days and for not getting rid of him again when it was pretty obvious that John was in no fit state to do his job properly. Another manager might have handled that situation differently but Mr O'Connell was loyal to his staff and his staff respected him for that.

'Morning, Trevor. You wanted to see me.'

Without answering, the manager shot out of his chair and bustled over to the door. He peered out and called gently, 'Dawn.' Then he gestured for the person whose attention he wanted to catch to come to the office. He returned to behind his desk and sat.

'Yes, yes. I'll just wait for Dawn to join us. Sit down, please.'

John sat. Something was definitely wrong. In walked Dawn from Human Resources, with a folder clutched to her chest. She sat on a chair in the corner of the office.

'Morning, Dawn. It must be serious if you're needed as well.'

She smiled, thinly, and set the folder on her lap.

'I have some awkward business to discuss with you, John. Some regrettable information has been brought to my attention by my superiors over the weekend.' Mr

O'Connell was stern-faced and agitated, making eye contact only fleetingly.

'A large amount of money has been misappropriated and this office is believed to be the source of it.'

John was initially happy it was nothing to do with his impending court appearance, but the obvious gravity in Mr O'Connell's words struck him. This must be serious.

'Oh, really. What sort of amount are we talking about?'

'Eighty-six thousand pounds.' Mr O'Connell looked straight at John as he announced the detail.

'A lot of money.'

'Indeed.' He held his stare.

'How does that sort of sum go missing?'

Mr O'Connell looked down and thumbed through the papers in front of him.

'It appears to be a campaign of small-scale frauds. A number of our older customers have been targeted, ones who had not previously shown an interest in online banking, whereby online accounts have been set up for them without their knowledge and loans for sums ranging from two thousand pounds to seven and a half thousand pounds have been processed on their behalf, again without their knowledge. The transactions were verified using email addresses which appear to have been falsely set up especially for these purposes but the loan amounts were then diverted to a different account. Therefore, the repayments for the loans were being taken directly from the customers' accounts but without the loan sums ever actually having been paid into them.'

John sat back in his chair. It was a fairly smart con but not foolproof. It was always highly likely to be quickly uncovered. Whoever pulled it off must have reckoned on a quick hit and then attempt to get away with the money before their deceit was discovered. A kind of high-tech smash and grab. But you would have to be prepared to give up an awful lot if you were trying to embezzle from within the company on the back of that scheme and it was hardly a life-changing sum to run away with. The chances of getting away with it must be slim.

'I see. What kind of timescale are we talking about?'

'Several weeks, it seems. The loans were all arranged on dates covering only a few days and we began to get the first enquiries from customers noticing unexpected amounts leaving their accounts last week. The fraud department were quickly on to it and moved to contact all the customers who we have so far been able to establish as being caught up in this scam to reassure them. We believe we are on top of it now.'

'Good and do they think this has come from someone inside the building society or has our system been hacked?'

'From inside, we think.' Mr O'Connell stood and paced.

'They must have used passcodes and passwords to access privileged customer information to set this up and all that is traceable, surely. The fraud people must soon know who's responsible for this.'

Mr O'Connell stopped pacing and turned to face John.

'John, the passcodes and passwords used were yours.'

So that was why he had been summoned.

'Shit.'

'Precisely.' He began pacing again. 'Do you have any inkling as to how your security information might have come to be used?'

John did not have to consider the question for long. He was very keen on matters of computer security. 'Not at all. I never write my details down anywhere and certainly don't tell anyone what they are. The only way anyone else could know them is if they infiltrate the computer system but we're supposed to have safeguards to prevent all that. I don't know how they would have got around those safeguards.'

Mr O'Connell nodded. 'As I said, the fraudulent loans were paid into a different account instead of being paid to the customers and our people have traced that account and have shut it down. Fortunately, all the money, the eighty-six thousand pounds, was still there. The account was set up, again using false identification which the fraudster had been able to verify, sidestepping the usual security checks, in the name of a Miss Pauline Smith from Lincolnshire.'

He again turned to look directly at John. This was beginning to feel like an interrogation.

'Does that name mean anything to you?'

Of course it did. Did Mr O'Connell already realise that?

'Yes. It's my mother's maiden name. My mother and father live in Lincolnshire.' John's heart sank. He did not like the way this was heading.

'You can see this leaves me in a very difficult position.'

He could.

'Trevor, I promise you I had absolutely nothing to do with this. I've never done a dishonest deed in my life. I couldn't do this to the company and especially not to you after you've been so good to me. I hope you believe that. I'll do everything I can to help you get to whoever is responsible.'

Mr O'Connell bowed his head and sighed. 'I do believe you, John, but it has been decided that you should take a period of leave, on full pay of course, until we get to the bottom of this.'

'You're suspending me?' He was indignant. 'I've done nothing wrong, you can't do this. Everybody will assume I'm implicated.'

'It's out of my hands. The police are involved now. It's only until they have completed their investigation. It's for the best. I'm sorry, John.'

He could not look up as he uttered the words. This was painful for both of them.

There was no point pursuing it further. The decision had been taken and that was it. John stood to leave. Mr O'Connell also rose to his feet and the two men looked straight into each other's eyes. The situation was not what either of them wanted but that was no reason for either to compromise their dignity.

'If you have any personal items in your office, you can collect them before you leave, of course, but I'm afraid our security man will have to accompany you.'

John nodded and held out his hand as a gesture to show he held no personal grievance. The manager stretched across his desk to grip it firmly.

He turned to go.

'John.'

He turned back.

'I need you to leave me your ID badge and keys.'

Pavel had remained at his post, like a vigilant oversized Rottweiler. There was no change in his stance or expression as John exited the manager's office.

'I have to go downstairs first to pick up a few things.'

The slightest of nods showed that this suggested course of action was acceptable to Pavel and he followed his charge back down the stairs. John was less concerned with collecting personal property than taking the opportunity to let Stella know what was going on.

He glanced over towards her desk as he skirted the main office floor but she was caught up in a conversation with one of the juniors.

I'll see her on the way out.

The door to his office was locked. It was never locked. He went to go into his pocket but then remembered he had just surrendered his key. He turned to Pavel and gave a shrug to convey that he had run out of options.

Pavel said nothing but opened his jacket to get to the clutter of keys attached to a lime green spring cord from the belt around his waist. He thumbed through them until he found the one he wanted and used it to open the door, stepping back to allow John to enter the office.

The computer screen was there but the stack had gone. No doubt it had been impounded to be scrutinised for incriminating evidence. He sighed. This was all so depressingly unnecessary.

He sat in his chair and opened drawers, looking for a few token bits of belongings he could gather to justify having dragged Pavel on the diversion.

The big security man filled the frame of the door, watching impassively.

'OK, let's go,' said John and he stood.

This time, Stella was not distracted and she saw him. She peered quizzically at the sight of John with his hands full, followed by an imposing Czech security man, and immediately headed towards him.

'One minute,' said John to his guard, who stopped and stood to attention, his arms folded.

'What's going on?' she asked, glancing down at the items in John's grasp.

'I've been suspended.'

It generally took a lot to disturb Stella's veneer of calm control, especially at work, but she was clearly shocked.

'Suspended? What on earth for?'

He tried to remain composed.

'It's all right, Stell. They've uncovered a fraud with a lot of money going missing and the only clues they've got about who's done it are all pointing in my direction at the moment, so they want me out of the way while they sort it all out and find out who really did it.'

'But that's outrageous! I'll take this up with O'Connell.' She was raging.

He shook his head.

'Leave it, Stell. This has come from above his head. I just want to get out of here before anybody notices. The last thing I want is a fuss.'

Her expression mellowed. 'OK. I'll ring you at lunchtime. I want to know exactly what was said.'

She leaned forward and gave him a peck. He attempted a look of reassurance and walked towards the exit, pursued by a bear.

28

The buzz from the security door stalled the steady descent of his mood, which was approaching what could be officially classified as 'foul'. He hated feeling helpless and out of control because he knew where feeling helpless and out of control had taken him last time and he did not want to go back there.

Someone is trying to ruin me. If not that, then someone is using me and doesn't care if that ruins me. Either way, there's someone out there who has to be stopped. They have to be caught so that I can clear my name but there's bugger all I can do to get to them. Nobody could have got to my details unless they had infiltrated the system – but who? It could be anybody. It doesn't have to be somebody in a senior position with higher access clearance. You hear about these clever little sods who hack the Pentagon security systems from their bedrooms, so the Ridings Building Society must be child's play in comparison. Who's done it? I'd love to get my hands on the bastard.

The intercom buzzed again. John rose reluctantly to his feet and walked to the door.

'Who is it?' he said flatly.

'It's me.'

Her voice pierced the darkness. He looked at his watch. Almost quarter past one. She must have been worried.

'Sorry, Stell. Come on up.'

He pressed the button to release the security lock on the outside door.

She looked flustered. She strode straight over and took hold of him, pulling him close.

'I've been trying to call you but your phone was switched off.'

She released her grip but held her arms over his shoulders. He slid his hands onto her hips.

'The police took it. They were waiting for me with a warrant when I got home. Four of them – from the fraud squad. They went through the flat, opening every drawer and cupboard, emptying files and looking through all my documents, and they seized my phone, laptop and tablet. Took them away in evidence bags and they took a load of stuff dating back to when I set up the business as well. I can't believe this is happening, Stell.'

She kissed him. 'Come and sit down and tell me about it.' She led him by the hand to the sofa.

'I'm so angry. I'm always so careful not to write down passwords and such, so the only way anybody could have got to my details is through the internal computer system and that's supposed to be secure – but obviously it's not. And now I've got this hanging over my head and if the police don't clear it up soon, what then? This could stop me setting up the business again because you can't go out there and tell people what a great IFA you are if they know you've been investigated for fraud. This kind of shit sticks.'

His agitation concerned her. She wanted to say something to take away his anxiety but knew the only way to deal with it was to allow him to get it all out in the open.

'Let's take it a step at a time. Tell me what O'Connell said to you.'

He took a deep breath.

'He said my security information had been used to set up online banking for some older customers – he didn't say how many – and arrange loans in their name but instead of paying the loans to them, all the money was diverted into another account. That was another thing. The account that all the money was filtered into just happened to be in my mother's maiden name. It's quite a common name but there you go; another little clue which makes it looks as if I'm the mastermind. And the address given for this fictitious person with a bank account is in Lincolnshire, which is where my mother lives. You can see why I'm their prime suspect but, the thing is, it's not a very clever con. I don't know whether this person thought all old people are oblivious to what goes in and out of their accounts but any fool would surely see that the alarm would be raised, sooner rather than later. The best of it is that all the money – eighty-six thousand quid, by the way...'

Stella raised her eyebrows.

'... all the money was still there in the account when they traced it and blocked it. I think we can fairly assume that whoever devised this little scheme isn't really as bright as they would like to believe. I could no more try to steal other people's money than I could attempt to run for Pope but I'd like to think that if I was going to try to pull off a fraud on this scale, I'd come up with a better con than this.'

'I dare say.' It seemed an odd boast but she was prepared to indulge him at a time like this.

'But that might be a good thing. If they weren't able to think through the plan properly, they must have left a trail that the authorities can pick up on and nab them. I bloody hope so, anyway. First the ABH thing and now this. Talk about it never rains.'

'Well...' Stella hesitated. 'I've been thinking about this. You know how you told me you don't believe in coincidences anymore, do you think this could be your friend influencing events again?'

He paused. 'I had the same thought but I don't think so. I can't see how that would make any sense. Everything that has happened to me since Stef came back into my life has served a purpose but these two events just don't fit the pattern. I can see how having me go to the police station to be charged at that precise time, which meant I ended up walking instead of driving and meant I caught up with the killer again – I can see how that served a purpose in a weird kind of way but then it might just be that the ABH charge was totally out of Stef's control and he just took advantage of me being in the right place at the right time. I don't know but I can't believe Stef suddenly has the power to micro-manage everything that touches my life. There has to be some scope for somebody else cocking it up – like whoever it was at the CPS who thought it was a good idea to bring charges, for example.

'It's the same with this fraud. Somebody has had a half-baked idea for stealing money and it's my bad luck that they used my details. I can't see it being anything else. It wouldn't make sense for it to be Stef. All his influences have been positive. This wouldn't serve any positive purpose.'

She put her arms around him and pulled him close again. 'I'm sure this will all work out, John. Stay strong and we'll get through this together.'

He held on, trying to draw all the strength he could from her. From her and from their baby.

'I'm so lucky to have you. I love you so much.'

She smiled. 'I love you too. We will get through this.'

'Yeah. Yeah, you're right.'

They separated and she checked the time.

'Look, I've got to go back. Just try not to let it get on top of you.'

He nodded.

'I'm going to head out as well. I need to find myself a pay-as-you-go phone to get me through until the police have finished with mine. You'd better write your number down so I can let you know what my new number is.'

She unfastened her handbag and took a business card from her purse, then took out a pen and wrote her personal number on the back of the card. He slipped it into his pocket.

'I'll send you a text. It'll be strange having a phone that can only make calls and send texts again.'

'Very retro.'

They kissed again. He opened the flat door for her and she left.

The little Romanian lady was at her usual pitch, outside the supermarket, selling *The Big Issue*. She always seemed to be dressed in about a dozen layers, even in the summer, but she needed every one of them on a day like this. He reached into his pocket for change.

'Hi, how are you today?'

She rolled her eyes. 'Cold. Nobody buys today. It's too cold.'

He handed over his money and she gave him a magazine.

'I hope you sell the rest soon.'

'Yes, I hope so too. God bless you. Have a nice day.'

'You too.'

Not too late for it to start getting better, at least.

As he turned to go through the supermarket door, he bumped into a younger man on the way out.

'Oops! Sorry, pal.'

The younger man glared back at him and made no attempt to either return or accept the courtesy of the apology. John held the eye contact for a second, maybe two. There was something in that face that said it was not healthy to look for longer. It was the expression of a person who had become too used to being quick to anger, with dark, heavy-set eyes too often used to spot opportunities to vent the malevolence which simmered behind them. They were cold, menacing, animal.

John moved on. It was an encounter best kept brief.

Past what remained of the day's pre-packed sandwiches in the refrigerated display, he eased through the small gap left by an old couple's shopping trolley, as they obliviously pondered which newspaper they were going to buy, to get to the selection of mobile phones on the end of the electronic items aisle. John scanned them to see which appeared to be the cheapest.

He was being stared at. He could feel it. He looked up and there, towards the exit, was the man he had bumped into, in his black tracksuit with three gold stripes down the side of the arms and legs. There was a second man with him, maybe slightly older and stockier, defying the weather in his white t-shirt and jeans, though he had made the small concession of wearing a grey beanie hat. Black tracksuit man was staring hard, scrutinising, challenging. Beanie was glancing up and back down to his phone as he tapped on the keypad with his thumb.

John tried to give the appearance that he was still taking a close interest in the phone display but his heart had started to beat just a little quicker. It was only an accidental bump. Surely there was no need to take offence because of that?

He stepped out of view, making as if something else on the electronic items aisle had caught his attention. He left it for close to a minute, though it seemed longer, then he stole a quick look as he went back to the phones. They were still there. Both of them were gazing over now, broodingly, belligerently.

What the hell?

He could barely distinguish one mobile phone offer from the next now but he stared at them still, trying to think what to do, hoping the men would just go away. He slipped further down the aisle again, sheltered from their intimidation, and attempted to clear his mind.

Go to the end and head towards the hair and beauty products section, stay out of view and then disappear into the main body of the supermarket. Just hang around for a bit. If I can just walk around for a quarter of an hour or whatever, they'll get bored and want to leave to bite the heads off a few puppies or something by then. Maybe they've gone already. I might just be getting paranoid.

He waited longer, thumbing through the selection of phone charging cables to keep up the impression of being a shopper. He was steeling himself to take another look. He had to do something.

They had not moved. As John peered towards the exit, as unobtrusively as he could with his head bowed, a third man, taller than the other two in a dark zipped-up puffer jacket, entered the building and stepped between them. Beanie nodded over in John's direction and puffer jacket stared over too.

Jesus! They're not going anywhere. They're sending for reinforcements.

Jarvis' lot. They could be. Shit. Got to get out of here.

John walked towards the exit, as nonchalantly as he dare. Just beyond the newspaper stand, he turned sharply right and quickened his pace as he headed for the long and winding ramp which shoppers used to wheel their trolleys to the car park. Satisfied he was out of sight of the main exit, he began to run, almost slipping on the wet surface as he negotiated the sharp one hundred and eighty-degree turn and then startling an old lady as he rushed by. Not daring to look back, he ran towards his car, fumbling in his pocket for the key and pressing the keypad to open the door before he got there. He jumped into the driver's seat, turned the key in the ignition, then pressed the button to lock the doors from the inside, just in case. As he reversed out, quicker than he should, a car driving towards the car park exit braked hurriedly and gave him a blast on the horn but John did not acknowledge it. He slammed the gearbox into first and squealed away. Heading towards the main road, he saw puffer jacket getting into the back seat of a black car in a lay-by, parked facing the opposite direction. John tried to mask his face by turning his head from them as far as he could without losing sight of the road in front of him.

As he reached the roundabout for the main road, he looked in his mirror to see the black car mount the pavement on the far side to complete a U-turn and set off after him. John cut out to turn right, earning an irritated insult from the driver of the car he almost clipped, and pressed much more heavily on the accelerator along the open road than he would normally. He hoped the black car would be held up at the roundabout.

If I can get to the next junction before they are able to see which way I'm going, I can use the back roads to get home.

The junction loomed quickly and he began to decelerate. There was a car in front waiting to turn right and not enough room to get past him to turn left.

Come on! Come on!

He glanced nervously at his rear-view mirror. The black car was in view. The chance was gone. Can't head back towards home now. Can't let them know where I live. Shit.

He drove straight on.

The black car was closing. John tried taking random turns without indicating but his pursuers had plenty of time to react and pick up the trail. He was close to panic, unable to see a way of giving them the slip, wary of not taking an unknown turning which might be a dead end. Must keep moving.

Though he had lived in the city most of his life, he was in unfamiliar territory now. He scanned the road ahead for a landmark he knew, all the time glancing into the mirror to check. The black car was still there. There was a car between them but they could still see each other.

A police station. There must be a police station somewhere close by. Pull into the police station and they wouldn't dare follow. If I had my phone, I'd be able to call the police and get them to help me.

Up ahead was a large pub whose name he recalled but he struggled to locate it in relation to the landscape of his mind. For no reason other than to attempt something to end the chase, he turned left just after the pub. A long straight hill rose in front of him, which John reckoned would give the black car too long a run to catch up, so he turned sharply right, the tyres screeching as he did.

This road was narrower, with cars parked on either side. He thought about pulling in to the next space he saw, then lying flat to get out of sight, hopefully unnoticed as the black car sped by but, looking back, it was on his tail again. He turned left, his thoughts growing ever more frenzied in his mounting alarm and desperation. As he pressed hard on the accelerator, he looked in the mirror again. The black car was not there yet. Still not there. Still not there. Did they miss the junction or not notice him turn? Still not there. Still not...

The noise, a heavy thud, made him squeeze hard on the steering wheel and jump on the brake, the shock of the dark shape which suddenly loomed towards him and cracked against the windscreen on the passenger side scrambling his brain and making his heart leap into the back of his throat.

As his senses recalibrated, he began to speed away again but his reason regained control and he jammed on the brakes. Wide-eyed, he gazed ahead, panting, for several seconds before daring to look into the rear-view mirror.

Back down the road, he saw the black car reverse into a side street and drive away in the opposite direction.

But then he became aware of the screaming. Piercing cries. He looked and saw a young woman dragging herself towards the pavement on her right side, her left leg straight and pathetically lame as she pulled herself along. All the time screaming, crying.

'My baby! My baby!'

Then he saw the overturned pushchair.

29

The first of them rushed to the woman within seconds, alerted, no doubt, by the sound of the impact and the screaming. Soon, there were around a dozen of them, emerging from the shops. One was on the phone, two knelt by the woman's side, but all she wanted was to know.

'My baby! My baby!'

A man had set the pushchair back on its wheels and was fumbling to unbuckle the harness before picking out a small child and holding it to his chest. The child cried and held out its arms for its mother but appeared none the worse for the trauma.

John watched by the side of the car, barely daring to breathe, as the child was handed to its mother and she caressed it immediately, then held the child slightly away from herself to check for obvious signs of injury and, reassured, gripped it close again, all the time muttering comforting words as the child cried loudly.

Thank Christ.

She remained, resting on her right side with her left leg stretched out straight, on the cold, dark pavement surface. A man took off his coat to put around her shoulders and she glanced up to thank him. A woman came from a shop with a bottle of water and offered it to her. Some stood around, showing their willingness to help if needed, maybe, or perhaps just because they were curious. Others passed by, satisfied everything was in hand.

John thought about going over to join the small huddle around the woman and her child, but he could not find the courage. What do you say? Sorry for knocking you down. Glad your child isn't seriously injured. He thought it best to stay away, in case anyone turned nasty against him, so he stepped away from the car and skulked in anonymity beside a bookmaker's shop window, consumed by his wretchedness, scorned by the bare flicking bulb of his nearside front hazard light which was now exposed by the damage of the impact.

A police car was first to arrive. The officer pulled up before the crowd and left his blue light flashing. He strode purposefully to the scene and crouched beside the woman. The ambulance came less than a minute later from the opposite direction and carefully pulled in as close to the gathering as it could as the policeman made sure everyone was safely back far enough from its line of approach. One paramedic jumped out of the passenger side and went straight over to the woman, while another opened the back doors of the ambulance.

The policeman stood back to let the paramedics do their job and John saw him talking to the people on the front row of the growing crowd, those who had been quickest to the scene. The woman who had made the phone call pointed towards John's car and the policeman began to walk to him.

He left the shelter of the shop and ambled, shamefully, towards his damaged car.

'Is this your car, sir?'

The officer surveyed the signs of impact to the front wing and the windscreen as he asked the question.

'It is, yes.'

'And were you driving the car at the time of the incident?'

'I was.'

The officer continued to assess the damage, then took out his notebook, looked at the licence plate and scribbled down the number.

'Could I have your name please, sir?'

'John Baldwin. B-A-L-D-W-I-N. The woman, how is she? And her child. How are they? Are they all right?'

The officer was writing and wasn't about to offer any quick comfort.

'The paramedics are making their assessment now, sir. From what the lady says, she was able to push her child out of the way when she realised you were not going to stop and then had the wherewithal to jump slightly just before the collision. If her feet had been planted I'm sure her injuries could have been a lot worse. She is a lucky woman and you are a very lucky man.'

He looked up from his notebook and fixed John with an accusing stare which burnt straight through him.

'Did you not see the pedestrian crossing lights at red?'

John shrivelled even further into his self-inflicted misery. Everything he could think to say was so inadequate, but he had to say it.

'No, I didn't. I was distracted. I was being chased.'

'Chased?' The tone bordered on mockery. This is a new one.

'Yes. I was threatened after I got caught up in an assault a couple of months ago.

The police are aware of it. Three men – I'm assuming it was the people who made the threats – saw me at the supermarket and I tried to get away from them but they were following me. I was panicking. I wasn't concentrating on what was in front of me and then... Then this happened.'

The officer flicked over the page of his notebook to finish writing down the burbled explanation, which somehow sounded unconvincing even to the ear of the speaker. He tapped an exaggerated full stop as he completed his writing and closed the pad.

'I need you to stay here until I get back, understand?'

With that, he walked back to the scene around the woman, who had an oxygen mask over her mouth and nose and had given up her now-placated child to be cuddled by a bystander. The second paramedic had lowered a stretcher to ground level, ready to lift the injured woman on to it.

A couple passed and gave the damaged car an inquisitive look over. John slipped back into the shadows.

The policeman was taking more notes, presumably witness evidence, as the paramedics lifted the stricken woman on to the stretcher. She gave a muffled cry of pain as they manoeuvred her over and John winced as he watched. A second police car then arrived, with two officers on board. One of them stepped over to talk to the colleague who was first on to the scene. After delivering a briefing of what had been done and what still needed to be done, he left the two newcomers to it and returned towards the damaged car.

'Mr Baldwin,' he called.

John was already walking towards him.

'I'm going to need to take more details from you and I need you to take a breathalyser test as well please.'

'I haven't been drinking,' he replied, defensively.

'Nevertheless, sir, it is standard procedure to require you to take a breathalyser test when you are the driver of a vehicle involved in a traffic offence. I should warn you that you can be arrested for refusing to comply with a request to do a breath test unless you have a reasonable excuse to do so, such as a medical condition.'

The threat of even more trouble was the last thing he wanted.

'No, no, of course I'll do the test, I just wanted to... No, there's no issue.'

The officer's body language suggested his patience was not to be stretched. He had seen too many incidents such as this – and much worse – to have retained a great deal of tolerance in dealing with the perpetrators, who always tried to sound so sorry after their stupidity had brought such suffering upon the innocent. He took out a device – about the shape of an old-style mobile phone – which was sheathed in a protective clear plastic cover, with a white tube protruding at ninety degrees from the top.

'Blow into the tube please, sir, and carry on blowing until I tell you to stop.'

A group of four teenagers were watching closely, intrigued. John felt his sense of indignity go up a further notch as he moved to the tube and blew hard.

'That will do it,' said the officer, just as John felt he could not possibly draw another ounce of breath from his lungs. He sucked in deep to fill them again.

'Hey, copper. Is he pissed?' shouted one of the youths.

Just go away, you little pricks. At least there would be the slight consolation of a negative reading to throw back at them. This is so embarrassing.

The officer scrutinised the reading on his device and snorted in an 'I thought as much' sort of way.

'Seventy-two,' he announced.

John felt the blood drain from his face. He was bemused, temporarily stunned. He didn't know what seventy-two was but he knew it was more than nought.

'Seventy-two. Seventy-two what? What does that mean?'

The policeman was already returning the breathalyser to the pocket of his heavy yellow jacket.

'Seventy-two micrograms of alcohol per one hundred millilitres of breath. That's the reading. What it means is that you are more than two times over the legal limit.'

'No, no, no – that's not possible. There must be something wrong with your gadget. I haven't had anything to drink for two and a half months. Not a drop. This can't be right.' He was agitated. Cold beads of sweat burst through the skin of his forehead and he felt sick.

The officer was really beginning to dislike this one. *First he tries to spin me some load of bollocks about a car chase and then he lies about not drinking. Does he think we're stupid? It's going to be a pleasure to take this one in.*

'The devices are completely reliable, sir. You're going to have to come with me to the station. John Baldwin, I am arresting you on suspicion of a driving a motor vehicle with alcohol concentration over the prescribed limit and with dangerous driving. You do not have to say anything but it may harm your defence if you do not mention, when questioned, something which you later rely on in court. Anything you do say may be given in evidence. Do you understand?'

John nodded, though he was in no state of mind to take it all in. *How the hell can it show I'm over the limit?*

'Ha, ha, ha! You're nicked, mate!' yawped the youth as he and his friends began to move away, laughing.

What do I do? This is ridiculous. Shouldn't I contact somebody?

'I can't...how can? This is unbelievable.' He looked all around him, distressed. The whole world was collapsing in around him. 'Do you want me to move my car out of the way?'

Even as he said the words, he knew it was an absurd offer to make but nothing was really making much sense.

'You're not to go anywhere near the wheel of a car in your state,' warned the officer. 'It's not to be moved until we've completed our scene assessment and then it will be towed away. That's not for you to think about, you're coming with me.'

He gripped John's forearm firmly and began to march him towards the police car. The ambulance was just pulling away and the small crowd, some of them still giving their statements, watched it go, before their attention was drawn to the officer leading the guilty man their way.

They glared at him, despising. He could not meet their eyes as they denounced him.

'He wants locking up.'

'You should be ashamed of yourself.'

It was almost a relief to reach the police car. The officer opened the back door and put his hand on the top of John's head to guide him in, then slammed the door shut. He kept his head bowed. This was all too much.

The policeman climbed into the driver's seat and took off his cap, flinging it on to the passenger seat like a frisbee with a flick of his wrist. He reached for the seatbelt, clicked it in and turned on the engine. As he checked over his shoulder and pulled out, he turned off the blue flashing lights and John was grateful to be spared the extra attention. Small mercies.

The silent journey lasted only three, maybe four, minutes before the car turned into the police station parking area and John realised how close he had been to the sanctuary. Maybe if he had driven on instead of turning off at the pub he would have spotted the station and the chase would have had a much happier conclusion. The thought only made the sour taste in his mouth worse.

'Hey, sarge.'

The veteran officer looked up from his computer keyboard and peered down at the two of them from his elevated position behind a curved desk, which was like a hotel reception desk but with posters warning against the recklessness of carrying offensive weapons. The room was grey and cold and another policeman in a protective vest was thumbing through a drawer of files behind the sergeant.

'PC Wood. Who have you brought me today?' He looked John up and down.

'This is John Baldwin, who has been arrested on suspicion of driving with excess alcohol and with dangerous driving. Mr Baldwin was the driver of a car which was in collision with a young woman and her small child in a pushchair on a pedestrian crossing on New Albert Street at approximately 2.45pm. He was breathalysed at the scene and was found to be over the legal limit.'

John felt his sense of humiliation could not have been greater if he had been stripped naked in the street and made to perform a little dance.

'I see.' The sergeant tapped his keyboard again. 'My name is Sergeant Anderson and I'll need to take a few details from you. Let's start with your full name.'

He stood meekly, the miscreant schoolboy before the headmaster, and surrendered all the information required of him for the record of his misdeed, all the time longing for when the full excruciating process would be over and he could go home. Go home and hide. Shut himself away before this dreadful day had the chance to get worse still.

'Right,' pronounced the custody sergeant, looking up from the computer keyboard. 'You have been arrested by this officer on suspicion of driving with alcohol concentration over the prescribed limit and with dangerous driving, is there anything you would like to say at this time?'

John shook his head.

'I need you to empty your pockets if you could, please, Mr Baldwin.'

Further indignity.

'OK, we've got one wallet, containing ten, twenty, twenty-five pounds in notes, one credit card, one debit card and various business cards, three pounds and fifty, sixty, sixty-five, sixty-seven pence in loose change, one opened packet of mints, one wristwatch, one further business card and – is that it? No mobile phone?'

That really would be too complicated to explain at this stage.

'No. No phone.'

'Anything else?'

John opened his coat to check the inside pockets. 'Oh, there is this.'

'One copy of *The Big Issue* magazine. Is that it?'

He frisked himself. 'That's it.'

'Your property will be returned to you when you are released from custody but, right now, I need to inform you that you have the right to contact a solicitor if you wish to do so or one will be provided for you upon request. Do you want us to make that call at this stage?'

He couldn't think why he would need one yet. Later, certainly. After all this is over.

'No, that'll be fine for now, thanks.'

'As part of our investigation, we need to conduct a further breath test. Is there any medical reason why you are not able to do a breath test?'

'No.'

'Have you consumed any alcohol or used any mouthwashes in the last twelve hours?'

'No. Mouthwashes?'

'Many of them contain alcohol which can affect the reading.'

'Oh, I see. No, I haven't.'

'In that case, this officer will accompany you to the room where we will conduct the breath test.'

John was encouraged by this news. Surely this machine will be more accurate than the last and it'll show I haven't had anything to drink. Then I'll be able to go home.

Down the grey corridor, the officer opened the door to a side room and gestured for John to step inside. The room was barely big enough to be called a cupboard, enclosed by bare, windowless grey walls broken only by a single grey noticeboard which had three sheets of paper pinned to it. On a battered office table stood a machine that looked like a small grey printer which ought to have been thrown out as obsolete in the 1990s. A single blue plastic chair was set before it. The officer clicked a switch on the machine and a display of red LED letters and numbers proved that it was, indeed, still functioning.

The officer had a form and he leaned on the desk to start filling it in. 'Just need to give it a couple of seconds to warm up.'

As it went through its range of buzzes and whirs, John decided he might as well sit down. Presumably, the chair was for whoever was about to use the machine. He imagined some of them probably needed to be seated.

'OK. You've had the procedure explained to you and you've told us there are no medical reasons why we cannot carry on with the breath test, so if you would like to step up beside me please.'

He stood.

'And blow into the tube until I say to stop please.'

He blew.

'Right, that's fine. Just have a seat please.'

He sat.

The machine performed another series of buzzes and whirs as what appeared to be a till receipt began to emerge from a slot on its right side. The officer tore off the paper and another strip started printing behind it. He inspected the paper.

'What does it say?' Come on. This time, surely.

'Seventy-five.'

'Seventy-five? Oh, for fuck's sake! Sorry to swear, but this can't be possible. I promise you I haven't had anything to drink.'

The policeman tore off the second print-out and gave that the once-over too.

'Must have been a very heavy weekend, then.'

'No, I mean I haven't had anything to drink for weeks. Two and a half months, actually. It can't still be picking up alcohol on my breath from two and a half months ago. Jesus!'

The officer's expression remained deadpan. He was used to hearing earnest expressions of innocence in the face of all evidence.

'I need you to blow into the tube again please. We need to take two readings.'

John stood again and blew again, though he was now stripped of the expectation of impending redemption.

Another till receipt emerged.

'Seventy-seven.'

'Of course it is.' His indignation had overtaken his humility. He felt as if he had fallen into an elephant trap and could now see that kicking at the steep earth sides was utterly futile.

'Perhaps we should try a few more. I feel like I could go on to get a century.'

The officer ignored the comment.

'The lower of the two readings will be the one we use...'

'Oh, that's something, then.'

'... but that does mean you are currently more than two times over the legal limit for driving of thirty-five micrograms of alcohol per one hundred millilitres of breath.'

He leaned to fill in more of the form and then offered John one of the duplicate print-outs.

'This is your copy of the readings, Mr Baldwin, for you to retain. Could I ask you please to sign to show that you have received a copy?'

John was feeling bullish now. The hunters were pointing their guns at him from the lip of the trap and he wasn't about to go down without giving them a piece of his mind.

'Actually, I don't think I will. I don't accept these findings. I know I haven't had anything to drink, no matter what everybody else appears to believe or what your crappy machine says. I want to do a further test to prove there's nothing wrong with me. A blood test. I demand a blood test.'

The policeman remained unmoved.

'I see. In that case, I'll take you back to the custody sergeant and you can tell him yourself.'

'I will.'

John was on his feet and already making for the door. The officer led the way.

'Sarge.'

He looked up from behind the reception desk. 'Right then, Luke, what're the scores on the doors?'

It never bothered him that most of the junior officers were too young to understand the reference. They simply accepted it as one of the odd things the sarge said.

'The readings were seventy-five and seventy-seven, but Mr Baldwin says he doesn't accept them and has asked if we could conduct a blood test.'

The sergeant stiffened. 'Does he now?' He glared straight at John, ready to accept a challenge.

'Look, I'm not trying to be a trouble-maker here but I know these readings can't be right because I know I haven't had a drink in two and a half months. I can't just shrug my shoulders and say it's fine to prosecute me for something I haven't done. I thought a blood test would be more conclusive, tidy this up for good.'

The sergeant held his stare.

'Can I remind you, Mr Baldwin, that you have the right to contact a solicitor if you wish to do so or free legal advice can be provided for you. Do you wish to have a solicitor present?'

'Not at the moment, thanks. I'd like to see a doctor please.'

'John Baldwin, you are charged that on Monday February the 19th you drove a motor vehicle with alcohol concentration over the prescribed limit contrary to section five of the Road Traffic Act 1988. You do not have to say anything but it may harm your defence if you do not mention now something which you may later rely on in court. Anything you do say will be given in evidence. Have you got any comments you would like to make?'

'Only what I've been saying all along. I haven't had anything to drink and I have no idea how these readings have come back positive. Could I please have a blood test to prove that I am innocent of this charge?'

He watched as the sergeant wrote the comments on a pad. If being hit by the charge was intended to take him down a peg or two, he was determined he was not going to let it show.

'Summon the doc, will you please, Luke, and take Mr Baldwin down to our executive suite to wait until he arrives.'

The young officer stepped forward to show the way.

'Thank you,' John said firmly to the sergeant, who kept his eyes on him as he was led away again.

They followed another grey corridor to where another officer, middle-aged and wiry, was sitting at a desk.

The younger policeman handed over his paperwork. 'This is John Baldwin, charged with driving with excess. We're leaving him with you, Chris, until the doc gets here to do a blood test.'

'Righto.' The older officer looked up and smiled as his colleague turned to leave.

'OK, Mr Baldwin. If you would remove your coat, shoes and belt for me please.'

John looked around. He couldn't see any x-ray security machine.

'What for?' He began to take off his coat anyway as a gesture of compliance.

'Safety, sir. We don't want you attempting to do yourself any harm in the cells.'

Cells? Oh, right. Executive suite. An exposure to custody sergeant humour.

'We'll keep everything here for you in a locker, so that you can put your shoes back on when you go to see the doctor.' He smiled again. A friendly jailor. John didn't know whether to be thankful or wary.

He followed the detention officer to a row of heavy grey doors, his feet chilling against the concrete floor, and the first of them was pushed open for him to step into the cell.

It was every bit as miserable as he could have imagined it to be, had he ever envisaged a time when he might be faced with being shown to a police cell. Across the length of the far end of the narrow room, underneath a small lattice-barred window, was a blue plastic mattress – like a gym mat and about as thin – on a concrete ledge. The walls were white tiled, like an old public convenience and, as if to complete the comparison, there was an aluminium toilet bowl and wash basin just behind the open door to his left.

If the aim was to strip all sense of humanity from whoever was shut behind its door, then it surely suited the purpose.

'There is a buzzer here if you need us for anything,' said the detention officer, pointing to the right of the door. 'We'll come to fetch you when the doctor arrives. I'm sure they won't be long. In the meantime, can I get you a cup of tea?'

They were about the kindest and most welcome words he had heard in hours.

'That would be much appreciated, thank you. White, no sugar, please.'

The detention officer smiled again and moved to leave.

'Excuse me.'

The officer turned back.

'There was a woman hurt in the collision I was involved in. Is it possible to find out how she is?'

Another smile. 'I'll put in a call.'

With that, the officer left and closed the heavy door behind him. John was utterly alone.

He stood completely still, trying to take in his new surroundings. Bleak did not even come close.

A blink of a red light high in the room to his right caught his eye. It blinked again. A camera. Great. Solitude with no hiding place. He decided to sit on the mattress.

The cries of the woman on the crossing rang in his ears again and her pain as she was lifted onto the stretcher stabbed at his conscience.

Oh god. I hope she's all right.

What if she is seriously hurt? What if she had been more seriously hurt? What if the child had been hurt? Or killed? Oh god. I wouldn't be able to live with that.

The contemplation was too terrible. He tried to blank it out but everywhere his mind turned, it ran into another awful scenario. What if her injuries are life-changing? What if she is on her own and can't work anymore? How would she manage with a small child, no support and limited mobility? He was drowning in a torment of his own making.

Eventually, the door opened again and in came the detention officer with a polystyrene cup.

'I called the hospital,' he announced. 'The lady has been treated for bumps and bruises but that's all. They said her husband is going to be allowed to take her home soon.'

She is OK. She's not alone.

'That's a relief, thank you.'

'The other news is that the doctor is about five minutes away.' He handed over the cup of pale brown warm liquid. 'Just time to drink your cuppa.'

John rolled up his left sleeve, as instructed. The doctor looked as if he was from the Middle East. Somewhere in that region anyway. North Africa, possibly. Wherever he was from, he was washing his hands and his demeanour shouted out that he felt he had much better things to do with his time than this.

'Could I ask you something please, doctor?'

He began to dry his hands on paper towels. 'You may.'

'Is it possible for alcohol to stay on your breath for a couple of months?'

'Not in my experience.' He took out a small white plastic tray from his bag and a white paper packet.

'Even if you used to drink quite a lot?'

'Not in my experience.' He opened the packet and pulled out a pair of purple Latex gloves.

'Can the alcohol stay in your blood over that length of time if, as I say, you used to drink quite a lot?'

The doctor pulled on the gloves and began to arrange other small white packets on the tray. 'That would depend on your age, weight and how much you have had to drink but it would normally be a matter of hours rather than days.'

Good. John was glad he had insisted on a blood test.

The doctor was securing a tourniquet around his upper arm and then he pushed one end of a needle into a small plastic container. He eased a plastic sheath off the other end to reveal a sharp metal point.

Time to look away.

'Just a small scratch.'

He felt the needle going into his arm. The doctor took a small bottle and attached it to the other end of the needle inside the container. John glanced briefly round to see the red liquid being drawn into the bottle and quickly looked away again.

'One done. One more.'

The second bottle was filled and removed, then set next to the first on the tray. The doctor clipped off the tourniquet, eased out the needle and pressed a small square of padding over where it pierced the skin.

'Press on this please.'

That was easy. John pressed his middle finger against the padding.

'Thank you. How soon do you get the results?'

The doctor was peeling off the gloves. 'Six weeks, usually.'

'Six weeks?' He did not want this hanging over his head for six more minutes, never mind six weeks.

'Usually six weeks. Can be a little longer.'

'Jesus!'

The doctor threw the gloves in a metal bin and began to tidy up his discarded packets.

'This second sample is available for you to take away and send for independent analysis if you choose. These results will generally be processed more quickly.'

'Definitely. I will do that.' Jesus! Six weeks!

The young officer who had taken him for the breath test came into the room.

'All done, doc?'

The doctor nodded, repacking his bag.

'Could I have a quick word, then?'

The two men left the room but left the door ajar.

'Do you think he's in a suitable state to take him into interview?' asked the officer.

The doctor considered. 'Well, he appears lucid but the breath sample reading was seventy-four?'

'Seventy-five,' corrected the policeman.

'That's quite a lot for so early on a Monday, isn't it?'

The policeman leaned forward, as if to pass on a confidence.

'The sarge reckons it wouldn't do this one any harm for him to spend the night.'

They glanced together at the figure on the plastic chair who was still wondering why it should take six weeks to analyse a simple blood test.

'I'm fine with that,' said the doctor and he bustled away to complete more worthwhile tasks.

'Is that it? Am I free to go yet?'

It was a plea made more in hope than expectation. No doubt there were more formalities to complete yet.

'I'm afraid not, sir. You are to be held in custody overnight with view to conducting further interviews in the morning.'

Another dagger.

'Is that really necessary? I'm hardly incapable, am I?' He knew it was a vain attempt to change the decision. The die had been cast. Could this day get any worse?

Even the detention officer's unshakeable cheeriness could not lift him now. He was returned to the same cell to begin his night of incarceration. Through the barred window, he could see it was barely turning dark.

'Now, I'll sort you out with a pillow and blanket and we'll get you some food in a short while. Is there someone you would like to call to let them know where you are?'

He had not thought of that. All he had thought about was calling Stella to ask if she could pick him up when he was being released.

Oh, Jesus! What would I say? I'm too ashamed.

'Or we could call them for you instead?'

'Actually, that would be very good of you. It's my girlfriend. Her details are on a loose business card which was with my things that the desk sergeant took off me. Her mobile's written on the back. I don't think I could...'

The officer smiled. 'Leave it with me.'

The door slammed shut and the lock fixed with a clunk. He was alone again, with only remorse, guilt, self-pity and a huge helping of a sense of injustice for company.

As he sat back down on the thin plastic mattress, he reflected on all the times, in the months after Stef died, when he was drinking lord knows how much and still carried on driving when he must have been permanently over the limit, yet he hadn't been involved in an accident once and hadn't been stopped once. The irony was not lost on him but the real irony was that through two and a half months of allowing nothing stronger than concentrated orange squash to pass his lips, he had never felt more in need of a drink than at this moment.

It was going to be a long night.

30

When, at last, he felt he should attempt to sleep, he spent what felt like an eternity trying to find a position to lie where he could be comfortable for more than five minutes without seriously impeding blood flow to his lower limbs, on a mattress which creaked with every movement, with his head resting on a hopelessly inadequate pillow and his body covered only by a coarse blanket which itched every time he pulled it as far as his exposed neck. He did not even have the comfort of being able to watch a clock as time trickled barely discernibly towards daylight like a thick, glutinous liquid on an almost perfectly flat board.

Yet he must have drifted into sleep for a short while at least because he woke at one stage with a sore hip and the memory of a bizarre dream fresh in his mind. He was in his childhood home, watching *The Flintstones* on TV, and could hear the crackle of the coal fire and could see the picture above the hearth of the seascape painted on black velvet which his mother had bought one year on holiday. It was all as he remembered from his youth but he was a fully grown adult and there was no sign of his parents.

Through the door walked Amy. She was so heavily pregnant that she looked as if she might burst at any moment and she was pressing her hands into the small of her aching back for support. She reminded him that they were going away and that if he didn't get a move on they would not get to the airport in time. He had no recollection of having planned to go anywhere with Amy and thought it odd that they would be travelling when she was plainly so close to giving birth but reckoned that they must have discussed it previously and so he decided he had better pack a bag.

Upstairs, in his old bedroom, there were model aeroplanes suspended by cotton thread from drawing pins in the ceiling and a half-painted line-up of British infantry soldiers from the Battle of Waterloo on his table. He could practically smell the enamel paint and turpentine. He looked around for a case to pack but could not find one, so he started to pull clothes out of the drawers but they were not the ones he wanted to take. Then he realised that he would need his passport but he couldn't remember where he had put it and he was getting nowhere as, all the time, his feeling of urgency grew because he would make them miss the plane and they wouldn't get to where they wanted to be.

That was when he woke up, his face flushed even though his feet were cold and cramping. That was the only time he was aware of being able to drift off to sleep.

That was the only time his turbulent mind had allowed him to sleep. For the rest of the time, the possible repercussions of his situation rolled endlessly around his consciousness like a roulette ball which never lost its momentum. Ceaseless, nagging, tormenting thoughts.

Everything depended on the blood test. Everything. That was what it all boiled down to. The blood test had to come back negative or he was ruined.

It was not so much the danger of a driving ban and a fine. He could handle that. He could find a way to make that work, even though it would not be easy to manage without a car.

The stigma was a problem. If he was prosecuted for causing the accident, he would have to take that one on the chin because he was at fault, though he would hope the mitigation of being chased by three psychos intent on revenge for the accidental death of their psycho friend would carry some sway. It was the same for the ABH thing, though he still could not believe that charge would stand up to close scrutiny in court. As for the fraud investigation, his connection to that was so laughably flimsy that it did not bear serious consideration.

But if the blood test somehow came back positive...if the blood test somehow came back positive, that was a different matter.

If he was convicted of drink-driving, the local media would most likely pick up on that and, because of the profile he had acquired through the firewalk and the aftermath of the firewalk, the news would capture more interest than if their only point of reference was some bloke who worked for the building society. The publicity would reflect badly on GameOn and so he would have to resign from his position. He did not want to do that. It meant too much to him.

Even more scary than that, if the blood test came back positive, what would those closest to him think? They would think he was a liar. What other conclusion could they come to? They would think 'hang on, he's been telling us that he hasn't had a drink in two and a half months but the blood test and the breath tests clearly prove that he's still on the booze'. They would think he had been sticking it away in secret. There's no one more deceitful than an addict. That's what they do. They hide their nasty habits away and deny to everyone that they have ever been there in the first place. He knows. It's what he used to do.

And Stella. Stella. She would feel betrayed. How could she trust him again? They were only just beginning to get to know each other properly anyway and this, this would make her feel she didn't know him at all. If he was lying about his drinking, what else was he lying about? She might even wonder if he really was behind the building society fraud. And all the promises, what were they worth? Could she even believe him when he said he loved her?

It would be the end of them. How could they start a life together – with a new baby – if she could not trust him? It would be over. And the thought of that really was too much to bear.

There would be nothing more to live for.

Max Monaghan was already waiting in the room, wearing a purple shirt with an orange and yellow tie. They were given time for a consultation before the police quizzed John about the accident.

He told his solicitor about the three men in the supermarket and how they had followed him in the black car, about how the accident had happened because he was trying to shake them and how he had been distracted from watching the road ahead, about how the breath tests were clearly unreliable because he hadn't had anything to drink for so long, about requesting a blood test and about getting the feeling that they had held him in custody because they wanted to teach him a lesson rather than because they needed to. Max Monaghan listened and scribbled on a pad, nodding and grunting occasionally.

'The blood test – did they offer you a sample for you to have tested independently?' He scribbled some more, his eyes fixed on the pad as he asked the question.

'They did, yes.'

'Good, good. I'll have that picked up and sent to the lab. Cover all bases. Did they mention CCTV?'

'CCTV?'

The solicitor looked up. 'CCTV from road traffic cameras, to verify your story about the black car.'

'Oh, I see. No, not yet. I only mentioned the car to the officer at the scene and I think he thought I was making it up. I didn't really feel in a position to press the point at that stage.'

'Fine. We'll get them to pull some footage when you've mapped out the route you took from the supermarket to the crash scene. Once we can show that you were, in fact, being pursued we can look to push for a lesser charge, when we have the results of the blood test anyway. As it stands, however, they are going to ask the CPS to go with a charge of dangerous driving and they intend to get you in front of the magistrate today on the charge of driving with excess.'

'Today?' How can it go ahead so quickly? They won't have the blood test results for six weeks. Why today? I feel absolutely knackered, I hardly had a wink of sleep and I'm finding this whole experience quite terrifying, to be honest. All I want to do is get away from here, have a long shower and go to bed.'

'Just the plea hearing. Nothing to worry about. Five-minute job.' He dismissed the concern in John's voice with a waft of his hand. 'They ask you to confirm your personal details, the legal clerk reads out the charges, you plead not guilty, you're bailed until the date of the trial and you go home. Simple as that. Best to get it out of the way as quickly as.'

'Oh, OK.' It still sounded pretty unpleasant.

'Do you think you will be able to keep it together for another couple of hours?' Max Monaghan sat forward in what he hoped was a reassuring manner.

John sighed. 'Yeah, sure.'

'Good man! Let's get on with the interview, shall we?'

'Is it on?' the senior officer asked her younger colleague. He double-checked the machine into which he had just loaded the two discs and nodded.

'My name is Inspector Jane Hinchcliffe and it is (she looked at her watch) 9.18am on Tuesday February the 20th two thousand and 18. I am in interview room two at Woodseats Police Station in Sheffield and with me is...'

Prompted, her colleague leaned slightly forward. 'Police Constable Aaron Neville.'

'Could I ask you to state your full name and date of birth please?' She looked towards John.

He cleared his throat. 'My name is John Baldwin and my birth date is 8th May, 1980.'

'Max Monaghan, solicitor, of Toombs, Tonks and Taylor.' He needed no prompting.

'We are here to conduct an interview with Mr Baldwin over his arrest on Monday February the 19th on suspicion of an offence of dangerous driving, relating to an accident on New Albert Street in Sheffield at approximately 2.45pm on that day. I must caution you, Mr Baldwin, that you do not have to say anything but it may harm your defence if you do not mention, when questioned, something which you later rely on in court. Anything you do say may be given in evidence. Do you understand?'

John nodded.

'If, at any time, you want to stop the interview to consult with your solicitor, you are free to do so. Now, could you tell me, in your own words, about the events which led to the accident on New Albert Street?'

So he told the inspector about the three men in the supermarket and how they had watched him and then followed him in the black car, about how the accident had happened because he was trying to shake them and how this had distracted him from watching the road ahead and how sorry he was that the poor woman had been hurt and that he was just thankful that her child had not been injured.

The inspector listened without acknowledgement as she made notes, then, shortly after he stopped speaking, she looked up at him again.

'Did anyone see you with these men at the supermarket?'

He thought for a moment.

'There was the lady who sells *The Big Issue*. I don't know her name but she's from Romania. She told me that once.' He realised that was not especially helpful information. 'That's her regular patch. She might have seen me bump into the one in the black tracksuit just after I bought a magazine from her.'

'And did you recognise this man or the other one (she glanced down at her notes) who you said was wearing a white t-shirt and beanie hat? Had you ever seen them before?'

'No, but I got the distinct impression they knew who I was. As I said, I had a threatening letter from friends of Kyle Jarvis and Craig Thomas, the two men involved in the assault I stumbled on in December, which said they were going to take revenge against me. I'd never actually encountered any of them but they gave me every reason to suspect they recognised me – probably from seeing my picture in the papers and such – and that they were keen to get me somewhere less public.'

'But you didn't *know* they were connected with Jarvis and Thomas?'

'No I didn't but when the third one turned up – the one in the dark jacket – I wasn't going to take any chances. That was when I decided to make a run for the car.'

'You say you saw the three men getting into a car as you left the car park at the supermarket. Can you tell us anything else about the car?'

He shrugged. 'I'm sorry, I can't. I'm not very good at telling cars apart. It was black and a hatchback, I think. It looked a bit old and battered.'

'OK. Where did you drive to after you left the supermarket?'

'I tried to get to the junction where I normally turn left towards home before they had the chance to see where I was going but there was a car in front of me turning right and I saw them in my mirror, so I drove straight on instead. After that, I'm not entirely sure where I was going. I could possibly trace out something like my route on a map and then you could check out CCTV footage, couldn't you?'

The inspector did not look up from her note-taking. 'We'll arrange that.'

'I was mostly just taking turnings in hope that I might lose the black car but then I saw the big pub on the main road – the Saracen's Head – and turned left, then right, then the next left again. That was the road where the accident happened.'

'Do you know how fast you were driving at the time of the accident?'

'I don't know. Not very fast but I can't say for sure.'

'We have statements from witnesses who have told us they estimate you were travelling in excess of forty miles per hour and were still accelerating as you approached a built-up area with shops on either side of the road and the pedestrian crossing showing a red light.'

Jesus! Was I?

'I...I don't know how quickly I was going. I can't say for sure.'

'And you did not notice the red light on the pedestrian crossing?'

'No, I didn't. As I said, I was looking at my mirror to see if I was still being followed. If I'd seen the red light I'd have stopped, of course. I wish I had.'

It felt like the right thing to say but he also meant it. None of this would have happened if he had been watching where he was going.

'You failed a roadside breath test after the accident. Can you tell me approximately when you last drank alcohol before then?'

'I can. It was probably just before midnight but it was definitely Friday the eighth of December.'

The inspector was incredulous.

'The eighth of *December*?'

'That's right.'

He was unlikely to ever forget that date.

'You failed a roadside test and two subsequent breath tests at this police station. How do you explain that? Are you suggesting someone may have spiked your drinks?'

'I haven't been anywhere near a pub, so I can't see how that could have happened.' He sat back in his chair. 'Look, I can't explain the readings, not in any kind of way which would make sense. Some kind of freak medical thing, I don't know, but I had a blood test and I'm confident that will corroborate my story.'

'OK,' she said in an unconvinced tone and completed her note.

The inspector recapped the details of the statement again before the interview was closed and the two discs put in sealed envelopes, which they all signed.

'This record of our interview will be sent, along with witness statements and the report of the arresting officer, in a file to the Crown Prosecution Service for them to consider whether charges will be brought against you. Is there anything else you would like to ask about at this stage?'

'I don't think so,' he added, contemplatively. 'I would like you to see about getting hold of CCTV footage of the black car coming after me if you could.'

'PC Neville here will get a map to see how much of your route you remember but you may like to speak with your solicitor again now. I understand we're getting you in at the Magistrates' Court later this morning.'

John stood in the dock and attempted to suppress a yawn. Waiting in the police cell after his solicitor had left, he had barely been able to keep his eyes open, even in his continued state of high anxiety, and the motion of the van on the way to the court had not helped. The adrenaline was beginning to kick in again now, however.

Max Monaghan was busying himself with his papers and, further along a bench, the man John presumed to be the prosecution solicitor had turned around and was talking to one of the court officials. The three magistrates – a grey-haired man flanked by two middle-aged women – gazed austerely down from their raised position of authority, waiting for the start of the proceedings.

At the other end of the courtroom, John had noticed Stella and Jas huddled together in an otherwise deserted public section when he first walked into the court. He acknowledged them with a sheepish smile but had felt too ashamed to hold eye contact with them for long, even though all he wanted to do was to go over to them both and hold them. He looked over to them again and Jas offered a subtle encouraging wave. Stella sat still. John could feel the pain in her expression. He would have plenty of explaining to do very soon but was looking forward to paying that price.

'Could I ask you to confirm your full name, date of birth and address for the court, please?'

The woman at the bench in front of the magistrates had decided it was time to begin the hearing. John struggled to force the words of his reply past the welling tightness in his throat.

'Your worships, Mr Baldwin has been charged with driving a motor vehicle with alcohol concentration over the prescribed limit, contrary to section five of the Road Traffic Act 1988.'

The expressions of the three magistrates remained unchanged but John imagined he could feel their distain. Another drunkard for them to keep away from decent folks.

'Mr Baldwin, are you ready to enter a plea?'

'I am. Not guilty,' he pronounced. The male magistrate arched his eyebrow as he peered above his glasses.

'Mr Robinson.'

The prosecution solicitor rose slowly and composed himself.

'Your worships, Mr Baldwin was the driver of a Ford Focus car on New Albert Street in the Woodseats area of Sheffield at approximately 2.45pm on February the 19th when he was in collision with a young woman who was pushing her one-year-old child in a pushchair across a pedestrian crossing showing a red light to stop traffic. When he was breathalysed at the scene by a police officer, he was found to be over the legal limit and arrested.'

He sat slowly down again. What more needed to be said? He is clearly guilty. Make sure this reprobate is never allowed to sit behind the wheel of a car again.

Max Monaghan was upright.

'Your worships, I ask that my client be released on bail until the date of the trial. Mr Baldwin is a respected employee of the Ridings Building Society who has held a driving licence since the age of eighteen and has not previously had any endorsements for motoring offences. He maintains that not only had he not been drinking on the day of this incident but that he had not taken any alcoholic beverages for some two and a half months before it and has submitted a blood test for analysis to prove that this is the case. Moreover, we intend to prove that the reason my client was distracted on this occasion and was involved in this unfortunate collision with the lady, who mercifully suffered only minor injuries, was that he was being pursued by three men in a car who were intent on doing him physical harm and that was why his attention was not entirely on the road ahead and not because he was under the influence of alcohol. My client is of impeccable character and highly respected, as I said, has no criminal record and represents no likelihood of interfering with witnesses or evidence in this case, so I therefore respectfully request that bail be granted.'

Thanks, Max. In a modest sort of way, John began to feel a little better about himself.

'Your worships, the prosecution opposes the application for bail in this case.'

He stared towards the prosecution solicitor. Max appeared unperturbed, but this is not what he had said would happen.

'Not only was Mr Baldwin found to be more than two times over the legal limit in his breath test, the police are to pursue a charge of dangerous driving against him as the cause of the accident and a file is shortly to be sent to the Crown Prosecution Service. Moreover, I am advised that Mr Baldwin has recently been charged with assault occasioning actual bodily harm, relating to an incident on December 17th last year, and is currently awaiting trial for this offence. In addition, he is currently the subject of a police investigation regarding an allegation of fraud following the misappropriation of some £86,000 from his place of employment, the Ridings Building Society.'

The alarm was clear in the face of Max Monaghan as he glared towards the dock. John could not meet his stare.

I forgot to mention that. Shit.

'In light of all these impending charges and allegations, the prosecution would submit that there is a real likelihood that Mr Baldwin will abscond and that, therefore, bail should not be granted.'

Max Monaghan was on his feet again. 'Your worships, could I have a moment to consult with my client please?'

The male magistrate held up an open palm. 'Be brief please, Mr Monaghan.'

He bustled over to the dock and leaned close. 'What on earth?' he whispered.

'I'm sorry, it only happened yesterday morning and with everything else that was going on I forgot to tell you. I'm sorry. I had a really bad day.'

'Is there anything in it? The fraud allegation. Will it stick?'

'No, of course not. I've never stolen anything in my life.'

'Right.' Max Monaghan returned to his place and attempted to convey in his posture that everything was under control.

'Your worships, my client is keen to prove that he is not guilty of all the allegations made against him and is intent on vigorously defending his good name in court. He is in a settled relationship with plans to start a family and it is therefore nonsense to suggest that there is a danger he will abscond if bail is granted.'

The male magistrate had his head bowed and was writing. He leaned towards each of his colleagues in turn and whispered a few words. They nodded back to him. He set down his pen and looked straight over towards John.

'Mr Baldwin, for a man with no criminal record, trouble appears to have developed an uncanny habit of seeking you out.'

John did not know what he was meant to say in reply, so he remained silent. He felt a knot of tension in his stomach.

'In light of all these allegations and despite Mr Monaghan's entreaties on your good character, I agree that the risk of your absconding is a concern and therefore we order that you be remanded in custody.'

'What?' The word broke involuntarily from John's throat as the blood drained from his face. He gripped the railing of the dock, suddenly unstable like a man who had stepped ashore but still felt the pitch of the boat in his legs.

A stifled cry of 'No!' from the back of the room pierced his consciousness and he turned to see Stella and Jas wrapped together in their mutual distress. The tears welled in his eyes and seemed to be sweeping the two women, the two most important people in his life, further away from his grasp with the unstoppable force of a storm. He was adrift.

'Sir, I must protest...' Max Monaghan was appealing dramatically towards the magistrates.

'That is the decision of the bench, Mr Monaghan. Take him down, please.'

A policeman was at John's shoulder, encouraging him to move. He gaped imploringly towards his solicitor, angry and confused, but he knew there was nothing anyone could say to change his plight now.

I'm going to prison.

As the door shut and enclosed him in the dimly lit tiny cell under the court, he felt stranded beyond reach; isolated and alone, betrayed by his faith that fairness would always prevail. How can this be happening?

He sank to his knees and wanted to cry out; scream in frenzied rage in desperate exasperation at the injustice which was tearing his world apart.

But no sound and no tear would come.

Instead, as he crouched on the cold floor of that bleak cell with his head bowed, he began to feel the unexpected warmth of a strange sense of calm which wrapped around his body until he was enveloped completely.

He was allowing the surge to carry him away. There was nothing to be gained by pawing at the water to try to escape its currents. He was helpless against its power. He could only be taken by it and wait to see where it would wash him up. He understood that now.

He also understood how it was that he had got there. What he did not understand was why.

31

Helplessness can bestow a rare kind of clarity, the type which can prove elusive to those who still believe they have options, can still control their own destiny.

Confined in the court cells, waiting an age for the heavy door to be unlocked, knowing that when that time arrived it meant only the inevitability of swapping one incarceration for another, John had ample opportunity to pick up and examine from all angles the smooth curves of his new clarity, forged from the chaos. He embraced his helplessness in the way you would give yourself up to a white-knuckle ride at a theme park, knowing that the machine controlled everything and that the best way to survive intact was to succumb completely.

John's life was no longer his own. He did not control it. Stef did. Stef was the machine.

For the last two and a half months, John had been happy to accept the gifts – the opportunities to make a difference, the people who had enriched him, the wrongs he had put right, the wounds he had healed – but this...what had he done to deserve this?

The embezzled money was not the work of some devious hacker or dishonest employee, it was Stef. The breath test readings were not technical malfunctions or a medical anomaly, they were Stef too. He accepted that now. He was not even too concerned with *how* Stef had managed to pull off these deceptions, it was *why?* Why is he swinging a huge wrecking ball through everything he has helped me build? Why? It makes no sense.

Max Monaghan came to see him in the cell. Poor Max. His face was practically the same colour as his shirt as he vented his disapproval of the decision and his long-standing misgivings about the compassion of this particular magistrate and made his vow that he would have the blood test processed as quickly as was humanly possible even if he had to take it to the laboratory personally and his assurance that they would appeal this outrageous custody order when he appeared before the magistrates again in seven days and his guarantee, on his honour and the good name of Her Majesty's legal system, that he would get his man out of prison. It's just for a few days. Just a few days.

John listened and was not once tempted to castigate the solicitor for another confident judgement which had proved unreliably inaccurate. He could tell Max was embarrassed and, besides, it was not his fault. How can you fight forces which you cannot comprehend? You can't. You lie back, try to keep your head above the water and see where the surge washes you up. That's all you can do.

Eventually, they did come to collect him from the cell to take him to prison. He was handcuffed to a security guard – handcuffed! What the fuck did they need to do that for? Did they think he was going to attempt to cosh the guard and make a run for it? Anyway, he was handcuffed to a security guard and led to a white truck in an enclosed courtyard.

The inside of the truck was partitioned on either side and sub-divided into narrow compartments. As he passed the lines of rigid doors, making his way cautiously up the aisle, he could hear from the coughs and grumbles within that some of the compartments were already occupied.

'This is you,' said the security guard as he pulled down the handle of a door to his left. He unshackled them and stepped aside for John to enter.

Squalid did not come close. The space was barely more than three feet by three feet, though there was room to stand in it without stooping. Its amenities consisted of a battered plastic seat, fixed to the back wall to face forward, and the overpowering stench of body odour and stale urine – an inescapable cocktail which had met his nose as he first climbed the steps into the van but which was concentrated here – made him want to retch.

The door slammed behind him and the lock was turned with an unforgiving click. In front of him was a small window of darkened glass, now his only means to connect to the world beyond this tight confine apart from a gap of a few inches at the bottom of the fastened door.

He stood and waited for maybe twenty minutes, listening as more inmates were loaded into their boxes, feeling the cold penetrate his bones and the rancid smells pollute his lungs, before reluctantly lowering himself onto the dirty seat, trying not to make any contact with it with exposed flesh. Eventually, the engine chugged into life and the truck began to move, making its way onto the open roads beyond the courtyard and jolting its cargo with every turn, making it a challenge to avoid banging his shoulders against the sides or lurching forward to hit his head against the snot-encrusted partition in front of him every time the driver jumped on the brakes.

The whole sensory ambiance was like spending too long in the toilet on a train.

But that was not the full extent of the torment. Turned up to ear-splitting levels so that it drowned out even the roar of the engine was the sound of a radio show on which an irritatingly chirpy man and his female foil were discussing, in excruciating detail, the events of a reality TV show the previous night. It was the sort of conversation which, if it was happening close by in a pub, you would move to avoid but there was not that option here. The inanity of it all was almost mesmerising and John wondered how it could be that people found such fascination in the sight of washed-up D-listers demeaning what remained of their faded reputations.

The only relief from the empty chatter was the interruption of maddening advertising jingles or some tuneless offering from the music charts and it was all simply impossible to shut out, leaving John to speculate that there must be some sort of human rights legislation governing prolonged forced exposure to such fatuous nonsense.

Before long, they were on the dual carriageway heading towards the motorway and the dim view through the window became almost as monotonous as the view inside. The road stretched on and the minutes ticked by, leaving John feeling like a forgotten slice of bread in a broken toaster. Like a novice greyhound wondering what will happen when the trap's door springs open.

Like a barren farm animal on its way to the slaughterhouse.

The truck pulled through a series of security gates and came to a halt. The engine was silenced and so too was the radio, which was some form of relief at least. John was lifted by the anticipation of being released from his claustrophobic cubicle but that did not come straight away.

He could hear the guards open a door and the sound of someone leaving the truck but then there was a long wait before the process was repeated. There was nothing more to do than to try to blank out the growing chill of his body and to listen to the cries of the other internees as their patience wore thinner.

'Come on, how much longer?'

'Get on with it. I'm busting for a piss.'

The whole trip had been torturous but, as he waited still, John realised it had left him in a far less passive state of mind than he had been in the court cell. Though there was still nothing he could do to change his situation, he pledged to himself that it was not going to break him.

At last, his door was unlocked.

'Baldwin!' barked the guard before gesturing, with a flick of his head in the way you would give direction to a dog, that it was time to get up and get off the truck.

What light there had been on a chill, gloomy February day was fading in the late afternoon and John drew in deep, cleansing breaths, glad to be out in the open. The modern brick buildings around him looked more like a council house than a house of correction but, as he followed the guard across the yard, his anxiety began to grow again. This is it.

'It stinks in there,' he said, attempting, unsuccessfully, some sort of connection with his escort.

Inside, a younger man with a thick dark beard was sitting behind a reception desk at a computer screen. John was ushered in front of him and stood silently, waiting for instruction.

'Name?' The man looked only at his screen.

'John Baldwin.'

The man scrolled down the screen with his mouse.

'Date of birth?'

'Eighth of the fifth 1980.'

The information was typed in.

'Have you already been issued with a prison number?'

John paused for a moment. 'Not so far as I know.' He hoped the reply didn't make him sound like he was trying to be a smartarse and it appeared to be accepted at face value.

'Go and stand over by that wall.' The man pointed vaguely over John's shoulder. He turned and wandered over, wondering what sort of test he was about to be asked to perform which required him to stand by a wall.

'Here?' It seemed as good a spot as any.

The man came from behind his desk.

'Look straight towards me.'

In one movement he raised a camera and released a flash of light which made John blink. In seconds, he was back behind the desk and connecting a cable to the camera.

'Do you have any special needs we need to be aware of – religious, dietary, medical, disabilities?'

John assumed he had no further need to stand by the wall. 'No, none of those.'

After more typing and scrolling, the man reached to the floor and brought up a clear plastic bag, which he dumped on the desk.

'Your personal possessions will be held in secure storage until the time of your release. Could I ask you to confirm that these are your possessions?'

John opened the bag. His wallet, his watch, his belt, the magazine. It seemed like so long since they had been taken from him at the police station.

'Yes, they're mine. Hold on.'

The man paused just as he was about to snatch back the bag.

'This card. Can I take that with me?' It was the business card Stella had given him at the flat.

'It's my girlfriend's number. I need to call her.'

The man stared blankly, as if trying to come up with a good reason why he should deny the request.

'Yeah, whatever.'

John swiftly retrieved the card and pushed it deep into his trouser pocket.

'Thanks.' It was the most valuable item he could wish for right now – a connection with his real world. What must Stella be going through? He wanted to call her as soon as it was possible.

The man had swivelled in his chair and was waiting for a printer to dispense whatever was now going through its processes. He scooped up a small card as it popped out of the machine and slapped it onto the desk. An image of a slightly startled, unshaven, dishevelled man in his late thirties with heavy eyelids stared back at John.

Jesus! I look like shit.

'This is your prison number and this is your prison card. Keep it with you at all times and don't lose it.'

He slid the card off the desk.

'Take the first door to the left through there and wait.' The man pointed. John headed towards the open door and turned into the next room, which was empty apart from half a dozen orange plastic seats.

He sat and looked at his face on the card.

It all seemed somehow much more frighteningly certain now. He was being processed through the system and Christ knows how long it would be until the system spat him out again. Until he could clear his name. Until he could be a free man. Until he could go home to Stella.

He stared at the picture.

Until he could have a shower and a shave.

The prison guard strode purposefully down what appeared to be an endless stretch of interconnecting corridors and John walked slightly gingerly as he struggled to keep up.

The strip search was something he could have lived without. He certainly hadn't expected it to be so rigorous. Between the guard, who must have had fingers like cricket stumps, and the unnerving metal chair he had to sit on while it scanned him, it appeared to have been established that he did not, after all, have a mobile phone or drugs or a weapon shoved up his arse but John now felt as if the object of the exercise had instead been to leave some sort of large object up there.

The guard had clicked on a torch as he gave the instruction to bend over and John couldn't recall seeing it again after the examination.

He followed, as best he could, clutching a pile of bedding and trying not to drop the cup, cutlery, toiletries, carton of orange juice and small packet of custard cream biscuits which were balanced precariously on it, waddling like an overloaded bellboy in the wake of an uncaring hotel guest.

He managed to make up ground as the guard swiped himself through the last of the security doors and there they were, on the wing.

It was not as he expected. John was not sure what he had expected, having said that. Something resembling the set of *The Shawshank Redemption* or *Porridge*, maybe, but not this. Two storeys of cells like motel chalets were set around a bright and airy triangular open space, on which men were casually occupied in games of pool on the three tables, as if they were just a load of mates at the pub. Dotted around the perimeters of the open space were tables and chairs, where men sat chatting or playing games. Everyone seemed to be in their own clothes.

The pillars, stairs and railings were painted blue and white, trimmed with orange. Definitely not the uniform drab grey he had been given the impression, over the last couple of days, that all custodial facilities were painted.

It was all almost pleasant and yet curiously out of place, as if someone had bought out the old Wild West saloon in Dodge City and reopened it as a falafel wrap cafe.

John was aware that he had become the new focus of attention. It was an intimidating sensation. The setting may be bijou and cosmopolitan, but these people were all here because they had committed Christ knows what type of unspeakable crimes and so he deliberately avoided any chance of eye contact as he bustled by, staying as close as he could to the now-comforting presence of the prison guard.

He led them up the flight of steps to their left and then to the far cell at the end of the row.

The acrid dryness caught in the back of his throat within seconds of walking into the cell and made him cough. Tobacco smoke had infested the air and wrapped itself around everything within the room like ivy. He could already feel it seeping into his clothes.

The barred window was bigger than he might have imagined it would be but the cell was not. There was barely space to walk through it without having to turn sideward between the single bed, with its thin gym mat mattress, and a very basic grey office desk, which had no chair. The desk had two shelves and there was another cupboard fixed to the smoke-tinted wall at the far end of the cell.

Be it ever so humble.

'You got lucky. You haven't got to share,' offered the guard. The words were no great consolation.

'I'm afraid the bloke in here before you left the toilet in a bit of a mess, so you should request some cleaning products tomorrow and give it a bit of a once-over but if I was you right now I'd go down to the servery to see what they've got left because there's...'

He checked his watch.

'...twenty-five minutes until lock-up. Don't forget to collect your breakfast while you're down there because the doors stay locked until midday, so it's a long time until you'll next get a chance to eat.'

It had been a long time since John had eaten and breakfast at the police station hardly qualified as a good meal. They had offered him a sandwich and a cup of tea before going to the Magistrates' Court but he hadn't felt much like eating then. What he wanted now, more than food, was to speak to Stella.

'Is there somewhere I can make a call?'

'There are phones by the far wall, as you look out of your cell, and you can make a call there, if you look sharpish. They tend to be very busy during recreation time.'

He had to speak to Stella but he was reluctant to run the gauntlet of all the prying eyes again.

'Is everybody here on remand?'

'Some are, some have already been sentenced.' The guard could see that this one was finding it difficult to come to terms with a very strange environment.

'Don't worry. This is a category B, so no serial killers or terrorists. They're generally a docile bunch but you might want to watch your step all the same and don't get caught up with the wrong sort. Don't go looking for trouble and you'll be fine.'

John had hardly moved since he first stepped into the cell. It was so spartan and yet there was so much to take in.

'I'll leave you to it,' said the guard. 'The first night is always the worst. If you're struggling, there's a buzzer on the wall near the door. There's always somebody about.'

He left. John stood a little longer.

This is a nightmare.

Come on! You need to get to the phone.

He set down his bundle and then sat on the bed beside it.

There was a small TV on a shelf beneath the cupboard. And a small kettle. That's nice. No complimentary biscuits, though.

He remembered the custard creams he had been issued with after he declared he was not a smoker during the booking-in process and opened the packet. He took a bite. It tasted really good.

As he chewed on the biscuit, savouring its sweetness, he sighed. The thought of being shut in this space all night until midday, breathing in its foul air, was not appealing.

How long will I have to put up with this?

He sighed again.

Come on, John, you have to get through it.

Whether it's seven days, seven weeks, seven months or whatever – you have to get through it. You cannot let this break you. Keep yourself to yourself, stay out of trouble, get through it.

'Fuck it,' he declared to the wall and rose to make his phone call.

There was a queue at the phones but there was only one more person in front of him now. John was nervous. He couldn't think of what he might say to Stella. He would have to say it quickly because there could not be much time left until everyone was ordered back to the cells, according to the time frame the guard had given him. Just to say anything and to hear her voice back would be enough. He wanted to tell her he loved her. He comfortingly stroked the business card in his pocket between his thumb and forefinger.

There was suddenly a man beside him. He was staring, though John dare not turn to look back at the man. It was unnerving, a deep glare which seared into him.

'I fucking knew it.' The voice was full of spite.

'You fucking wanker. I fucking knew it was you.'

John had to look. The hatred in those eyes! He had seen the face before but it was darker then and there wasn't that fresh scar above the right eyebrow. It was the night he saved Gregory from a beating. He knew that face.

'I saw you coming in and I thought to myself, "that's the bastard who killed my mate, got me put inside and cost me a bollock", but I couldn't be sure because my eyes haven't been as good since you broke my eye socket.'

John was floundering, as vulnerable as a kitten trapped in a wolf's lair.

'I heard they were going to do you in court for what you did to me but this is better. This is priceless.'

'Look, let's just...that night...it was just... I...'

He wanted to placate Thomas in some way but there were no words. There was no way out.

'What the fuck is he doing here?'

There was a second voice, behind Thomas' shoulder. John turned to see who it was and his agitation grew.

The copse behind the garages. The bandstand. The firewalk. The night on White Lane with Stef, near the gap in the hedge where you could get on the path to the golf course. Chaplin.

'You know him as well?' asked Thomas, his mouth opening into a wide grin.

'He got me nicked,' said Chaplin. 'Nearly shit himself before the coppers saved him. You should have stuck me when you had the chance, pal.'

Both men inched forward to close the gap between them and their prey, cranking his unease to intolerable levels. This is beyond a nightmare.

A buzzer sounded. At the tables, prisoners reluctantly began to get to their feet and make their way towards the cells as the guards ambled into position to usher them along.

'What are the chances, eh, meeting up with your two best friends again? This is going to be so sweet.' Thomas stepped closer still and grasped John by the testicles, squeezing.

'We are going to beat the shit out of you, you fucker, then I'm going to cut your balls off and watch you bleed to death.'

He gave John a final sharp squeeze and then released him. John gasped in pain and wanted to buckle, but he stayed upright.

'And do you know what?' Chaplin pushed his face into John's. 'Look at those men on stepladders on the first floor. They're trying to fix the CCTV because it broke again. You know what that means? It means nowhere is off-limits. It means we can get you any place we like and nobody will be looking in. It means you're dead, pal. You're going to get what's coming to you.'

The two tormentors moved slowly back, keeping their eyes on their intended victim.

John stood, petrified and in pain. He felt a dark, warm patch of urine spread on the front of his trousers.

32

He led me here to die.

The cell was bathed in the pale blue light of a full moon and John sat, as he had for hours and hours and hours, on the edge of the bed, becoming reconciled to his fate.

He led me here to die.

It was sort of obvious now. The last few days had been a condensed effort to discredit him, destroy his reputation, so that the news of his sudden death would not be such a tragedy. Who would mourn a man who could endanger innocent lives by driving when he's pissed, who could steal from the company which had stood by him through the rough times, who was looking at five years in jail for ABH? He had revealed himself to be a bad man. He had probably brought it on himself.

And Stella, Stella would move on. She would probably come to realise that she'd had a lucky escape. She had been conned into falling for a man who had been living a lie and had taken advantage of her trusting nature. She wouldn't be fooled again. The baby? She won't keep it. It was early enough. Who would want to bear the child of a liar and a thief? She'll terminate and move on with the rest of her life. So will everyone else. He won't be missed.

Only he would know how cruel this was. He would and Stef would.

Had he let Stef down that badly? Were the choices he made so wrong as to deserve this? They were best friends. He would have given anything for the chance to save Stef that night but, when it came down to it, he had not been prepared to do everything to avenge him. Maybe that was why he was being punished.

Stef granted me a second chance so that I could wipe his killer from the face of the earth and I failed him. Everything else he gave me were inducements to put me in his debt and I failed him when he asked me for a repayment. My ingratitude has brought me to this.

Maybe I should have been dead anyway, if I'd stayed on the course I was following, and I've been living on borrowed time, so now that I've outlived my usefulness... But he didn't have to end it in such a brutal way. Not like this.

He shivered and turned to separate the blanket from the pile on his still-unmade bed, pulling it over his shoulders.

It has been quite a journey, these last couple of months. Quite a roller coaster. It was great to feel alive again, though. It's a pity it has to end so soon, when there's still so much left to do, but I would say I've been a good man, for the most part, and I can face whatever comes next with my head high. I did my best but I guess when your time's up, that's that.

When your time's up.

What was it Stef said that night outside the flat? That night a year after he was killed? He said everybody has a time to die and there's nothing you can do about it when your time comes. But he said I still had time. He said I had a new destiny.

So much for that.

He stood and walked to the barred window. It was a crisp, clear night and he could see frost forming on the roofs of cars parked in the courtyard below him.

It was too clear a night for snow. They hadn't had much snow this winter and it won't be so long until it's spring, then the work will really pick up to get ready for the concert. August the 25th. They announced the date a week or so ago. That was going to be awesome. Alison, the person they had been working closest with from Gregory's office, had promised them they were close to announcing a headliner soon, just before the ticket details were due to be released. Alison said she thought it would sell out in no time. GameOn would make a fortune and they would be able to put so many of their plans into motion then, start making a difference to so many people's lives. That's not a bad legacy.

The last time they spoke – the last time! – Mike had told him that he was thinking of handing in his notice at work to take on the running of GameOn full time. He asked for John's blessing. It was a good idea, the right thing to do. Mike was the man for the job. He's an excellent bloke. It won't be so long until they need to take on other people on salaries. The Trust had grown much bigger and far more quickly than they could have imagined. He hoped Jas would decide to stay involved. She would be doing it for two others now.

I wish I could be a part of it. There's so much more we can do!

He gazed at the moon and the points of starlight glistening against the endless darkness and it was beautiful. There was not a sound and he became lost in the vastness above, just as he had that night while he was waiting for Stef, on the road just over the county border on the way back from the pub.

If only he hadn't wasted time looking at the stars that night and had stayed closer to Stef. How different their destinies might have been. It was too late to do anything about that now but this time...maybe it's not too late this time.

What was it Stef said that time at the playground? The time when I was knocked out and was drowning in a puddle? He said he could protect me and guide me but that he couldn't do everything for me. He said the decisions were mine to take. He said I could still take control.

The final act hasn't been played out here yet. It doesn't have to end with another man lying in a pool of blood as his life ebbs away.

I don't want it to end that way. I don't accept this fate.

'Fuck you, Stef!' he roared at the moon.

'You're not a god. You don't get to decide if I live or die. I don't deserve this. I've got a future. I deserve to live. Fuck you!'

That's right. First thing in the morning, I'll buzz for one of the guards to come up, tell them about Chaplin and Thomas and their threats to kill me and give them the background so they know why the danger is real and they'll take steps – switch me to another wing or move me to another prison. Get me to safety, well out of the reach of those two mentalists. They've got a duty to protect me. I haven't done anything wrong. In days, I'll be able to prove that I'm an innocent man. I'll be able to get on with my life the way I'd planned – with Stella and a new baby and my own business and GameOn. I'll put this behind me. It'll be a bad memory. A life experience. It'll be in the past.

There was a click and a thud. John spun to face the source of the sudden noises. The door. It must have been someone on the other side of the door.

He stared. He couldn't see anyone looking back at him through the observation hatch.

'Hello?'

No reply. Silence.

There was another thud and slowly, with a creak, the heavy steel door began to swing open.

John backed up until he felt the coldness of the solid wall against his body.

Oh Jesus! They're coming for me!

He waited for the sight of his two adversaries, his breathing quickening, heart pounding.

This is it. I'm not going to get the chance to get out of this. It's going to happen now.

Not without a fight.

His eyes darted to his left and right, looking for something he could use to defend himself. He grabbed hold of the kettle, ready to offer stern resistance. As ready to offer stern resistance as it is possible to appear when you are a man armed only with a small domestic appliance.

'Come on! Bring it on! I'm ready for you.'

But no one came. His breathing slowed, his heartbeat steadied. He could see through the door across to the opposite row of closed cell doors but he could see no one.

He was confused and scared, but the long seconds ticked by and still nobody came. His curiosity grew and his fear abated. He edged closer to the open door, holding the kettle in front of him.

He stopped again when he came within a yard of the door frame. They could be lurking out of sight, waiting for him to emerge, trying to lure him out of the cell.

He drew a long, fortifying breath and inched forward stealthily before lurching through the open door with a leap, turning sharply to both sides to assess the danger.

Nothing.

What the hell?

The wing was completely still. The light of the full moon shone palely through the large skylight windows, joining the dimmed electric lights in gently illuminating the eerily silent central area where he had lately seen so many men taking their brief recreation period. The pool tables were empty and the chairs were leaned against the tables like a cafe closed for business. There appeared to be not a soul around. He peeked over the railing to be sure but could see no sign of a guard. It was almost as if he had the whole prison to himself.

The faint sound of a television playing in the next cell to his left dispelled that illusion but John was spellbound. He was in prison but felt free. It was as if he could wander wherever he liked, perhaps even just walk straight out through the main gates, unchallenged, and walk all the way home.

He put down the kettle and stepped softly along the landing, his feet making no sound, as if in a dream. All the other doors were securely closed. This was his world and his world only. He was invisible, undetectable, a ghost.

But opposite the opening to the steps to the ground level there was a dark shape to break the sequence of metal doors. He walked closer. It was open. Another door was open.

What now? He glanced back, tempted to retreat to the safety of his cell, shut the door and hide. His world had been infiltrated. He might not be alone.

But there was still no sound, nor a sign of anyone else outside their cell. He was drawn to the open door and peered inside.

He could not make out any form but he could hear the regular rhythm of deep sleep breaths, slow and rattling. He could make out two distinct, low snores, each blending with the other in a languid tuneless harmony.

He edged further into the cell and his eyes began to adjust to the muted light.

The layout appeared much the same as his cell but there were bunk beds and their occupants were completely still. His foot touched against a soft object on the floor and he squatted down to look what it was. A pillow.

In his lowered position he was almost at the same level as the bottom bunk. The man in it was on his back, his head turned towards John, utterly lost in sleep.

Chaplin. John squinted, trying to sharpen his focus. It was him alright.

He rose to his full height and stretched to see if he could distinguish the face of the man in the upper bunk. This one was lying on his front but he too was turned towards the centre of the cell.

Thomas.

It was a vipers' nest. John backed away half a step and stumbled over the loose pillow at his feet. Reaching back with his left hand to steady himself, he flipped the edge of a plastic plate on the desk and it spun into the air, landing with a clatter on the solid floor.

He quickly grabbed down to stop the plate before it could rattle to a natural stop and held his breath, staring back towards the two prone forms on the beds, fearing he had revealed himself.

The men moved not one muscle. How did they not hear that?

He inched closer to the beds. Thomas lay completely still, his head resting on the mattress, dead to the world but still definitely alive.

So too was Chaplin. They must be on something. They must be out of their heads on drugs or whatever. They were gone.

John stood straight and smiled.

Now I get it.

Stef didn't lead me here to die. He led me here to kill. He led me here to finish the job.

He wasn't trying to ruin me, he was raising the stakes. He was reminding me how much I have to lose so that I'm completely aware of how much I have to gain. He is saying: 'look how easily I can take it all away from you but do this for me and I can just as easily give it all back'.

It's not a death sentence, it's a choice. I could do nothing and wait until I feel the blade between my ribs or the first boot against my skull or I can take control of my own destiny.

Kill or be killed.

Jesus, he must really need this.

'You bastard, Stef. I love you like a brother but I hate you right now.'

He thought of the war memorial in the church. All those men. Ordinary men. In normal times they would have discovered their enemies were ordinary men just like them but when, angry and scared, they faced each other a bayonet's length away in a trench in a foreign land, only one thing really mattered – to survive. To see home and see their loved ones again. To live a life.

Whatever the rights and wrongs, survival is the instinct which is stronger than any other and they will have learned then that everything they were told about setting their moral compass according to what they were told in church and about obeying the ten commandments was not the whole truth because the most important of those commandments had an addendum attached all the time.

Thou shalt not kill – except when those who have declared themselves your superiors tell you to.

And the ones who did survive, the ones who didn't end up as names carved into a stone tablet in a church, how did they adjust to stepping back into their ordinary lives? How did they live with the horrors they had to be a part of in order to survive? How did they rationalise the terrible things they had to do?

They had to adjust. Of course they did because whatever they had to do to make sure they came home, it was better than the alternative. That was all the justification they could have needed.

And so John stood at his own crossroads. More of a T-junction, really, because his choice was clear. Putting his faith in the law to give Stef justice was no longer an option. Stef had made it plain that was not the justice he wanted. He had said it all along and had spelled it out again in recent days – don't rely on man's justice because it is flawed, just as men are flawed. It will let you down. Innocent people get hurt and guilty people get away with it. Man's justice had let Stef down.

John's choice was as stark as that facing those poor frightened boys in the trenches. Kill and live or do nothing and die.

This is what fate had driven them to, him and Stef. That night, on the road just over the county border on the way back from the pub, had turned them both into lost souls.

John had been no more than a dead man walking when Stef came to him to save him and John saw now that his friend had been every bit as lost all along. He still was. They were two lost souls who needed to save each other. That is why the killer must die. Until he dies, Stef cannot find peace.

Today is judgement day and I am the reaper.

John looked at the plate he was still holding. He rolled down the sleeves of his shirt and pulled them over his hands, then wiped the plate vigorously to remove trace of his fingerprints. Best do this thoroughly.

When it was done and the alarm is raised, it will look like these two got stoned and that Thomas, in so much of a stupor that he has no recollection, used his own pillow to suffocate his cell-mate. There would be no need to look for any other suspects. It's a locked cell with two men in it and one has killed the other. Case closed.

No one will miss Chaplin and no one will doubt that Thomas was capable of the act. Not a man with his record.

John put the plate back on the desk and bent to pick up the pillow with his sleeved hands.

I'll close the cell door on the way out, go back to mine, shut myself in and wait until the morning. Stef unlocked these two doors so he can lock them again. Then it will all be over. Stef will see to everything else. Make it all right again.

All I have to do is put this pillow over his face and hold it down. Hold the pillow down and then it will all be over.

Acknowledgements

I must have written millions of words through my career as a journalist but nothing quite prepared me for the process of writing this debut novel.

I leaned on many people, for support and to fill the gaps in my knowledge, but none more so than my love and life partner, Sue. I am eternally grateful for her constant availability as a sounding board, her good sense and for her tolerance as I shut myself away for countless hours to pursue this daft ambition when I should have been doing something more worthwhile.

Likewise, my sons, Jack and Tom, deserve huge thanks for indulging their old man and for nodding at all the right times while I blathered on about what I was up to. What both of you have given to achieve your goals is inspirational.

My old friend, Tom Gray, did a grand job when confronted with the task of being the first to read and assess the completed novel and my sister, Jane, was a tremendous help when I struggled to get my head around proper procedures and terminology. Others who assisted greatly along the way by feeding me precious information I did not possess were Ian Craigie, David Cusack, Richard Gerver, Ty Mitchell and Martin Naylor, while I'm grateful to Richard Cusack and Clifton Mitchell for setting up information-gathering meetings.

Apologies are due to Felix Frixou for borrowing the concept of his excellent charity, The Titan Children's Trust. You're a saint.

Towards the end of the process, the support of the Society of Authors was invaluable, while the professionalism of Nicky Lovick (editing) and Vanessa Mendozzi (cover design) was just what I needed to take this over the line.

My thanks to you all.

Printed by Amazon Italia Logistica S.r.l.
Torrazza Piemonte (TO), Italy

11935443R00148